LOVE, AND HONOR

THE BORODINS
BOOK I
LOVE and HONOR

LESLIE ARLEN

A JOVE BOOK

Copyright © 1980 by Leslie Arlen

All rights reserved. No part of this publication may be reproduced or transmitted in any form or by any means, electronic or mechanical, including photocopy, recording, or any information storage and retrieval system, without permission in writing from the publisher.

Requests for permission to make copies of any part of the work should be mailed to: Permissions, Jove Publications, Inc., 200 Madison Avenue, New York, NY 10016

First Jove edition published August 1980

Printed in the United States of America

Jove books are published by Jove Publications, Inc.,
200 Madison Avenue, New York, NY 10016

Except where identified historically, the characters in this novel are invented, and are not intended to represent actual persons, living or dead.

LOVE AND HONOR

Chapter 1

A GROUP OF HORSEMEN WAITED ON THE HILLS OVERLOOKING THE little harbor of Pi'tzu-wo. Behind them the mountains of the Liaotung Peninsula carved a serrated silhouette against the lowering May sky; in front of them the waters of Korea Bay surged restlessly, awaiting the wind which the heavy cloud formations indicated was coming.

Visibility was good. From their vantage point the watchers could make out details on the Elliot Islands, ten miles out into the bay. Closer at hand, between the islands and the shore, they could count the ships, the heavy cruisers and the destroyers, the myriad transports, many of which were hardly more than open boats shepherded by a few steamers belching black smoke. Each transport was crowded with soldiers. Through telescopes these too could be identified, eager little men with yellow-brown faces, wearing khaki uniforms and oddly incongruous white gaiters over their black boots.

Colonel Prince Roditchev closed his telescope with a snap. "The Japanese Third Army," he said over his shoulder to his secretary.

Like most of his companions, Prince Roditchev wore the green uniform of the Russian army and sat his horse with careless arrogance. But then, he was clearly an arrogant man; it was apparent in the curl of his mustache, the gleam in his eye, the carriage of his broad, heavy shoulders. A handsome man, too, with cleanly etched features, prominent nose and chin, and, when he wished to use it, a graceful smile. He was not smiling today.

"Nogi's army. A risky venture, to disembark so close to our forces, would you not say?"

He glanced at the faces surrounding him. No one commented. Since the Japanese navy had already bottled up the Russian Pacific fleet inside Port Arthur, it was difficult to determine where the risk would come from.

"And what do you suppose is their destination, gentlemen?"

"Port Arthur."

The reply came from the one civilian in the group, and he spoke Russian with a Massachusetts accent. George Hayman wore a silk hat and a red jacket over his white breeches. When they had first met, Prince Roditchev had been tempted to inquire if the American confused warfare with fox hunting.

"You suppose so, Mr. Hayman?"

"I do, prince. In any event, he is going to throw himself between the fortress and General Kuropatkin."

Hayman smiled at the prince, endeavoring to soften the impact of his suggestion. He smiled easily; he had little to frown about. Twenty-seven years old, he was tall and slender, and kept his face clean-shaven. It was a pensive face in repose, long and serious, dominated by the softness in the huge brown eyes, and equally, and paradoxically, by the firmness of the flat mouth. The eyes seemed to be smiling all the time; when the mouth joined them, as now, his charm was irresistible.

Except to Prince Roditchev. The prince was discovering that he disliked the man more with every second. He disliked the way he sat a horse, with such graceful evidence of having been there all his life; but then, he also disliked the huge American saddle. He disliked having any newspaper correspondent with him on such an occasion, and for that correspondent to be an American was worse; Hayman could not even be treated like the common dirt he was, because his confounded father owned the newspaper. "Be nice to Hayman," the viceroy had said. "We shall need a good press when we make our demands at the victory conference."

And worst of all was Hayman's habit of being strategically right. Despite his youth he had already attended two wars, one of them as a combatant. This strange confrontation in the spring of 1904 was Roditchev's first.

"And what, Mr. Hayman, do you suppose General Kuropatkin will be doing about this intrusion into our position?"

"I wish I knew, prince. I wish I knew."

Roditchev snorted, but said nothing: they had both been present when the Japanese crossed the Yalu, only two days before. Easy to say that the Russians had been outnumbered, had had no alternative but to fall back. It was the manner of the retreat that had been galling, the lack of coordination, the men wandering around aimlessly trying to find their units. A bad advertisement for the Russian army in its first test in a generation.

Below them the Japanese were beginning to disembark. The prince pulled his horse round. "Time to go, gentlemen. Captain Solowzow, you will ride to Port Arthur and inform the viceroy. The rest of you gentlemen will accompany me to Liao-yang. Mr. Hayman?"

"I will go with Captain Solowzow, if you'll permit me, prince."

"You may go where you choose, Mr. Hayman," Roditchev said. All the way to hell, he thought. "But if you are right, and Nogi intends to mount a siege, you will be cut off from the main theater of war." It was his turn to smile. "Hardly the place for a war correspondent."

"I regard Port Arthur *as* the main theater of war," Hayman pointed out.

"Indeed?"

"I don't imagine the Japanese reckon they can conquer Russia, prince. They want their place in the sun here, in Korea and Manchuria. And Port Arthur is the only ice-free port around, right? I figure once they get that they'll be willing to call it a day."

Prince Roditchev inspected him as if he were an insect. "Once they get it, Mr. Hayman? You have clearly not been to Port Arthur."

"I landed there three months ago, prince."

"Ah, but you have not seen the defenses. You are perhaps not aware that it is garrisoned by fifty thousand men. That it is commanded by the viceroy himself. Port Arthur, Mr. Hayman, is impregnable."

"Let's hope it is, prince."

Roditchev began to go red in the face. "And suppose I told you, Mr. Hayman, that General Kuropatkin and the viceroy are equally aware that it must be Japanese strategy to seize the port, if only to deny our Baltic fleet an ice-free harbor? That it is General Kuropatkin's intention to permit the Japanese to set up their siege and commit their armies to this desperate and unsuccessful course while we mobilize our forces at Mukden in preparation for the decisive stroke?"

"I'd say that is as good a plan as you have, prince."

"But you still suppose the Japanese will take Port Arthur?"

"Just an opinion, prince."

"Bah!" Roditchev wheeled his horse once more and looked over his shoulder. "Then why are you not down on that beach, welcoming them?" he shouted. "What is the point of being with the side you think is going to lose?"

George Hayman raised his hat. "I was with the Boers, Prince Roditchev. I always ride with the side that's going to lose. They are so much more interesting than the victors."

"Vodka, Mr. Hayman?"

George sat up, rubbed the back of his head and inhaled the crisp mountain air. They had camped for the night in one of the narrow valleys that cut through the Liaotung like a series of knife wounds, but even so were over a thousand feet above sea level, and the early morning mist surrounded them like a shroud.

"I'd prefer coffee," he said without much hope. He had ridden with Solowzow before.

"Vodka," the captain said firmly.

George grasped the flask and held his breath. Taking a swig of the colorless liquid, he had to repress a shudder. It was not a pleasure he would ever appreciate, he supposed.

Solowzow reclaimed his flask, drank in turn and observed the orderlies who were busy cooking breakfast. "We shall be in Port Arthur for luncheon, Mr. Hayman."

"That'll suit me. Any water for shaving?"

"Cold," Solowzow said, and snapped his fingers. An orderly hurried forward with a bowl, and George unpacked his shaving gear. He had just finished scraping his chin when he was alerted by a shout. He raised his head to see half a dozen horsemen looming through the mist, not more than half a mile away. And he did not need a second glance at the white gaiters or the high-crowned khaki caps with the red bands to know that the riders weren't Russians.

Solowzow had also realized it. "Mount up!" he bawled. "Mount up!"

A shot rang out and then another. One of the orderlies gasped and crumpled to the ground. Without thinking, George ran forward to see how badly hurt he was; the man was already dead.

From behind him came the crack of Solowzow's revolver, but now the Japanese patrol had dismounted, and bullets sent spurts of dust rising to either side. Another cry proclaimed that a second Russian had been hit. George abandoned the dead man and ran to the boulders behind which the Russians had taken shelter. His heart pounded and he was sweating; but it was as much from excitement as alarm. For the past six years he had campaigned almost without pause; he could imagine no other way of life.

"I do not understand," Solowzow said. "I do not understand at all. They only landed yesterday. We were in front of them."

"Maybe they're in a hurry."

Solowzow gave the American a disgusted look; several times during the previous afternoon Hayman had suggested that the Russians make a little more haste; in fact, he had been against stopping for the night at all.

"What are we to do?" the captain wondered aloud.

"Mount up and ride like hell," George suggested. "Unless you want to wind up a prisoner. Where there's one patrol there'll very likely be more."

"Yes," Solowzow agreed. "You and you," he said. "Crawl over there and unhitch the horses. The rest of you, prepare to mount."

"What about the tents, your worship? The equipment?" his sergeant asked.

"They'll have to be left here," Solowzow decided. He ducked his head as another series of shots rang out, and bullets crunched into the rocks. "Haste, man, haste!"

Two of the orderlies got up and ran for the horses, which were moving restlessly against their hobbles. The Japanese immediately commenced firing again, but now the Russians were returning the fire, and the orderlies reached their destination safely. Returning with the horses, however, they were not so lucky, and one of them tumbled to the ground with a grunt.

"Quickly," Solowzow snapped. "Help Apraxin." The sergeant and an orderly rushed to pull the wounded man to his feet.

"Mr. Hayman?" Solowzow demanded.

George sighed. But he had elected to ride with the Russians, and he was not going to change his mind now. He stood up and ran for his horse. Beside him a third Russian gave a howl of pain and started to fall, as blood spurted from his leg. George threw his arm round the man's shoulders, got him up to the horses, and threw him across the saddle. Then he himself mounted, and wheeled away from the firing.

"Ride," Solowzow screamed. "Ride!"

They galloped into the mist, chased by the bullets of the Japanese.

* * *

Captain Solowzow drew rein and wiped the back of his sleeve across his forehead; in strong contrast to the snows of only a few weeks before, the day was already warm. "You'll have a drink, Mr. Hayman?"

George shook his head. "When we're inside your lines, maybe."

Solowzow grinned and lifted his flask to drink. "It is there," he pointed. "Port Arthur."

George walked his weary horse to the crest of the hill and looked down on another harbor. But Port Arthur made most other harbors look like coves. Beyond the isthmus the headlands curved towards each other to enclose a vast area of sheltered water, while in the center a third spit of land jutted forth to sustain the town itself. Here the remains of the Pacific fleet lay at anchor, together with all the merchantmen which had made shelter; the commercial harbor of Dalny, situated on the outside of the peninsula and close to the isthmus, therefore vulnerable to a Japanese raid, had been deserted. At sea, the Japanese ships lay at anchor or steamed slowly to and fro. There were not very many of them. George could not believe that an American fleet would permit itself to be bottled up in this way, even if it *had* suffered enormous casualties on the first two days of the war. But of course, the Russians had endured an even greater disaster than their loss of ships; Admiral Makarov had gone down with the *Petropavlovsk,* and the heart of the Russian navy had gone with him.

So it did, after all, come down to the land defenses, at least until the Baltic fleet could make the long journey around Africa. He looked at a gigantic beehive of activity. The peninsula itself was composed of low hills, and from several of them, situated perhaps three miles from the town, rose the silhouette of forts; the open spaces between the forts were being turned into field fortifications by battalions of hastily recruited Chinese laborers. Closer at hand, the neck of the peninsula, dominated by Nanshan Hill, was also fortified.

"There is no army in the world could storm those defenses," Solowzow said. "But you do not agree?"

George shrugged. He had no wish to offend Solowzow, who was not an aristocrat but a professional soldier, destined to spend the rest of his life at best a major because of his lack of connections. And George was well aware of a tendency to speak out of turn or press too hard in pursuit of an objective. Remarkably, in view of the confident and laughing demeanor he presented to the world, this trait was a symptom of inadequate self-esteem. He recognized it honestly enough. He was an only child. His grandfather had emigrated from England following the failure of the Chartist movement in 1848, disappointed in his hopes for a republican Britain where every man would have a vote, and had carried that disappointment through a failed life. George Hayman senior had begun his business career selling newspapers on a street corner and had risen to own the paper itself. There did not seem a great deal left for his son to do except prove himself, despite his parents' doubts, to be the greatest war correspondent of all time.

"It makes no sense," Solowzow pointed out. "Do you know how many men there are in the Russian army?"

"Four and a half million," George said.

"And in the Japanese?"

"Three quarters of a million, I would say."

"Well, then. . . ."

"But only a quarter of a million of your Russians are in Manchuria."

"The rest are coming, Mr. Hayman."

"At forty thousand a month? That one-track railway of yours can't cope with any more than that."

"Yet they will be here eventually, Mr. Hayman. No matter how long it takes."

"So all you have to do is keep the Japanese out for a year or so, captain."

"And you do not suppose we shall do that?" Solowzow took another long swig of vodka.

Not if you keep drinking at that rate, George thought. Behind them one of the wounded men groaned. "I am sure you will try, captain," he said. "Let's get down there."

They approached the scene of activity and gazed at the guns bristling out of Nanshan. "Captain Solowzow," the captain identified himself to the sergeant of the guard. "With dispatches for the viceroy. And Mr. Hayman, of the Boston *People*."

"General Borodin was asking for you, your worship," the sergeant said.

"Well, I have three wounded men here," the captain said. "See to them. You'll come with me, Mr. Hayman."

Their horses were removed by grooms, and they were escorted up stone steps carved in the hillside, toward the command position. They passed huge casement walls, gun emplacements, and sweating Russian soldiers, reinforced by Chinese coolies, who muttered to themselves—and drank vodka. George had spent only three months with this army, but never had he seen such concentrated drunkenness. And once he had supposed the Rough Riders, with whom he had assaulted San Juan Hill half a dozen years earlier, had been a wild lot.

The two men were taken inside the fortress itself, through narrow, damp corridors and reinforced doorways. Junior officers stood to attention, and they found themselves in the presence of the general.

With the careful preparation that he gave to every assignment he managed to wheedle out of his father, George had studied General Count Borodin. He knew that Dimitri Borodin, although only a divisional commander and subordinate to both the viceroy and General Stoessel here in Port Arthur, was the son of the Prince of Starogan, and of even higher rank than Roditchev; he was also a personal friend of the tsar. He was, in fact, too highly ranked to be dismissed as arrogant even by the most rampant Boston republican who ever lived. Dimitri Borodin was big and bluff and utterly confident; he shrouded his face and chin in a blond beard and mustache, but that he was good-looking could not be doubted. Bold was the word, George thought, already mentally composing his next dispatch. Bold forehead, big nose, thick lips, thrusting chin—and amazingly sleepy blue eyes. And a voice like a rumble of distant thunder.

"Solowzow," he said. "Where are they?"

"Landing in Pi'tzu-wo, your excellency."

"That is only fifty miles away."

"Yes, your excellency. And their patrols are already probing in this direction."

"Has General Kuropatkin been informed?"

"Colonel Prince Roditchev and his staff were there, your excellency. They were returning to Liao-yang."

"And I must inform the viceroy at once." Borodin stood up and turned his sleepy gaze on George. "You'll be Mr. Hayman."

"Yes, sir."

"You should be with the main army."

"I prefer to be with this army, sir."

"Mr. Hayman supposes Port Arthur may well fall, your excellency," Solowzow remarked.

"Indeed?" This time the eyes came to life. "We must talk about that, Mr. Hayman. Have you a billet?"

"No, sir."

"You'll stay with us."

"Sir? I couldn't possibly impose."

"Nonsense." Dimitri Borodin smiled. "I like Americans. I have visited your country, Mr. Hayman. Besides, we have something to discuss, have we not? Lieutenant Borodin."

One of the officers standing beside the desk came to attention, and George realized he was looking at an image of the general thirty years ago. This boy—he was certainly not more than twenty-two or three—was clean-shaven and superbly handsome. He was as tall as his father, but needed filling out. A soldier's son and the grandson of a soldier, as George recalled, his dress and his manner were immaculate; and despite his presently being assigned to his father's staff, his dark green uniform jacket had the red facings of the Preobraschenski Guards, Russia's premier regiment.

"Yes, your excellency," he said.

"You'll take Mr. Hayman up to the house and introduce him."

"Yes, your excellency." The lieutenant opened the door. "Mr. Hayman?"

For one of the rare occasions in his life George had to think of something to say. "You're being too kind, general."

"Just be honest with me, Mr. Hayman. Haha! I shall be straight with you too. At supper."

George nodded and followed Lieutenant Borodin into the open air. Immediately three orderlies came to attention. "Mr. Hayman's horse and mine," Borodin said.

They mounted and walked their horses down the roadway at the rear of the fort. Now they were in the narrowest part of the isthmus, with gentle surf rolling onto the beaches to either side, not fifty yards away.

"The name's George." If he so immediately liked the father, George did not doubt he would also like the son.

"I am Lieutenant Peter Borodin," Borodin said.

"And you are on your father's staff. But did I understand him to say that your mother is also here?"

"My mother and my sisters," the lieutenant said.

"Shouldn't they have been evacuated?"

At last the head turned; gloomy blue eyes were directed at him. "This is our home, Mr. Hayman. My father has been here for six years. Why should we leave?"

"Point taken."

They were past the narrows and riding into the city. It was difficult to believe there was a war on, and that the besieging army was only fifty miles away. A great number of soldiers were to be seen, but then Port Arthur had always been a garrison town. For the rest, the city appeared to be occupied with business as usual; as the sun began to loom above the hills, shutters went up on the shops and the street filled with chattering Chinese, among whom the taller, more dignified Russians appeared like scattered adults in a world of children.

The two men heard shouts and reined their horses at a crossroad. Past them marched a platoon of green-uniformed soldiers in whose midst was another soldier being prodded on his way by a sergeant. The man panted, and his red face streamed sweat; he was unsteady on his feet.

"What would be his crime?" George asked.

"Drunk on duty," Borodin replied.

"It seems to be a problem."

"It is a problem. We permit a good deal of latitude, but when a man becomes incapable of duty, he must be punished. That man will be flogged."

"And will that cure him?"

"It may."

"Wouldn't it be better to ban vodka altogether?"

Again the quick glance. "A man must drink, Mr. Hayman."

There did not seem to be an immediate answer to that.

"Tell me, Mr. Hayman. Is it true what Captain Solowzow said, that you believe the Japanese will win?"

They had passed through the shopping district and turned away from the docks toward the residential area, on slightly higher ground and open to the breeze. Immediately the houses became more elegant, the gardens more evident.

"I'm afraid I do, lieutenant."

"Will you tell me why?"

"There are several reasons. Perhaps they come down to two, here in Port Arthur."

"Yes?"

"Inert defense. That is never good."

"Inert defense?"

"Lieutenant, there are fifty thousand men in this fort, so I'm told. There are thirty thousand Japanese landing, not fifty miles away. Yet you sit here and let them do it. You let their patrols ride as they choose, all the way to the isthmus. That is inert defense."

"I see. And the other reason?"

George Hayman sighed. "Vodka, lieutenant."

Another glance. Then Borodin pointed ahead. "My father's house."

George Hayman did not have to remind himself that the Russians had only occupied Port Arthur for half a dozen years. This house must have belonged to a Chinese mandarin at one time; the architecture was Chinese, as was the layout of the garden, a mass of little ponds and streams over which flimsy bridges, carved with intricate care, curved like toys. He guessed the delicate bridges must reflect the Japanese influence imposed during their brief occupation.

But the Oriental façade ended at the patio, where Russian grooms assisted them in dismounting, and where they were greeted by a short, plump man with a flowing white beard and an equally white smock over his loose breeches.

"This is Mr. Hayman," Peter Borodin explained. "Nikolai Ivanovich is my father's steward, Mr. Hayman."

Lieutenant Borodin had used the familiar form of address meaning, George recalled, that Nikolai was the son of Ivan; his surname would have to be discovered.

"Welcome, Mr. Hayman," the steward said. "Michael Nikolaievich will take your bags."

A groom waited with the saddlebags, and now these were hefted by a young man, clearly the steward's son; apart from his name, there was a physical resemblance, although the son was considerably taller, and about Peter Borodin's age. He hardly seemed to look at the guest at all, and yet George had the feeling that he himself had been absorbed into the depths of a very keen intelligence.

"I cannot stay," Peter Borodin explained. "With the enemy so close, duty requires me at the fort. Is my mother at home, Nikolai Ivanovich?"

"She went shopping, Master Peter. With Mademoiselle Ilona."

"Well, show Mr. Hayman to a room, and introduce him to Tattie." He held out his hand. "We shall see you at dinner, Mr. Hayman."

"I'll be here," George agreed. He waited with the servants while the lieutenant swung back into the saddle and walked his horse to the gate.

"Michael Nikolaievich will show you to your room, Mr. Hayman," the steward said.

"Thank you, Mr. . . . ?"

"My name is Nej, sir."

George nodded and followed the young man into the house, and was suddenly transported to the world of Moscow, or more likely, he supposed, St. Petersburg. Here were thick carpets on the floors, incidental tables laden with brass ornaments and two enormous and valuable-looking icons which frowned at him from the wall as he was led, not up the stairs, but along a succession of corridors toward the rear of the house.

"Have you been here long, Michael Nikolaievich?" he asked.

"We came with the general. Six years ago, in 1898."

A door was being opened, and George was in a large and airy room whose walls were hardly more than screens. One of these, on the far side, had been opened to give access to the garden and, beyond, the beach and the waters of a secluded offshoot of the harbor. In these surroundings the four-poster bed was as absurd as the dark-stained oak furniture.

Michael Nikolaievich carefully placed the saddlebags on a low table. "Would you like me to unpack for you, sir?"

"Why not?"

George threw his hat on a chair and stood in the window, inhaling the sea air. But he was more interested in the man. Michael Nej worked quickly and neatly, selecting where he wished each garment to go, concentrating and yet, George suspected, thinking about something else. George found his face fascinating, the gleam of the brown eyes softening the thrust of nose and chin, and they themselves softened by the wide mouth which reluctantly, George felt, kept turning up at the corners as if he would rather smile than weep. A man who thought deeply, even intensely, and yet optimistically. Forty years ago he would have been a serf. And he was still a serf, George reckoned, even if legally he was as free as air. He was a representative of ninety percent of all the Russian millions, and yet he was more than that; for if all the Russian millions were as intelligent as this lad seemed to be, they would hardly put up with the almost medieval system of social injustice which prevailed throughout their country.

It was something about which George felt strongly, and which had led him into a study of the Russian language as well as Russian history. Indeed, his eagerness to cover this war, and to cover it from the Russian side, had been dictated mainly by a book which he intended to write in the not too distant future. It would be called something like *The Decline and Fall of Russian Imperialism*. And it was not a subject that he could reasonably discuss with his hosts; he was being sufficiently dishonest in accepting their hospitality.

Would it therefore also be dishonest, or even treacherous, to engage this young man in conversation, try to find out exactly what he thought and felt, what he had experienced in the past and what he dreamed of for the future? Would Michael Nej even be prepared to talk to him, an apparent friend of his employer?

Michael Nej straightened. "Will that be all, sir?"

"Stay a moment. I am an American."

"Yes, sir."

"And a war correspondent. Did you know that?"

Michael Nej allowed himself a glance at the elaborate writing case. "I had assumed so, sir."

"I'd like to find out something of what the ordinary people of Port Arthur think about the war, about the prospects of being besieged."

"Of course, sir. I am sure that General Count Borodin will see that such information is found for you, sir." He half-turned his head. "Mademoiselle Tatiana, sir."

George snapped his fingers in irritation—he felt he might just have got the man going—and then as quickly found himself smiling in delight. Tatiana Borodina entered the room like a burst of sunflowers gone mad. The girl, and she could not be more than twelve, was hatless; her pale blond hair was scattered, her blouse was open at the throat, and her skirt was crushed. She exuded health and sweat and sheer animal spirits as she stood before the door and peered at him, hands on hips.

"You're the American journalist," she accused.

"Guilty."

She came closer and held out both her hands. "I think you're awfully nice-looking."

George turned to give Michael Nej a startled glance, but Nej was already gone. As he held her hands uncertainly, he felt himself being dragged forward for a kiss on each cheek. He discovered she had magnificent fingers, long and slender and amazingly strong.

"Illie will like you too," Tatiana confided.

"Illie?"

"My sister. What a lovely jacket." She fingered his sleeve. "Is it velvet?"

"I'm afraid it is."

"Red velvet. I adore red velvet. They've given you this room? Do you like it?" She released him and went into the garden.

"I think it's delightful." George followed her, aware that something was wrong. This girl was too natural, too utterly entrancing, to be a serf-flogging mistress. And yet that was what she would surely grow up to be, to preserve her proper station in life. He frowned. Was Dimitri Borodin a serf-flogging master? He could not believe it, any more than he could believe that Michael Nej, or his father, had ever been flogged. He had to remember to be fair. If the Russian social and political system was utterly rotten, that was no reason to condemn every member of the aristocracy. That fellow Roditchev had been too easy to dislike, that was the trouble.

"I think it's boring," Tatiana said, turning around twice and sending her hair flying again. "I think Port Arthur is the most boring place on earth. Nothing ever *happens* here."

"I can't believe that."

"It's true." She turned to face him. "Except you. You're the first thing that's happened here for . . . oh, for ages." She put her hand to her mouth to cover a guilty laugh. "But you're not a thing. Papa says he's going to take us all to St. Petersburg when this horrid war is over. We were going this summer, but he has to stay here and fight the Japanese. Peter has to stay too. But when it's over, next summer, we're going to St. Petersburg. Will you be there?"

"I don't know. Next summer is a long way away." He smiled in turn. "Let's get through this summer first." And suddenly he felt quite depressed. Suppose the city fell to an assault? Japanese infantry, maddened by danger and by seeing their comrades killed, would run wild through these streets, surging across these exquisite gardens . . . encountering glorious creatures like this child.

She blew him a kiss. "Oh, this is going to be a good summer, George. You're here. What is it, Ivan Nikolaievich?"

George turned, and regarded a younger edition of Michael Nej, except that this boy wore spectacles, rimless circles of glass hiding the gleam of his eyes. And his mouth definitely turned down. He looked sly, while his brother had merely looked intense. Probably because of the glasses, George rationalized.

"The countess is home, Mademoiselle Tatiana. She wishes to meet Mr. Hayman."

"We'll run," Tatiana declared, seizing George's hand. "Let's run."

He found himself hurrying behind her, but turned long enough to throw a glance over his shoulder at Ivan Nej. He found the boy staring after them. But not at him, he realized. Ivan had eyes only for Tatiana Borodina.

Sly eyes.

Countess Olga Borodina had clearly played her part in creating her family's physical splendor. As tall as her husband, with hair as fair as his, her features were softer and her whole demeanor was less brusque. She wore white muslin, yards of it, so far as George could see, over what must be still more yards of petticoats, and hid her face from the outside glare beneath an enormous straw hat.

As did her elder daughter. For in Ilona Borodina, George saw all the promise of her parents come to fruition. Here was the height, allied to the slenderness of a girl; he estimated that she was about eighteen years old. Here was the yellow hair, magnificently smooth, perfectly gathered in an enormous loose pompadour which only just hid her ears. Here was a grace which perhaps the others lacked, although no doubt Tatiana might one day achieve it, combined with an already full figure; George, however, who was inclined to cynicism where women were concerned, wondered how much the small waist owed to her corset, or the deep bosom to some of the other aids currently prevalent among girls seeking the fashionable hourglass figure. But here, more than anything else, was also a perfect meld of features, the flawless Borodin bone structure overlaid and rendered beautiful by the disproportionately small nose, the soft chin, the breathtakingly deep blue of the huge eyes. George supposed, with the reactions of a journalist who aspired to be a historian, that here was six hundred years of Russian aristocracy gathered together in a single flawless model.

He had to remind himself that he did not like these people, or at least, what they stood for.

"Mr Hayman." Olga Borodina's voice was as soft as her face. "You are here to tell the Americans about our little war."

"I am that, ma'am."

"Can there be such a thing as a *little* war, Mama?" Ilona held out her hand, and he gave it a gentle squeeze. Her gaze was very direct, nor did she indulge in any feminine ploys such as blushing when he returned it.

"I'm sure it will not last very long," the countess declared, and removed her hat. Without George's noticing it, the room had filled with servants: Nikolai Nej waiting just inside the door, Michael standing beside him, and a girl who was clearly his sister hurrying forward to take the hats and gloves now being discarded by her mistresses. "Tea, Mr. Hayman. Do you like tea?"

"I do, ma'am," George lied.

"Then we shall have iced tea on the terrace, Nikolai Ivanovich," the countess said, without bothering to turn her head. "Mr. Hayman?"

He walked beside her, Ilona on the other side.

"Have you practiced?" the countess asked, again without turning her head.

"I've been too busy," Tatiana explained. "Mr. Hayman was here."

"Well, I am sure he has been sufficiently bored with your company for one afternoon," her mother declared. "And you must practice every day. Off you go."

Tatiana made a face but retired into the house. The countess sank with a sigh into a reclining bamboo chair. "Do sit down, Mr. Hayman. What part of America are you from?"

"Boston, ma'am." George sat on the edge of his chair, acutely aware of Ilona. She had remained standing, half-turned away from him, and was looking out to sea, where a Japanese destroyer was slowly steaming by.

"Ah, the eastern seaboard. A nice place, I have heard. My husband was in America for a while, as a young man. He was a military attaché in Washington. Ilona Dimitrievna, do stop standing there like Cassandra and sit down."

"They make me shiver," the girl said. "They make me think of sharks, swimming up and down, waiting to get at us."

"And they will go on waiting until Admiral Rozhdestvenski and the Baltic fleet get here, when they will be destroyed," the countess pointed out. "This situation should of course never have arisen. That madman Makarov brought it about."

George opened his mouth, glanced at Ilona, and discovered she was looking at him. He closed it again instead and listened to the distant notes of a sedate Bach fugue suddenly alter to an infectious rhythm which might just have come from Tin Pan Alley.

"Wretched girl," the countess declared, and got up with surprising energy. "You'll excuse me for a moment, Mr. Hayman."

By the time George had reached his feet she had swept through the drawing-room doors and was gone. He glanced at Ilona.

She smiled. "My mother is a traditionalist, Mr. Hayman. Poor Tattie—she wishes to be a composer of popular melodies, and Mama will have none of it."

"And are you a traditionalist, Mademoiselle Borodina?"

She tilted her head to one side in a gesture of consideration that he found enchanting. "I think we are forced to be, by circumstances. I mean . . ." For the first time a trace of color crept into her cheeks. "We only exist by force of tradition. Isn't that so, Mr. Hayman? People like Papa and Mama, I mean." She gave a little shrug. "People like me."

"Well, I . . ." For the second time that day he found himself in the unusual position of having nothing to say. The piano playing had now ceased altogether.

"And because of our position," Ilona said, looking away from him and out to sea again, "there is something in every generation which makes us turn more and more to what we have, and what we are determined to hold. The year Mama was born, the serfs were liberated." She gave George a quick glance. "You may think that was a step in the right direction for a Russian government, Mr. Hayman. I may agree with you now, after forty years. But it must have seemed like the end of the world then, to Mama."

"And what is *your* particular circumstance, Mademoiselle Borodina?"

"Oh, this war."

"A little war."

She gave him a quick glance.

"I apologize," he said. "Although I suspect that is a commonly held opinion."

"But not by you?"

"I agree with you, Mademoiselle Borodina."

"And if we were to lose?" she asked.

"Is that possible?"

"Oh, *Russia* cannot lose. Except its reputation as a great military power. But we, here in the east . . ." another little shrug. "We have been here for six years. Port Arthur is my home."

"Do you believe Port Arthur can hold out until General Kuropatkin defeats the Japanese? Or until the Baltic fleet gets here?"

"I am just a girl, Mr. Hayman. My opinions count for nothing. Mama calls me her Cassandra, as you have heard." She gave a self-deprecating smile, but it was the first time he had seen her smile, and he was enchanted. "I'm just a pessimist. I don't see why there have to be wars at all. There were never any wars in Starogan. I do remember that much. There was never anything in Starogan but peace. My family grows wheat, Mr. Hayman. I cannot tell you how many acres of wheat there are. It is like an ocean which never gets rough, just rustles in the breeze. You fall asleep to the rustling, and you wake up again to the rustling. And you know you are going to do that for the rest of your life. I adore Starogan, Mr. Hayman."

"I can see that. Will you ever return there?"

"Of course. Papa is Grandfather's eldest son, so he will inherit. Fairly soon, I imagine; Grandfather is very old." Another quick smile. "So I will have a year or two there before I marry. I hope."

"Are you engaged?"

"Of course not."

"I apologize again. It's the way you spoke of marriage, as if it were just around the corner."

"Well, it is," she pointed out. "I imagine Mama and Papa have already decided who it should be." A third smile, yet again different from the others. "They haven't told me yet."

"And you'd go along with that?"

"Go along?" This time a quick frown. Her face was so mobile, each expression so deliciously different, he thought he could sit all day, just watching her. "You'll soon be making me believe all the stories they tell of America, Mr. Hayman. Mama and Papa are . . . well, Mama and Papa. They must know what they wish me to do."

"And you'll always obey because you are a Borodin."

He supposed he had been trying, consciously, to annoy her, to entice yet another type of reaction from her. His instincts as a reporter, again getting out of hand, were instantly regretted. But he had succeeded. Her frown deepened, and again she flushed slightly. Her gaze dropped away from his and returned to the sea.

"As you say, Mr. Hayman, I am a Borodin. Ah, Michael Nikolaievich. Have you met Mr. Hayman?"

Michael Nej placed the tray of iced tea on the low table. "We have met, Mademoiselle Ilona."

"Michael is my best friend," Ilona confided. "He taught me to climb trees."

"And was beaten for it." Michael observed, without rancor.

"But so was I," she pointed out, with a little tinkle of laughter. "I was twelve. We had just come here. It was that tree over there, Mr. Hayman."

George Hayman gave a polite smile. Suddenly he was a complete outsider, shut away forever from a world of shared intimacies. Once again, mistress and serf. But mistress and freed serf. Michael Nej had rights, if he ever dared attempt to exercise them. He wondered just what other activities this pair had shared as children. It occurred to him that investigating the relationship between the Borodin children and the children of their servants might be a fruitful starting place for his book.

"Port Arthur is impregnable." Dimitri Borodin leaned back in his chair and smoked a cigar. "Properly defended, of course. It is effectively surrounded by sea, and it cannot be taken by assault from the sea, so there is no flank which can be turned. The isthmus is totally commanded by Nanshan Hill, and it is quite impossible to take Nanshan by direct assault. It is not a question of training or bravery or morale, Mr. Hayman. It is a simple matter of mathematics. There is insufficient room for enough men to launch a simultaneous assault in enough force to overwhelm the garrison. Surely you must agree with that."

"The only way would be if they could drop shells on the fort from above," Peter Borodin said, and passed the port.

"You mean from balloons?" Not for the first time in his brief spell with the Russian army, George was experiencing a sense of unreality, that life should be proceeding at so leisurely and luxurious a pace, from the fresh salmon and roast duckling they had enjoyed for dinner to the crystal goblets from which he was now drinking his port, with the enemy all the while actually preparing for their assault.

"I don't think balloons would be very effective," the general said. "The wind is freakish over those hills. They'd never find themselves over the fort at all."

"And if they did we'd bring them down," Peter said. "I was thinking of an airship. Have you ever read Jules Verne, Mr. Hayman?"

George nodded.

"Well, then, something like that."

"Which doesn't exist," his father pointed out. "If every general were to base his strategy upon something that might happen a thousand years from now, military science would come to a halt."

George drank some port. He needed a little Dutch courage to put the next question. "Can you tell me, sir, if it is true that Admiral Alekseev has left the city?"

Dimitri Borodin's brows gathered in a frown which extended from his nose to his hairline. "It is true."

"Is there a reason, sir?"

"Humph. The viceroy does not have to give reasons, Mr. Hayman, for any of his actions. But I can tell you why he went. Here in Port Arthur we have nothing to do but stand firm. The real war is being fought at Liao-yang, with General Kuropatkin's army. Naturally the viceroy wishes to be there, to make sure that the campaign is mounted in accordance with the wishes of the tsar. *He* has no fears for Port Arthur." He stubbed out his cigar and pushed back his chair, which was hastily pulled aside by Nikolai Nej, tonight wearing a butler's black coat and looking almost British. "Shall we join the ladies?"

Michael Nej was waiting to take George's chair. The American put out his cigar and got up. Perhaps he had pressed too hard. But the viceroy's departure at the very last moment before the Japanese sealed off the peninsula was the rumor of the moment.

He followed the general into the drawing room, where the ladies were enjoying their coffee. No more politics or military talk tonight, he told himself. He just wanted to sit and look at Ilona, splendid in an evening dress of apple green silk with dark green velvet trimmings and a lighter green crepe bodice; like her mother, she wore a rope of pearls and there were more pearls in her hair, together with a flowered bow to hold it all in place.

"Have you solved the problems of the universe?" Olga Borodina asked, dispensing coffee.

"I should think we have increased them," George said.

Dimitri Borodin smiled. "I have just thought, Mr. Hayman, that perhaps you should have accompanied the viceroy. If it is true that our enemies have now sealed the isthmus, and as they have certainly sealed the sea, your dispatches have no means of reaching America."

"I think it's horrible," Ilona said, "to be completely surrounded. I'm almost afraid to take a long breath."

"Oh really, my dear," her father said. "Being surrounded is a figure of speech. One is always surrounded, by people, by hills, by water, and one is not actually aware of it."

"Do you suppose they will assault Nanshan, sir?" Peter asked.

"I imagine they will make a show of it. After all, they cannot just sit there. But I do not think they will try it more than once." The general glanced at his wife and received a clear signal. "We shall not talk of war any more tonight. Ilona Dimitrievna, tomorrow you and Tatiana must take Mr. Hayman on a tour of the peninsula. Go across to Dalny as well. You may use the trap. Michael Nikolaievich can drive."

"Would you like to look at our town, Mr. Hayman?" Ilona asked.

With you, he thought, I'd like to look at hell. "I think that would be very enjoyable," he agreed. "And informative."

"You'll have to ask Mama," Tatiana said. "She's gated me for three days."

"Really?" her father asked.

"I do wish you wouldn't use absurd words which have no meaning," her mother said. "It's all these ridiculous books you keep reading. And it is past your bedtime. Say good night."

Tatiana got up, pouted for a moment, then threw her arms around her father's neck and kissed him on each cheek. "May I go tomorrow, Papa?"

"I'll discuss it with your mother."

"Because you couldn't let Illie go alone," Tatiana pointed out in a loud whisper. "Not with Mr. Hayman." She kissed Peter on the cheek, then held out her hand. "Good night, Mr. Hayman."

"I'm not exactly a monster, you know." He squeezed her fingers.

"No, but Illie is. Bye." She hurried from the room, Michael Nej opening the door for her.

"Wretched child," her mother remarked. "I do not think Madame Riquet is strong enough to give her the discipline she requires. I think she should be sent to that convent we were talking about."

"Humph," her husband responded. "It will have to wait until next year, anyway. I will think about it. What did she do today?"

"Oh, that stupid music she keeps trying to play. I do *not* know where she gets her ideas from."

"But do let her out tomorrow, Mama," Ilona begged. "I should so like to drive over to Dalny."

"I shall consider the matter," the countess decided. "Listen."

"Thunder," Peter suggested.

"Guns," his father said. "From the sea. Michael Nikolaievich!"

Michael Nej hurried forward and opened the patio doors. It was a warm, still night, and the rumbling could now be heard distinctly.

"They do this from time to time, Mr Hayman," the general said. "Just to remind us that they are there."

Ilona got up, pulled a shawl round her shoulders and went outside. George hastily used the excuse to follow her. Now they could even see the flashes, lighting up the sky beyond the hill.

"Isn't it *absurd*," Ilona said, "that they should be there. Wanting to kill us."

"I am sure no one wishes to kill you, Mademoiselle Borodina," he said.

Her head began to turn, and was checked. "I am sure no one on any of those ships has the slightest idea that I exist, Mr. Hayman," she said. "That is the worst thing about modern war. A shell is thrown into the air, and the gunner has no idea who it is going to destroy." Shivering slightly, she pulled her shawl tighter. "You will be thinking I am the family coward." She laughed softly. "And you would be right. I am going to bed, Mr. Hayman. Until tomorrow."

He touched her fingers. "When the sun will be shining, and all will be well."

"Yes, Mr. Hayman," she said. "All will be well, tomorrow."

Michael Nej waited in the doorway of the bedroom. "Is everything to your satisfaction, Mr. Hayman?"

"Nothing could be better." George opened the window, looked out at the sea and the flashing lights. "How long do they keep this up?" he asked, listening to the growl of the explosions.

"Sometimes all night. But none of the shells ever falls here."

"I had figured that," George said. "There isn't a damaged house for miles. Do the shells frighten you, Michael Nikolaievich?"

"No, sir."

And undoubtedly he was telling the truth. His face was quite relaxed.

"And suppose the Japanese forced their way into the city?"

"That is impossible, sir."

"Suppose it happened, Michael. You have an imagination; use it. Suppose in some unthinkable way the Russian defenses collapsed and the Japanese came boiling up that street out there, all bristling bayonets and yells of *banzai*. What would you do?"

Michael Nej gazed at him. "I would protect the family, Mr. Hayman, to the best of my ability."

"The family, Michael?"

"Of course, sir. And my own, as well. Good night to you, sir."

"Good morning, Mr. Hayman. And you were right. It is a lovely morning, is it not?"

Ilona Borodina wore a promenade gown of dull pink silk with white lace frills at neck and hem and matching insertions on the sleeves. In one hand was a hat of navy straw to which was attached a voluminous veil to be lowered when she went outside.

"It grows lovelier by the moment," George confessed.

Her gaze was cool. "You are a flirt, Mr. Hayman." She smiled at him. "I also read Tattie's books, you see."

"And are we visiting Dalny?"

"Oh, yes, Mr. Hayman. My sister has been forgiven. For this morning, at least. Will you breakfast?"

She walked in front of him into the dining room, where her mother was seated, gazing absently at the sea. The Borodin men had already left the house for their posts on Nanshan Hill.

"Good morning, Mr. Hayman," the countess said. "Did you sleep well? Not disturbed by those dreadful guns?"

"Not in the least, ma'am. I slept like a log. And I'm looking forward to Dalny."

"It is a nice day. Michael Nikolaievich."

Michael hurried forward. "Mr. Hayman?"

"Just some eggs, please, Michael. Oh, and that kedgeree looks rather pleasant."

"Michael caught the fish himself." Tatiana entered the room like a runaway horse, holding her hat on her head. "Aren't we going?"

"When Mr. Hayman has breakfasted, my dear. And do go and brush your hair."

Tatiana gave a most audible sigh, and flounced from the room.

"Some coffee, Mr. Hayman," the countess decided, waving Michael Nej forward with the pot. "And then . . . what on earth is that?"

The rumble of fire spread across the town; the house shook. George barely swallowed a mouthful of kedgeree as he got up and ran to the window to look out at the sea. But the firing was coming from behind him. Nanshan Hill. He turned and found himself gazing at Michael Nej.

"They are assaulting Nanshan," he said.

"Oh, my God," Ilona said.

"You knew it would happen," her mother pointed out. "Your father told you it would happen. I do not suppose it will go on for very long."

"I must get out there," George said. "You'll excuse me, ma'am, but this is my job."

"Of course, Mr. Hayman. But won't you finish your breakfast?"

"I really must go." He hesitated by Ilona's chair. "About our ride, Mademoiselle Borodina. . . ."

She smiled and rested her hand on his for a moment. "Dalny will still be there tomorrow, Mr. Hayman. But do take care."

"Take Michael Nikolaievich," the countess said. "Yes, that would be best."

George glanced at the young man.

"I will saddle the horses, sir," Michael Nej said.

Progress was slow through the streets, which were crowded with civilians staring toward the mountains of the Liaotung, listening to the rumble of the guns, exchanging rumors which grew wilder by the moment. Michael Nej rode first, pushing people out of the way with his crop as well as with his horse's shoulders. But at last they left the houses and were in open country. It too was busy enough, with platoons of soldiers marching to take up their positions. The road to the commercial harbor of Dalny was to their right now, and in front of them was the isthmus, dominated at its landward end by the fortified hill. Now they could see the rolling smoke and the flashes of the heavy guns, and even hear the cries of the combatants.

"Halt there." A sergeant stood in front of them. "You cannot cross the narrows."

"I am a war correspondent," George explained. "I belong over there."

"You cannot—"

"He is a guest of his excellency General Count Borodin," Michael Nej said.

The sergeant pulled at his mustache and shrugged. "It's very dangerous, on the isthmus. You should know that."

"You'd better stay here, Michael Nikolaievich," George said.

"I was told to accompany you, sir," Michael pointed out.

"Okay, then. Let's go."

He cantered his horse forward and drew rein to survey the scene. The causeway up to the rear of the fortress was deserted except for one or two bodies lying strangely inert in the morning sunshine. The causeway was constantly swept by gunfire, as Japanese destroyers on either side ventured as close inshore as they dared. The causeway was only about a mile across.

"I reckon it's a case for a gallop, Mike," George said. "Charge!"

He kicked his horse in the ribs, at the same time slapping its rump with his crop, and the stallion bounded forward with such energy he nearly lost his seat. Then he was bending low over its neck as the animal galloped along the road. He did not look back, but assumed Michael was at his heels. Guns rumbled and he reminded himself that you never heard the shot that killed you. He was aware of some sand scattering over him and of the horse checking and sidestepping before regaining its stride and balance. A moment later he was straining on the rein to bring the panting animal to a halt before the parapet leading up to the fort.

Here there was a platoon of infantry, looking quite amazed to see the two horsemen. "George Hayman, war correspondent for the Boston *People*," George explained as he dismounted. "General Count Borodin is expecting me."

They stood aside, and he ran up the slope, aware of moving into the loudest noise he had ever heard. At the crossing of the Yalu he had been a spectator from a distant hilltop; here he was surrounded by the roar of rifle and machine-gun and cannon fire, by the screams of men. The morning had become deathly hot and sweat was rolling down his face.

"Over there," Michael said at his elbow; he had apparently left the horses with the sentries. George turned to his left and emerged onto an observation platform. Instinct sent him falling to his hands and knees as several bullets seemed to whine past his head. Cautiously he looked in front of and below him at a line of Russian soldiers in their concrete trench, rifles resting in the embrasures as they fired; then his gaze traveled beyond, to the slopes of the hill covered in barbed wire, and covered too in little khaki-clad figures with arms and legs thrown wide, with chests and heads dissolved into bloody messes, with rifles lying around them like discarded matchsticks. The wind was from the land, and already the smell of death was creeping toward the fortress. But already, too, another assault force was grouping at the foot of the hill, forming lines, bayonets bristling in the sunlight.

"They keep coming," Peter Borodin said at his shoulder. He remained on his feet, and rather shamefacedly George also stood up. Michael stayed in the shelter. "It does not seem to matter to them how many men are killed. They just keep coming."

The screams of *banzai* drifted up the hill, and the khaki mass surged forward. The Russian soldiers did not seem to hurry. They aimed and fired; then they drew the bolts on their rifles back, and they aimed and fired again. Only the rattle of the machine guns to either side was in keeping with the haste of the Japanese advance. On they came, hurling themselves at the wire. But once they reached there they could go no further, except very slowly. Peter offered George a telescope. He leveled it, focused almost reluctantly and stared at the eager yellow faces. He watched a man catch himself on the razor-sharp barbs and rip his trousers, watched him turn around in mingled anger and pain to disengage himself, watched his shoulders explode into flying red and his body collapse, draped across the wire like a piece of cloth. Because that was all he was now, George thought. Nothing more.

And still they came, closer and closer, threading through the wire.

"You had better leave," Peter suggested. "It's going to be hot work."

He ran down to the parapet below, leaving George and Michael above. Bullets whistled about their heads and struck the stonework with echoing thuds.

The two men exchanged glances, and George smiled. His initial concern for his own safety had disappeared in the exhilaration he always knew when under fire. But today there was an added quality, of what he could not be sure.

"Look there," Michael called.

The Japanese had climbed the hill and reached the parapet. Now the shouts and shrieks grew louder and more desperate as bayonet met bayonet, fist met fist, and Japanese blood mingled with Russian.

"Look out, sir," Michael cried, and George turned to see a khaki-clad soldier on the platform beside them, leveling his rifle to take aim. George dropped to his hands and knees. The sound of the shot deafened him; he had no idea where the bullet had gone. But now the Japanese soldier was running forward, bayonet to the fore. George's hands, scrabbling over the ground, found a stone dislodged from the wall, just the size of a baseball. He stood up and pitched with all his skill and strength. The stone struck the soldier between the eyes and he fell backwards as if shot.

"My God." Peter Borodin stood beside him. "You're not supposed to fight. And with a stone?"

"I pitched for my college," George said. "What's happening?"

"Our men—they're retreating. Look there." Peter pointed, then swung round as a bugle call rang out.

"What the devil . . ."

"They're sounding the retreat," Michael said.

"That's impossible." Peter turned back to look down the slope, where the Japanese assault had been brought to a stop. The khaki-clad mass was beginning to surge back, once again leaving many of their comrades scattered about the field. But in the trenches immediately beneath their vantage point, the Russian soldiers were also looking over their shoulders in consternation.

"There must be a mistake. Or we have been betrayed," Peter said. "By God, I'll—"

"Look there, sir," Michael pointed.

George ran to the end of the parapet and gazed down on the sea. It was the strangest sea he had ever seen, because it was dotted with heads, and arms holding their rifles clear of the water. The Japanese were wading past the hill. He ran to the other end of the parapet and looked east. There too the sea was full of soldiers. A flank which could not be turned—except by men so intent upon victory they did not mind drowning to achieve it.

Peter was on the level beneath them, trying to bring some order to the retreating soldiers. But it was difficult. The men nearest to him slunk by in a pretense at discipline. Those further away were openly running. And now the Japanese were beginning to return up the hill for yet another assault.

"We had better leave, Mr. Hayman," Michael said. "Or we could be taken prisoner. This fortress is lost."

He spoke in a very matter-of-fact voice. But there was no doubt he was right. And therefore I was right, George thought. My God, how I wish I'd been wrong.

He followed Michael along the platform and through the doorway onto the parade ground. A mass of officers were milling about, calling for their horses. And here was General Count Borodin. The general was weeping.

Ivan Nej polished the general's boots slowly and carefully, and with much enjoyment. He truly enjoyed the work, took pride in it, pausing occasionally to spit on the leather before resuming his slow, luxurious movements. "They say the retreat had been arranged beforehand," he remarked. "That it was all part of the plan."

Michael leaned against the wall, arms folded. He had been staring out the window, but now he gave his brother a pitying glance. "It might have been arranged. But still they ran. Russian soldiers, running away."

"Why should they stay and fight? Why should they die? Who wants this place, anyway? I want to go home to Starogan."

"Why should you kneel there polishing boots?" Michael asked.

"It is my duty to the count."

"It was those men's duty—to the count, to the tsar—to stay and fight."

Ivan stopped polishing and rested his hands on his knees. His spectacles glinted. "Do you really believe that, Michael Nikolaievich?"

Michael flushed and looked out of the window again. "There is the American. With Ilona."

Ivan got up to stand at the window with his brother. "He fancies her."

"Bah."

"He does," Ivan said. "And you know it."

"He can fancy whom he likes," Michael declared. "She is a Borodin. She will marry a prince. She *must* marry a prince."

"And where will you be then?" Ivan asked.

"Me?"

"Do you never dream?"

"Of what am I supposed to dream?"

"Of women," Ivan said. "Of Ilona. I dream."

"Of Ilona?"

"Oh, yes. I dream. I dream of us going back to Starogan, by ship."

"Why should we go by ship?"

"It is all part of the dream. For some reason we must go by ship. And we are overtaken by a typhoon in the South China Sea, and the ship is lost, with everyone on board, except Ilona and me."

"What, you mean Mama and Papa and Nona and me as well?"

"Well," Ivan flushed. "I'm sorry, Michael. It is a dream, you understand. Only we survive, clinging to a spar. And we are washed ashore on this desert island, and we live there for the rest of our lives. In the beginning she is very arrogant and dignified, as arrogant and dignified as she is now. But it is only me and her, and I know that. I have to teach her that she is my servant now. And more than that, that she must lie with me and do everything I wish her to. It is hard and it is long, but it is very enjoyable."

Michael Nej gazed at his brother. "You are a despicable little rat, with a mind like a sewer. I ought to box your ears."

"For thinking about a woman? You think about her. Have you ever seen her legs?"

"Of course I have not seen her legs. Neither have you."

"I have," Ivan said. "That night the count was taken ill at dinner, remember? You and Father put him to bed, and then he sent down for some hot chocolate, and I took it up. The girls had just retired, and when I was coming back down the stairs Ilona's door was open. Tattie was just saying goodnight. She had her back to me and didn't see me, and I was standing above her on the stairs, so I could see past her. Ilona had taken off her clothes, and was standing by the bed. She was facing the door."

"You saw everything?"

"Well . . . she was putting on her nightgown, and it was already past her shoulders. I couldn't see her tits. But I saw her belly, and her hair, and her legs . . . Michael, there can be no woman in all the world with legs like hers."

"What did you do?"

"I stood very still in the shadows by the stairs. And when Tattie closed the door she never saw me. It was only seconds, but I shall never forget it. Never."

"Go polish your boots," Michael said, and went outside. He didn't want to look at her, walking with Mr. Hayman. He didn't want to look at her at all, because then he would start to imagine legs. But he had never seen any woman's legs in his life except his sister's, and Nona's legs were thick.

But Ilona's legs . . . suddenly he hated his brother.

It would soon be time for tea, an English habit imported by the countess because the tsarina, who had been educated in England, had tea every afternoon. Michael went into the pantry to prepare the cart and the cutlery, the cakes and the sandwiches, the china pots and the crockery. English tea, in the middle of a collapsing world. The Japanese were across the isthmus; they had taken Dalny without firing a shot. The American had never had his ride in the trap, sitting beside Ilona. Now the rumble of Japanese guns could be heard all the time, as they bombarded the outer forts, only four miles away from this house. But tea must still be served, just as Ilona must still walk on the terrace with Mr. Hayman. Couldn't they understand? He thought Mr. Hayman did, because of the question he had asked him, the day before yesterday. Now the unthinkable was about to happen. There could be no doubt about it.

Therefore were not all unthinkable thoughts now thinkable? He could forget about Ivan's silly dream. But what of when the Japanese stormed the fortress? Michael could read. He had been educated at the village school in Starogan, and he had maintained his education, in a manner of speaking, by reading the books in the count's library. All without permission, and all liable to earn him a thrashing if he were ever discovered. But without books he would go mad.

And books had told him all about what happened when fortified towns were sacked, after a desperate resistance. It would then be Ilona, and himself, against the world. At least, he saw it that way.

It was not a situation he had considered before. And yet, ever since he could remember, Ilona had been there; she was only a year younger than himself. They had played together as small children, and had romped together as older children. Then he had seen her legs often enough, although encased in stockings, and he had not been interested because he had not known that he should be interested. That the two of them were different, and not only on account of their different stations in life, had been brought home to him with alarming force on the occasion of the tree. Ilona was a girl, apart from being the daughter of a count and the future wife of a prince. And girls did not climb trees with boys, even boys they had known almost from birth.

Especially when those boys were their servants.

From that afternoon their relationship had changed. But the change, he realized now that he thought about it, had been all on his side, in the way he regarded her. Ilona had had it brought home to her that girls did not climb trees. Nothing more than that. She remained as innocently friendly to him as she had always been. But he had been made to understand, between each stroke of the strap, that she was a creature as far above him as was the moon. Whatever she wanted, she must have. Whatever he wanted had had to be relegated to the realm of dreams.

So it was better not to dream at all. It was better to read, things which could not possibly concern Ilona, and which could sufficiently occupy his mind. There were some very strange books in the count's library. Military history by the volume, and several histories of Russia; these were the most interesting. There were also large volumes on economics, and a good number on politics. The count was a liberal, by Russian aristocratic standards.

Thus there were also books on anarchy, and the socialist movements which had been growing in Russia these past few years. The count was not liberal enough to approve of socialism; he was merely a conscientious man well aware of the position which would be his when his father died, and he intended to know all there was to know about every aspect of the society he might well be called upon to govern. He had no idea that the more controversial ideas in his library were being studied by the son of his steward. But there was a world of men and women who had not been content merely to wonder why some people were born to wealth and power and others to poverty and servitude, but had actually stood on street corners and asked if it was truly the preordained nature of things.

Well, that was not something Michael Nej ever intended to do. As far as he could make out, those who had were either cooling their heels in Siberia or were dead. Nor did he have much use for organizations like the People's Will, which had carried out campaigns of organized assassination thirty years before. It was absurd to suppose that a handful of people, by meeting and talking, or even occasionally killing, could ever hope to change Russian society. Besides, he wasn't at all sure he *could* kill a man.

But it gave him an enormous sense of belonging to know that there were other people who thought as he did, who wanted the same things he did. It was not something he could discuss within his family. His father and mother would be horrified at the very idea that a son of theirs could think socialist thoughts; Nona never thought about anything, so far as he could tell; and if Ivan did spend a lot of time thinking, it seemed to be entirely about women. If Ivan ever took part in a revolutionary movement, it would be with the idea of gaining possession of Ilona's legs for himself.

"Ah, Michael Nikolaievich, there you are."

He swung around guiltily. Ilona had managed to get rid of Mr. Hayman.

"You were with Mr. Hayman at the isthmus yesterday," she said in a tone he found accusing.

"Yes, Mademoiselle Ilona."

"Was it as terrible as he says? Did our people run away?"

"I'm afraid they did, Mademoiselle Ilona."

"And now the Japanese are on the peninsula. Michael, Mr. Hayman thinks Port Arthur may fall. Do you believe that?"

"I think it may well fall, Mademoiselle Ilona."

"My God! What will become of us?"

"I . . . I will see that no harm comes to you, Mademoiselle Ilona."

She had been inspecting the tea cart. Now her head came up and for a moment she gazed at him. She smiled. "I know you will, Michael Nikolaievich." She left the room.

What do *I* want from a revolution, Michael wondered—even a revolution as inconceivable as a Japanese victory here in Port Arthur—what do I want, if not possession of those legs?

Chapter 2

ONLY SOUTH AFRICA, DURING THOSE LONG DAYS OF THE BOER WAR, had ever been hotter, in George Hayman's experience. The August sun, boiling down from a cloudless sky, seemed to be perched directly over Port Arthur. The city steamed, and stank, and rumbled. A large part of the stench came from untreated sewage, several of the reservoirs having been taken by the enemy. The rest was the stench of death. From his vantage point, on the summit of 203-meter Hill, the highest and strongest point in the Russian defenses, George looked to the north and west at the Japanese, once again surging to the assault on the hill immediately beyond, known as 174-meter. They had now been climbing that bloodstained slope for nearly a week, and for nearly a week they had been hurled back, leaving their trail of dead and dying men. This was the daytime operation. At night they bombarded or tried flank assaults, only to be picked out of the darkness by the unceasing Russian searchlights, and then submitted to another hail of rifle and machine-gun fire. While all the time, day and night, another battle was waged beneath the ground: the Japanese engineers trenched relentlessly into the Russian positions and the Russians in turn countertrenched, until the converging tunnels met, and another vicious encounter would take place only feet above the hell it all so closely resembled.

George had known nothing like it. Cuba had been bad, because of the mosquitoes and the fever, but neither side had possessed quite the weight of armaments, nor quite the determination to die. The South African war, he now realized, had been almost a holiday, fought over vast areas of open country, where one could leave the battlefield to the vultures. In Port Arthur the smell of the dead, the moans of the dying, the wails of the bereaved, were always with you.

And he was, after all, being proved wrong—partly because the Japanese had taken an inordinately long time to launch their assault. They had reconnoitered the massive defenses before them with enormous care, had wasted week after week while they had brought up more and more men and more and more guns. Then the attack had come, and it was being held. He knew that, just as the elated Russian officers knew that, just as the Japanese generals—even old Nogi himself, who had taken this same city from the Chinese only ten years before—must know that as well. The attack was already losing momentum, and would die of its own accord soon enough. And all the while the Baltic fleet was coming closer, while Kuropatkin's forces around Mukden were growing stronger. The Japanese were being proved unwise after all, to have challenged the European colossus.

Where did that leave George Hayman? It was time to pack up his writing case and his sketching block—there was no means of getting his copy out of the city in any event—and return to the house for tea. He was learning to accept that it was possible to conduct a war in this utterly civilized manner and still win it. Just as he was now prepared to accept that it was possible to belong to the richest aristocracy left in the world, to be absolute lords over all around them, to leave millions of people in hopeless poverty and subservience, and yet be utterly charming, utterly attractive, and even, in their own way, utterly good. In the three months he had spent as a guest of the Borodins he had grown to like every single member of the family, just as he had grown to like every single member of the Nej family. Well, not *every* member. He still found Ivan sly, felt that Ivan was capable of betraying the loyalty that the other Nejs were prepared to give to their employers. But old Nikolai Nej was a treasure, just as his wife was a charmer. And the girl Nona, a constant bubble of embarrassed laughter, was a joy. Michael, waiting for him now and holding their horses, was as good a companion as any man could wish.

But he had come here prepared to like people like the Nejs. It was his reaction to the Borodins which was at once surprising, delightful and also a little disturbing. But how could one dislike a man like Dimitri Borodin, a soldier's soldier if ever there was one, a man with the courage of a lion, but who at the same time wore his emotions on his sleeve, not ashamed for the world to see them? Or the countess, showing equal patience as she coped with her husband's idiosyncrasies, the growing shortage of food and water or Tatiana's wild ambitions? Or Tatiana herself, who wanted only to sing and dance her own compositions?

Or were they all shining with such brilliance because in them was held the reflected light of the sun? His heartbeat was quickening with every step his horse took through the town, and out onto the slightly cooler slopes beyond. With the perversity of a man in love he actually enjoyed departing in the mornings for his survey of the battlefields, in order to feel the pain of leaving her side, and to know the utter pleasure of returning to her at the end of the day. Because he *was* in love. He supposed he had fallen in love the first time he had seen her, last June. And he had not troubled to resist the emotion for a moment. George Hayman, in love with a Russian princess. What would the class of '97, which had once taken a collective midnight oath to oppose monarchism and its offshoots wherever it might be encountered, say to that?

George did not suppose they would ever find out about it. It was not an emotion he had even considered communicating to her. That was arrant cowardice—but also the forbearance required by their respective stations. She *was* a princess, and a Borodin, and she had made her position clear on their first afternoon together. Nor had she ever, in any way, suggested that she might reciprocate his passion. She seemed to enjoy his company, but no doubt that was because he was different from those officers of the garrison who had been her usual escorts before the commencement of the siege; he often got the impression that she found him amusing.

But even if she had revealed a reciprocal interest in him as a man rather than a foreign visitor, now was surely not the time for declarations of love. Apart from the circumstance of warfare being waged around them, they were both far too busy. She was even busier than he, because as a Borodin she must play her part in the life of the city. That meant donning her uniform every day, concealing her glorious hair beneath her starched white cap, and hurrying down to the hospital to grant the solace of that smile and those hands to wounded soldiers. If there was undoubtedly a touch of patronage in a Borodin acting the nurse, her efforts were nevertheless inspired by a genuine desire to help.

And then, when she was at home, there again seemed so much for her to do. Her father insisted that life continue as normally as it could; after all, no Japanese shells had yet reached the city itself, or the harbor. Thus there would certainly be tea waiting when he dismounted. But it would be a strange tea, because instead of whitebread sandwiches there would be dark-bread sandwiches, and the little cakes would be made from corn flour instead of wheat, and the tea itself would have been carefully saved from the day before and reboiled, and would therefore be weak and tasteless. And all these changes and economies, from the grinding of the corn flour down to the reboiling of the tea, would have been supervised by the countess and her elder daughter. Without apparent concern or regret they had turned away from the life of balls and concerts and stately tea parties and great dinners which had been their usual existence up to this catastrophic year; they were content to do their duty and await the coming of better times. As aristocrats they might not deserve to survive; as human beings George could not see how the world—this world, anyway, the world of Port Arthur—could possibly do without them.

And there she was. As he swung from the saddle she came round the corner of the house, carrying her basket filled with flowers she had been cutting for the dinner table. As it was August she was dressed with the utmost simplicity, pale blue skirt, white blouse above with the sleeves pushed up to her elbows, fingers lost in greenstained gardening gloves, face shaded beneath a huge straw hat, and best of all, hair undressed and loose, gathered only on the nape of her neck with an enormous blue bow before being allowed to drape past her shoulders. It was not a garb she would have dreamed of allowing herself to be seen in, by him, three months ago. But now, the intimacy of having him constantly in the house, combined with the even greater intimacy of sharing in a war, had brought them into an intimacy he once could only have dreamed of.

And therefore, into an intimacy which could never be spoiled by attempting to secure a relationship even more intimate.

Now she waved and hurried toward him. "George," she cried. "I'm so glad you came back early. We're having a special tea today. A celebration tea."

"And what are we celebrating?"

"Why, today you have been here three months exactly." She tucked her arm through his. "We have been waiting for you." She glanced over her shoulder. "Hurry along, Michael Nikolaievich. As you have looked after Mr. Hayman these three months you must be there too."

George glanced from Ilona to Michael. Whenever they looked at each other he was aware of the depth of understanding between them. And he had just been congratulating himself on the closeness *he* had achieved. He supposed the class of '97 would laugh.

"Next," said Dr. Alapin. He was a young man, given to premature stoutness, and over the past few months, to premature aging as well; the bushy hair beneath the military cap was speckled with gray. But this might well be from sheer fatigue; as the senior surgeon left in Port Arthur, he worked almost around the clock, removing shattered arms and legs, tying up lesioned veins and arteries, bandaging heads and abdomens, and he did it all with complete impartiality, almost disinterest, except that he preserved an overwhelming pride in his work and was never satisfied unless things were just so. This standard was becoming increasingly difficult to maintain as medical supplies grew shorter.

He expected a similar professional disinterest from his chief nurses. He had selected *them* himself, and in choosing Ilona Borodina as one of them after only five months' experience, he had been counting on her character and on the effect her presence would have on men in desperate pain and consuming misery. It was not merely her beauty, which was widely admired, that made her services so desirable, it was the fact that there were no other princely families resident in Port Arthur. Her rank made her hands seem twice as soft as anyone else's.

Ilona was well aware of the reasons behind her selection for surgical duty as the doctor's assistant. In the beginning she had been immensely flattered, and she was proud of the fact that she had not once fainted or even vomited. She had felt the instinct to do both those things, but she had merely reminded herself that she was Ilona Borodina, and that it was up to her to set an example. Now, after three weeks, she did not even feel like vomiting.

But she did not enjoy the work. Having overcome her initial repugnance at seeing human beings reduced to bits of meaningless flesh, and having become absorbed in the technical mastery revealed by Dr. Alapin, she might well have grown to enjoy the medical side of her duties for revealing an aspect of life of which she had previously been unaware. What she could never accustom herself to were the men themselves. She had had little to do with men before this spring. Peter was three years her elder and was an aloof, withdrawn boy in any event. Michael Nej had been equally standoffiish ever since the mishap with the tree six years ago, and in any event it had always been impossible to consider Michael as a *man*. He was Michael Nikolaievich, who had been there ever since she could remember, and who would be there for the foreseeable future. The same was true of his brother, Ivan.

But the men who were brought into the hospital were different. Often their clothes had to be cut away, and there was no avoiding contact with their masculinity—their odors, their beard-stubbled faces, the dirty, matted thatches on their chests, the lice which might be embedded in their hair or between their legs and which had to be carefully removed, the organ which lay between their legs, sometimes flaccid against the sweating flesh, sometimes rearing at her when her fingers brushed against it. Worst of all, of course, was when, helpless in their misery, they leaked urine or feces.

It was not a subject which could be discussed, and thereby relieved. There was no one to discuss it with. She had no real friends in Port Arthur. She was the granddaughter of a prince, and besides, the Borodins had always been an intensely self-contained family. Nor did she dare mention any of the things she had seen, and heard, and been forced to do, to her mother, because she reasoned that Olga Borodina would immediately have her removed from the hospital. Mama did not believe that there were any really unpleasant occurrences in life beyond giving birth and dying, and these were necessarily private events. Presumably, as she was the mother of three children, she knew *something* about men, but as she had never discussed the matter with her daughters it was impossible to decide how much; at eighteen, Ilona, for all her recently acquired knowledge, was still not *precisely* sure what happened between a man and a woman when they were married, although like her mother before her, she was ready to play her part to the best of her ability whenever her father chose her husband. But undoubtedly Mama had not the slightest idea what happened inside a hospital full of dying men.

So Ilona was obliged to return to the house every evening and assume as carefree a demeanor as she could, while endeavoring to forget all the horrors she had witnessed during the day. If occasionally it was impossible to be as gay as she would have liked, the family usually put it down to her innate pessimism.

But now the last casualty of her day's term of duty lay on the table, shirt and coat cut away while Dr. Alapin probed for the bullet which had lodged in his chest. The man was almost unconscious. The doctor was using his dwindling supply of anesthetic with increasing care, saving adequate doses for the most seriously wounded; this patient certainly bore a serious wound—in fact, it was doubtful whether he would survive at all—and for now he was drugged rather than unconscious. His head turned from side to side and his eyes rolled. At each stab of pain resulting from one of Dr. Alapin's thrusts, his hands twisted convulsively; once he caught one of Ilona's and squeezed it so hard she had to bite her lip to stop from crying out. But she made no sound; Dr. Alapin did not like to be disturbed at his work.

And suddenly the strength left the fingers holding hers. Perhaps he had fainted. But she knew better than to hope that, and a glance at the man's face told her she was right.

Dr. Alapin had recognized it before she had. He turned away without a sound, waved his fingers at the orderlies in a most disturbing gesture of finality, looked at the clock at the same time, and then at the door, where Alla Godneva was already waiting to begin her duty.

"Thank you, Ilona Dimitrievna," Dr. Alapin said. "Sleep well."

Ilona gave him a brief curtsey and Alla a quick smile, then hurried into the nurses' changing room to strip off her bloodstained uniform and wash her hands and face. Then it was on with her own gown, and off with her cap, to allow her hair some freedom. Other girls came in to wash themselves, but they remained at the far end of the room. Ilona Dimitrievna must not be disturbed.

Her hair was a mess, tumbling past her shoulders as the restraining pins were withdrawn. She gathered it up as best she could and tied it with a ribbon, crammed her hat on her head, said good night and hurried down the stairs into the comparative freshness of the cold evening air. Already the first gathering clouds were reminders that the sunlight over Port Arthur was not eternal. Nor was the air really pure. The stench of death and decay, the gloom of a city living from hand to mouth, was everywhere; for the first time in her life she almost prayed for one of the monsoon-driven typhoons to come roaring out of the China Sea to dissipate the stench of Port Arthur. Why, she thought, it might blow the Japanese away as well.

The trap was waiting for her, Ivan Nej sitting on the box. Another unique occurrence, that every evening a nurse should be met by an expensive trap. She supposed she was the first Borodin woman ever to consider these things. But how could she not? Just as a general and a private soldier looked exactly the same when they were stretched on Dr. Alapin's table, bled the same and groaned the same and howled with pain the same and smelled the same, so did she sweat just like any other girl, and feel sick like them, and suffer menstrual pains and blood like them, and certainly she did not possess any more courage than any of them. She thought, and hoped, that she might possess a greater sense of duty, since it had been drummed into her ever since she could remember. But that had not yet been proved.

So she was an ordinary woman, different only by an accident of birth. There was a sinister thought for a Borodin. But she could no longer convince herself that Papa or Peter would be any different—any more noble, any more stoic—on Dr. Alapin's table than anyone else. That was a thought she refused even to consider, lest it happen, and yet it lurked at the back of her mind all the time.

And had recently led her into other, even stranger thoughts. As now. Ivan was down from his perch to wrap her legs in the traveling rug, fussing about her like a mother hen. He was not only a servant, he was also a man. Or he would be, in a couple of years. A man no different from any other. She shut her eyes, to reject the possibility of envisioning him on the operating table, and of course saw him there the more clearly. She opened her eyes again and stared out of the trap at the people closing their shops for the night—an easy task, this, as there was not much left to sell.

These thoughts, disturbing, even obscene, but so provocative, had been haunting her with increasing strength over the past few weeks. Thoughts today of Ivan, certainly, but also of Michael, who was already a man and who clearly worshipped the ground on which she walked. He knew nothing of her. She knew everything of him, by proxy. And Michael *was* only a servant; having left the realities of the hospital she could again attempt to convince herself that he did not really matter. It was George Hayman who disturbed her most.

He had come as a stranger, and by his infectious good humor and personal charm, not less than by the way he had instinctively fought with the Russian soldiers on the day Nanshan had fallen, he had become a friend, almost a part of the family. The only thing she would regret about the arrival of the Baltic fleet and the subsequent lifting of the siege—because that was what would happen; everyone, even Papa and General Stoessel, in overall command of the entire garrison, insisted on that—would be the departure of George Hayman. She had liked him from the first, even if he did seem to possess rather odd ideas. But those ideas were refreshingly new to her. Thus she had flirted with him. That had been before October, though, and her promotion to the operating theater. Since then they had seen less of each other. Life had quickened for both of them as the Japanese assaults grew more determined. When they did meet, he continued to be as charming as ever.

But meanwhile she saw him on the operating table—not wounded, surely, however many risks he took—but lying there, with his clothes cut away.

She knew him too.

"Many happy returns of the day."

Dimitri Borodin stood and raised his glass, and his family and their guest stood with him. He smiled at his daughter, but it was a forced, tired smile, and even as he did so he swayed. But he had come home for her birthday, because it was a family event; he had bathed and changed his dirty uniform, and he had stayed for dinner and to give the toast. Now he sat down, and Ilona stood in turn. George Hayman thought she had never looked more beautiful, for all that she was plainly as exhausted as everyone else. She was wearing her favorite green evening gown, the one she had worn on his first night here; it had become necessary for even a Borodin to trot out an old gown from time to time.

In Boston, his mother and father would be sitting down to Christmas dinner, drinking a toast to their absent son. They would not be too worried. They were not a worrying family, and they knew he could take care of himself. Here in Port Arthur, as all over Russia, Christmas was still nearly a fortnight away, and instead they celebrated Ilona's birthday.

She was nineteen. The beautiful girl was daily becoming a more beautiful woman: the hollows in her cheeks, the shadows under her eyes, and even more, the shadows *in* her eyes, gave her face a maturity, an understanding, she had previously lacked. And George, who had been in military hospitals in both Cuba and South Africa, was appalled at what she daily experienced here in Port Arthur. Now her gaze, drifting round the table, met his for a moment. She never revealed any strong emotion, or even any very great interest; another concomitant of her recent experiences was that she had learned to control that delicious mobility of expression which had first attracted him. But in the strangest fashion he had gained the impression over the past couple of weeks that when she looked at him her eyes were speaking to him, almost as he had always felt they were speaking to Michael Nej, rigid as ever behind the general's chair. Was it because, without sharing anything personal, they were sharing so much of life just by being in this besieged city? If he could believe that, he thought, then this ordeal would have made one man happy, at least. And one woman? Something not to be considered.

Her smile had passed on, to come to rest on her mother. "I thank you," she said. "I thank you all."

"There is no present," her father said. "That will have to wait until the siege is lifted. Then there will be a present." He leaned back in his chair and surveyed the table. "When the siege is lifted," he said, "I am going to take the leave that is due to me, and we shall go home to Starogan. All of us. Back to Starogan." He smiled at George. "You too, Mr. Hayman, if you will. Would you like to visit Starogan?"

"I should like that better than anything else in the world, count."

Dimitri Borodin laughed for the first time in several months. He leaned forward, his elbows on the table. "Do you know, Olga, I think we have converted this young man? Come now, Mr. Hayman, tell the truth. When you came here, you expected us to be beaten, did you not?"

"I did, sir."

"And you felt that would not be a bad thing. Am I not right, Mr. Hayman?"

"Well, I. . . ." George felt his cheeks burning and glanced from left to right. He dared not look at Ilona.

"Be straight with me, Mr. Hayman. You promised me that, remember? Besides, I have read the Boston *People*. I know the gist of your father's editorials."

George regained control of his composure. "I am surprised you put up with me, sir."

"I did it because I *wished* to convert you, Mr. Hayman. I wanted you to see us and know us as we really are. And I wanted you to learn how the Russian soldier can fight. Would you agree that he can fight, Mr. Hayman?"

"He can fight, count," George said. "I never supposed he couldn't. I only wondered if there were enough in his life, and especially here in Manchuria, for him to fight for."

"He fights for the motherland, Mr. Hayman. For the tsar, God bless him. For the weight of history that has made Russia great. I know that is something you Americans find hard to understand. You are a new country, scarcely a hundred years old. You emerged as part of a great wave of change, which spread across Europe as well. Therefore you stand always for new ideals, new beliefs. You would *rather* change than continue on the same road your ancestors trod for centuries. Am I being unfair?"

"I don't think so, sir."

"But here in Russia, you see, no revolutionary movements came to disturb the even tenor of our lives. We have progressed slowly but surely, liberalizing our institutions in our own time, and with far less upheaval and indeed bloodshed than characterized the revolutionary movements in America, and France, and Hungary, and Italy and Greece. Russia is like a great river, Mr. Hayman, flowing on its way to the sea. It can be whipped into a frenzy by a storm, but the frenzy is only on the surface. Dive beneath the surface and you will find the true strength of the river, flowing, always flowing, never changing in itself, intent only upon deepening and widening its bed, to make itself even stronger. And this river is made up of every drop of water in it, Mr. Hayman, all moving toward a similar goal, all content to be a part of one immense whole. Will you write that in your newspaper?"

George's gaze had wandered to the head of the table. There Nikolai Nej was standing, eyes shining as he listened to his master speak. Clearly *he* believed. But what of his son, standing beside him? Michael Nej's face was expressionless, but little muscles at the base of his jaw were jumping.

"I shall write of Russia as I find her, count," George said. "But I will tell you this. You *have* changed my ideas. So in reply to you, sir, I would like to ask you to rise and drink a toast with me." He stood. "To Russia. May she ever prosper."

They were on their feet immediately. "The Motherland."

Dimitri Borodin put down his glass, came around the table and held out his hand. "For that, I thank you, Mr. Hayman. You will come with us to Starogan, and we will show you even better things. Now I must return to my post. Peter."

Peter hurried forward and Michael Nej opened the door for them. The three women watched them go with varying expressions of concern; neither Peter nor his father had slept in the house for six weeks, but came home only occasionally for a change of clothing or a bath.

"You aren't going off again tonight, Mr. Hayman?" the countess asked. "Surely there is nothing left for you to write about."

George sat down, and at once his glass was refilled. "I feel I'm very much of a supernumerary, eating rations which could be used for someone else."

"Nonsense," the countess insisted. "There is plenty of food left in Port Arthur. General Stoessel is being unnecessarily pessimistic in not allowing more to be available. Admiral Rozhdestvenski has been delayed, that is all. But he will be here. I can assure you of that, my dear Mr. Hayman. I know him well. And besides," she said with a roguish smile, "you are fulfilling a very important function, which is keeping my girls happy. Ilona, I think you and Mr. Hayman should go for a walk in the garden. It is your birthday, and a young woman must be escorted for a walk in the garden on her birthday. That is absolutely essential."

Ilona opened her mouth, then seemed to decide against speaking. Instead she turned to George. "Would you like to walk in the garden, George? I imagine it is very cold."

"A short walk," her mother said.

"I'll come too," Tatiana announced.

"You will not, Tatiana Dimitrievna. You have had far too much wine. You will go to bed."

Tatiana made her usual face, got up and ran from the room. Olga Borodina also rose. "Talk to her of America, Mr. Hayman. It is her birthday. A young woman should not have to think about war on her birthday. Tell her of America."

"Your mother is a very thoughtful woman." George allowed Nikolai Nej to drape him in his coat. Ilona already wore hers and had concealed her hair beneath an enormous chiffon headscarf.

"She is a romantic," she remarked. "But I must apologize for Papa. A birthday party is not really the place for a patriotic speech."

"Perhaps not, but Port Arthur is, wouldn't you say?"

Nikolai opened the terrace door for them, and they stepped into the chill December air. Immediately their heads turned in the direction of the unending noise, where flashes of light flared over the hilltops to the west. The Japanese had been probing forward following their recent success in capturing 174-meter Hill, and the fighting would clearly go on all night. Of course 203-meter Hill was impregnable, George reminded himself. But so had Nanshan Hill been impregnable.

"I do not think patriotic speeches are going to help Port Arthur." She walked away from him to the edge of the terrace and turned from the noise to gaze at the sea.

"Now isn't that strange," he said. "I came here convinced this city would fall, and now I almost believe it may hold. When I came here you were equally sure it would hold, and now you are beginning to have doubts."

"I never thought it would hold, George. I just didn't have the courage to say so. And what you really believe is summed up in that *almost*. Those guns get closer every night."

"And more men get killed every day. Or wounded."

He wondered if he should have said that. It really was unforgivable to remind her, tonight of all nights, of what she must return to the next day.

"I sometimes wonder which supply will give out first," she said. "Men or days." She turned so suddenly he had no time to step back, and her arm brushed his. "No war tonight, George. I am so glad you will come with us to Starogan."

"Do you think your father was serious?"

"Of course he was serious, or he would not have said it."

"I was wondering . . . well, here in Port Arthur we're all in the same boat, so to speak. We're captives of the siege. When it's all over, your father will again be the son and heir to a prince, and I will again be a rather scurrilous reporter, at least in his eyes."

Her face was very close to his. "Do you not think some of us may have been changed by sharing all this?"

"I suppose it's a matter of how much."

They had moved away from the light glowing from the terrace doorway, and her face was only just visible. Yet he could see the expression in her eyes, the expression he thought he had seen so often before but which this night was unmistakable. And as he watched, her tongue stole between her lips, briefly, before returning. Oh my God, he thought. This isn't what the countess intended at all. But it was going to happen, because they both wanted it to happen, so very much, and because this night they had both had too much wine, for the first time in six months, and because those months had stretched their emotions to the limit, time and again.

"I. . . ." She hesitated, and then suddenly and without warning it was as if a dam had burst. "Too much," she said. "Too much. Every day, watching men die, watching men . . ." She half fell against him, and he caught her around the waist and held her close. Her head rested on his shoulder. "Watching men . . . oh, my God, watching men." Her voice broke, and he put his fingers under her chin to tilt back her head so that he could kiss the tears which were rolling down her cheeks. Her mouth was his, and yet he hesitated, more sober, more aware of the enormity of the step she was contemplating.

"Men," she said, and turned, once again taking him by surprise. His hands, slipping from her chin to her shoulders, slid across her breasts and he hastily released her, allowing her to move away, if she wished. But instead she leaned her back against him, and he could listen to her breathing—long breaths.

"Every day," she said. "Every day I think I am going to go mad when I enter that operating theater. Every day. Every day I think I cannot go on."

"But you do go on," he said against her ear. "Because you are Ilona Borodina." Sanity. For God's sake, sanity. But he could not be the only sane person in a world gone mad. She had to be sane, too.

"I don't want to be. God, I don't want to." Once again she turned, and this time she was in his arms, his hands closing on her shoulder blades to hold her close, her face tilting back to be kissed. There was no great difference in their heights, and he found her lips without difficulty. They were closed, but a moment later open, wide, to allow him inside, to take his entire tongue into her mouth, and then to release him in order to breathe. "I don't want to be Ilona Borodina, George. Not ever again."

Her body was against his, pressing even closer than he was prepared to hold her, breast against breast, belly against belly, thigh against thigh, and groin against groin. She had learned, these past few weeks, what bodies were for when a man and a woman wished to share them, and she had learned about erections, too, because she only pressed closer as he rose against her.

But what was George to do, but thrust her away, hurry her inside the house, and remind her again and again, that she was Ilona Borodina until she understood it? And then . . . speak with the general. The general liked him and—at the moment, at least—was prepared to treat him as an equal. The general might even be prepared to accept him . . . betrothed to Ilona Borodina? The entire night went into a spin.

Her mouth was back on his, her tongue thrusting. There was no aspect to her being at this moment except passion, a passion which had been building for six months of tension and forced intimacy, forced knowledge. But if they remained out here a moment longer they would hate themselves. He half carried her, hands on her waist, across the terrace, still kissing her so she would not know what he was doing, fumbled for the catch on the door, opened it and stumbled into the drawing room. The door slammed shut behind him, and his head jerked back, expecting to see Nikolai Nej appear, or worse, Michael . . . why worse?

But no one came at all, and Ilona was making a soft moaning sound as she reached for his mouth again.

Oh God, he thought. "Ilona. . . ." But his mouth was lost against hers yet again, and now she was half pushing him, so that he touched the edge of the settee with the backs of his knees and fell over, the girl on his lap.

She is mad at this moment, he reminded himself. And therefore I am also mad. But I am criminally mad, because I understand what we are doing, and yet I will not stop. I cannot stop.

And besides, I love her.

It was not an emotion that he had ever understood before. He had never made love to any of the few women with whom he had previously supposed himself to be in love, and thus with the few with whom he had shared a bed, there had always been present an element of guilt or, in the case of prostitutes, self-disgust. The profane and the sacred had never before come together, and in the case of Ilona any thought of the profane had been rejected even before he had rejected the possibility of a sacred relationship. But suddenly the two were together, here, and desired as much by the woman as by the man.

She was uncertain. This was understandable. She was nervous and probably terrified by what she was doing. Yet she could no more stop herself than he could stop himself. She placed his hand on the bodice of her gown, and when he lowered his head to kiss the tops of her breasts she herself dragged on the material to expose the nipples.

Her own hands were even less controllable. They were already moving across his trousers, finding the hardness and staying there, while she shuddered against him. His brain seemed to cascade emotion, terrifyingly mingled with the common sense which was commanding him to stop, even more terrifyingly mingled with the desire which had him falling back and pulling her on top of him, and allowing his hands to slide down her back and thighs. Ilona Borodina's thighs, her legs, her bottom, all his, if he wished to take them. And he knew then the greatest experience that can befall any man, that of suddenly realizing that the woman he considers the loveliest and most desirable in all the world is willing to reciprocate, willing to allow him to take possession of all the magnificent gifts a kindly God had bestowed. The thrill of ownership.

Added to the thrill of exploration. Where on previous occasions everything had been haste and anxiety, here he was almost reluctant to reach a consummation; he wanted to linger, wanted to understand just what he was gaining, just what she was yielding. He wanted to *see,* and instead could only feel. And flesh was hard to find. His fingers played over entrancingly muscular thighs concealed beneath rippling silk, and when he pulled skirt and petticoats past her knees, he found only more silk, her stockings, and moving up again, her drawers. Her mouth moved on his as she squirmed tighter into his arms. The silk was on the back of his hands now, and here at last was what he sought, tight buttocks overflowing in his caress, great heat, and damp hair as silky as her clothes. He felt himself about to burst, and had to pull himself from beneath her, to rise on his elbow and release his own clothes. Her mouth fell away, and he could at last look at her face, eyes flopping open to match her mouth, cheeks flushed, soft golden pompadour dissolving as the headscarf slid around her neck to form a pillow.

He sat up, gazed at breasts bigger than he had ever dreamed surging out of the disordered bodice, then at the long slender legs, and on an impulse leaned forward to release one of the garters and push it, and the stocking, down past her knee, and kiss the flesh of her thigh, so white it might have been carved from ivory, but for the trembling muscles. Then his face was at the lace edging of her drawers, loose enough to allow his mouth and tongue in there as well.

Ilona gasped and sat up, forcing his head against her, hugging him into the secret warmth of her body, tearing his collar open to drive her fingers down his back, inside his shirt, kissing his neck as she arched above him. Thus contorted they clung to each other for perhaps a second, then seemed to fly apart like released springs.

Now all was haste and purpose. They had passed the point of no return. The girl lay down again, on her back, she herself pulling her skirt about her waist, keeping her legs together only to allow him to slide her drawers down and drop them on the floor, and then spreading them to allow him between. He knelt above her as he removed his own clothing, and looked down on the pulsing white belly, the dark hair at her groin. Then he was upon her and in her in a long surge of heat and anxious passion, a soaring ecstasy which seemed an eternity but could only have been seconds, an explosion of animal power which had his mouth slipping away from hers to leave his lips sucking at her neck, embedded in the marvelous scent of her hair.

He became aware of being disturbed, without understanding the cause. He pushed himself up, once again kneeling between her legs, and looked from right to left. But the room was unchanged. It had been his conscience.

Because now passion was spent—by him, at least. He looked down at her. One leg had slipped off the cushions onto the floor, the other was pulled up and pressed against the back of the couch; his thigh was marked by the imprint of her boot. And there was a trickle of blood, staining the white flesh from vagina to buttock. To him she was girl-become-woman, displayed and exposed, waiting for man. But the man was spent, and gradually her breathing returned to normal, and her eyes, which had been shut, opened. Now was the moment of reckoning, when she must either adore or loathe the creature who had done this to her.

Her arms, which had been thrown above her head, raised slowly and came down. "Oh, my darling," she said. "My darling, darling, George."

He still could not believe it. It could be no part of his destiny, which already encompassed so much health and strength and vigor, so much wealth and position and so much achievement, at twenty-seven, also to have the love of the most wonderful woman he had ever known or could have imagined. He had to be existing in a dream, and even the dream was beyond belief. But she was again in his arms, sitting up to hold him against her, and he was again kissing her, knowing her, possessing her. For whatever he did, wherever he stroked, was where she wanted to be touched. It was as if their minds had melded equally with their bodies, and could never again be separated. Perfect love, he thought. Out of all of this bloodshed and mayhem, there has come a perfect love. Obviously, a girl like Ilona Borodina would have to know a perfect love. But for that love to be George Hayman. . . . "I'll speak to your father," he said. "Today."

Her head moved away. "Are you sure?"

"Sure? Me? Are *you* sure, you mean?"

"I am sure, George. Sure, sure, sure. I meant . . . now?"

"My dearest, darling girl," he said. "We have . . . we have already consummated our marriage. In advance of consecrating it. We dare not wait a moment longer in obtaining his permission."

For the first time a shadow passed over her face. "You'll not tell him?"

"Only that we love each other. I will have to confess that I have not gone about it the Russian way. But I have gone about it the American way, in making sure of *your* love before speaking with him. He will understand that. He respects my Americanism as I respect his Russian point of view. He does like me, Ilona. I think he does, at the least. I will speak with him today."

"Oh, my darling, darling," she said, and clung to him again. "If anything should happen to separate us. . . ."

"Nothing can separate us," he insisted. "Not now. Nothing can ever separate us again. I'll make sure of that, I promise you." He pushed himself off the sofa, held her hands, raised her to her feet. Her clothes fell back into place and everything that had happened might never have been, except that she was again in his arms; when he released her, she stooped to pick up her drawers, then crushed them into her hands.

"George. . . ."

"There is nothing to fear."

"I am not afraid. I would like you to love me again. Come to my room, George. No one will know. Spend the night with me, George."

For a moment he hesitated. The temptation was enormous. But what had happened had been necessary; without it they would not have understood the depth of their love. It must not now be abused, reduced to the level of a purely physical desire. They knew that they loved, that they were suited, that they were inseparable, from this moment. When he held her naked in his arms it must be as his wife.

He shook his head, kissed her on the nose. "That would be wrong, my wonderful girl. We'll be married soon. We must have your bed to keep as the seal on that."

She gazed at him, her eyes deep pools of desire. Then she held him close and kissed him on the mouth. "If Papa refuses you, we shall elope. Swear that to me, George."

"No one on earth is ever going to come between us, Ilona. I'll swear to *that*. But your father isn't going to say no. You go to bed, and I'll get dressed and go out to the hill. I must talk with him the very moment he comes off duty."

"You'll go to the hill tonight?"

"I go to the hill most nights."

"But . . . my God, if you were to be hurt. Swear to me you'll not be hurt, George."

"I'm not going to be hurt, my darling. Go to bed, and when you awake, we shall be betrothed. Officially."

A last kiss, a last long look into his eyes. Then she was moving across the room, her drawers in one hand, her shoes in the other, her gown half off her shoulders, her hair a golden cascade partly covering her face. A sight he could never forget, even if it had been a dream.

But it was no dream. She blew a kiss and disappeared, and it was time to gather up his own clothes, and hurry along the corridor to his room, change into his riding habit, and go down to the stables. The house slept, the Nejs slept; thank God the Nejs slept. He saddled Long John, walked him out of the garden, and suddenly he was aware that he was reentering the real world, the world of explosions and gunfire, of distant flames and fighting men. Or was *that* not the dream world, the nightmare world, and reality only to be found in the arms of a beautiful woman?

And this night even war could not dull the soaring pleasure of his senses. Once away from the house he kicked Long John into a trot, sent him down the slopes and into the town, there discovering that although the Borodin household slept, Port Arthur seethed. Everywhere were troop movements and anxious civilians, shouted rumors and simmering panic.

"The hill has fallen," he heard someone shouting. "The hill has fallen."

Oh, Christ, he thought. While I was lying on that couch, while we were all celebrating Ilona's birthday . . . He sent Long John into a gallop, careening through the darkness, having to swerve aside as more and more men were hurried to block the enormous gap which had suddenly been torn in the Russian defenses. It was too immense a catastrophe to be comprehended so suddenly.

"Halt there." He gazed into the gloom. The firing was dying down; probably the Japanese were too exhausted to press home their immediate advantage. Besides, why did they have to? 203-meter Hill overlooked the entire town and port.

"You can go no further," said the officer. "The hill has fallen."

His men straggled past him and the solitary rider. They carried stretchers or gave arms to the walking wounded. They did not look at the war correspondent; his red jacket had become a familiar sight over the past six months. And now they were defeated. Utterly and irrevocably.

George dismounted. "But what *happened?*"

The officer shrugged. "They just kept coming. They came from in front and from the side and even from under the ground. It did not seem to matter to them how many men they lost. They just kept coming. And when the general fell. . . ."

George's heart seemed to constrict. "General Borodin? Where is he?"

"Dead, Mr. Hayman. General Borodin is dead. He fell at the head of his men."

Only the rumble of the drums disturbed the quiet of the morning—the drums and the whipping of the eagle-crested flags in the cold breeze coming off the bay. The Russian soldiers stood motionless at attention, their officers waiting before them.

And with the officers, the family. Olga Borodina held her coat close, collar turned up against the wind. Ilona stood immediately beside her, holding Tatiana's hand. The girls' faces were serious, and there was evidence of tears, but for the moment they were on parade.

Peter Borodin stood on his mother's other side, wearing full dress uniform, white tunic and breeches, gilt breastplate, gilt helmet with a nodding plume. He had been at his father's side when the fatal shot had found its target.

In front of them the Japanese soldiers approached slowly, marching with rigid discipline beneath an enormous white flag. Four of them carried the stretcher on which lay the shrouded figure. An act of gallantry, certainly, George reckoned. But they could afford to be gallant. Behind them, on the top of 203-meter Hill, the Rising Sun fluttered proudly in the breeze, and the rim of the hill was crowded with their soldiers. More than that, it was already lined with guns, some captured from the Russians and now turned around, others dragged up the rocky slopes beyond. The guns were silent for this moment, but when they decided to speak there was no part of Port Arthur, no ship in the harbor, which would be beyond their range.

So this was the end, even if the defenders still hoped for a miracle, for a glimpse of smoke on the horizon to tell them Rozhdestvenski's fleet was here. And what did *he* hope for? His miracle had taken place last night. There had been no time to be alone with her since, no time for them mutually to take stock of their positions, of their futures. The man who had had the power to make or mar that future was dead. Therefore their path might be eased. Olga Borodina certainly liked him, and Peter was his friend. But it was not to be thought of at this moment, and certainly not discussed. This was one of the most closely knit families he had ever known, and today their world had crumbled into dust.

The Japanese party reached the Russian lines, where the gun carriage waited with the coffin already in place. General Stoessel remained mounted, a disturbing sign, George thought, of the man's anxiety to maintain his dignity even in the presence of death. But he had had the courtesy to remove his hat. George wondered what he was thinking. He was the senior officer, though Borodin had been the higher in social rank, and thus they had loathed each other. Now the death of the one had exposed the other to catastrophe.

The Japanese came to attention and presented arms. The Russians responded. The officer commanding the Japanese party saluted. George studied his face. He knew the Japanese people well, had spent several months in Tokyo and had sampled the delights of the Hakone lakes beneath Fujiyama. It was this knowledge, as much as his understanding of Russian weakness, that had made him prophesy a Japanese victory in this war. Now he realized, watching the frozen face in front of him, that the outcome had never been in question. There was dedication and determination and iron discipline, for no hint of the triumph the officer must be feeling was permitted to show at his mouth or even in his eyes. He was a soldier, paying a last tribute to a gallant foe.

And now his task was done. A crisp order, and the Japanese turned and marched back up the hill. The Russians watched them returning to the safety of their gun muzzles.

And therefore time was short. No one knew for sure how much time General Nogi would allow for a funeral, even one of a princely general like himself. The gun carriage was wheeled back into the Russian camp, and at a signal from General Stoessel the family moved forward. Ilona's head started to turn, as if to see what George was going to do, and then straightened again. George remained still, in the ranks of civilians. This was not something into which he could intrude.

Peter leaned over the coffin and turned back the shroud to allow his mother a last look at her husband's face. Tatiana and Ilona made the sign of the cross and the younger girl suddenly started to weep, not noisily or violently; great tears simply began to roll down her cheeks. But they are fortunate, George thought, because it is happening so quickly, and there is no time for a long lying in state and mourning.

The general raised his hand and the carpenters moved forward to nail the lid of the coffin in place. The banging of their hammers sounded dully as the drums ceased, for the moment. Then the band struck up Chopin's funeral march, and the soldiers fell into column behind the family as the carriage was led up the roadway toward the cemetery.

George found himself in the midst of the civilians straggling behind the cortège, between the ranks of Russian soldiers who waited only for them to depart before taking their places in the hastily improvised earthworks west of the town.

The procession entered the cemetery, where the priests waited, suitably sepulchral figures in their black robes and tall black hats. In a city about to be blasted out of existence, there was no time even for a church service, only for a brief celebration of the Eucharist. The priests prayed at the grave side, the family falling to their knees on the earth beneath them, the soldiers standing with bowed heads. General Stoessel at last dismounted to stand beside the widow. George removed his top hat and waited; he could only barely hear the words. Had I had the time to speak with him, he thought, I might have been able to give them my support as their future son-in-law. How he wished he could be there, how he wished he could belong to their grief and their misery. George Hayman, republican, wishing to become a pillar of imperial Russia.

The rifle bolts clicked, and a moment later the first volley echoed into the air. The second followed immediately, and the firing party came to attention. There were several seconds of silence, and then heads began to turn, slowly but irresistibly, to the hilltop and the Japanese flag and the staring gun muzzles, still silent.

General Stoessel remounted. "To your positions, gentlemen," he said, and wheeled his horse. The crowd broke up, the civilians returning to the town, the soldiers hurrying for their stations, the officers calling for their horses. George watched Peter Borodin embrace his mother and each of his sisters in turn and then mount, his horse's bridle held by the faithful Michael. And what did *he* think of it all, George wondered? Where he had belonged to the father, he now belonged to the son. But he and Peter had been friends all of their lives, just as old Nikolai had been Dimitri's friend.

George had left his own horse at the house, preferring to walk. But the trap would have to pass him on its way back to the town, and he remained standing at the roadside while those around him melted away, until he was alone, watching them approach. Michael sat guiding the horse, and now was tugging on the rein to stop. There was no welcome in his face, merely a stony acknowledgment of his duty. Could he really feel that much grief for the general?

"Mr. Hayman." Olga Borodina's voice was quiet. "You'll ride with us."

"I'd not intrude."

"It is no intrusion, Mr. Hayman. You are our friend. We need our friends at a time like this."

George climbed up beside Ilona, facing the countess and Tatiana. He did not dare look at her, but looked instead at Tatiana, her cheeks red and swollen. Tattie met his gaze for a moment, then looked away.

"It seemed that you were right, Mr. Hayman," Olga Borodina remarked. "About the outcome of the siege."

"Believe me, countess, I wish I had been wrong."

The countess gave him a sad smile. "I know that, Mr. Hayman. As my husband said. . . ." She paused, and sighed. "Last night, we converted you. And now you must share our destruction with us."

"I shall, ma'am. I promise you that."

Her gaze was as direct as her daughter's. Did a mother's instincts give her any clue to his and Ilona's feelings? "I had no doubt you would, Mr. Hayman. And we may well need you."

His hand dropped beside him, and he touched Ilona's glove. She sat bolt upright, her face shaded by the huge dark hat with its flopping brim which kept being blown up by the wind, and stared ahead. What could she be thinking? She had been as happy as he, last night. But undoubtedly what they had done was wrong, however they intended to put it right in the future. And almost at the moment of orgasm her father had been shot. What *could* she be thinking?

The carriage entered the garden and came to a stop. Michael was down immediately to assist his mistress alight. George got out on the other side and helped Tatiana down, then hurried around to walk beside Ilona. She must speak soon. *They* must speak.

"When will the bombardment begin, Mr. Hayman?" Olga Borodina asked.

"When General Nogi is ready, ma'am."

"And what is he waiting for?"

"Perhaps he is hoping the garrison will surrender, now that it is so exposed."

The countess's head came up. "This garrison will never surrender, Mr. Hayman. My husband died that they should never surrender. My son may die as well. We shall fight to the bitter end. You must be prepared for that, Mr. Hayman." She went into the house, Tatiana following her. Ilona hesitated, and he took her hand. She glanced, not at him, but at Michael Nej, standing beside the horse, his face still cold. Then she turned and went into the garden, still holding George's hand.

"I don't suppose there is anything I can say now that won't sound banal," he said.

She turned with that suddenness which always took him by surprise. "You can say you love me."

"Love you? My God, my darling, how I love you!"

"Because if you stop loving me now," she said, "I have nothing. You do understand that?"

Her face was serious, and there was only a suggestion of lurking tears in her eyes. Her complexion was unblemished, even by the fury of their lovemaking. But her body was not unblemished. It could never be the same again.

"I understand that," he said. "I will speak with your mother as soon as it is proper."

"Six months," she said.

"We cannot wait six months."

"We must," she insisted, her voice suddenly fierce. "We cannot discuss marriage while we are mourning Papa. Can you not wait six months?"

"I can wait forever, so long as I am at your side."

"You will be at my side, George Hayman. Always. Now I must go to Mama. Now—" She checked, as the first explosion burst into the morning sky.

"Aaagh," screamed Nadia Nej. "Aaagh." She rocked back and forth, hands pressed to her ears, body shuddering. Her husband threw his arm round her shoulders, hugging her close.

"Hush, my love," he begged. "Hush. You will distress Madame."

Lost in the paroxysm of the following explosion, Nadia subsided into huge, raking sobs which seemed to travel from her head to her heels. The explosions were not close now, but continuous. The Japanese were not interested in the destruction of houses or civilians; they aimed at the harbor, and only those shots which fell short disturbed the town itself.

But the noise alone, Michael thought, would bring about their destruction. Nona certainly would not last much longer than her mother; she was crouched on the floor, her hands also covering her ears. Ivan looked as though he might already have surrendered; his body and head were humped, his hands drooped over his knees, his eyes were shut and face expressionless.

Then what of the family at the other end of the cellar? Only three of them now. The general was dead, and perhaps Count Peter, as he now was called, had also been killed. And perhaps even the American, who had gone out to record the destruction of the city, was lying dead in a gutter. Michael stared into the gloom, at the three figures huddled together, not screaming—yet. But *they* too would be screaming soon. Because he now knew that they were no different, no better than Mama or Nona. He had never thought a great deal of the countess and had always been certain that Tattie was weak in the head, but presumably those misfortunes could overtake even princesses. On the other hand princesses could always look forward to bearing children like Ilona, with the beauty and the poise and the aloofness of a goddess—and the lust and abandon of a Tartar whore.

Legs. He wondered if Ivan, hunched beside him, was thinking about legs. About the only legs he had ever seen. Well, he's seen nothing. I have seen legs, Michael thought. I have seen legs thrown in the air, stretched to one side in ecstasy, a white backside between them. A male backside. An American backside. I have seen legs, and I have seen tits, and I have seen golden hair loosed as it should only be loosed for a husband.

All in a split second. He had opened the door, wondering whether they had gone to bed and whether he should douse the candles, he had seen, and he had closed the door again. All before he could draw breath. The breath had come when he was leaning against the outside of the door, sucking for air like a drowning man. A goddess, straight from the pit of hell. Giving herself to a casual acquaintance, a man she had known for only six months, and a man who was not even an aristocrat, but belonged to a nation which had abolished aristocracy. His idol, reduced to the stature of a fishwife.

Supposing the American were dead, in a gutter, where he belonged, why should she not then surrender to *him*, as she lusted so hard, and was so quickly prepared to surrender? But did he still want her, after the American?

He got up, nearly lost his footing as the entire house shuddered, and walked across the cellar. "Is there anything you would like, madame?" he said. He looked at the countess, but his eyes could slide sideways to look at Ilona also, for she had raised her head.

"You are very good, Michael Nikolaievich," the countess said. "I would like some tea, if it is possible."

"I will fetch some, madame. May I make some also for my mother and father?"

"Of course, Michael Nikolaievich. But . . . is it not dangerous to go upstairs?"

"I do not think so, madame."

"I will come with you," Ilona said.

"You, Mademoiselle Ilona?"

"You cannot," her mother said. "You'll be killed."

"Killed," Tatiana wailed. "We'll all be killed."

"Oh, do be quiet, Tatiana Dimitrievna," the countess snapped.

"I will not be killed," Ilona said, getting up. "I wish to see what is happening."

Michael held the door for her; with it open, the noise—the continuous crackling explosion—seemed much louder.

"Be careful," the countess shouted.

Ilona gathered her skirts and ran up the steps. The cellar exited beside the kitchen at the back of the house, away from the garden and the view over the sea. She hesitated for a moment, then pulled the cellar door open, stepped outside, and at once shrank against the wall: there was a long, slow whine, followed by a shattering explosion from close at hand.

"Come," Michael said, and took her hand. Michael Nej, holding the hand of Ilona Borodina—and she had taken off her gloves in the cellar and forgotten to replace them. But she made no demur, followed him in a stumbling run round the side of the house and into the kitchen. Then she lost her balance and tumbled to her hands and knees, and as he helped her up he inhaled her perfume, and felt her lean against him for just a moment. Oh, he wanted her. Even if she were the lowest whore in all the world, if her entire gown were composed of prostitutes' yellow cards, one from every municipal authority in the empire, he would still want her.

He held a chair for her, and she sat down. He busied himself at the stove, stoking up the fire that was still simmering, then went outside to fill a kettle from the pump. His brain was teeming. If she wanted so badly, then she would want him as well. He was sure of it. They had been friends, close friends, all their lives, not like the intruding American. All he needed was the right approach, the right moment. And the right words. Confess that he had seen her that night? No, that might shock her, and make her angry. She was Ilona Borodina; no one could ever be told that the granddaughter of a prince could give herself on a sofa in her mother's drawing room. It was only possible for him to know that she *would* do that, for all her upbringing and her poise and the beauty which had seemed to make every man no more than a cipher. That secret belonged to him—and to the American. So, find the right approach, and know that she would surrender to him.

The kettle was full. He should not have filled it, but he hesitated to empty it, just in case they should run short of water at a later stage of the siege. The siege was certain to go on. The countess had said so, and Michael never doubted her for a moment.

Slowly he hefted the kettle back toward the kitchen. Ilona was the countess's daughter. Suppose she refused him? She might have yielded to the American because he was a foreigner. She would never yield to the son of a serf. So much for that dream. He knew her secret, and he knew her for what she really was, but he could never possess her. His elation disappeared in a cloud of despair, and he banged the door behind him.

She was gone. Michael dropped the kettle, ran through the house, and reached the terrace, where he stopped to stare beyond the girl at the harbor, plumed with white cascades of water where the shells had entered; at the ships, burning, listing, one sinking even as he stared at it, its stern dipping and its bow pointing at the sky, its specklike crew leaping from the decks into the seething sea; and at the waterfront, a sheet of flame through which collapsing buildings could dimly be discerned, while the shrieks of burning men and women drifted through even the thunder of the guns.

And nearer at hand the girl. She stood quite motionless, both hands clasped to her throat, watching the scene before her, not even trembling any more at the whine of the shells passing overhead. She gave the impression of having lost her soul to the god of battle, of having been sucked into the vast cataclysm which was consuming Port Arthur.

He went nearer. "Mademoiselle Ilona. . . ." He hesitated, and cursed himself. Then she turned, and he saw her gaze go past him to the doors of the drawing room.

"George."

"Ilona."

She stepped past Michael and ran toward the doors. Michael Nej watched the pair, his face twisted.

"General Stoessel has sent out a flag of truce," George Hayman said. "He is asking for terms."

Ilona, already in his arms, seemed to arch backwards.

"It's true," Hayman said miserably, and sighed. "There was nothing else he could do, my darling. The Japanese have sunk the fleet. They can just sit up there and destroy the town at their leisure. And everyone in it."

"Surrender," she whispered, her voice suddenly clear. For the guns had ceased. The tremendous roaring had stopped as suddenly as if one had awakened from a bad dream. Only the burning houses, the sinking ships testified to its reality, Michael thought.

A horse galloped up the drive. Peter Borodin threw himself from the saddle and ran up the steps to the terrace. He still wore his full dress uniform—he had not changed his clothes in the week since his father had died—but the gilt was stained black and there was a rent in the dirty white sleeve.

"George," he cried. "Thank God you are here. You've heard the news?"

Hayman nodded.

Peter paused before them, still panting. "Where is Mother? Where is Tattie?"

"In the cellar," Ilona said. "They are all right. But Peter—what is going to happen to us?"

"You will be leaving here. There is nothing to worry about. General Stoessel has obtained honorable terms. All civilians will be allowed to leave the city with whatever they can carry."

"All civilians?" She stared at her brother for a moment, then gave a wailing cry. "Peter!" She threw herself into his arms.

"There is nothing to be afraid of." He stroked her hair and looked over her head at Hayman.

"But . . ." She looked up. "You?"

His smile was twisted. "I will be a prisoner of war. It will only be for a little while. When General Kuropatkin defeats the Japanese they will be happy to sue for peace." Still he gazed at Hayman. He does not believe a word of it, Michael thought. He knows they are defeated.

"You are an accurate military observer, George."

"I wish to God I weren't."

Peter disentangled himself from his sister. "Nonetheless it has happened. Now I must ask a favor of you."

"Whatever I can do."

"Take my mother and my sisters back to Starogan."

"Of course. It will be an honor."

Peter gazed at him for a moment, then nodded. "I know I can trust you."

"I . . ." Hayman looked at Ilona. Michael could read the message passing between them. They loved, and shared, and understood. And she was telling him, now is not the time. Wait, and be sure. "I wish I could tell you how I feel," Hayman said. "About what has happened. About this . . . this tragedy."

Peter Borodin gave another twisted smile. "Tragedy," he said. "It is more than that, my friend. It is a catastrophe on a scale none of us ever imagined possible. Russia will never be the same again, and neither will any Russian. My father's deep running river has reached the rapids, at last."

Chapter 3

"ONCE," GEORGE HAYMAN WROTE, "I THOUGHT THE UNITED STATES a large country. Once I thought I had seen the greatest plains on earth. Once I felt I was traveling forever, with no end in sight. Now I know better."

He laid down his pen, stared out the window of the first-class smoking carriage. Houses. More than just houses. This was a city. Kharkov.

There had been towns, even cities before. It was difficult to say how many. Travel by train on this scale made time meaningless. His brain was filled with images, first of the surrender itself: the Russian garrison, bowed and beaten, marching from the burning city past the martial splendor of the entering Japanese. It had been the greatest triumph of their brief renaissance as a modern power, the coping stone on the revolution which had begun in 1867.

They had been the most courteous of victors. Determined to prove themselves fitting members of the concourse of great powers, they had overwhelmed the ladies with their kindness, by providing their own soldiers to assist the Nejs in packing up the household. General Nogi had himself received the Countess Borodina, her daughters, and their American friend, had himself served them tea. But they had never been allowed to forget for a moment that they had been defeated; Lieutenant Count Peter Borodin was already on his way to a Japanese prison camp.

Nor had any of the women—countesses, ladies, or washerwomen—been allowed to forget their position when they had been passed through the lines to rejoin the main Russian army under General Kuropatkin, waiting at Mukden for the decisive encounter of the war. Again, no officers could have been more courteous. But their expressions said more clearly than any words could have: your husbands and sons and brothers were given a sacred task to perform, and they have failed. Colonel Prince Sergei Roditchev put it into words. He was an old friend of the Borodins, and had spent the evening with them the night before the train had left for the west.

"No blame can be attached to Count Dimitri, my dear Olga," he said. "To die fighting for one's country is the most honorable fate a soldier can desire. But there were mistakes. There will have to be an inquiry. Stoessel says he was forced to surrender because of the risk of his noncombatants being slaughtered. Why were those noncombatants there at all?"

"Would you have me desert my husband, Sergei?" Olga Borodina demanded.

"A woman has a duty no less than a man," Roditchev insisted. "And in war it is to avoid inflicting unnecessary burdens on him." He gazed at Ilona reflectively, as if considering that it might be a pleasure to teach her what duties a woman should have, then was recalled by the presence of George beside her. "And you, sir, should have known better than to clutter up the defenses, or the ration strength, with an unnecessary mouth."

"Even wars must be reported, Prince Sergei," Ilona said.

"Wars? Bah. Mr. Hayman is a harbinger of disaster. And why are you running off now, Mr. Hayman? You claim to be a war correspondent. Why are you not staying to report on the coming battle?"

"Even war correspondents have duties, prince," George said, refusing to lose his temper, although it would have been a pleasure to punch the fellow in the nose, if only for the way he was looking at Ilona. Almost as if he owned her.

"Mr. Hayman is pledged to escort the girls and myself back to Starogan," the countess explained. "It was Peter's wish."

"Indeed?" inquired the prince, giving George the full benefit of his close-browed stare.

But then the Borodin family had been on their way, chugging east, slowly following the route through enormous pine forests. Every few miles, gangs of soldiers, supervised by warrant officers mounted on enormous tricycles pedaling before the train, had to disembark to clear the track of snow.

It had been possible to imagine oneself in another world. Wherever the eye could see there had been nothing but snow. When they reached Lake Baikal, where the railway line was broken, they had crossed that enormous inland sea by sledges traveling on ice. Then it had been another train, and more snow as they had slowly approached the Urals, before turning south toward the basin of the Don. But always there had been the snow.

It had taken ten days for them to reach this far—the most entrancing ten days of George Hayman's life. Quite apart from the otherworldly scenery and the emotional experience of being so small a being in such an enormous wilderness, the time had been spent entirely in the company of Ilona Borodina. There had been no intimacy; there had been no opportunities for it in the crowded train— George was sharing his first-class sleeper with three wounded Russian officers—but it would not have happened anyway. Apart from his own resolution, there was the reason for their presence on the train. That reason was not only the death of Dimitri Borodin; the ladies seemed to be slowly absorbing the immensity of what had happened to them. Nearly *all* the twenty-odd women aboard had left husbands or fathers or brothers behind in Port Arthur, whether dead or in prison. So they talked about familiar, reassuring subjects, discussed the St. Petersburg social scene, the latest fashions—latest being the last time any of them had been to the west, two summers before—grumbled about their children, who played up and down the corridors of the train with shrieks of careless pleasure. But they never talked about the future. The future, whether as a widow or knowing that one's husband had been defeated, was not to be considered.

Except by the couples who were young, and in love. And fortunate enough to have their loved one on the train beside them. They, too, did not really wish to discuss the future. It was enough to be able to sit next to one another, to stand on the rear platform and watch the snow-covered scenery dropping away behind them, to touch hands and to exchange looks as they made ready for bed. It was enough to be in love. And they *were* in love. If he had feared that the intensity of her emotion might not equal his own, might have been diluted by the tragedy which had so suddenly entered her life, he feared no longer. They loved, and the future was theirs.

And now they were in Kharkov, where the train was to divide, the larger half, and therefore by far the greater number of passengers, turning north for Moscow. The rest—the fortunate ones, in George's opinion—would change to a small train for the journey to the south, to the Crimean peninsula. And on the way, Starogan.

"Starogan," Tatiana announced, bursting into the male sanctuary of the smoking carriage, her nostrils twitching as she inhaled the tobacco-filled air. "We're coming to Starogan."

Predictably, Tattie had been the first to recover from the depression which had haunted the journey. Equally predictably, she had managed to span the gap between the adults and children. If she began every day the neatest young lady imaginable, her ribbon descending from exactly the center of her hat, her pale blonde hair waving gently on to her shoulders, her blouse neatly pressed, her skirt smoothly elegant, by midmorning she was hatless, her hair scattered and her blouse open at the throat. She had spent this morning, as she had every morning, dominating the game of hide-and-seek played by the smaller children, and using her opportunities to wander the length of the train, even as far as the third-class compartments, where the muzhiks slept eight to a compartment, men and women and children on bare boards, talking to anyone who would listen.

Her enthusiasm was infectious. George was on his feet in a moment, smiling apologetically to the few remaining Russian officers on their way to the hospitals of Sevastopol. Peering out of a window, his first impression was one of disappointment: a slightly larger village, but still a village like any of the others they had passed through, and it was surrounded by the same endless sheet of snow. Presumably, beneath the white was black earth—this was the most fertile part of the entire Russian empire, according to his books. And presumably that earth, come summer, would be the sea of wheat that Ilona had described. But for some reason which he could not now understand he had imagined that Starogan was at the seaside. Here he could see only a river, a broad sheet of ice.

The train was stopping, and Michael Nej appeared in the doorway, holding George's hat and coat. Michael had not been himself on this journey. George had supposed that over such a land voyage, with Michael obviously now regarded as his valet, they would have had endless opportunities for talk. Instead they had hardly exchanged half a dozen words a day. The fault was partly his own, he knew. He no longer wanted to encourage a Russian servant to tell him how much he resented his station in life, how much he dreamed of a change, perhaps even a revolution, which would elevate him to some dignity and prosperity. However much he tried to convince himself that love had nothing to do with politics, George had quite unintentionally joined the elitists. But Michael had also changed. If he had always been suspicious of George's overtures, for the first six months of his stay in Port Arthur, George had felt they were as much friends as master and servant could ever be. But since the general's death Michael had drawn away from him, drawn away from everyone, so far as George could determine, and become introverted and silent, brooding on some immense tragedy. So there had gone another theory, George realized: Michael Nej, even Michael Nej, could be overwhelmed by the enormity of the catastrophe which had befallen the Russian army. Perhaps old Dimitri had been right after all, and every Russian *was* happy merely to be a drop in the deep running river that was his country.

It was far more likely that, since Michael was a muzhik, he was afflicted with guilt that, not being a soldier, he had not been allowed to follow his master into captivity.

But Michael Nej's problems were no concern of his. They were at Starogan, and here was Ilona to squeeze his hand as they took their places immediately behind the countess, in the line waiting to leave the train. "You're seeing it at its worst," she said. "It's lovely, really. If only for the peace of it. Wait until spring."

A conductor opened the door and assisted Olga Borodina down the step and onto the platform. George realized that for all the elegance of the house overlooking the Charles River, and Father's butler and Mother's three maids and a cook, he had never understood the true meaning of the words wealth and power when taken together. On the snow-covered platform stood a line of officials: Father Gregory, the stationmaster and his flunkies, the head of the village council, or Zemstvo and his senior householders. A little girl in her best gown hastily presented a bouquet, and beyond, at a proper distance from the carriage on which two top-hatted grooms were waiting, the rest of the village, shivering in respectful silence, waited to gaze at the widow of their lord's heir and her children.

But there was no member of the family waiting to greet her; George was pretty sure he would have recognized one on sight. No doubt this was an act of mourning. The plumes behind the horses' ears were black.

Olga Borodina paused next to the headman. "You are too kind, Alexander Ivanovich," she said. "My husband would be grateful."

The old man's eyes filled with tears, and he fell to his knees to kiss her gloved hand. "Oh, my lady," he said. "My lady. . . ."

As if he had given a signal, a slow wail arose from the watchers, and they too fell to their knees in the snow. George helped Ilona down and watched a tear escape her eye as well. She brushed it away with the forefinger of her glove and glanced at him in turn. "They love us, George. Truly they do."

"I never doubted it," George said, escorting her down the line of waiting dignitaries, who gazed at him in suspicious bewilderment. Olga Borodina was already seated in the carriage, and Tattie was scrambling up beside her, ignoring the helping hand offered by the postilion. George and Ilona joined them and the door was shut. George watched the Nejs wrestling with the baggage and wondered how they would get it to their destination. No carriages for them.

"How far is it to the house?" he asked.

"Why, it's just there," Tatiana said, pointing out the window.

The snow-covered road led away from the village in a straight line, marked by hedges to either side. The fields continued to stretch left and right, but ahead of them, and rising out of the white, he could see the roof of a house. A very large house, made of wood, and quite grotesquely unattractive; a rectangular box four stories high, with verandas surrounding the ground floor, and great windows above intended to let in all possible light—and air, no doubt, for the summers would be as hot as the winters were cold—but yet a house lacking the slightest spark of architectural beauty.

The frozen river suddenly reappeared again beside the road. Now they were driving through an orchard of heavily pruned apple trees, and beyond were snow-draped lawns and more trees. Here at last was something to admire. But always the house loomed in the near distance, growing every second, towering above the landscape. Now he could see the outbuildings, the stables and the kitchens—built away from the main structure to lessen the risk of fire, but connected to the house by a covered passageway—then the servants' houses, and even the farm which lay about a mile farther on, safely downwind.

The carriage stopped at the foot of the short front staircase and was surrounded by a small army of footmen, opening doors, helping the ladies down, bowing to the countess. From their pen behind the house, dogs barked excitedly. George was the last to leave his seat, but Ilona waited for him, and together they followed the countess and Tatiana up the short flight of wooden steps to the people who stood at the top. And George was struck by a sudden sense of foreboding, as much by the expressions of the three women he had come to know so well as by the expressions on the rest of the family.

At the top of the steps was the Princess Marie Borodina, a tiny, wizened figure; Ilona had told him she was seventy-seven years old. It occurred to George that as she was so small, and her children and grandchildren so large, her husband must have been a mountain of a man. Must have been? His heart constricted.

Marie Borodina wore a very plain black gown, and no jewelry except a gold wedding band and a huge string of pearls looped twice around her neck and lying gracelessly on her dwindled bosom. She had been married to the prince of Starogan for more than fifty years. Fifty years ago . . . George frowned as he tried to think. Fifty years ago, when the elder Peter Borodin first brought his bride to this house, Tsar Alexander II had just come to the throne. The serfs had not even been emancipated. My God, he thought, when I marry Ilona, suppose, just suppose, that we return here for a visit in fifty years. 1955. And this house, presumably, would still be standing, as the younger Peter Borodin's wife would be standing here, to greet her sister-in-law and her American husband.

"Mama?" said Olga Borodina.

The princess held out her hands and Olga kissed them each in turn; then she was swept into an embrace and hugged close. The princess did not weep, but in her face was all the tragedy of a lifetime.

"But Mama," Olga said, releasing her. "Where is Papa?"

The princess sighed. "The prince is dead." Her voice was hardly louder than a whisper. "He had a heart attack when he heard of the surrender of Port Arthur."

Yes, Prince Peter Borodin of Starogan had been a big man. George guessed he must measure well over six feet; and he had been broad and fleshy, despite his age. His face in death was composed; only the slightest twist of the lips, half-concealed beneath his white beard and mustache, indicated the anger and the pain he had felt at the moment of dying.

And what would he have made of me, George wondered? What does he make of me now, from his perch on a cloud, as I solemnly walk past his coffin as if I were a member of the family? Is Dimitri there with him?

He took his place with the other Borodin men. Count Igor, Dimitri's younger brother and temporary head of the family, had the

Borodin height but none of its breadth. He wore rimless pince-nez and a worried frown. In his black frock coat he resembled the undertaker more than a Borodin. By contrast his wife, Countess Anna, was a large woman, thrusting at both hip and bosom, wearing the inevitable double loop of pearls, but with the addition of a hat filled with feathers, and fingers glittering with diamonds. George supposed he had never seen anyone so vulgar in his life. At last he was encountering a typical female Russian aristocrat, he thought; a fitting complement for a man like Sergei Roditchev.

Their sons took after their father. Tigran, Ilona had told him, was already assigned to the Foreign Office; his ready smile belied his carefully cultivated gravity of demeanor. Viktor was younger than Ilona and still at school. He wore glasses and appeared to be a silent, introspective boy, but that might just be his reaction to the consecutive tragedies which had afflicted his family.

Xenia Borodina, Count Igor's daughter, was an older and coarser edition of Ilona. She took after her mother, and her gush of titian hair, deep bosom and wide hips, pealing laughter (which threatened at any moment to disturb the solemnity of the occasion) and mobile, welcoming mouth gave ample indication of Count Igor's reason for marrying Anna years before.

But today they were an unhappy lot. And their unhappiness, George was realizing, was not altogether because of having lost a father, grandfather, brother or uncle. It had to do with the drastic change in the family circumstances. Presumably Count Igor Borodin's family had known all their lives that eventually Dimitri Borodin would be prince of Starogan. Now they had to come to terms with the fact that the new head of the family was a twenty-two-year-old lieutenant in the Preobraschenski Guards, a boy they had not seen for several years, and who was at present in a Japanese prison camp. Watching them, George wondered if they hoped, in the deepest and darkest recesses of their minds, that he might possibly stay there, forever.

Unworthy thoughts. But his mind kept filling with absurd, dangerous and even obscene thoughts. Two people had grasped at happiness, throwing aside convention and family considerations and at least a hundred years of carefully nurtured differences in background and belief. And, it seemed almost as a direct result, the heads of her family had been decimated. She stood close to him, wearing a black gown as did her mother, grandmother, sister, aunt and cousin, hands clasped in front of her, watching the black-clad men placing the lid on the ornate coffin. She had seen it all before, only five weeks ago.

Here, however, there was no haste, no lurking fear of what might be coming next. That at the least Starogan had accomplished, even for a stranger like himself. Starogan was a good place to die.

"The dowager princess tells me you are a newspaper correspondent." Count Igor Borodin, leading the men back from the family cemetery, had indicated that George should be at his side.

The dowager princess—now there were two dowager princesses in this family. But George no longer found their preoccupation with titles absurd. In the cemetery he had been able to glance at all the headstones. Borodins had been buried here for centuries. And since Tsar Peter the Great had inaugurated the granting of princely titles for achievement or merit, they had been princes and princesses; a Borodin had fought at the autocrat's side at Poltava. But even he had not been the first Borodin to lie in that cemetery.

He cleared his throat. "Yes."

"I was not aware that Count Dimitri had any American friends," Igor said, half to himself. "Although of course I do know that he visited your country as a young man." He glanced at George.

"Before my time, count. I just happened to be in Port Arthur, reporting the war for my father's paper, the Boston *People,* and we became friends." Snobbism, awareness of position, was contagious; George had never before considered it necessary to establish, this early in an an acquaintance, that the *People* was owned by his father.

"I see." This time the glance was more open, suggesting that Count Igor was finding it difficult to deduce what the American possessed to make Dimitri wish to make a friend of him. "And now . . . ?"

"Well, Count Dimitri was kind enough to have me stay in his house. So when . . . all this happened, with Peter being a prisoner of war, I felt the least I could do was escort the ladies back."

"*Prince* Peter," Igor remarked. Again he might have been speaking to himself rather than administering a rebuke. "I must apologize for your misfortune in having been involved in my family's bereavements."

"I only hope I'm not intruding."

They were walking between the lines of villagers and servants, who waited with bowed, bared heads despite the bitter cold. The Nejs were there, no longer the family servants, but merely servants. Starogan had its own butler and his family at the head of the line. George wondered if Michael were contemplating what the future held for *him;* whether the new prince, when he returned, would elevate his people to the top of the servants' social ladder.

"Intruding," Count Igor echoed, showing no sign of noticing the human wall through which he was passing. "What do you propose to do now?"

"I haven't considered it."

"Of course I shall be happy to arrange your passage to wherever you wish to go," the count said. "From Sevastopol ships visit every country in the world." He paused. "Even America. And it is only a short train journey from Starogan."

They were walking through the orchard and the house was in sight. The two dowager princesses and the other women were already climbing the steps. In a little while it would be possible to be alone with Ilona. They had not been alone since this new tragedy had entered her life; the family had known the day they were due, and the funeral had been already arranged. Even in the depths of winter it was not wise to keep a body for more than a week.

After he had spoken with Ilona it might be possible to reply to the count without being rude. My God, he thought; suppose it had been the younger branch of the family garrisoning Port Arthur? He continued to be amazed at the fickleness of fate.

The ladies had retired to change their clothes, and George did not know where all the bedrooms in this rambling house were.

"You must not be concerned about Father." Tigran Borodin smiled at him. "He is naturally overwhelmed by what has happened."

"And you are not."

The butler was bringing in a tray with neat little balloon glasses of brandy. George sat down, crossed his knees, and sipped one. He desperately needed a drink; he might even be able to appreciate one of Solowzow's nips of vodka. Poor Solowzow—he had been one of the first victims of the siege.

Tigran Borodin sat beside him. "Old men die. And soldiers get killed when there is a war."

"A sensible point of view. But easier to preach in the abstract than to believe in the concrete, wouldn't you say? Especially if you happen to be either an old man or a soldier."

Tigran Borodin smiled. "Evidence to the contrary, Mr. Hayman, I am not entirely callous, or shallow. I am just trying to explain that I am prepared to look a little further ahead than my father. Would you tell me about Port Arthur?"

"Don't you read the newspapers?"

"Our newspapers are rather strictly controlled by the government. Oh, not even the tsar can pretend that the fortress has not surrendered. But I wonder if there *were* any mitigating circumstances? May I be frank with you?"

"Shoot."

"A quaint expression. But I don't suppose I am telling you anything you do not know, or suspect, when I say that things are not good in Russia today. There is unrest. You know, liberalizing a country can be a tricky business. The great and good Tsar Alexander II believed in a liberal regime. That is admirable. My grandfather and my uncle Dimitri supported him. And he was blown up by the very people he was hoping to serve. On the very day, in fact, that the law ending serfdom was passed. An almost Grecian development, would you not say?"

"I'll go along with that."

"So his son, Alexander III, inheriting such a situation, ruled the nation with an iron hand. He was the man for it, Mr. Hayman. And Russia prospered, even while it seethed. Then he died, as all men must die, and now we have his son. Believe me, Mr. Hayman, I am the most loyal of men. How could a Borodin be otherwise? But the plain fact of the matter is that Tsar Nicholas II has not yet made up his mind whether he wishes to emulate his father or his grandfather. I think he is essentially a liberal man, but one who is afraid to be taken advantage of. Thus the country seethes even more, and we are left with a succession of ministers who, themselves uncertain of the tsar's aim, bumble from mistake to mistake. Like this ghastly war. I suspect it was provoked for purposes of prestige, to bolster the reputation of the government. And it has not gone well. This is known to the people. Only two weeks ago there was a massive demonstration in St. Petersburg. The tsar was not there, so no blame can be attached to him. But when the mob marched on the Winter Palace to present a petition, the guards opened fire. Several hundred people were killed. Do you know, many revolutions have started with just such a situation? Had you heard of the incident?"

"No," George said.

"Well, I am not suggesting Russia will have a revolution. The people—I mean the peasantry, the backbone of the nation—are far too loyal for that. These disturbances are caused by intellectuals and factory workers. But if we lose at Mukden, we shall lose the entire contest, and be the laughing stock of the world. This is a serious consideration for a nation which has never lost any war in recent times. Even in that Crimean disaster we gave as good as we got. But this war . . . do you sail, Mr. Hayman?"

"What? Why, yes, I do. My father has a yacht."

"We keep one in Sevastopol. In the summer I spend a lot of time on the water. But the Black Sea can be treacherous, and before putting out it is essential to have some idea of what the weather might do. I should like you to give me a weather forecast for this coming summer, Mr. Hayman, based upon what you saw and heard in Port Arthur. I think it may be important. I feel there is a touch of thunder in the air."

"The tsar."

Everyone stood, even the ladies.

"The tsarina."

Once again the lifted glasses, the solemn intonation.

"The tsarevich."

George discovered he had been drinking each time, and his glass was empty. The others had done nothing more than touch their lips with the rim. What to do? Tatiana had noticed and was going red as she attempted to stop herself from laughing.

The butler, resplendent in blue and gold livery, stood at his elbow to pour, while Count Igor waited, his expression weary.

"The tsarevnas."

Another sip. He had no idea how long this continued. But Count Igor was gazing at Dowager Princess Marie, who was sitting down. George caught Tigran's eye, and sank into his seat, only to stand again immediately as the dowager princess rose again. Her chair was removed by a footman and she walked to the door. The other ladies followed her. Ilona's cheeks were pink. She had also noticed.

Count Igor sat down and waited for Alexei Alexandrovich to clip the end from his cigar and strike the match. He blew smoke as he watched the two young men receive their smokes; Viktor was apparently considered too young.

"News arrived by telegraph this afternoon," Count Igor said. "General Kuropatkin has at last launched his attack."

"At Mukden?" Viktor was eager.

"He has been victorious, it appears." The count raised his glass of port. "Another toast. The Russian army."

"The Russian army."

George could not believe it. But he dared not suggest the news might be only a rumor.

"The Japanese are retreating?" Tigran asked it for him. He thought he might just get to like Tigran, eventually.

"One assumes so," the count said. "The wire merely said that General Kuropatkin had achieved all his objectives."

"Sounds like headquarters material to me," Viktor said.

His father glared at him. "It is past your bedtime. Off you go."

"Tattie is still up."

"I doubt that. And do not speak to me in that tone. Good night."

Viktor hesitated, then stood and bowed to his father. At the door he hesitated again. "Good night, Mr. Hayman."

"Good night, Viktor," George said.

Count Igor stubbed out his cigar and pushed back his chair so suddenly he took the butler unawares. "Shall we join the ladies?"

They found the ladies still sipping their coffee. "Where is Viktor?" inquired Dowager Princess Marie.

"He has gone to bed," the count said. "It is ten o'clock." He looked at Tattie who turned to her mother.

"Yes. Well," Dowager Princess Olga said, "I suppose it is late, and you have had a tiring day."

"Oh, Mama . . ."

"Bed," pronounced Count Igor.

For a dreadful moment George thought she was going to stick her tongue out at her uncle, but instead she slowly wandered round the room, kissing each person on both cheeks, with only her uncle excluded. She got to him last. "Now that Peter is prince," she said, "will you still come here to visit, Uncle Igor?"

His head jerked, and she fled from the room.

"I am sorry, Igor," Olga said.

The count cleared his throat, a slow and noisy process. "Brandy," he said.

Instantly the butler placed the tray on the low table and carefully poured the correct measure into three balloon glasses. The ladies continued to sip their coffee.

The count seemed to realize for the first time that he no longer had a cigar, but he dared not call for one in the presence of his mother. "That girl is spoiled," he remarked, looking at Ilona. "Dimitri spoiled her. It does no harm for a young girl to be whipped occasionally. None at all. Ilona was whipped."

Ilona flushed, and put down her coffee cup with a clatter. She stood up. "If you'll excuse me, Mama, Grandmama, I should like to show George something of the house."

"George?" inquired Dowager Princess Marie.

"We are old friends, Grandmama," Ilona assured her. "George?" George excused himself and followed her into the billiard room.

"Do you play?" she asked.

"I do."

"Well then. . . ." She placed the balls and selected a cue. "I am full of hidden talents."

It was the first time in three weeks that he had actually been alone with her, even if the door to the hall was still open. He touched her hand, and a moment later she was in his arms.

"Oh, George, George," she whispered. "I thought it would never happen."

He kissed her mouth, each eye, her nose, her chin, each cheek, and her mouth again. "May I close the door?"

She shook her head. "We must be patient."

"Patient? With your uncle determined to get rid of me?"

"I brought you out here to explain that," she said. "Uncle Igor can insist on whatever he pleases. It cannot affect us. Peter is prince of Starogan now, and in his absence Mama makes the decisions. Anyway, they will soon be leaving. They hate Starogan, especially in the winter."

"Have you spoken with your mother?"

Ilona released him. She bent over the billiard table and made a distinctly good shot. The butler walked past the open door as she did so.

"You must have ears like a cat," George remarked.

"It is your shot. I have not spoken with her. How could I, my darling?"

"Of course. I'm being impatiently masculine. But to have you right here, to be able to touch you. . . ."

"I wish you to come to my room tonight," she said. And frowned. "No, I will come to yours."

"Now, my darling, I did explain—"

"I must explain to you, George. We have only this life to live. And it is passing us by, through no fault of our own. I must continue to mourn my father for six months, and I do so genuinely. I cannot pretend to mourn my grandfather. I have not seen him for six years. But I love you, and here we are together. I cannot live without your love.

You talk about being able to touch me—how masculine. Do you not think I want to touch you as well?"

"My darling."

"Anyway," she said, "as soon as Peter comes home, we shall be betrothed. I promise you that."

"Peter?" He took her in his arms again, his resolution disappearing.

"Well, you see, it is Peter who now has to give his consent."

"But he won't be back until the war ends."

"Which we must hope will be soon, if General Kuropatkin is at last starting to win battles. As you have said time and again, the Japanese were only interested in Port Arthur. Now that they have it they will be happy to make peace at the first opportunity."

"And do you suppose your people will wish to make peace, if they see a chance of getting it back?"

"I don't know. You've heard the news from St. Petersburg?"

"Tigran told me this afternoon." He sighed. "It seems hard to believe here in Starogan. Hard to believe there should be a war on, even."

"I told you it would be like that. Starogan is a place for peace. But what is happening out there is real." It was her turn to sigh. "And so absurd, that people should wish to kill each other. That workers should wish to cause trouble. Don't they know that the government is trying to help them as best it can?"

"Perhaps they don't have your patience. You have everything already, they have nothing yet."

"Oh, you . . ." She pushed him away. "I'd forgotten you are a radical. All Americans are radicals."

He smiled at her. "Well, maybe by Russian standards."

"And will you change me?"

"I love you just the way you are, my precious girl. Do we have to talk politics?"

"No," she said. "Not ever again. It's just that . . . sometimes I get frightened. These last two weeks I have been frightened. No, this last month. We have so much, we are going to have so much . . . George, don't ever let anything happen to what we are going to have."

She was in his arms again, billiards forgotten. "I promised you that, didn't I? We Haymans keep our promises."

The Japanese orderly stood to attention. "The colonel will see you now," he said, the Russian words sounding odd in his high-pitched singsong.

Peter Borodin straightened his collar and glanced down at his boots. The officer prisoners were very well cared for; they had a dozen Japanese girls to do their laundry, and indeed perform any other duties the Russians might require, yet inevitably, after two months of prison, clothes were beginning to look overworn and boots were beginning to crack.

The door was open; the colonel, an elderly man with a long mustache, was on his feet to greet him. He was hardly more than half Peter's size, yet matched him in the rigidity with which he stood at attention. But Peter no longer had any temptation to be contemptuous of the Japanese for being either small or Oriental. "Come in, Prince Borodin. Sit down."

Slowly Peter removed his hat. "That is not correct, sir. My grandfather is prince of Starogan."

"Sit down, Prince Borodin," the colonel said again.

Peter lowered himself into the chair.

"I do not enjoy being the bearer of bad news. And I am equally sorry it took so long to get to us. Your grandfather died two months ago."

Peter gazed at him. It did not make sense. Papa and Grandpapa both dead?

"I understand it must be a great shock to you," the colonel said. "A great inheritance, a great responsibility, and you are not there to grasp it. Those are the fortunes of war, my dear prince, but at least you have the satisfaction of knowing that your return to Starogan will not now be long delayed. In view of the circumstances, negotiations are already in progress for your exchange. But in any event, this war will soon be ended."

Peter's head came up. "Your government has sued for peace?"

The colonel smiled. "I do not see his imperial majesty suing for peace. But it is expected that your tsar will do so."

"Because our army has suffered a few defeats? The tsar will never accept peace except as a result of victory." He realized he was speaking too loudly and made himself lower his voice. "The situation will change after General Kuropatkin completes his concentration."

The colonel's smile was triumphantly sympathetic. "General Kuropatkin has completed his concentration, Prince Borodin. There has been a great battle at Mukden. I have to tell you that your army has been overwhelmingly defeated."

Peter stared at him, brows slowly drawing together. "That cannot be."

The colonel's smile faded. "Japanese officers are accustomed to speaking the truth, Prince Borodin. I understand that this is bad news for you. But at least it must mean the end of the war."

"There is still Admiral Rozhdestvenski and the Baltic fleet, sir. When he gets here—"

"He too will be defeated, my lord prince."

"It will not matter," Peter declared. "The tsar will never make peace."

The colonel allowed himself a sigh at such wrong-headed optimism. "I think he will have to, Prince Borodin. Your country is in a state of serious unrest. You know there has been fighting in St. Petersburg?"

"A riot," Peter said.

"No doubt," the colonel agreed. "But do you also know that one of your grand dukes has been assassinated? Blown up by a bomb. Grand Duke Sergei Alexandrovich, the tsar's uncle. These are serious times, Prince Borodin, for Russia. As I said, you are returning to a great responsibility. You need peace, to save your country from revolution."

Peter stood up. "Permission to withdraw, sir."

"Of course, prince." The colonel also stood. "I am sorry to have been the bearer of ill news. But I congratulate you on your inheritance. Good day."

Peter set his hat on his head and saluted. The orderly held the door for him. He walked across the lawn separating the command buildings from the prison block and felt the winter sunshine on his neck. He did not really doubt the truth of what the colonel had said. But he found it difficult to accept. Not necessarily the murder of Grand Duke Sergei—the grand duke had been possibly the most detested man in St. Petersburg; still, his death, coming on top of the riots, suggested the home front was in a state of collapse. But another defeat for the army—and this time not in a skirmish, but in the major clash on which all the prisoners had been pinning their hopes— this was almost beyond comprehension.

He gazed beyond the wire fence at the calm waters, at the islands and the fishermen with their nets and their straggling beards, at the little houses on the shore opposite, where women laughed and children played. The Japanese were happy in a way the Russians were not, except when drunk. He wondered if they were happy because their armies were winning, or if they were winning because they were happy?

He started guiltily, less at having drifted into unpatriotic thoughts than at having drifted philosophically, an absurd frame of mind for a soldier.

He entered the lounge and gazed at his fellow officers. Most of them were his seniors in rank.

"Well?" Colonel Oblomov hurried to his side. "Not bad news, I hope?"

"General Kuropatkin has been defeated," Peter said. "At Mukden."

Heads turned, and other officers got up to gather around him.

"That cannot be true," someone said.

"It is true," Peter insisted.

General Stoessel himself stood in front of him. "The colonel called you, Lieutenant Borodin, to impart this news?"

Peter came to attention. "No, sir. He called me to inform me that my grandfather is dead."

Stoessel stared at him. "Your grandfather? Then you are now prince of Starogan?"

"Yes, sir."

Stoessel snapped his fingers and an orderly brought a tray of vodka. His most junior officer had suddenly become the highest ranking noble in the army, short of the grand dukes themselves. "Then I must congratulate you even as I offer you my condolences, my lord prince. What else did the colonel tell you?"

"He expects the tsar to seek peace, sir. Do you believe that?"

Stoessel's mouth turned down at the corners. "I would not be surprised. Things are bad. Bad." He looked around the room at the serious faces. "I have not told you before, but that trouble in St. Petersburg has spread to Moscow. And other places. Things are bad." He slapped Peter on the shoulder. "But you, prince of Starogan, whatever happens you will soon be exchanged. Oh, yes, you will be going home, my lord prince. You are the fortunate one."

Peter gazed at him for several moments, then turned and walked away, leaving a hubbub of disturbed conversation behind him. He opened the door and stepped outside, blinking in the sunshine. The meaning of what he had been told was only just sinking in. He would be going home. To Starogan. He had not seen Starogan for six years, and now it was his. Three hundred thousand acres of wheat, twenty thousand sheep, fifty thousand acres of beets, all his. And several hundred people, all his responsibility, even if they no longer actually belonged to him.

And he would be returning there a soldier, released from prison camp. A defeated soldier. But there was no soldier in all Russia who would not be defeated after this war. The greatest army in the world, he had always been told, and had always believed. And it had been defeated by a horde of little men who had not been afraid to die.

Russia was the greatest country in the world—no question about that. And yet it had been defeated. Or had it defeated itself? This trouble the general had spoken of—strikes and riots, the murder of the grand duke—absurdities, and especially so in time of war. Such things should never have been permitted. The men who fomented them should have been shot as traitors.

Such decisions would be his to make now. Would he have the determination to make them?

A hand touched his; he looked down at the Japanese girl. She was a pretty little thing, with more aquiline features than most of her compatriots, and an eager heathen body allied to a matching mind. She found the big, handsome Russian attractive, as she had made plain almost from his first day here. And last week he had succumbed to her charms and her invitation. It had been an unforgettable experience. But one he suddenly, desperately wished to forget. Had he really done it? Was that not a symptom of everything that was wrong with Russia, everything that had caused this defeat? A moral and physical weakness, spreading through the nation like a cancer, a concern with material comforts rather than with duty.

And he was now prince of Starogan.

He pulled his hand free and walked away from her to the edge of the compound, to look at the sea. Prince of Starogan. He had greater responsibilities than almost anyone except the tsar himself. Duties to his family, to his people, to his nation. A nation of drunkards, George Hayman thought. Damn George Hayman for being so observant. He realized he was still holding the half-full glass of vodka and he turned it over, allowing the liquid to splash to the ground.

He inhaled, filling his lungs to their uttermost capacity. Suddenly he felt good again. The blood tingled in his veins. Everything was going to be all right. It had been necessary for Russia to lose this war —which, after all, was not a very important war, not like losing a European war—in order that the weaknesses in the Russian people be found out and exorcised. That was the sacred duty of all those placed by God in positions of authority, to restore the people to their old concepts of duty and obedience to the will of the tsar.

A fitting responsibility for the prince of Starogan.

"You'll take another glass of vodka, Michael Nikolaievich?" Feodor Geller smiled at his guest as he poured and Michael smiled back. With every day his importance was growing. The wheels had been set in motion, and Prince Peter was to be exchanged. Why, he'd be home in a month, it was said. And then, no one had any doubt at all, he would wish to elevate his late father's servants to their proper station. With old Nikolai Nej clearly approaching the end of his life, Michael Nej would be the most important muzhik in the village.

And so even the schoolmaster was anxious to be his friend. But Feodor Geller was obviously working according to a plan. He had only lived in Starogan for twelve years, which meant he was still considered a stranger, and he desperately wanted to be accepted. And he had a daughter, who was presently seated in the far corner beside her mother, watching the two men, attempting to hear what they were saying, smiling anxiously whenever she discovered Michael looking at her.

Her name was Zoe, and she was attractively ugly. She had a round head and rounded features, and a distinctly round body. Michael supposed her legs would be plump; certainly they were short. But he had made a resolution never to think about legs except when he was alone. So, not thinking about legs, or about breasts, because here she was well endowed, she was quite an appealing prospect, young and eager to please, and desperate to marry the man her father had chosen—who was clearly Michael Nej.

He supposed he could do a good deal worse. The Nejs had always been family servants. There was no record of a Nej ever progressing to the dizzying intellectual heights of even a village schoolmaster. Feodor Geller was preparing to sacrifice his daughter on the lower social scale in the hope of achieving some entirely local advantage. Nor could there be any doubt that Prince Peter would be delighted. Michael supposed he should also be delighted. Because here was comfort on a scale enjoyed by no one else in Starogan, except Alexei Alexandrovich, the butler who actually lived in the Borodin house, Father Gregory and possibly Alexander Ivanovich, the headman. The Gellers' floor was wood, not earth; the great porcelain stove provided a good deal more warmth than that in the Nej household; there were four chairs, so that the women could be seated when a guest called, providing there was only one guest; and there were no animals sharing the warmth. In their privileged position during the years in Port Arthur, the Nejs had forgotten just what they were returning to at Starogan. When they moved up to the house they would regain that stature and comfort. But Feodor Geller enjoyed it all the time.

"Lenin is his name," Feodor Geller was saying. "Nikolai Lenin. It is not his real name, of course. I knew him as Ulyanov. But as you were in Siberia as well . . ."

"I was not in Siberia, Feodor Alexeievich," Michael said patiently. "I was in Port Arthur. That is Manchuria."

"Ah, but to get to Manchuria one must pass through Siberia," Geller said triumphantly. He was the schoolmaster, and not about to be given any geographical runaround by the son of a servant. Even the son of a prince's servant.

Michael drank some vodka and smiled at Zoe. His return to Starogan had been a disappointment, in more than the half-forgotten family hut. He loved the place, but he had never supposed an entire community could be so ignorant. While he had spent six years reading Count Dimitri's library, nobody here seemed to have advanced their knowledge at all. Even old Feodor supposed that because one traveled across a country several thousand miles wide one must necessarily meet every political exile hidden away in every little village.

And why would a village schoolmaster be asking after a political exile in any event?

That an explanation might be necessary had also occurred to Geller. "He is no longer in Siberia, of course," he explained. "But he was there a few years ago. Now he has left Russia, and is living abroad. England, and Switzerland." He lowered his voice. "He is a most dangerous fellow. A socialist."

A socialist. Michael had not given much thought to socialism during the past few months. Events had been too immense for socialism.

"A friend of yours, Feodor Alexeievich?"

Geller looked suitably shocked. "Of course not, Michael Nikolaievich. As I have said, a dreadful man. A criminal. Why, his brother was hanged for conspiring against the late tsar. No, no, no friend. But we were at college together. A sinister fellow, even then. Redheaded. Redheaded men are always troublemakers."

"I do not understand," Michael confessed. "You say he was in Siberia, and is now in England . . . ah, he was involved in that business in St. Petersburg."

"A dreadful affair," Geller said. "Oh, dreadful. Mobs marching on the Winter Palace. They should have shot more of them. It wouldn't surprise me in the least if this Ulyanov was involved. But I do not think he was. It is just that he recently came to my notice again. He has written a book called *Two Tactics*. Pure revolution, my dear Michael Nikolaievich."

"You have a copy?"

"Good heavens, no," the schoolmaster protested. "I was shown a copy, but I gave it back, of course."

"Who showed it to you?"

Geller's face took on a peculiar expression. "I do not think I can share that confidence with you, Michael Nikolaievich. I merely asked if you had come across this Ulyanov during your stay in the east."

"Well, Siberia is a large country," Michael pointed out. "And as I have said, I was in Manchuria." He finished his vodka and got up. "I must take my leave, Feodor Alexeievich. Your hospitality has been most kind." He bowed to the ladies.

"You'll fetch Michael Nikolaievich's coat and hat, Zoe Feodorovna," her father commanded, and the girl hurried to the back of the house. "You'll come again, Michael Nikolaievich?"

"It shall be my pleasure." He allowed himself to be wrapped in his cloak, then adjusted the peak of his cap. Even if the worst of the winter was clearly over, the nights remained cold. Zoe accompanied him to the door, but his thoughts were already drifting away. He smiled at her before trudging off down the street.

So the schoolmaster was a socialist at heart, even if he dared not reveal his beliefs. But he thought that in Michael Nej he might be able to find a kindred spirit. Now, however did he deduce that? However could he suppose that the prince's servant might also be a revolutionary?

The lights of the house dominated the night sky, every window a candlelit blaze. It was a discouraging thought that one day, and it might be one day soon, he would be responsible for all that wax and all those polished floors, all that cutlery and all that crockery, all the footmen and all the upstairs maids and downstairs maids and kitchen help.

And much more besides. It was still early in the evening, and as he was now walking through the gardens—his father's house was on the farm side of the family residence—he could hear the tinkling notes of the grand piano. Tatiana was being required to entertain her family and their guest. Poor Tattie; she would much rather be playing her own senseless but pretty little melodies.

Michael thrust his hands deep into his pockets and listened to the dogs barking; they were penned up at night, but they could still let the world know there was someone in the yard. And the world would ignore them, because this world was Starogan, where there were no strangers, and therefore no intruders.

Except for those who were invited. The American had now been virtually a member of the family for nearly a year. It did not appear as if he were ever going to leave. And why should he, as he had those magnificent arms and legs, that even more magnificent body to call his own whenever he wished? Michael felt quite angry when he thought of that, and then quite faint when he remembered that in the excitement of his new-found knowledge and of the noise and fear of the collapse of Port Arthur, he had actually dreamed of the possibility of possessing that magnificence himself, had actually thought that things might be different following such a catastrophe. Had actually, now that he came to think about it, looked at life with the eyes of a socialist, of this Ulyanov who now called himself Lenin.

Thank God Michael had lacked the courage, or *he* might have found himself exiled to Siberia, and eventually sent from Russia altogether, under a false name. It might have been possible to feel that things could never be the same in Port Arthur, but Starogan was reality, the finest of all examples of the unchanging face of Russia.

All the same, when he thought of that American enjoying Ilona, while his best prospect was Zoe Geller—and that only after they were well and truly married—he could not stop the anger returning. Why should the American enjoy Ilona's charms? He was not a prince, not a nobleman, not even a Russian. Perhaps his father was a wealthy man; there were many wealthy Russians the Borodins would not permit to enter their doors. Should Master Peter—correction: Prince Peter—ever even suspect . . . but why should he not *know?* Why should he not be informed? And who could do that but the one man who knew the true situation? His faithful servant, with whom he had grown to manhood. He could not, of course, be told the whole truth —that might be to involve Ilona in disgrace. But he could be warned that this upstart Yankee was paying court to his sister.

Michael strode through the darkness, filled with virtuous anger. The Borodins were *his* family, to be looked after, protected from a bad influence.

How odd that Geller, who knew nothing of what had happened in Port Arthur, should consider him to have socialist leanings.

* * *

"Half an hour. Do hurry."

George realized he had never before seen Olga Borodina so agitated. But then, she was no longer just the mother of a lieutenant in the Preobraschenski Guards; she was the mother of a prince, who was about to return to claim his inheritance. So she fussed about Tatiana and even dared to adjust Dowager Princess Marie's hat.

Ilona stood by herself, a picture in a sealskin coat trimmed with fox, and a velvet hat. Ilona Borodina. A tall and dignified and incredibly lovely girl, who was also his mistress. George found this impossible to believe when he saw her in the presence of the rest of her family, utterly composed, given to long moments of introspection, and then to startlingly direct and frank remarks. But of course he was realizing that this summed up the woman herself. She thought deeply and privately, resolved her problems and her doubts with the aid of no counsel but her own, and then implemented her decisions, again without reference to any advising or restraining influence.

The truly amazing thing was not her character at all. That character had been molded by centuries of omnipotent decision-making by her ancestors, just as her beauty had been molded by centuries of omnipotent selection by those ancestors of the most intelligent and beautiful girls they could discover, to be their brides. The amazing thing was that she had chosen to bestow this beauty and this determination—indeed, this omnipotence—upon one George Hayman, a foreigner, and a liberal foreigner at that.

But she had. She came to his room almost every night. So much for his pious resolutions. But he did not suppose he would ever be able to sleep again without waiting for the soft opening of his door, for a glimpse of that tall, white-shrouded figure who without a word would drop negligee and nightgown on the floor beside his bed, and before he would even have the time to appreciate the beauty that was about to be his, would be beneath his blankets and against him.

Sometimes he doubted. Ilona Borodina wanted love, physical love, with a yearning he, with his strict Massachusetts upbringing, had not supposed possible in a woman. No doubt she had wanted for a very long time, and had always rejected the thought. Once the desire had been released, it could not again be subdued. But what had been the cause of the release? George Hayman? Or her experiences as a nurse in Port Arthur?

Unworthy doubts. Because whatever had been the cause of the release, her love for him was the effect. He could not doubt that love.

If she gave him her body, wanted, with utter desperation, for him to *use* her body, he could have no doubts about the time afterwards, when she lay with her head on his shoulder, and made him tell her about Boston. About the life she was going to. She had no doubts about that, and neither should he. She was concerned with his own future, though. She could see no reason for him to continue being a war correspondent. Apart from the danger to him there was the probability of her loneliness while he hurried around the world. He would inherit the paper. It was time for him to settle down and familiarize himself with the editorial and managerial side of publishing.

And of course she was right. Mother had been hinting that very strongly for some time. He did not even have to be persuaded. What, find himself somewhere up the Congo covering a bush war while Ilona was left to her own devices in Boston? Besides, what war could ever equal the thrill of entering a crowded ballroom with Ilona on his arm? Ilona Hayman.

He was, as usual, looking at her, and she was, as usual, returning his gaze and giving him a little smile which brought him back to himself. The dowager princesses were satisfied, Olga even pausing in front of George to make sure all was well. Alexei Alexandrovich and his minions were waiting with top coats and umbrellas and George's silk hat, for it was raining outside with a ferocious persistence that almost made one wish for the endless snow of only a few weeks ago.

"There," Olga Borodina said. "Shall we go?"

More umbrellas were held by the dripping footmen as the family waited in turn on the veranda before hurrying down the steps, one at a time, into the shelter of the waiting coach. The suddenly warm interior was at once damp and crushing. The two elder ladies sat on one seat with Tatiana between them; George and Ilona enjoyed slightly more space opposite. George had suggested that he remain at home on this family occasion, but Olga Borodina had insisted he come. He was more than just a friend of the family now, she said. He continued to wonder if she suspected. Of course she must suspect the attraction between Ilona and himself, but certainly she could not suspect the relationship they enjoyed. No one must ever suspect that. It must be their secret, to the grave.

The real reason he was being taken to the station, he knew, was that all Starogan had to be there to greet their returning prince. The platform was crowded, far more crowded than when they had returned at the end of January. He wondered if the wooden boards had been intended to withstand this strain. Everyone was in his best, sheltered beneath somewhat worn umbrellas. But at least the official party were better off than the muzhiks, who huddled in the square beyond, already soaked to the skin and feeling their finery slowly soaking into a sodden ruin. Feathers and hats drooped, boots squelched in the mud, noses sneezed and throats coughed. Prince Peter might be returning to a village of chronic invalids, but this mattered nothing beside the fact that he must be met.

George was aware that he was slipping into a dangerously ambivalent way of thinking. Everything about Russia was wrong. But because Russia had produced Ilona, nothing could be less than right. For the future owner of one of the great reforming newspapers in the world, that was a dangerous prospect.

A rustle of anticipation went through the crowd at the sound of the whistle. Now the craning heads could see the smoke, and a moment later the train itself came into view. Father Gregory muttered to the headman before coming across the platform to stand with the family. The headman muttered to his aides, and the aides muttered to the station master. Together they hurried for the storeroom and fetched the red carpet, up to now kept dry. This they slowly unrolled up to the edge of the platform, completing their task just as the train pulled to a halt. But it was not a moment too soon, either; immediately the red dye started to run across the wood.

The doors were opened. The crowd held its breath, and Peter Borodin emerged. He was wearing his Preobraschenski full dress uniform, but beneath a cloak which served at once to keep off the rain and to hide the threadbare condition of the cloth and leather beneath. He carried his helmet under his arm, again neatly concealing the dent it had received on the day Port Arthur had fallen. It occurred to George that it was out of character for Peter not to have delayed long enough in Kharkov to have a new uniform made; he must be in a tremendous hurry to seize his inheritance. His face was composed and serious; he looked around him with a slight air of surprise, as if he had not realized that all his people would be here to greet him. He bowed his head at the outburst of clapping which greeted his descent.

The headman pulled his speech from his pocket, then watched the paper dissolve into an inky smudge before his eyes. He opened his mouth, closed it again, turned in desperation to look for Father Gregory, who immediately stepped forward, arms and icon raised high. With an enormous sigh the entire concourse sank to its knees, the squelch of those in the mud outside drowning the hissing of the train. George knelt as well. It would have been absurd to be the only one to remain standing.

Father Gregory's words rolled across the morning, deadened by the rain, and yet loud enough to be heard by the people outside. Father Gregory was sufficiently used to having to preach while the rain battered on the tin roof of his village church. And here he was blessing a prince, a new prince, a prince who, God willing, would be ruling over them long after the father was dead.

Then the blessing was over. The headman muttered a few hastily remembered words, and the prince was free to greet his family. A bow and a kiss on the hand for Dowager Princess Marie. A bow and a kiss on each cheek for Dowager Princess Olga. A hug for Tatiana, whose hat fell off. A sudden stare for Ilona, but no greeting and no kiss. And an abrupt drawing back of his shoulders as he discovered himself opposite George.

"Hayman," he said. "I am surprised to find you still here." He turned and walked across the platform, his family trailing behind. George tried to catch Ilona's eye, but she was staring at her brother's back. Instead, he found himself gazing at Michael Nej, peering from the ranks of the crowd.

Chapter 4

OLGA BORODINA MADE CONVERSATION. AS SHE HAD TO COMPETE WITH the rain pounding on the roof of the coach, her booming voice precluded thought.

"Spring is always the best time of the year," she remarked. "A beginning. A good time for you to come home, Peter, my dear. The plowing has just started. It will resume as soon as the rain stops."

Peter nodded. For the return trip he was squeezed between his mother and grandmother, and Tattie was squeezed between George and Ilona. This made it difficult for Peter not to look at one or the other of them, so he preferred to look out the window at the endless sweep of freshly turned black earth—such a strong contrast, George thought, to the endless sweep of snow of only a month ago. But he was not really interested in the observation. He wanted to look at Ilona, gauge her reaction to her brother's demeanor; but to do that, with both dowager princesses looking at him, would have been too obvious.

"You will find everything is as it should be," Dowager Princess Marie said. "The prince attended to everything that needed doing, up to the day he died. It was very sudden, you know. He just died in his chair. Very sudden."

"Mercifully sudden, Mama," Olga pointed out. "Like dear Dimitri. Mercifully quick." She squeezed Peter's hand. "But you, my dear boy, you are looking so well. Did the Japanese treat you well?"

"They did, Mama." He looked past Tatiana out the front window of the carriage, at the house appearing before them. Faint frown lines gathered between his eyes. Of course, George realized, it will be the first time he has seen it in six years. Perhaps his coldness was caused only by nerves, by a bracing of himself for the immense responsibilities that lay ahead. George hoped so.

After all, what other reason *could* there be for his coldness? It was merely his own nerves, his own guilty conscience, causing him to see shadows where none existed. Or his own anxiety over the talk that they must have, as soon as possible.

The carriage halted, and Peter stepped down first, as befitted his rank. Every house servant was lined up on the veranda for his inspection, marshaled by Alexei Alexandrovich, resplendent in frock coat and wing collar. "Welcome home, Prince Peter," he said.

Peter nodded and glanced at the servants, then went inside. Alexei Alexandrovich gazed at Dowager Princess Marie, but received no information and no solace. He snapped his fingers to dismiss the parade and hurried behind his new master. Peter stood just inside the doorway, watching a puddle of water slowly gathering on the polished floor. Alexei Alexandrovich twisted his hands together. "Whenever the spring rains come, excellency, they find out the leaks. I am making a list, and they will be repaired. As soon as the rain stops."

"They should be repaired now, Alexei Alexandrovich," Peter remarked, speaking quietly. "Or the house may drown, and us with it."

"Of course, excellency. Of course. It was remiss of me. I will have it seen to immediately. Will your excellency be shown your bedroom?"

"In a little while," Peter said. "Did the late prince not have a study?"

"Indeed he did, excellency. Indeed he did."

"I will go there first." He turned to face his family, gathered in the doorway rather like a small herd of frightened sheep, George thought. "You'll excuse me, Mama, Grandmama. But there is a great deal to be done. I will attend you at tea. Hayman, would you accompany me?"

It was not a request. George stepped past the ladies. "Of course."

Peter gave a brief nod, turned, and followed the butler. George hesitated long enough to glance at Ilona. Her cheeks were suddenly pink, but her eyes had no message save concern.

George squared his shoulders, handed his hat to a waiting footman and walked along the corridor which took him past the billiards room and the dining room to the back of the house. He knew where the study was, but in the four months he had spent here he had never entered it. Now he discovered it to be a large, comfortable room, redolent with the scent of good cigars and even better brandy, and completely lined with leather-bound books, except for the huge window which filled one wall. It looked out at the apple orchard and beyond—to the dusty road, today nothing more than a river of mud, which led to the farm.

The desk was also leather bound, and behind it Peter Borodin had already seated himself. The butler bowed and withdrew, closing the door.

"Sit down," Peter suggested, and George sank into the comfortable chair before the desk. "Cigar?"

George helped himself and clipped the end. "It was your father's wish, and yours, as I understood it, that I should return to Starogan with your mother and sisters. Having done that, and in view of the circumstances we found here in January, I felt I could do nothing less than stay until your return."

"It was my wish, certainly," Peter agreed, his tone suggesting that he must have been mad. "But now we have consumed enough of your time. I have ordered that the train remain at Starogan station for the rest of the day."

George frowned at him. "You have ordered that? What about the other people on it?"

"They can wait. I wished the train to wait so that you could board it this evening. Alexei Alexandrovich will see that your things are packed and transported. I will give you a note to my agent in Sevastopol, and he will secure you passage upon the first available ship to wherever you wish to go. The cost will be mine, of course."

George put up his hand to scratch his head and realized that he was still holding the cigar. "I'm afraid I don't understand. You wish me to leave Starogan today?"

"Yes."

"But . . . my dear fellow, I had intended to stay a while longer. I don't mean to impose, of course, but as a matter of fact there is something I wish to discuss with you, urgently. Perhaps now is as good a time as any."

"And I would prefer not to discuss the matter at all," Peter said.

"The matter? You don't know what it is."

"Let me say that you have overstayed your welcome," Peter said.

"You have abused both my hospitality and the position of trust in which I placed you. I prefer not to make an issue of these things, not only because it was my father's wish that you visit us here, but because you are an American and cannot be expected to know how to properly behave. Were you a Russian, Hayman, you would find me far less accommodating. Now I wish you to go, and I would advise you to leave without attempting to create a scene, and certainly without attempting to see Ilona again. I hope I have made myself clear."

George stared at him. Strangely, he was not surprised, only angry. "And were you an American," he said, "I would punch you on the nose."

Peter's head came up, and his cheeks turned bright red.

"All right," George said. "It is Ilona I want to speak with you about. But it has nothing to do with abusing any trust. Ilona and I discovered that we loved each other back in Port Arthur, before your father died. I was going to speak with him, but then he was killed, and Ilona wished to wait until a decent period had passed before approaching you. I love her, Peter, and she loves me. I wish to ask you for her hand in marriage. And don't suppose she'll be going slumming. My father is as much a millionaire as yours ever was."

Peter gazed at him for some moments while his color slowly faded. Then he rang the bell on his desk. "Were you a Russian," he said, "I would take great pleasure in killing you. A millionaire. Money! My God, is that all you Americans think about? Tell me this, Hayman—who was your great-grandmother? Oh, no doubt she is entered somewhere in your family Bible, but was she a princess, and was *her* great-grandmother a princess?"

"I don't see that that has a lot to do with it," George said, and listened to the door opening behind him.

"I would not expect you to. Mr. Hayman is leaving on the train, Alexei Alexandrovich. See that his things are packed and taken to the station. He will travel by the coach."

"Yes, excellency." The butler held the door.

"Now hold on just one moment," George said. "Hadn't we better get Ilona in here? She loves me, and I love her. Okay, so she's not twenty-one, and you can play the big bad wolf for two more years. But not forever. What are you trying to do, wreck your family?"

Peter Borodin placed his hands on his desk and leaned forward. "Were you a gentleman, Hayman, you would understand that we do not discuss our personal affairs before servants. Ilona is my sister, and until I am married and a father, she is my heir. She will do what I tell her to, and she will marry whom I tell her to. Now leave my house, or I will have my servants throw you out."

"He has changed," Dowager Princess Marie said. "He is a man. My God, how long ago it seems when last he was here. And to return in such circumstances. . . ." She sniffed into her lace handkerchief.

"Ring and have one of the girls bring Grandmama's smelling salts," Olga Borodina said. She was looking at Tatiana, but Ilona got up.

"I will fetch them, Mama."

"You? There is no need, my dear Ilona."

"I would like to." Sitting in the drawing room, listening to her mother and grandmother exchanging inanities, was no longer bearable. She had to know what was happening in the study. She had to know how Peter had found out, because quite definitely he had found out. But *what* had he found out? That was possibly the most important question of all.

She opened the door, stepped into the corridor, then paused to listen and to wait for her heart to stop pounding. Was she afraid of her brother? It was not a thought which had ever crossed her mind before. But she suddenly realized that she had allowed no thoughts of any substance to enter her mind for several months now. She was in love, and nothing else mattered. Her only consideration had been that George, so much older and more experienced and confident than she, might find her tiresome or silly, or not as exciting as the women he would have been used to. He had occupied her every moment, and she was realizing that he had done so from almost the moment he had entered her father's house, last June. She had almost hoped that he would never have to make a formal application for her hand. Why? Because she had known all along there would be difficulties?

But only difficulties. Surely no more. . . .

She tiptoed along the corridor, checked as the pantry door opened and the butler came out. He did not look in her direction, but continued on his way toward the study, knocked, and opened the door. She listened to her brother and George exchanging their angry words, and felt faint. She gazed at the open study door, at Alexei Alexandrovich's back, and crammed her knuckles into her mouth as chairs scraped. Her eyes met George's.

"Ilona—" He started forward.

"Ilona," Peter said at his shoulder. "Come in here."

"George." She extended her hands, and George took them. Alexei Alexandrovich waited patiently, looking toward his master.

"I will have no further discussion about this," Peter said. "Hayman, I have asked you to leave my house. Ilona, I forbid you to speak with him. Whatever promises he has made you, they are quite absurd. Go into the office."

Ilona stared from one to the other. Her brain seemed to be paralyzed.

"Will you come away with me?" George asked. "You told me once that if your father refused us permission to marry we would elope."

"I. . . ." She gazed at Peter.

"You seem determined to force me to act the tyrant," Peter said. "Elope? Would you compound crime upon crime? How do you propose to do that? Get out of here! Alexei Alexandrovich."

The butler touched George on the arm. George also looked from one to the other, then gazed at Ilona's stricken face. Oh, let me think, she prayed. Let me say something. Let me shout my undying love.

"I am going to Sevastopol," George said. "I'll not upset your mother on what should be a happy occasion. I'll stay in Sevastopol until I hear from you." He looked down at Alexei Alexandrovich's hand, and it fell away. "Until I hear from you," he said again, and went toward the stairs.

Ilona turned to look after him. "I'll come," she cried. "I swear I'll come. I love you, George."

He checked, and looked back at her. The angry serrations in his face dissipated, and he almost smiled. "I know that, my darling girl," he said. "As I love you. I'll wait for you."

"One would expect a Borodin woman to act with dignity," Peter said, more in sorrow than in anger. He held the study door for her.

Ilona walked past him, inhaling slowly and carefully. But he was only her brother. She could not be afraid of him. "I meant what I said."

Peter pointed to the chair, and she sat down. He sat opposite her, picked up his half-smoked cigar, and then stubbed it out quickly. "Young girls," he said, "often form absurd attachments, to their tutors, their physicians, even some members of their own family. You have led a life which has been at once sheltered and at the same time, because you happened to be in Port Arthur, more exposed than that of any other wellborn woman I can think of. And you were at a very impressionable age when these things happened. Therefore I am determined not to be angry with you."

"*You* are determined not to be angry with me?" she shouted.

"How could I be angry with you?" he asked. "I love you. You are my sister. But more important than that, you are my heir. Suppose I had died in Port Arthur or in that prison camp? Have you ever considered that?"

"Starogan would have gone to Uncle Igor. You are being absurd."

"You would have been my heiress, and therefore father's heiress. You would still have had your place in society, your duties and your responsibilities."

"Duties and responsibilities," she said contemptuously. "What duties does a woman have?"

"The same as a man, in her own sphere. You are certain to be appointed lady-in-waiting to her majesty the moment you are twenty-one. Do you suppose you can be a girl forever? What then of your social duties in St. Petersburg? And suppose I were to die without an heir? The estate would not go to Uncle Igor then. It would go to your husband."

"George would make a very good prince of Starogan," she declared.

"A foreigner? A liberal, as he proudly calls himself? What is a liberal, Ilona? Just another word for a socialist. You wish to marry a socialist? A man who openly prophesies that Russia will lose this war? Your husband must be a prince, someone who will care for his people. As will you. They are *your* people, Ilona Dimitrievna, as much as they are mine, or were ever Father's or Grandfather's. From the day you were born they accepted you as their princess, their lady. You have forgotten. You have spent too long in Port Arthur. But the women of Starogan will need you, will turn to you, will expect you to visit them when they are sick, to praise them when they have babies and to console them when their babies die. To sew with them and to pray with them, and on saint days to laugh with them and sing with them."

He paused for breath, and Ilona could only stare at him, taken aback by his vehemence.

"But most of all," he said, "they will expect you and your husband to bear children, that the line may be perpetuated."

She refused to be subdued. "For God's sake," she said. "Isn't that what I'm trying to do? I love George. He loves me. All we want to do is get married." She flushed. "And bear children."

"I have said that he is quite unsuitable. Apart from anything else, what is his religion? Is he going to change it? Or are you going to turn your back upon everything you have been taught to believe?"

"I. . . ." She bit her lip. "That would have worked out. Everything would have worked out."

"Worked out? You are even talking like an American!"

"Everything will work out," she shouted. "Because I *am* going to marry George, and I *am* going to be an American. There is nothing you can do to stop me. Even now. If you lock me up, I'll appeal to the tsarina."

"I think you will find that the tsarina will support my point of view. But I am not going to lock you up, Ilona. You are nineteen years old. You should have been married years ago. If Father ever failed in his duty it was in being too easygoing with both you and Tattie. It is those weaknesses which have brought the country to this sorry pass. Well, I intend to do my duty. In February Father will have been dead six months. You will be betrothed then."

Ilona found her back pressing against the chair. She could only stare at him in total consternation.

"I have not yet told Mother," Peter said. "But I know she will approve." He smiled briefly. "Oh, do not worry, my dear Ilona, I intend to sacrifice myself as well. You'd not have Uncle Igor really inheriting, would you? I have already sent a proposal of marriage to Prince Golovin."

Ilona sat up again. Despite her anger and her confusion and her misery, she almost wanted to laugh. "You intend to marry Irina Golovina?"

"I do."

"*You?*"

"Irina is a very pretty and charming and well-educated woman. She will make an excellent princess of Starogan."

"She's four years older than you."

"She is in the very prime of life."

"She's also, well . . . I don't suppose you ever listen to Petersburg gossip."

"If you say a word against Irina Golovina I *shall* be very angry with you," Peter said.

"Oh, I've nothing to say about her. Or to her." Ilona got up. "You can marry whomever you choose, Peter. Only let me do the same."

Peter pointed at her. "On June the twenty-seventh you will be betrothed to Sergei Roditchev. It is all arranged. The marriage will be in September."

Ilona's knees gave way and she slowly sank back into the chair. "*What* did you say?"

"I said you will marry Sergei Roditchev, in September."

"Sergei . . ." She drew a long breath. "Sergei Roditchev?"

Peter nodded. "He is an old friend of the family, and of Father's. He will make an admirable husband. And I happen to know that he has always been very fond of you. He was overwhelmed when I approached him."

"You . . . approached him?"

"Of course. I have given a great deal of thought to a proper husband for you. And he has been a widower for too long. As a widower he will be good for you. He will be able to guide you through the intricacies of marriage."

"As a widower?" Ilona shouted. "As a man old enough to be my father!"

"Sergei is thirty-eight."

"That is twice my age."

"No bad thing. Certainly he is not old enough to be your father."

"I won't," Ilona declared. "I absolutely refuse. Marry Sergei Roditchev? I'd sooner go to a convent."

"Don't be childish. You are going to marry Sergei, if I have to keep you under lock and key until then. I am the head of this family. I have our position and our future to think of. Believe me, it is a grave responsibility, but it is a responsibility I intend to bear to the best of my ability."

Ilona got up again. "You can bear what you like, Peter Borodin. I am not going to marry Sergei Roditchev."

"Now, Ilona. . . ."

"And he is not going to marry me. Shall I tell you why?" She placed her hands on the table and leaned forward to stare at him. "Because he will never marry a woman who is not a virgin. Will he?"

Ilona held her breath, horrified at the enormity of what she had just said—perhaps the enormity of what she had done, and had been doing for the past six months.

She watched Peter lean back in his chair. For a moment his face was quite expressionless, as if he could not take in her meaning. Then bright spots flooded his cheeks, and she could hear his breath rasp as he inhaled. Slowly she sat down.

"Do you expect me to believe that?" he asked.

Her chin came up. It was done now. She no longer had any option but to face it out. "What is the usual procedure?" she asked. "To call in a midwife?"

The pink was beginning to fade, and fade and fade, leaving his face quite pale. "Hayman?"

"I am not a prostitute, my dear Peter. I am a woman in love."

Peter pushed back his chair and got up.

"Will you challenge him?" Ilona asked, keeping her voice low. "He has been a soldier too, you know. He has seen more action than you. He would very likely kill you. And you would be making it public to the world."

He stood beside her chair. Suddenly he swept his hand sideways, driving his fingers into her hair to turn her face around, and slapping her across the cheek with his other hand. Her hair was being held too firmly for her to ride the blow, and she was aware only of a wall of pain on one side of her head, of the sharpness of teeth cutting the inside of her cheek, of the sudden blood which filled her mouth. He released her hair and she fell over in the chair, arms and legs suddenly flopping. Her eyes filled with tears and she could only just see him.

"I ought to kill you," he said, and went outside.

Ilona fumbled in her sleeve, found her kerchief and held it to her mouth. Then she dried her tears. It was necessary to move very slowly and carefully. She was not at all sure of her actual physical state, but she was only too sure of her mental state. She was about to become hysterical, and that would do no good at all. She remembered the first time she had stood at Dr. Alapin's shoulder and watched a man being prepared for an operation. She had thought then, I am about to scream and scream and scream. But she had not. She was Ilona Borodina.

And no matter what had happened, she was still Ilona Borodina.

Cautiously she moved her tongue. Miraculously it had not been cut. And slowly she was becoming able to think. She had never been hit on the face before. Being hit on the face was not a possibility for a princess of the Borodins. And it was several years since she had suffered any physical pain at all. She did not suppose she could ever be the same again. Certainly not in regard to Peter.

She got up, then sat down again. Her knees were still unsteady. But now her thoughts were running wild. George! In her careless defiance she had endangered George. Suppose Peter had sent after him to have him arrested. . . . Peter had that power, as prince of Starogan. She would have to fight all over again, insist upon telling her side, insist that it could never have been rape, that she had wanted it, wanted it, wanted it.

The study door opened and she got up. She stood with her thighs pressed against the desk, to gaze at her mother.

"My God," Olga Borodina said. "Are you badly hurt?"

Ilona put up her hand and realized that she had rubbed blood from her mouth into her eyes when she had wiped them. "My lip is cut. That is all."

"You should be held down and whipped," Olga said. "That is what your father would have done." She closed the door behind her. "If it is true."

"I am not accustomed to lie, Mama."

Olga Borodina glared at her. "When?"

"It began in Port Arthur. But it has happened here as well. Often."

"My God! You can stand there, and say something like that?"

"It *happened*," Ilona said. "We are in love. Where is he?"

"At the station by now, I should think."

"Has Peter sent after him?"

"No. We did not think that would be wise. Better to let him go, and be forgotten, than to turn this thing into an international scandal. Oh, Ilona, my little pet, how *could* you?"

"We love each other," Ilona repeated stubbornly. "It did not seem wrong, since we were going to be married. We *are* going to be married. You can't stop us now. We are already husband and wife, in all but the eyes of the church and the law. You cannot interfere with that. Why, I might be carrying his child."

"You . . . tell me you are not! For God's sake, tell me you are not."

"Well, I don't think so. But I could be. Mama, speak with Peter. Make him understand. Make him see that I cannot possibly marry Sergei Roditchev."

"Well, of course you cannot marry Sergei Roditchev," Olga Borodina agreed.

"Thank God for that," Ilona said. It was all going to be all right. Even the slap was worth it. Perhaps George had been right all the time, and it would have made more sense to have spoken with Mama from the beginning.

"You cannot marry anyone," Olga Borodina said.

"Except George Hayman."

"George Hayman? Do not be absurd. He is an American."

An icy hand seemed to close over Ilona's heart. "What do you mean, an American? What's wrong with being an American?"

"Everything is wrong with being an American. They are not like us. They do not believe in the same things we do. They are—"

"There are hundreds of Russians in America. Thousands of them. Millions of them."

"Oh, indeed. Jews and socialists and radicals. *That* is what is wrong with America," Olga said triumphantly. "It is full of people who have been expelled from their own countries."

"It is full of people who have *left* their own countries in search of a better life than they could hope to find had they stayed," Ilona shouted. "Don't you understand? It is all very well for us, sitting here in Starogan or at the house in St. Petersburg, doing whatever we wish, eating and drinking whenever we want. It is not like that for the muzhiks. It is not like that for Nikolai Nej and his family."

Olga stared at her, eyes opening and shutting as if she had been exposed to a strong light. "I am glad Mr. Hayman has left," she said at last. "Now, I wish you to go to your room and remain there. We shall have to make arrangements. I shall have to tell Mama. She is well aware that something is happening. But I do not wish her to see you with a cut lip. And there's Tatiana. I shall have to send her away. Yes, she will have to go and stay with Anna for the time being. She really must not find out about this. I had planned to send her to school in any event, but not so soon. Really, Ilona, you are the wickedest child. Think of the trouble you are causing. It won't end even after you have left."

"After I have left?" Ilona asked, speaking very slowly.

"It will take some time," Olga said. "I will have to write to St. Petersburg . . . no, no. You cannot go to St. Petersburg. Or even Moscow. That would be too dangerous. You will have to go somewhere like . . . oh, dear, I will have to think about it. Minsk. No, Minsk is too near St. Petersburg. I will have to discuss the matter with the tsarina. Yes, that is what I shall have to do."

A monstrous suspicion began to creep into Ilona's mind. "Where are you sending me?"

"Why, you will have to go to a convent, my dear. I really cannot see anything else."

"A convent?" Ilona kept her voice down with an effort. "A prison, you mean? How long am I to spend in this convent?"

"Why, my dear girl, the rest of your life. You will have to take orders and become a nun."

* * *

A knock on the door. Ilona sat up. She had hardly been aware of being taken to her bedroom. Escorted by Peter and Mama, like a prisoner. Because I am a prisoner, she thought. Oh, my God, I *am* a prisoner.

She stared at herself in the mirror. Her face, swollen on one side, looked lopsided. She had washed it clean of blood, but she could still taste blood. Her hair was starting to come down. It was lovely hair, her proudest possession. But they would shave it off, conceal her blooming figure beneath a black robe, and wait for her to grow old and sour. How carelessly had she shouted that she'd rather go to a convent than marry Sergei Roditchev. She'd rather marry the devil than go to a convent for the rest of her life.

They couldn't do it. This could not be happening. It had to be some dreadful nightmare from which she would awake in a cold sweat and with a great feeling of thankfulness. But she was awake now. Her mouth hurt too much for her to be dreaming.

Oh, why hadn't George stayed, and made a fuss? Why hadn't he defied Peter and insisted she leave with him? Because he had not supposed any society could be so archaic? Because she had promised to go after him, no matter what happened?

And because he knew that he would not have succeeded. Even George Hayman could not fight all of Starogan.

And because God had decided otherwise? Had decided they had sinned? She could not believe that. They wished to obey God's law, to be married, to live the rest of their lives in his grace. She could not really believe that he would punish them for believing in different versions of himself. But she had never confessed George to Father Gregory. That was a deadly omission. She had not dared. She had told God all about it in her prayers. He would understand.

Or had he felt they were just *too* happy? Living was meant to be a sorrowful business.

The knock came again, gentle but insistent.

"Come in."

The door opened; Nona Nej stood there awkwardly, shifting her weight from one foot to the other. She wore her housemaid's uniform, and her normally smiling face was serious.

Ilona stared at her for some seconds. "Nona Nikolaievna," she asked at last, "what are you doing here?"

Nona closed the door and clasped her hands in front of her. "The countess. . . ." She bit her lip and flushed in embarrassment. "The dowager princess sent me, Mademoiselle Ilona. She says I am to be your personal maid. She says you are not to leave this room, and that I am to fetch anything you wish."

Ilona frowned at her. "You? What of the housemaids?"

"I am to be your maid, Mademoiselle Ilona," Nona repeated. "The dowager princess said you should have a friend serving you."

"Oh, Nona. My darling Nona." Ilona held out her hands, and the girl came forward hesitantly to take them. She gasped in amazement as her mistress kissed her on each cheek. "A friend," Ilona said.

"Yes. I should have a friend."

Suddenly her brain was no longer dull or frightened. It teemed with thoughts and schemes and hopes. Because she did have friends. She had the entire Nej family, who worshipped the ground on which she walked.

"Your face is all swollen, Mademoiselle Ilona." Nona peered at her. "Can I get you something?"

Ilona shook her head. "Prince Peter hit me."

"Prince. . . ." Nona's mouth formed a disbelieving O.

"I wish to marry Mr. Hayman, you see," Ilona explained. "And Prince Peter wishes me to marry Prince Roditchev. Do you remember Prince Roditchev?"

Nona nodded.

"Which of the two would you rather marry?"

Nona's concern dissipated into a giggle.

"And now they say that if I refuse to marry Prince Roditchev, they will lock me up in a convent."

"Oh, Mademoiselle Ilona." Nona's eyes filled with tears.

Ilona held out her hands again. "Will you help me, Nona?"

"Help you, Mademoiselle Ilona?" Nona's O returned, and Ilona remembered that she was not the brightest girl in the world. She would need someone more intelligent. And could they really be trusted? They adored her, but did they not adore the entire family? Her savior would have to be someone who loved her more than anyone else in the world. Michael. Michael Nikolaievich. Of course, it had to be Michael. And of course he would help her.

"Listen," she said. "Prince Peter has brought you up to the house. Has he brought your father and mother as well? And Michael and Ivan?"

Nona's head bobbed up and down, and she gave another giggle. "I do not think Alexei Alexandrovich is very pleased."

"Do not concern yourself with Alexei Alexandrovich. Listen to me. I want you to do two things for me. Will you do that, Nona?"

"Yes, Mademoiselle Ilona." But she looked doubtful.

"First, I want you to promise me that you will not repeat a word of what I have told you to a soul. Promise."

Nona looked disappointed. "Not anyone, Mademoiselle Ilona?"

"Not a soul. Promise?"

"Yes, Mademoiselle Ilona."

"Good girl. And second, I wish you to bring Michael to see me, tonight, when everyone is asleep."

"Mademoiselle Ilona?" For the first time Nona looked truly frightened.

"I wish to talk with him. Will you do that for me, Nona?"

"Well . . . can't I tell Michael what has happened, Mademoiselle Ilona?"

"No. I will tell him. Will you bring him to my room?"

"Oh, but Mademoiselle Ilona, if anyone were to find out . . . Prince Peter. . . ."

"No one can possibly find out if you are careful, Nona. It doesn't matter how late it is, I shall be awake and waiting for him. But you must make him promise not to tell a soul either. Do you understand?"

"Yes, Mademoiselle Ilona," Nona said doubtfully.

"Good girl. Then off you go to find him. And Nona . . . don't forget your promise."

"I won't break my word, Mademoiselle Ilona." Nona closed the door behind her, and Ilona lay back on the bed, gazed at the ceiling and even smiled. Now was no time for fear, or remorse, or guilt. Now was a time only for action. Whatever she had done in the past, whatever might happen to her in the future, her first and only duty at this moment was to avoid the living death she had been promised. It was a duty both to herself and to George.

"We escorted him to the station, and put him on the train."

Alexei Alexandrovich leaned back in his chair and drank an after-dinner glass of vodka. He smiled at the eager faces surrounding the butler's table. It was all very well for Prince Peter to summon these upstart Nejs to the house; if he had not done so, in fact, it would have shown that he was not a reliable master, was too much given to change or was not really interested in his people. But it was he,

Alexei Alexandrovich, who had had to handle the first crisis which the new prince had faced.

"Did he not protest?" Nikolai Nej leaned forward.

"How could he, Nikolai Ivanovich? We would have made quick work of him."

"But . . . the reason?" asked Nadia Nej.

Heads turned to peer at Nona, seated at the foot of the table. She turned bright red. "I . . . I know nothing," she protested. "Mademoiselle Ilona is to stay in her room. That is all I know." She in turn gazed at her eldest brother.

Silly cow, he thought angrily. She will give it all away. Give what away? He did not know whether he was standing on his head or his heels; was sure he was going to suffer violent indigestion after this meal. He was to go to Ilona's bedroom tonight. He did not wish to consider why. He waited only for the moment when her door opened, in the middle of the night, with everyone else in the house asleep.

She was nothing more than an aristocratic whore. He knew that. Her lover had been sent away, so she wanted someone else. It had to be that. She could be treated with contempt.

But oh, how he waited for that door to open.

"Do you think they were planning to *elope?*" the cook asked in a stage whisper, as if the very walls would be shocked to learn of such a suggestion.

"What, Mademoiselle Ilona and an American?" Alexei Alexandrovich was contemptuous. "Impossible. The fellow insulted her."

"Then why is *she* being punished?" asked Ivan Nej, seated beside his sister at the foot of the table.

His elders regarded him as if he were a beetle. But no one could immediately think of an answer, and they were saved by the ringing of the bell.

Alexei Alexandrovich finished his drink and got up. The family was ready for bed, and the butler's dinner party was over. Michael held the chair for his mother. He had drunk little vodka; in fact, he was the soberest person in the room. And the family was going to bed. How far away that plump little schoolmaster's daughter seemed now.

The footmen had to wait for Alexei Alexandrovich to light the prince's way upstairs and then return, to lead them around the house as they doused each candle in turn. This was the first such occasion for Michael and Ivan Nej, and they watched patiently as they were shown exactly how to pass the brass cap on the end of its long holder over the very top of each candle, exactly how to check every door and every window to make sure it would not rattle should the wind blow. They were shown how to round up the dogs and escort them downstairs to their kennels for the night, how to sweep up the floors and polish the tables used for the after-dinner coffee; as if they had not done it all before in Port Arthur. The only difference was that this house was much bigger. There were eight footmen in all, including the Nej brothers, and yet it took them over an hour to put the house to bed.

"Very good," remarked Alexei Alexandrovich, as they stood to attention in front of him. "You may retire. Five o'clock. I will cane the man who is a minute late."

He mounted the servants' staircase to the butler's apartment on the third floor. Cook and old Nikolai and his wife—no one had yet decided what Nikolai's duties were to be; the new prince just wanted him in the house—had already gone up, and the housemaids and downstairs maids and kitchen hands were scurrying up to the attics, where the footmen also slept, two to a room.

"What do you think of it all?" Ivan asked as he undressed.

"It is not our business to think about our betters," Michael pointed out. He hoped this was not going to be one of Ivan's talkative nights.

"Well, I think they *were* going to elope," Ivan remarked. "They are in love with each other. You can see it in the way they looked at each other."

"What do you know of love?"

"Besides," Ivan said without taking offense, "it is the only thing that makes sense, with Ilona being locked up. Do you suppose he ever went to bed with her? Can you imagine those legs being in bed with a man? It makes me shiver. But you never saw her legs, did you?"

"Shut up," Michael said, and got beneath his blanket. The heat never really got to the roof, and even in the spring the attics were chilly.

"I'd like to see them again," Ivan said, lying down with his hands beneath his head. "Oh, I'd like that. But to have them in bed beside you—"

"Shut *up,*" Michael repeated angrily. "Go to sleep." Can you imagine? He did not have to imagine. And yet he was as hard as a rod just thinking about it. And in only a couple of hours. . . . "Go to sleep," he said, and turned his back on his brother.

Ilona waited for her mother to come in to say goodnight. "Prince Peter has already written to Prince Roditchev," she said. "The letter will catch the next train. He has had to explain the exact circumstances, of course, but dear Sergei is an honorable man and you may be sure it will go no further."

"Does it matter?" Ilona asked.

"Of course it matters. Have you no thought for the family? I really do not know what has come over you, Ilona. I had always thought you a good and serious girl. Now I wonder if you are not a changeling. No one must *ever* know the truth. They must just assume that you have decided to turn your back on the world. Lots of young women do, and then devote themselves to good works. To teaching, perhaps. You will make a good teacher, my dear."

"When am I to leave Starogan?"

"It will be a little while yet. I must make arrangements. I will have to go to St. Petersburg. Tatiana will accompany me. You will go as soon as I can arrange it." She held her daughter's face and kissed her on the forehead. "If only. . . ." she sighed.

"If only Papa were alive," Ilona said.

"You should thank your patron saint that he is not, or you would have been flogged by now."

"Papa liked George," Ilona said defiantly.

"There is a great deal of difference between liking someone and being prepared to allow him to marry your daughter. Why, Papa liked old Nikolai, and Michael and Ivan. Now go to bed, and try to think some decent thoughts. Prepare your mind for the life that lies ahead of you."

The door closed. Prepare my mind for the life that lies ahead of me, Ilona thought. Prepare my mind to turn my back on my family, my religion, my country, my upbringing, and my fortune, all for the sake of a man. But were any of those things equal to the man? And they had forced her to it, she reminded herself angrily.

But first of all, she must prepare herself for the hardships of the journey to Sevastopol. Leaving the house would not be difficult. Making the journey and finding George might be, especially as it would have to be done with speed; once she was discovered missing, Peter would certainly guess where she had gone.

But with Michael at her side she could hardly fail. Michael was probably the most reliable man she knew, excepting only George.

She got up and dressed, from stockings to petticoat, leaving off only her boots and her gown. Then she got beneath the covers, and closed her eyes. There was no possibility of her falling asleep. She was too excited.

She awoke with a start when her door opened. She sat up, pulling the blanket to her throat. The candle had burned low as had the fire, and the room was nearly dark. Had he come in without knocking?

She blinked at Tattie, wearing her dressing robe over her nightgown, her hair a pale cloud on her shoulders.

"Tattie?"

"Sssh," Tatiana said, and closed the door.

"What are you doing here?"

"I came to see you. I listened at Grandmama's door when Mama was speaking with her. Were you really going to run off with Mr. Hayman?"

Ilona sighed. "It is very wrong to eavesdrop."

"Not as wrong as it is to . . . did you really let him . . . well. . . ."

"Let him? I wanted him to."

"Ugh. You mean he . . . well . . . what *did* he do? Tell me, Illie."

"I shall not tell you. You are a very wicked child. Now go back to bed."

"I want to help you."

"You?"

"They're sending you to a convent. Can you *imagine?* A convent! They'll cut off all your hair, and they'll—"

"Oh, shut up, and go back to bed," Ilona snapped.

Tattie pouted. "Don't you *want* to be helped?"

"How could *you* possibly help me?"

"Well, I could. . . ." She turned as knuckles sounded on the door.

Oh, my God, Ilona thought. Oh, my God, my God, my God. Of all the luck.

Tattie's eyes and mouth were huge. "Who is it?" she whispered.

The door was opening, and Michael Nej stood there. He looked from sister to sister. His expression was as confused as Tattie's.

"Well, shut it," Ilona said.

Michael shut the door.

"Michael?" Tatiana found her voice. "I knew it. You *are* going to escape. You *are!*"

"Escape?" Michael inquired.

"Oh, very well," Ilona said. She threw back the coverlet and got out of bed. Michael Nej flushed as he stared at her, and she realized she was embarrassing him. "I'm sorry, Michael. I'll just put on my gown. I want you to go to the stables and saddle two of the best horses you can find. I want to leave Starogan tonight."

"Leave Starogan?" Michael's mouth was opening and shutting like a fish's. She thought he seemed very dense tonight.

"Leave Starogan?" Tatiana cried.

"For God's sake, be quiet. Help me with this." Ilona stepped into her gown, and Tattie fastened the buttons.

"But where will you go?"

"Sevastopol. George is waiting for me there."

"An elopement! I've always wanted to elope," Tattie said.

"You're not going anywhere, except back to bed."

Tattie pouted. "I'm coming with you."

"Are you mad?"

"I'm coming with you."

"Listen," Ilona said, forcing herself to be reasonable. "I am going to be with George. We are going to be married. Who are you going to be with?"

"I'll be with you. I'm your sister. I'll be George's sister, too, when you're married."

"But *why?* Why on earth do you wish to leave Starogan?"

"Because I want to," Tattie said. "I hate this boring old place. I hate Russia. It's all so boring. And in America they'll let me play whatever I like on the piano. They will, Illie. I know they will. If you don't take me I'll tell. I'll go outside and scream and scream and scream until the whole house knows what you're up to."

Ilona sat back down on the bed and pulled up her skirts to put on her boots. "Help me, Michael," she said.

He folded his body before her, took her stockinged foot as he might have lifted a baby from its cot and slowly inserted it into the boot.

"What are we to do with her?" Ilona asked.

Michael's head lifted slowly. His fingers slid round her ankle to make sure the boot was properly on before tying the laces. He had a curiously gentle touch. She realized with a start of surprise that his touch was even more gentle than George's. "I don't know, Mademoiselle Ilona," he said.

Ilona chewed her lip and allowed Michael to take her other foot. "Mama will miss you terribly," she said.

"She'll miss you as well. And we can come back," Tattie pointed out. "They'll be glad to have us back, afterwards. Once you're George's wife, they won't be able to do anything about it."

Ilona watched Michael tying the laces, head bowed. She had the strangest feeling that he had nearly kissed her toes, just then. Her entire brain seemed to be playing absurd tricks. Oh, blast Tattie for turning up. She meant well, but she was always doing the wrong things. And now she was sapping her powers of decision.

But what decision was there to make? Tattie was certainly capable of screaming the house down.

"All right," she said. "Go and get dressed. Warm clothes, now, and don't bring anything else. Meet me downstairs in ten minutes. Hurry now."

"Oh, you darling." Tattie threw her arms around Ilona's neck, pushing Michael's kneeling figure out of the way as she did so. "I'll hurry." She ran to the door, then hesitated. "You won't go without me?"

"Ten minutes," Ilona said. "Michael, it'll have to be three horses. Saddle them up and walk them out to the apple orchard. We'll join you there. Wrap yourself up warmly, Michael Nikolaievich. It'll be a long ride."

He stood up immediately in front of her. "But Mademoiselle Ilona," he said. "You can't run away."

Her head came up. "Why not?"

"This is your home. Your family. You belong here. You belong to. . . ." He did not finish the sentence.

"Not any more," Ilona said. "No matter what happens, not any more. They're going to send me to a convent, don't you understand? Starogan won't be my home any more. Besides, I love Mr. Hayman. Love, Michael." She smiled, and stretched out her hand to stroke his cheek. "I don't suppose you know the meaning of the word—the *true* meaning. It's when two people . . . well, when they cannot live without each other. I cannot live without Mr. Hayman, Michael. And he cannot live without me. That is love. You'll feel that way about someone one day, Michael, and then you'll know what I mean." Her hand slipped away. "Now go and saddle those horses."

* * *

Michael Nej stood on the downstairs veranda, his collar turned up and his cap pulled down against the chill night breeze. His hands were sunk deep in his pockets as he gazed into the darkness. What had he expected? To be treated as a friend? Had he really supposed she wished his company, his love? Was he that much of a dreamer?

She hardly considered him a human being. She had used him, indeed, as a facsimile of a ladies' maid, as if he were some sexless eunuch. As no doubt he was, to her. And now, carelessly, he had been commanded to throw away his entire life to take her to her lover. And not only *his* life: Prince Peter would certainly vent his anger upon Ivan and Nona as well, if not on the elder Nejs. These thoughts had clearly not entered Ilona's mind. And if they did, well, she would dismiss them. The Nejs were servants. They must expect to take the rough with the smooth.

And yet he knew that if she had proposed nothing more than escape from Starogan to avoid being locked in a convent, he would have abandoned his family and guided her to the very ends of the earth. To guide her to the arms of another man was more than she could expect, even from him. His interest—both his self-interest and his family interest—was to keep her here for as long as possible, where at least he could look at her every day. Once she joined the American she was gone forever, with all of Europe and an entire ocean between them. Whereas even if she were to be locked up in a convent, she would be allowed home to visit her family from time to time.

But how to keep her here? Tell her there were no horses? He chewed his lip. Ilona Borodina was not the sort of woman to be put off by so obvious a lie. Stop her by force? Then he would be lining himself up for a flogging, while earning her hatred as well. The only person who could stop her escape would be Prince Peter himself. That, too, would earn her hatred, but whatever he did to stop her would involve that. And telling Prince Peter might bring undreamed-of benefits to him and his family.

Betray Ilona. The woman he loved. Did he love her? Or did he just dream of possessing her, for an instant, before she disappeared forever? Then why not saddle up as she wished, and ride with her, and when they were out on the lonely steppe, knock her and her sister from their horses and rape her? Once she left Starogan she could never come back, never bear witness against him.

He turned violently and stared at the house. Another dream. He could never rape Ilona Borodina. He could never do anything, in her company, but worship and obey. He did love her—that was the plain, ghastly truth of his situation. If he would have any control over her life and her actions, it must be from afar, and through the agency of others.

He drew a long breath, opened the door, and went inside again.

"Be quiet," Ilona whispered. Tatiana's boots sounded to her ears like a herd of cattle descending the stairs.

"I'm so excited," Tattie explained.

"Sssh." Carefully, Ilona opened the outer door, stepped onto the veranda and closed the door behind her sister. The cold wind seemed to force its way inside her coat and through her gown and petticoats to chill her skin; she was not used to being out of doors at one o'clock in the morning. "Come on."

Tattie hurried to her side as they went down the outer steps onto the drive. "I've been thinking," she said. "Won't we need money?"

"I haven't any. Besides, it won't be necessary. Once we get to Sevastopol, George will take care of us." She looked up at the sky as the first drop of rain fell. "Oh, bother."

"We're going to be soaked," Tattie complained. "Let's go back, Illie. Please. Let's go back to bed. We can escape another night, when it's fine."

"*You* go back to bed," Ilona said, and strode across the lawn toward the orchard where Michael would be waiting. Dear Michael. He had asked no questions, had set about obeying her without a moment's hesitation. She could think of no more faithful servant. No more faithful friend.

Boots clumped behind her. "Aren't you going back?" she asked over her shoulder.

"We're going to be soaked," Tattie grumbled. "It's coming down hard."

Ilona could feel the drops splattering on the brim of her hat and soaking into the shoulders of her coat. It was a fur, for she had been more concerned at the prospect of cold than rain. But it would be warm and dry in Sevastopol. So warm and so dry.

And there was the orchard. "Wherever is Michael?" she muttered. But of course it would take time for him to saddle three horses and walk them out here. She was being too impatient. "Stand under the trees," she told Tattie.

"I'm scared." Tattie stood close to her, her back pressed against an apple tree. The rain poured through the leaves noisily, dripping to the ground with what seemed like huge thuds. The night became a gigantic whisper of sound. "Illie, suppose he doesn't come?"

"Oh, do be quiet," Ilona said, rubbing her gloved fingers together. Of course he was coming. If only it would stop raining. Then this adventure would be quite fun. But it was senseless to suppose that everything was always going to work out exactly as she planned. The only essential was to reach Sevastopol.

"Look!" Tattie's voice shook, and Ilona turned her head to look back in the direction of the house. There were torches flaring in the rain-swept darkness, and the glow of lanterns. Her stomach did a complete roll; she felt breathless and faint. "What'll we do?" Tattie's voice was high.

Ilona bit her lip to stop from bursting into tears. What'll we do, her brain screamed in unison? What'll we do? What had happened to Michael?

"I'm going to run," Tattie decided.

"Run?" Run where, she wondered? Oh God, what am I to do? But supposing it was Peter—what could he do to her but lock her up again? He was only her brother. When he had struck her it had been from sheer frustrated temper, and he was too much of a gentleman to hit her in front of the servants. "There's nowhere to run," she said, and stepped away from the trees to face the men. Tattie's hand stole into hers. Together they watched the lights coming closer, heard voices, and after a moment could identify them. Michael Nej walked beside Prince Peter.

Olga Borodina hid her hair under a cap and her nightclothes under a voluminous brocade dressing robe. Next to her, Marie Borodina was similarly attired. The two women looked like suddenly awakened avenging angels. Beside them Peter, fully dressed, merely looked embarrassed. Ilona realized that his concept of authority had taken him only so far—he had not envisioned open rebellion, and had no idea how to cope with it. He had not touched her, had hardly spoken to her, in fact. He had merely told Tattie to stop crying, and ordered them both to return to the house.

What did it matter? Michael had betrayed her. She could not believe it. Michael, of all people. He had not been able to meet her gaze. But if Michael would betray her, who in all the world would help her? Not even Mama, it seemed, judging by her expression.

"Close the door, Tatiana," Olga Borodina said.

Tattie sniffed, and obeyed.

"Well?" her mother demanded. "What have you to say for yourselves?"

"It wasn't Tattie's fault." Ilona was pleased to discover that her voice was quite steady. But what could they *do?* This was 1905, not 1705. They couldn't use the knout on her, or anything like that. The ultimate punishment had already been invoked.

"You persuaded her to leave with you?"

"I could not go alone."

"You hoped that Michael Nikolaievich would go with you."

"I could not go alone with him," Ilona said.

"You are a perfect lady," Olga said contemptuously. "But you agreed to go too, Tatiana. You should be flogged."

Tattie burst into tears.

"Your grandfather would have taken the skin from your back," Marie remarked.

"Please," Tattie sobbed. "Oh, please, Mama. . . ."

"I think she was led astray," Olga said. "You will go to your room, miss, and remain there until I send for you."

"Oh, yes, Mama. Oh, yes." Tattie turned to look at Ilona, opened her mouth and closed it again, and hurried to the door. They waited for it to close, and Ilona felt her knees touch in a shiver. She told herself it was because she was still damp and chilled from the rain.

"As for you, miss," Olga said. "I am deeply hurt, and concerned. No daughter of mine could possibly behave as you have behaved. I am trying to be charitable and convince myself that perhaps you have temporarily lost your reason. I wish you to regain it now. I will tolerate no more absurd scenes like tonight's, which will be the gossip of the servants' hall. Do you understand me?"

Ilona waited.

"So I wish you to take that icon over there between your hands and swear to your brother that you will not attempt anything so foolish again. Then I wish you to sit down and write a letter to Mr. Hayman, informing him that you were mistaken in supposing that you . . . were fond of him, that you bitterly regret what . . . happened between you, and requesting him to leave Sevastopol as soon as possible and never to return to Russia again."

"No," Ilona said.

Olga's head came up.

"I won't," Ilona said. "I won't swear not to escape. I am going to leave Starogan the moment I can, and I am going to join George, no matter where he is, no matter how long it takes me."

"You intend to defy me?" Olga demanded.

"I wish to be allowed to live my own life, Mama. Not to defy you. Or—" She glanced at her brother. "Or the prince."

"She should be flogged," Marie Borodina remarked. "Her grandfather would have had her flogged. So would my son."

"Papa would not have touched me," Ilona said, meeting her grandmother's gaze. "You cannot touch me. None of you. I am nineteen years old. I'm a woman, not a girl."

"Your brother is prince of Starogan," Olga pointed out. "He can do whatever he likes. The tsarina would support anything he chooses to do, especially to maintain the honor of his family."

The tsarina, Ilona thought. Always the tsarina. No one ever said what the tsar might say or do. It was eight years since she had met the tsar; he had seemed a kindly young man. She turned her head to gaze at her brother. There was no expression on his face at all. His eyes did not lower.

"I made a mistake," he said, "in letting Hayman leave. It would have been simpler to arrest him. It would still be best. Ilona thinks he is waiting for her in Sevastopol. I shall go there."

"And do what?" Ilona demanded.

"I shall place him under arrest," Peter said.

"On what charge?"

"That of seducing the sister of the prince of Starogan."

"There can be no such crime," Ilona said. "I will testify that I wanted everything that happened. I will go into court and describe everything that happened, in detail."

Olga threw up her hands in a gesture of horror.

"She should be whipped." Marie's voice rose as she resumed her favorite theme. "You must whip her, Peter Dimitrievich."

Ilona stared at her brother. You wouldn't dare, she said with her eyes. You wouldn't *dare*.

"I shall have to take legal advice as to Hayman's crime," Peter said, returning her gaze. "It is possible that I may not be able to have him imprisoned for very long. But I promise you this: I shall have him arrested. I shall have him locked up for at least a week. I give you my word that you will not recognize him when he comes out."

"You wouldn't dare." This time she spoke the words out loud. "His father—"

"Owns a newspaper," Peter said. "But whatever happens will have been an accident. Your paramour will have been set upon by the other prisoners, who will have been angered at the thought of Russia's most beautiful princess having been dishonored by a foreign liberal."

Suddenly Ilona knew that she was beaten. She was beaten because this time Peter had not lost his temper. He did not even seem to be very angry with George. But he was no longer either embarrassed or uncertain. She realized she was looking at the new prince of Starogan meeting his first crisis in the only way he could. She almost admired him, even as she hated him.

And he would not lower his gaze. Ilona turned away from him, walked to the desk, and sat down.

Summer in Starogan. When the notion that there had ever been a winter, or could ever be a winter again, did not exist. When, for as far as the eye could see, there was only the young wheat, already beginning to cover the rolling acres with pale green. When the cattle lowed as they were led to their pastures and the villagers sang as they worked their own communal acres. In the winters they grumbled. They huddled around their stoves and their samovars and they listened to their grandparents reminding them of how much better off they had been as serfs. Then they had still had their own strips of land, on which they had been permitted to work one or two days a week while giving the rest of their time to their masters. Now they had no masters; they had landlords. They must still work for the landowner, to pay the rent they could never afford in money. They had achieved nothing but debt.

And freedom. But freedom to go where, and to do what? Freedom demands an ability to earn, to sell one's skills, wherever one happens to be. Tied to thin strips of land mortgaged for the next fifty years, no man can be free. Tied to the responsibilities of being sons and brothers and fathers, no man can be free. How they envied the rich, the landowners, even the intellectuals, who at least seemed able to move from place to place. But were *they* really free? Was even Peter Borodin, prince of Starogan, free? However freely he might travel the length of Russia—from Starogan in the Don basin to St. Petersburg on the shores of the Baltic, was he not entirely borne down by his responsibilities? By the crushing weight of defeat which lay across the rulers of Russia since the annihilation of Admiral Rozhdestvenski's Baltic fleet by the Japanese navy in the Straits of Tsushima? After that disaster, following up on all the other disasters, the tsar had had to swallow his pride and ask President Roosevelt of America to arrange a peace conference. It was not something any

Russian nobleman, but most of all any Russian nobleman who had been at Port Arthur, could ever forget.

And certainly his family could never be free. His sisters least of all. Ilona stood at her window and listened to the sound of song drifting up from the garden, where some of the girls and boys from the village had reported for weeding duties, sent by their parents to make up a few days of rent. They at least were happy, with the sun shining on their backs, and the certainty that old Nikolai Nej would have jugs of cold lemonade for them to drink when they had finished their work. They were happy even to watch the high-stepping mares dragging the carriage back from the village, where the train had arrived only half an hour before.

It had been the sound of the horses' hooves which had lured Ilona from her bed. She spent most of each day lying on her bed, fully dressed. She was the least free of them all. Despite her oath, they did not trust her, and kept her under lock and key, allowing her out for an afternoon walk only in the company of four servants. As if she still had anywhere to flee. George would be back in America by now, cursing the day he had ever gotten involved with a Russian aristocrat.

And would he remember anything? She remembered everything, every word they had exchanged, every gesture, every caress. But she had nothing else to do but remember. Why should George, with all his life in front of him, with wars to be reported and women to be loved, newspapers to be edited and champagne to be drunk, remember anything? His life was to be spent anticipating.

Hers was to be spent in a convent. She was even anticipating that, now. There at the least she would be allowed to work, to occupy herself, instead of just sitting and waiting. It had to be soon, now. Tattie had been removed to a ladies school last month. Mama had gone with her, and Mama had also intended, Ilona knew, to consult the tsarina on the catastrophe which had overtaken her family. And undoubtedly this was Mama returning now, her decisions taken, her daughter's destination decided.

She craned her neck, but the carriage had disappeared around the front of the house. It would be necessary to wait a little while longer.

Ilona returned to the bed to lie down. At least, she thought, I have lived, if only for a few months. Many girls went to convents without ever having known a man. But she could remember for the rest of her life. She could remember love, and she could remember hate. And she could remember betrayal.

Michael Nej had been promoted from the ranks of the footmen to be Peter's valet. He was a man who would go far, because he knew what he wanted. He had always known what he wanted. And he had let nothing, not even friendship, not even intimacy—for she had supposed that in their lifelong closeness they had achieved something of that—stand in his way. As valet to the prince, he had a room to himself in the house. She saw him nearly every day—and preferred not to see him at all, however much his eyes begged her forgiveness. But when she was gone, she would remember him as often as George. It would never do to form an entirely idealistic image of the male sex.

Footsteps, on the corridor outside. Ilona sat up and dropped her legs over the side of the bed. The door opened, and Mama stood there. A happy Mama. A beaming Mama.

"Ilona, my dear child. Up, up. Brush your hair. Straighten your gown." Her teeth plucked at her lip, and she frowned. "Perhaps you should change. But no, no. You must come down now."

Ilona stood up. "Have you finally found a place for me, Mama?"

"A place. Ha ha. A place." Olga Borodina took her daughter into her arms, and kissed her on each cheek. "A place! You are the most fortunate girl on earth, my dear. Truly were you born under a lucky star. You will not believe this, my dear, dear girl, but Prince Sergei has decided to forgive you. In the fullest possession of the facts, he still wishes to make you his wife. Oh, bliss! Oh, joy! Aren't you the happiest girl in all the world?"

Chapter 5

"PRINCESS RODITCHEVA," SAID THE TSARINA, EXTENDING HER FINgers for the bride to kiss, and at the same time moving them upwards to indicate that Ilona should rise. "Truly you are the most beautiful bride in all Russia. My congratulations."

Easy words for the empress of all the Russias. Because Alexandra Feodorovna, Alix to her friends, had herself been the most beautiful bride in all Russia, eleven years before. Now thirty-three years old and five times a mother, she had put on weight and at the same time gained in assurance. From a lovely girl she had changed into a handsome matron, retaining her rich dark hair and strong, aquiline features, to which she had added the regal bearing of the most powerful woman in the world. Only a slight tightness at her lips, the way in which her eyes would occasionally become opaque as if she were suddenly lost behind a wall of private thoughts, suggested that she was not also the happiest woman in the world. Rumor had it that her youngest child, the Tsarevich Alexei Nikolaievich, her only son and heir to the throne, was sickly—as if a tsarevich could ever truly be sickly. Rumor also had it that she disagreed with her husband's decision, taken only the previous month, to summon the imperial Duma—as if tsarinas ever disagreed with their husband's decisions. Far more likely, Ilona thought, she suffered from the blight that hung over all Russia, but over the imperial family most of all: the fighting had stopped, the two countries had come together at Portsmouth in New Hampshire to discuss a peace treaty, and no one could have any doubts which nation had been the victor.

Portsmouth, New Hampshire. George Hayman would be there, covering the negotiations for his paper. But George Hayman was not to be thought about today. George Hayman was never to be thought about again.

"Princess Roditcheva." The tsar's face was grave, any softness at his mouth hidden by the neat beard. But his eyes were smiling.

"Your majesty." Another curtsey, the heavy folds of her gold-embroidered, white taffeta gown seeming to pull her down into a sea of sweat. It was early September, and the Baltic was calm. St. Petersburg sweltered in a heat wave, and even the Borodin town house, situated on the Nevski Prospekt overlooking the harbor and the islands beyond, and with all its great windows standing open, lacked air.

"Princess Roditcheva. Princess Roditcheva." The grand duchesses, younger even than she, smiled and kissed her on the cheek, one after the other. They trailed behind their parents wherever they went, invariably wearing white, like a gaggle of ducklings. Handsome ducklings, every one, but curiously interdependent: not one smiling except after a glance at her sisters to make sure they were smiling, too; often to be caught whispering to each other but never to anyone else; never, indeed, to be found very widely separated. But like everyone else, today they were all smiling. A society wedding, *the* society wedding not only of the year but of the entire century, so far, was just the event to end the summer with a flourish, make the possibility of better things during the winter seem just a little more likely.

"Princess Roditcheva." These were the other grand dukes and grand duchesses, making their way past the bridal party. And then the other guests, people she hardly knew but dimly remembered from seven years before, the last time she had been in St. Petersburg.

"Princess Roditcheva." A woman approached, as tall as herself and only a few years older, with a wealth of deep auburn hair shadowing curiously small, delicate features dominated by flaring nostrils and burning green eyes. She glowed, as she had just exchanged smiles with Prince Peter, who had acted as Roditchev's best man—to make sure I did not scream my defiance at the very altar, Ilona wondered?—and knew that her own wedding, which would take place the following spring, would outdo even this one in splendor.

"Irina," Ilona said, and was kissed on the cheek.

"I want you to visit me the moment you return from your wedding trip, Ilona Dimitrievna," Irina whispered. "I want to hear all about it."

Had Peter told her? She could not believe that. Although she was sure Mama had told the tsarina, which no doubt meant that the tsar himself knew all about her terrible crime. And how many others? She smiled at them all. They could think what they liked, whisper what they liked. She *was* the most beautiful bride in all Russia, and not even Irina Golovina could dispute that.

But why was she standing here today? Was she then a total coward? Or a total whore? Would she, after all her defiance, accept the caresses of any man, even Sergei Roditchev, rather than spend the rest of her life in a convent?

She glanced at him, smiling and bowing over someone's hand. He was a handsome man, and his family was one of the oldest in Russia. Yet she hardly knew him. She had met him only three times this year; once in January, when they had spent the night in General Kuropatkin's encampment before catching the train for the west, and he had been sternly critical of any civilian who had stayed in Port Arthur; once at their official betrothal, in June, when he had hardly looked at her; and then today. Today he had hardly looked at her either.

But he had been Papa's friend and was now, apparently, a friend to Peter also, and he knew he was getting a prize in a Borodin woman. But what was she getting? Certainly not freedom as Princess Roditcheva. She was beginning a life of domestic duty, domestic servitude and motherhood. Prince Sergei was thirty-eight years old, and his first wife had died in childbirth. He would be anxious to produce an heir, and as she had been told far too often during the three months since their betrothal had been announced, she might have been created by God especially for the business of childbearing. Her husband would be impatient for it to begin.

But at least she need not fear him physically, as she would have done had she been a virgin. She might even dream of enjoying some of the things which would happen to her. And she might even dream, since she was going to be a wife instead of a nun, and since she was not yet twenty and he was a soldier, that he might die while she was still young enough to pursue her own life. And visit America? She gave a little start with the guilt of the thought, and her husband rested his hand on hers. The line of guests had finally reached its end, and they could have a glass of champagne. She looked about and saw Tatiana using her sleeve to wipe sweat from her forehead, and her cousin Xenia, the other bridesmaid, looking bored, and Peter hurrying off to find Irina. Tigran, the second groomsman, asked Sergei if it were true that the socialists had already announced they were going to boycott the elections for the Duma because of the limited franchise, and Viktor, ridiculous in his high Eton collar and short jacket, endeavored to secure another glass of champagne.

Ilona turned around to find herself surrounded by Uncle Igor and Aunt Anna and Mama and Grandmama. She wondered if they were clustered there to protect her. They must be scarcely able to believe that their problem had actually been solved. The black sheep of the family was safely married, at last. Nothing else mattered. Today was a joyous occasion.

But one which continued to carry its responsibilities. While the guests enjoyed themselves, it was necessary for the bride and groom to go downstairs to be congratulated by the servants, both Roditchev and Borodin. Here was a row of faces she had never seen before in her life, but which she supposed she would soon learn to recognize. But nearly all of Starogan was present as well, brought to the great city especially for the marriage of the prince's sister: Father Gregory, waiting to bless her; headman Alexander Ivanovich, kissing her hand; schoolmaster Geller with his wife and his daughter, pink-cheeked and curtseying. And then there were the house servants themselves. Alexei Alexandrovich, who had been in on the scandal from the very beginning, and no doubt like everyone else was relieved to have reached the end of it, was first in line. Then came old Nikolai Nej and his wife, Nadia, and their children: Nona, Ivan and, at the end of the row, Michael.

"May this marriage bring you great happiness, Mademoiselle Ilona," he said.

She stared at him. Why should I feel anything but hatred for you, she asked with her eyes.

He bent to kiss her hand. "I could not let you go, my sweet princess," he whispered. "I could not let you go."

"You will be happy," Olga Borodina said. "I know you will be happy. You are a good girl, who needs only the influence of a good husband. Sergei is an honorable man. Remember always that he *is* your husband, and must be respected and obeyed, and you will have nothing to fear."

Nothing to fear? Ilona wondered. She looked around the eager guests. It was growing dark, and the imperial party had long since left. She had thrown her bouquet into the waiting arms of Irina Golovina, and she had changed into her going-away outfit, a mauve poplin bolero jacket and skirt trimmed with cream lace, worn over a white lace blouse. Her hat was a natural straw with mauve ribbons and flowers, and her parasol and gloves were cream. Her hair was secured in its usual pompadour, and she was very conscious of the feel of the gold band on her finger. Princess Roditcheva. With nothing to fear—why had Mama chosen those words?

There was a great deal of noise, melding together into a single roar as she went down the stairs. The servants were gathered at the foot, to cheer and throw rose petals. She looked for Michael, but could not find him in the gathering darkness. Had he really said those words? And what did they mean? What did anything mean today? Would it not have been better to have gone gracefully into a convent?

The carriage door was being held for her; a postilion handed her up. She sank into the softness of the cushions and watched her husband seat himself beside her. He still wore his uniform. Now he waved out from the window to the guests, and she did the same on her side.

"Are we going far, my lord prince?" she asked.

"No, no," he said. "I have a villa on the shore of Lake Ladoga. Not more than an hour's drive."

The flaring torches, the gleaming candlelit windows, the cheers, all faded as the horses clipclopped along the road. Passers-by stopped to wave and cheer, but it was too dark now for anyone to see inside the coach.

"I would have you call me Sergei," Roditchev said. "When we are alone."

Ilona began to feel relief seeping through her system. Perhaps it had been the uniform that had made him appear so stern and martial. And he had not looked at her. But he was looking at her now.

"I. . . ." She bit her lip. "I shall make you a good wife, Sergei."

"The tsarina assured me of it."

"The tsarina?"

"I obey my empress, my dear Ilona."

The relief receded at once, leaving little waves of alarm lapping at her mind. But things could not be left like *this*. "I. . . ."

"As she pointed out," Roditchev continued as if she had not spoken, "you are a very lovely young woman. Perhaps the loveliest young woman in the empire. And you are very wealthy, or will be when you are twenty-one. With such large assets, what is a blemish, even a serious blemish? Besides, my dear Roditchev—I am quoting her majesty, you understand—you are a widower. Pretend that this girl is a widow, and you are both marrying for the second time."

Ilona peered into the gloom, trying to see his eyes. But she could only see a glimmer of his face, and within it his mustache.

"All appropriate points of view," Roditchev said. "I am only sorry that you are *not* a widow. That concerns me. Do you think of him often?"

"I . . . I have not thought of him since our betrothal." A necessary lie at this moment.

"I disliked him from the moment I met him," Roditchev remarked.

"Do . . . do we have to speak of him, Sergei? On our wedding trip?"

"I had supposed that the thought of a wedding trip would make you think of him. However, I shall not mention the fellow again, I promise you. And I will make a confession to you, my dear Ilona. I am happy to have obeyed the empress. My first wife was not beautiful, and not even wealthy. Her father and mine were great friends, and that was sufficient. Now—why, I feel quite excited at the prospect of possessing you."

Relief, which had again started on its embracing journey, once more threatened to withdraw. What a strange word to use—although she supposed it was an accurate one.

But it was not a comment to which she felt she could reply. She looked out the window. They were almost clear of the houses now, and hurrying through the night. And her husband had not yet kissed her. The realization came as a shock. She turned her head to look at him, discovered that he was watching her, and attempted a smile. "Isn't it a lovely night?"

"Tell me," he said. "Did Peter whip you when you confessed your affair with the American?"

Oh my God, she thought. Oh my God, my God, my God. But if he intended to talk about George all night, then she must humor him. At least she did not suppose he would feel like "possessing" her while brooding on her lover.

"No," she said.

"My word," he said. "When were you last whipped?"

"I . . . my father did not believe in whipping us."

"But he must have done so."

She sighed. "When I was twelve, Sergei. For climbing a tree with a servant."

"A manservant?"

"I'm afraid it was."

He considered this for a moment, and she braced herself for the question, or at least the suggestion, that she feared was coming next. And how exactly would she answer it, now, after this evening? *I could not let you go, my sweet princess.* Had he really said it? But the prince merely said, "That would be more than seven years ago."

"Yes."

"I shall whip you tonight."

"You will *what?*"

"My father," he said confidentially, "whipped my mother every night before going to bed. He told me it brought out the best in her. Besides, women like it. They like to know their proper place."

She stared into the darkness. He was joking. He had to be joking. Even Sergei Roditchev had to be capable of making a joke. Well, she could joke too. The sort of joke he would be able to understand.

"I know my proper place, my lord prince," she said. "It is underneath you."

"Ha ha," he said. "Very droll. I am going to enjoy being married to you, Ilona Dimitrievna. I shall use a cane. When I beat a woman, I like to see the marks."

I am going to scream, Ilona thought. But she did not even open her mouth. Her stomach rolled and she felt sick. She turned to the window and inhaled great gasps of air. She felt better. Perhaps she should open the door and jump out. And break a leg, or even her neck? She was Ilona Borodina. Her brother was the premier prince in all Russia. No one could do anything to her she did not wish.

"I think our little game grows distasteful," she remarked.

"Game?"

"If it is not a game, Sergei, then I would like you to turn this equipage around and take me back to St. Petersburg."

"My dear Ilona, we are married. We are on our bridal trip. I had planned to spend a month at the villa."

"Beating me every night?"

"Ah," he said. "That is a point we shall have to consider. There would be little pleasure in it for either of us if you became used to it. Would there?"

"Pleasure in it?" Her voice started to rise and she made herself control it with effort. But it seemed quite incredible that she should be sitting in a bouncing carriage carrying on such a conversation, in perfectly matter-of-fact tones, with her husband. "Do you suppose I should enjoy being *caned?*"

"We shall have to find out. My father always told me that my mother did. My first wife did not. She used to cry. But you will not cry, Ilona Dimitrievna."

Ilona glared at him. "No," she said. "I shall not cry. Because I am not going to let it happen. I do not think my brother would like to learn of my being caned every night. Or at all. I think Prince Peter would be very angry to know that."

"Peter is an odd boy," Roditchev agreed. "But then, you know, old Dimitri was an odd fellow as well. I suppose that makes you an odd girl. Do you know, Dimitri actually used to argue in favor of a Duma? He used to say things like, 'at the end of the road it is the people who are the true sovereigns of our country.' In confidence, of course, and I have never repeated those words to a soul. They constitute treason, you know. But I should think Peter probably agrees with them. He must be quite delighted at the recent course of events. Not that this Duma will have any real powers, of course. We shall see to that. But there it is. I don't suppose your brother and I will ever really be friends. If you tell him that I abuse your body, no doubt he will, as you say, be angry. But then, you see, you are no longer only his sister. You are my wife. And I will be angry because you are relating the secrets of the marriage bed, which is one of the most unforgivable of all sins.

"So if we quarreled, Peter angry and me angry, it is very doubtful that I should ever see my way to visit Starogan, or even St. Petersburg. I have a house in Moscow, and in fact it is where my current duties demand that I live. Consider all of these points, my dear Ilona. A good wife considers everything from her husband's point of view, and makes sure that her point of view agrees with his." He pointed through the window at the lights which were appearing ahead. "The villa."

Ilona leaned back in her seat, hands tightly twined together. Oh God, oh God, oh God. But I am Ilona Borodina.

Only she wasn't anymore, as he had just pointed out. She was Ilona Roditcheva. For the rest of her life.

* * *

"Good morning, my lady princess. I have a glass of orange juice for you."

Ilona raised her head slowly, painfully. Every muscle in her body seemed to be aching, although the pain came together in a peak at her bottom and thighs. Thus she had been sleeping on her stomach—no, no, she remembered with a mental anguish equal to her physical discomfort, I am sleeping upon my belly because Sergei wished it so.

She rested on her elbows and pushed drooping yellow hair from her forehead. It should be white. It should have turned white last night. She rolled on her side and winced, looked at the young woman who waited, her professional smile tempered with just a hint of anxiety. "My lady princess?" She held a silver tray on which there was a large crystal goblet filled with juice.

Do you know what happened to me last night? Ilona wondered. Has it ever happened to you? It would have to have happened to her. Sergei Roditchev had been a widower for twelve years.

She took the goblet from the tray and drank. "What is your name?" She had been told all their names the previous night upon arriving, but she had heard none of them. Her mind had been chasing itself around in circles in apprehension of what was about to be done to her.

The maid gave a little curtsey. "Catherine Ivanovna, my lady princess."

Ilona inspected her. She was a pretty little thing. Oh yes, she would know what had happend last night. "And you are to be my maid, Catherine Ivanovna?"

Another curtsey. "Yes, my lady princess."

"Then I would like you to draw me a bath, before breakfast. Is my husband up?"

"Oh, yes, my lady princess. His excellency rises very early."

Ilona finished the juice and replaced the glass on the tray. "My bath."

"Yes, my lady princess." The girl crossed the room and closed the door behind her. Ilona rolled over again and sat up, then hastily lay down again on her stomach and burrowed beneath the covers, her body sinking into the softness of the bed, arms clasped around her pillow. That was how her husband liked her to lie, and when her husband had finished with her there was no other way she could lie. All that she had imagined to compose her beauty—her eyes, her mouth, her heavy breasts, her hair—had been meaningless to him. His interest in her, as a woman, began below her navel and ended above her knees. Into that small area of flesh he had concentrated all his pent-up passion, and all his pent-up hatred, too. As he had promised her in the coach, he had possessed her.

Had George ever *possessed* a woman like that? Never her. Whatever George had done had been gentle, almost shy. Oh, George, George. And oh, Michael Nikolaievich, for betraying her.

"I could not let you go, my sweet princess."

She realized she was crying; the pillow was wet. She had not cried last night. She had shouted with pain, and with anger, but she had not cried as the cane had stung her thighs. Now she cried with despair. Ilona Roditcheva. She was nearly twenty years of age. She might live for another fifty years. My God, she thought; suppose Roditchev also lives for fifty years?

"Still abed? Up, girl, up."

Her head jerked, and she watched him cross the room. He wore a crimson brocade dressing gown, and nothing else, she estimated; the robe kept opening to reveal bare legs. If he wants me again now, she thought, I shall go mad.

"Crying?" He frowned at her.

"A bride may surely cry on her first morning, Sergei." She kept her voice even.

"A bride should smile, and be happy. Get up."

Ilona pushed herself to her knees, feeling the covers sliding away from her shoulders and back. He was only the second man in all her life to see her naked. And he would be the last. The finality of her position seemed to be closing around her heart like an iron vise.

To her amazement he picked up her robe and held it for her. "Where are your slippers? Ah, there they are. Come along now. It is late." He stood behind her, gathered her hair, and scooped it on top of her head. "Have you a ribbon?"

Ilona gazed at him in the full-length mirror, behind the dressing table. His face was animated, happy, even handsome. She had not been able to see his face last night when he had been thrashing her, or when he had been driving his penis into her body with all the force at his command, hands tight on her buttocks to stop her from moving. Had he looked happy and handsome then?

"Where are we going?" she asked. "I have ordered a bath."

"A bath? A hot bath? My dear girl, as I suspected, you have been badly brought up. What are you, a hothouse flower? We Roditchevs go for a swim every morning in the summer. And the autumn too, when we can. Come along."

He had tied the ribbon around her hair so that the top of her head was an explosion of gold. Now he was holding the door for her. Last night might never have been.

She stepped onto the veranda and looked down at the sparkling waters of the lake, twenty feet below them. She had not realized, in the dark, how close they were to the water. From the veranda a flight of wooden steps disappeared below. Sergei was stripping off his dressing gown.

"The servants . . . ?"

"Are inside. They know that no one is to look out at the lake before nine o'clock. Which is why we must hurry. Come along now." He went down the steps carefully, launched himself off the bottom rung, and swam a few feet away. Ilona stepped out of her slippers, dropping her dressing robe on top of them. Suddenly the water looked deliciously attractive. The entire morning had become attractive. If only last night had not happened.

But it had happened; a cool swim was just what she needed.

The water was ice cold. She gasped the moment it lapped at her toes. But she was already pushing herself off, flapping her arms and kicking her legs to make sure her hair remained above water.

Roditchev laughed. "Makes the blood tingle, eh? Come on, now, swim. You *can* swim?"

Ilona did a breast stroke away from the steps. She had not swum for a very long time, and she had never swum naked before. The feeling of freedom was delightful, and now that she was in the water she was by no means too cold.

"Enough," Roditchev said, and climbed the ladder, water dripping from shoulders and arms and backside. He waited at the top to give her a hand.

"Bend over."

Oh, not now, she thought. Please God, not now, when I am feeling so much better. But she obeyed, and he touched her bottom.

"Hmm," he murmured. "Now, let us go and have some breakfast." He held her robe for her, then wrapped her in it, massaging the velvet over her wet flesh. She turned in his arms, and he continued to rub her back. "And after breakfast I shall make love to you. But I shall not cane you today. I do not think I shall need to." For the first time since their wedding he kissed her on the lips.

* * *

Princess Ilona Roditcheva sat at her desk in her private study, her gold-embossed notepaper in front of her. She wrote slowly, because despite the blazing fire in the grate behind her, her fingers were cold. Winter had come early this year, and already the city was blanketed with snow; from her window she looked across Red Square—so named for its connotation of boldness and bravery—at the gilded onion domes of St. Basil's Cathedral and those on the Kremlin, glittering in the pale December sunlight. It was peaceful, at least, here in Moscow. Winter had come early all over Russia.

"My dearest Mama," she wrote. "Your gift has arrived safely, and I am delighted and overwhelmed. Shall I be disloyal and say that I hope Sergei will give me the opportunity to wear it this Christmas? I am afraid that diamond tiaras are not really suitable for Moscow. When there are parties, which is seldom enough, they are very serious affairs. But Sergei places his responsibilities as garrison commander above all else, and in our present circumstances, I cannot really blame him, however much I may dream of either St. Petersburg or Starogan.

"Can I truly be twenty years old? I seem to have lived so long, if you will forgive me, to have actually completed so few years.

"And can this year actually be drawing to a close? Is it not the most terrible the Motherland has ever known? Sergei tells me that the strike in St. Petersburg is finally over, and that most of the leaders have been arrested. He says they will be shot or hanged. I think this is terrible, but how much more terrible must it have been in the Crimea and the Black Sea. Is it true that that terrible Schmidt man, when he took command of the *Ochakov,* signaled his majesty, 'I assume command of the fleet. Schmidt.'? He deserved to be hanged. And is it true that the crew of the battleship *Potemkin* turned their guns on the land? Did you hear them? My dear Mama, if you knew how I trembled for you.

"But apparently it was hardly less appalling in St. Petersburg. Sergei says there was no electric light, no water, no daily papers, no mail and no trains, for days. Have you heard from Tattie? I wrote to her, but I have had no reply. Still, I should think the convents were well enough; they are used to austerity!"

She chewed her pen. It was all very well to confine oneself to political matters, but Mama had asked certain questions which had to be answered. Truthfully?

"So here in Moscow we have been remarkably fortunate," she

wrote. "And now that winter is upon us perhaps the whole country will settle down and resume a more normal life. Especially with the concessions the tsar has made. Sergei is of course beside himself with rage, and regards widening the suffrage, and even more—agreeing to grant the Duma control of the finances—as total surrender to the forces of the devil. But if it gives the country peace, we should all be grateful.

"You ask about Sergei. He is well, as am I. No, I am not yet pregnant. I am coming to the conclusion that I am barren, in view of the circumstances. Again, forgive me.

"You ask of our lives together. As I have indicated, they are pleasantly dull here in Moscow." The first lie I have ever told you, my dearest Mama. My life as a woman and a hostess and a princess may be dull enough; Sergei wishes only to attend his office, and issue manifestos, and inspect the city; he regards the general strike in St. Petersburg with contempt, is sure that he would have ended that business in a matter of hours.

But as a wife, my dear Mama. You ask of my life as a wife. How can I speak to you of that? Can I tell you how he beats me, and loves me like a wild animal? How sometimes he *has* to leave me alone, because I am bleeding? How I lie awake at night and wish he were dead, or I were dead, or that we both were dead?

But as I am an honest daughter, my dear Mama, I would have to go on to say how he can sometimes love me as no other man has ever done. What a confession for a wife; no *other* man. And what disloyalty, for a woman who has sworn undying love to that other man. But a wife can have no other loyalty than to her husband, no matter what he might do to her or require of her. She is utterly at his mercy, as he had pointed out with quiet logic on their wedding night. She has nothing more to hope for than his occasional moods of gentleness, nothing more to anticipate than that, at Christmas, he might let her travel to St. Petersburg to see her family, her friends, to dance, and drink champagne, and know that she was alive.

"As I have said," she wrote, "I am hoping that the political situation will permit us to take some leave at Christmas, and come either to Starogan or to St. Petersburg to be with you all. I suppose the reason for my grumbling is that Sergei has no family remaining, and I am used to living always surrounded by mine. No doubt that will change in the course of time, but for the while, I hope you will kiss Peter for me, and tell Tattie that I did write, and remember me to Nikolai and Nadia, to Ivan and Nona, and to Michael."

She brooded at the page, wondered if she should change what she had written, or at least *how* she had written it. But Mama would think nothing of it.

"I could not let you go, my sweet princess."

A declaration of love, from a servant. Of all the absurdities. And yet, why should not a servant love? His crime was that he had allowed his love to shatter her dream of happiness. And to what end? That she should become the toy of another man? That she should be condemned to a lifetime of being treated as a slave, with only moments of promotion to mistress? And yet sometimes, insidiously, hatefully, those were becoming moments that she dreamed of and could not resist. I am a carnal creature, she thought.

And if I am hated by my lover for deserting him, and loathed by my husband for having had a lover, I am loved by my servant, who has never done more than touch my hand. So how can I hate *him*?

The door opened. Catherine Ivanovna stood there, holding the silver salver on which lay the day's mail. Ilona folded her letter, nodded, and the girl came closer.

"You have many friends, my lady princess," she remarked. "Many friends wishing you happy returns for your birthday."

Ilona took the heap of letters, flicked them through her fingers, sighed with relief as she spotted Tatiana's handwriting, felt a sudden glow as she came across a large envelope with the imperial crest, reached the bottom—and gazed at the American stamps.

General Prince Roditchev handed his hat and gloves and stick to his butler, waited for his cloak to be taken from his shoulders, his waist belt to be released, and the heavy weight of the revolver in its holster to be removed from his thigh. He nodded to the girl standing at the side of the hallway, and at once she came forward. The prince bowed his head to listen to her, then nodded again and walked on down the hall. The butler opened the double doors for him, and a footman hurried after with a silver tray on which stood a decanter of sherry and two glasses, already filled.

The prince entered the room and bowed to his wife, who stood in front of the fire, a tall, slender shadow crowned with the bouffant pompadour of her glorious hair.

"Truly, my dear, coming home to you is one of the great pleasures a man may experience. There can be no more elegant woman in all Moscow."

She extended her hand, and he kissed it. The footman placed the tray on the low table by the settee and backed out of the room. The butler closed the doors.

"How is it?" Ilona asked.

"Cold." Roditchev slapped his hands together. "But you are thinking of the city, no doubt. It is quiet. We will have no nonsense here. I do not think there will be any more nonsense in all Russia. Witte is, and always has been, a disaster. I remember him as minister of finance, you know. He all but bankrupted the country. Then he gave away the peace treaty to the Japanese, and now as prime minister he has very nearly managed to land us in a revolution. Now that he has been dismissed, you will see how things will settle down. This Stolypin seems to be a good man. A man who knows his own mind." He picked up the glasses of sherry and handed one to her. "A toast, to Monsieur Stolypin, and the Black Hundreds."

"The Black Hundreds?" She sipped.

"It is the name the newspapers are giving to the governmental reprisals. We are loosing the Cossacks and other irregulars in bands of a hundred men or so upon the various dissident areas. Believe me, the Jews will regret having started this business."

"The Jews? I was told the strikers were workers and radicals."

"And do you not suppose all the radicals are Jews? The entire Jewish nation is radical. But by the time we are finished with them this time, there will not be many left." He drained his glass and refilled it. "I am told you have received a large number of birthday greetings."

"My friends remember me, even buried alive in this place." Ilona's smile belied the watchfulness of her tone. She well knew what was coming next.

"Including one from America."

"Yes."

"I should like to see it."

Ilona reached behind her for the folded sheet of paper resting on the mantelpiece, and held it out. There was a distinct pause before Roditchev extended his hand and took it. He unfolded the note and read.

My dear Ilona,
  News of your wedding has only just reached me. I could not let such an event, or the approach of your birthday, pass unnoticed. However much I personally, may regret your decision last spring, I have no doubt at all that you acted in your own

best interests, and I would like most sincerely to wish you every joy in your marriage.

Yours,
George.

Roditchev raised his head. "You kept this to show me?"

"I do not think a wife should keep letters from men a secret from her husband," Ilona said.

"Letters from men," Roditchev said, as if to himself. "And suppose it had been a love letter? Would you still have shown it to me?"

"It could not have been a love letter. I wrote him myself, terminating our friendship."

"You wrote him on the instructions of Prince Peter," Roditchev said, putting down his sherry glass.

"I wrote him," Ilona said, keeping her voice steady. He had never before beaten her during the day. Indeed he hardly ever touched her during the day. But then she had never had a letter from George before. A letter from George. A cold letter. But why should he write at all, if he truly hated her?

And where would it get her, even if he still adored her? Nothing but a caning.

"And now he has written you. I would like a deciphering of what this letter really means."

"I have no idea what you mean. You are holding the letter in your hand."

Was she afraid of him? He could never do her any real harm. Even if she was, inescapably, Princess Roditcheva, she was still Ilona Borodina. Any marks inflicted upon her had to be in places no man—nor woman either, except her maid—could ever see. Nor could he starve her or take away her clothes and her jewels. His cruelty had to be confined to their bedroom, and to words.

But she *was* afraid of him. Constant unpleasantness, the constant assertion of male authority, was not something she was used to. Constant humiliation was also beyond her understanding. She feared his canings, less for the pain they caused than for what would happen after. Her sexual experiences before her marriage had all been gentle and restrained, and *shared*. She hated being played with, having her nipples flicked for minutes on end, having his fingers driven up her backside when he used her properly. Just as she hated, and feared, his delight in entering her from behind, less for the act itself—the feeling that she was being turned into some kind of a bitch to be mounted—than because she feared that one day he would actually sodomize her.

But most of all she hated herself for being aroused by him.

She feared him less for what he did to her than for what he made of her. But her instincts told her that the worst mistake she could make would be to reveal that fear. Let every night bring near rape. She must always be Ilona Borodina, must always object, always resist, always question his actions. Once she submitted entirely, there would be nothing left for her.

So she met his gaze and waited, knowing that after three months of marriage there were not even any telltale blotches of red in her cheeks.

"Hmm," he grunted at last. "I apologize, my dear. I should have known that a Borodin would never deceive her husband—a Roditchev even less so. Is luncheon ready?"

"I should like to go shopping this afternoon," Ilona said, gazing down the length of the oak dining table to her husband, who was selecting a cigar. She went shopping every Friday afternoon, but it was still necessary to ask permission, even on her birthday.

The butler struck the match, and Roditchev lowered his head. A moment later there came a puff of smoke and he leaned back with a contented sigh. "I should think that will be all right," he said. "Stay away from Kitai-Gorod."

"May I ask why?"

"Certain dissidents have appealed to the police commissioner for permission to hold a meeting there. Can you imagine, right in the middle of the market? They were refused, of course, but it is possible that some of them may attempt a demonstration. Nothing will come of it. I have informed the commissioner that I will have troops standing by in support of his people. But I think it would be safer for you to avoid the area entirely."

"Don't you suppose that to put soldiers on the streets before they are actually needed may provoke trouble?"

Roditchev pointed with his cigar. "There is typical female thinking. Unfortunately, it is typical of all the thinking in this country for too long. The way to provoke trouble, my dear Ilona, is to let the would-be troublemakers think they can get away with it. Once they see that they *cannot,* they will soon abandon any ideas of attempting a riot." He pushed back his chair and got up before his butler could assist him. "See that you are back by six." He left the room.

When Ilona had finished her coffee she drank a little brandy. Then she summoned Catherine Ivanovna and ordered her to get herself dressed for the street. Catherine Ivanovna—the spy with whom she spent all day, everyday. So why do *I* not beat Catherine Ivanovna, she wondered? She had never struck anyone in her life, and besides, what good would it do? Her best hope was to work at making the girl a friend, however long a task that might be.

Catherine wrapped her in her fox fur coat with its matching hat, removed her house shoes and encased her legs in fur-lined kid boots, placed the fur-lined kid gloves on her hands, then pulled on her own thick cloth coat and hat. The winter carriage was waiting for them, mounted on sledges and pulled by ponies rather than horses.

"We will begin at Kitai-Gorod," Ilona said.

The driver nodded and flicked his whip. Catherine, seated opposite, looked at her mistress with her mouth open.

"I am going shopping, Catherine Ivanovna," Ilona pointed out. "Should I not begin at the market?"

"But . . . we have heard there may be trouble there this afternoon."

"And his excellency has assured me there will be no trouble," Ilona said. "So there is nothing for you to worry about."

She gazed at the girl, and after a moment Catherine flushed and looked away. Why, then, am I doing it, Ilona wondered? In full recognition that it will make Sergei angry, with all *that* will entail. But she had to be her own woman, to be Ilona Borodina, to make her own decisions. She had to defy him from time to time.

Besides, even if he had asked her not to go, he had said there could not possibly be any trouble with his soldiers on the streets.

The sledge crossed the bridge over the Moscow River and rounded the walls of the Kremlin to reach the eastern part of the city and Kitai-Gorod. This area had been a market for hundreds of years; once it had been the meeting place for the trade routes from south Russia, a mart where merchants could exchange their goods securely beneath the massive walls of the citadel. Now it was a far more stable institution, and although in the summer there were many roadside stalls, they were less evident in December, when the emporiums lining the streets came into their own, great caverns of glowing gaslight, their shelves laden with goods ranging from weapons to bolts of cloth; since it was winter, the food stores were less well stocked. Scattered around the emporiums were the even more attractive restaurants, including some of the best in Moscow, already filled with cold and tired shoppers drinking tea from glass mugs.

As ever on a Friday afternoon the streets were thronged, and the driver was forced to slow to a snail's pace and crack his whip threateningly to clear a path through the crowd. The people seemed good-humored enough, and if there were policemen to be seen on every street corner, she could not immediately discover any soldiers.

"Which store are we visiting, my lady princess?" Catherine asked.

"I thought we would try Schiffers' Emporium in the square," Ilona said. "It is full of useless bric-a-brac and I am seeking a Christmas present for my sister. It is difficult to know what to give her, since there are not many things she would be allowed to take back to school with her. What has happened, Vasili Tigranovich?"

The driver had given up cracking his whip, and the sledge had come to a full stop. "There are too many people, my lady princess."

"Then we will walk," Ilona decided. "You will take the sledge back to the corner and wait for us."

"My lady?" The driver was astounded. "You cannot walk into the crowds."

"Oh, nonsense. No one will have any idea who I am. Come along, Catherine Ivanovna."

The girl looked as if she would have liked to protest, but she decided against it, no doubt reasoning that her best course was to obey her mistress and then make a complete report to the prince that evening. Little wretch. At the least she would have something to report.

Ilona stepped down, tested her boots on the snowy street, and decided it was not too slippery. As she waited for Catherine to step down, she peered into the semidarkness of the late winter afternoon, at the mass of people in front of and already surrounding her as more and more came. About fifty yards away the street led into the square, and there, beneath a street lamp, was a young man standing on some kind of makeshift platform, addressing the crowd. Oh, dear, she thought. Sergei was right. And that poor boy is going to be arrested, because in the steadily growing crowd there were more and more policemen.

"My lady, I think we should leave," Catherine muttered at her elbow.

Ilona turned her head. The sledge was attempting to turn to retrace its steps, but was finding it difficult. It was far pleasanter to be standing here in the freezing air then trapped inside the coach, with people peering in the windows.

"I think we will do better down a side street," she decided, and began to push her way into the crowd. People gave way readily enough, passing the odd remark at the obvious wealth of her coat and hat; but they were then attracted by a new voice. The young man had been difficult to hear, but this voice rang across the square like a bugle call. Ilona stood on tiptoe the better to see him. What she saw was a short, thick-set man, quite well dressed but wearing a flat cap from beneath which somewhat unkempt red hair bristled. His beard was also reddish in color, and gave to his already blunt features a curiously aggressive tilt.

But it was his voice which was his dominating aspect. It rolled across the crowd, not sonorously or inspiringly, but at once harsh and brittle, distinct and staccato in its pronouncements.

"It is a snare," the redheaded man said. "The tsar seeks to delude us. Things will not change, comrades. Electing Dumas to be imperial dupes is not the way to save Russia from the evil which has fallen upon us. We, the people, must take control. We must end forever this dreadful tyranny which would not be permitted for a day in other countries. We must reveal our true stature. We must—"

He stopped, as two policemen appeared on the podium with him. What they said could not be heard from where Ilona stood, but that they were arresting both speakers could not be doubted. Neither could it be doubted that the crowd resented their interference. There was a low growl of anger, and the people surged forward, carrying Ilona and Catherine with them.

"My lady princess," Catherine gasped, using her elbows in an attempt to stand still in the midst of so much movement. "There will be trouble. We must leave. Please, my lady."

Ilona stared at the struggling people on the platform, and as she watched, one of the policemen was seized by the arm from behind and pulled off balance so that he fell into the crowd, while a howl of approbation rose from around him. Her heart seemed to jump, and then lodge itself at the base of her throat. A shrill whistle cut across the noise, but the crowd merely roared its defiance, and other heads turned to see where the police reinforcements were coming from. Around the platform, which had now collapsed altogether, heads continued to bob and there was a steady growl of anger. She thought the second policeman had also disappeared.

But now there came a new sound, the clip-clopping of hooves. With everyone else Ilona turned her head, almost as if they were watching a play in which the action had shifted from one end of the stage to another. Now they looked at a hitherto unblocked street, a street in which many of the shops had been closed and which was therefore in semidarkness. But not so dark that they failed to see the ranks of horsemen riding forward, the glare of the gas lamps reflecting from their drawn sabers.

"Run," Catherine Ivanovna screamed. It was not a necessary exhortation. With a great wail the entire mob attempted to recede, at the same time trying to turn around to make their escape while there was yet time. Ilona found herself carried with them, but she was late on the turn. She watched the horsemen pouring into the square, and listened to the blare of their bugle. I am Ilona Roditcheva, she thought, wife of your commanding general. But it would do her no good to stand up and shout those words here. The horsemen were moving into a canter, and swords were being thrust forward.

Ilona turned and was struck from behind by a hurrying body; she fell to her hands and knees. Someone else kicked her in the thigh and fell right over her, and she sprawled on her face in the trampled snow. A foot was placed on her shoulder, and she gave a gasp of pain which disappeared as another boot kicked her on the back of the head and thrust her face forward into the snow. She inhaled, and her nostrils were blocked while her lungs seemed about to explode. My God, she thought, I am suffocating. I will be trampled to death.

Hands grasped her arms and dragged her up, and another hand slapped her on the back to make her gasp and spit snow and mucus and free her nostrils. She looked right and left seeking Catherine, and found two strangers, a boy and a girl, for they were not more than that, urging her onwards toward the nearest shop, where shutters were hastily being erected.

The crowd's wail rose to a scream, and she looked over her shoulder as they reached the temporary shelter of the shop doorway, and was then lost in the drumming of hooves. Ilona saw the horsemen crashing across the square, sabers slicing through the air. She watched men, women, and children falling to the ground, and even in the gloom she could tell that the snow was stained with blood. She glanced at the girl who had saved her. The face, whose solemnity enhanced rather than detracted from her good looks, watched the dreadful scene before them with glowing dark eyes, while the wide mouth twisted and seemed to spit. "Scum," she said. Then she felt Ilona's glance, and looked at her in turn. "We cannot stay here," she said. "Come."

She seized Ilona's hand and gave it a squeeze. "You must come."

Ilona looked at the boy on the other side, clearly the girl's brother. Where was Catherine? Where was Vasili Tigranovich? But the girl was right; she could not possibly stay here.

She nodded. "I will come with you."

The girl looked back at the square. The horsemen had finished their charge and were regrouping in the center of the bodies they had struck down, and were still carelessly trampling. Why, Ilona thought, there must be over a hundred bodies. Cut down just for listening to a man speak? And soon there would be more. The commander was clearly selecting a new direction for a charge. He raised his sword, and a shot rang out.

A great silence fell over the square, and the girl released Ilona's hand. Together with everyone else cowering in shop doorways and gutters, they watched the mounted officer seem to sit very straight in his saddle, his sword still pointing, and then, with inexplicable slowness, he leaned backwards, and backwards, and backwards, until he lost his balance and fell from the saddle to hit the cobbles, one booted foot still caught in its stirrup.

And still no one moved, not even the dead man's horse. The Cossacks themselves looked utterly bewildered, and Ilona realized that they had never suspected that someone might actually attempt to kill one of them. But then, no one in the crowd had considered such a possibility either. The girl beside her was watching the scene with half-opened mouth, while she slowly, absently, pulled the shawl from her head as if the cold no longer mattered. She had fine hair, thick and long and dark. She was a splendidly strong, healthy girl, for the first time in her life watching a man die. But it was a man she hated, without even knowing his name, and therefore she was enjoying the sight. Ilona suddenly felt utterly lonely, for the first time in her life.

There was another shot. This was even more surprising. It might have been possible to regard the death of the officer as an assassination, but this was rebellion. This shot too had struck home, and another man was tumbling from his saddle. And then there were several shots, and two more men fell. The Cossacks began to edge their horses toward the dark street from which they had charged, and when a shouted command rang out, they turned and rode off, chased by yet more bullets.

Ilona looked at the people around her, slowly emerging from their hiding places, from the shop doorways and the gutters and the suddenly darkened restaurants. There was no cheering, no shouting, only a gigantic murmur. The girl and the boy who had saved her life also moved forward into the square, to stare at the young men who led them, hands filled with rifles and revolvers, not all of which could have come from the gunsmiths down the road. Ilona realized that several of these men had come here today determined to make a fight of it. Oh, my God, she thought. What will happen now?

More tragedy, certainly. One of the Cossacks was not dead, but raised himself on his elbow, blood dribbling down the front of his tunic as he asked for help. The crowd came to life. With a roar several men and women descended upon him and lifted him from the ground. He screamed as they clutched at him and carried him toward the nearest lamppost. They tore at his clothing, and he screamed again and again. Then a rope was found and he was hoisted from the ground by the ankle, head bumping along on the cobbles to be kicked by those who stood nearby, while others cut away his straps and his buttons, ripped off his pants and underclothes to leave him as humiliated as a man could be.

Ilona found herself in the square, kneeling beside a corpse as she watched the Cossack die. Around her the night went mad. Now they had understood their victory. Men and women held hands and danced and sang together, round and round the lamppost with its obscene, dangling victim, while others began to loot the shops on either side of the square, and yet others saw a policeman attempting to escape down a side street and gave chase with catcalls which ended in another dreadful screaming as they caught him.

It is the end of the world, Ilona thought. My God, it is the end of the world.

"You should not be here," said the girl, standing beside her. Had she helped to hang the soldier? Ilona wondered. "You are not one of us. You are too well dressed to be one of us. Hurry away before anyone notices."

Ilona got to her feet. Looking at the girl's strong features, she guessed she could be little more than sixteen. And this was no muzhik face, nor were those muzhik clothes, beneath the shawl. "Do *you* belong here?" she asked.

"I *am* here," the girl said. "I want to be here. You do not. Come. I will show you how to get away." Once again she held Ilona's hand, and began to drag her toward a side street. That meant passing the dangling body of the Cossack.

"And what will you do now?" Ilona asked.

"We shall have to talk about it," the girl said. "When they have enjoyed their victory."

"Their victory?" Ilona shouted. "Do you think this is a victory? Do you not suppose those Cossacks will be back? Hundreds of them? Thousands of them? How can you fight an army? You will all be killed. Or taken and hanged. *You!*" She paused, and looked around herself in dismay. She had been speaking loudly, and others had heard. Now they clustered round the two women.

"What she says is right," someone said. "They will be back. With machine guns."

"My God, my God," a woman cried. "We must get away. Hurry. We must go home."

"And do you not suppose the Cossacks and the police will follow you to your homes?" It was the redheaded man, suddenly reappearing in their midst. "There can be no flight for us, comrades. We have killed soldiers and policemen. We have struck the first blow for the freedom of our people. We must build on this victory, not run away."

"How can we fight an army?" Someone echoed Ilona's words.

"With courage and determination," the redheaded man said. "We will seal them from this part of the city, our part of the city. We will build barricades. Tear up these cobbles to block the streets. Take what you require from those shops. This night we will light a torch that will burn from one end of Russia to the other."

Once again they sang, an enormous chant which drowned out the clash of pick and shovel, the orders and the occasional grumblings. It was a chant which must be audible for miles, Ilona supposed. Certainly it must be audible to the soldiers who by now must be gathering beneath the Kremlin. A single horseman had returned, walking his horse down the street to observe what was happening. Someone had fired at him, and he had turned and walked his horse away again.

So they worked with increased urgency, sang with increased fervor, Ilona Roditcheva among them. She lifted cobbles which they had torn from the earth, and she carried them to the head of the street to be placed on top of other cobbles. She rubbed shoulders with foul-smelling peasant women, and she sweated beneath her fox fur coat. And she sang with the rest of them.

And drank vodka, because the liquor stores had all been looted and buckets of the strong white alcohol were being carried around and around the square, each bucket with a cup for dipping. So whose lips have touched the cup immediately before mine, Ilona wondered? That prostitute's over there, or that butcher's over there, or that old man's over there? It did not seem to matter, because she had never even tasted vodka before. Dimitri Borodin had served only wine and champagne. Now her senses seemed to be swinging in time to the music.

It all added to the feeling of unreality. She was sure she was not the only person here who felt unreal. That ordinary people should actually have driven off a squadron of the tsar's Cossacks, should actually have killed four of them—no, no, killed three of them and executed the fourth—had to be unreal to everyone here. The vodka could only perpetuate the sense of unreality, maintain it until the moment of reality arrived.

So why was she here, waiting to be killed with everyone else? Because of a tremendous sense of guilt, that her husband had *caused* all these deaths, because of the certainty that if these people knew who she was they would carry her to the nearest lamppost and hang her by one leg? Or certainly use her as a hostage to secure their lives. Perhaps, she thought, as she lifted another cobblestone with torn gloves, her back starting to hurt, I want that to happen. Perhaps by being here and declaring myself I can save all their lives, those that are left. Supposing I have the courage. Supposing I believe that Roditchev will surrender to these people in order to save me.

"What are you doing?" It was the dark girl.

Ilona straightened. "Working, like everyone else."

"You? You do not belong here. Do you wish to be killed? You must get away. Come with me."

"With you? But . . ." She looked past the girl at the redheaded man.

"What is the trouble?" he asked.

"This woman is here by accident," the girl explained. "She was caught up in the crowd. She should not be here. She belongs on the other side of the river."

The redheaded man peered at her, at her coat. Even covered in snow and mud he could identify the fur. "Why are you here?" he asked.

"I . . . I am here," Ilona said.

"The young lady is right," the man said. "You do not belong here. You must leave at once. The soldiers will soon be upon us." He held her arm, marched her across the square to the head of one of the streets where the barricade had not yet been completed. "You will go a little way with her," he told the girl. "See that she is safe."

"But . . ." Ilona checked herself, shook her head to clear away the vodka fumes. "You need me here."

"We need people who can work and fight. Not people who will faint at the sight of blood," the man said. "And not bourgeoisie, in any circumstances."

"Bourgeoisie? You don't understand." She tossed her head. "I am the Princess Roditcheva."

They both stopped together, and released her. "Oh, my God," said the girl.

The man looked from right to left to see if anyone had overheard. But no one had. "Victory," he said. "This night we *will* gain a victory."

"No," said the girl.

The redheaded man frowned at her. "What do you mean?"

"I mean that she is a false hope. You will bargain for her? With her husband? Of course he will bargain with you. He will wish to save the life of his wife. But the moment she is surrendered to him he will break every promise he has made. Do you not know that, comrade?"

"Yet we have her," said the redheaded man. "That must be worth something."

"It is worth nothing," said the girl. "Not here. You must either let her go or hang her."

Ilona looked from one to the other. My God, she thought; they are speaking about *me*.

The redheaded man was chewing his lip.

"But if you let her go. . . ." the girl said.

"I should have betrayed our people," the man said.

"You might have saved them, in the long run," the girl argued. "She is here. She is working with us. She sympathizes with our cause. She must."

They looked at Ilona.

"If she sympathizes with us," the girl said, "she can help us much more than by dying here with us." She seized Ilona's hand. "Will

you help us? Will you persuade your husband to be lenient with us?"
"Why do we need leniency?" the man demanded. "We are not going to be beaten."
"Do you really believe that, comrade? Well, consider this. If we win, we are going to need no friends, anywhere. If we lose, we are going to need every friend we can find."
The man considered. Then he nodded. "You have a wise head on those young shoulders. Escort the princess outside our lines. And you, Princess Roditcheva, tell your husband that there are many thousands of people here, men and women, who will die before they surrender to be hanged or transported to Siberia. I have been to Siberia, but I am here now, and I will not be sent back. You tell your husband that." He marched into the crowd.
"Come," said the girl.
Ilona was led down the street. The men on the half-completed barricade stood aside to let them through.
"And tell him, when he has beaten us down, that he should be merciful," the girl said. "That the day may come when he will be glad to have shown mercy to the people of Moscow."
"You believe you will be beaten?"
"I think so. Today has been too spontaneous. There has been no preparation, and besides, conditions are not right. The French Revolution succeeded because the States-General supported it. The Austrian Revolution failed because it was only a mob, like this. Do you suppose the Duma, as it is presently elected, will support revolution?"
Ilona considered. "I suppose not," she said. "But then . . . why are you here? You are no more one of these people than I. You are only a schoolgirl." She frowned at her. "I do not even know your name."
The girl hesitated, and then shrugged. "My name is Judith."
"That is not a Russian name."
"It is a Jewish name, princess. That is why I am here."
"Oh." She did not entirely understand. "The redheaded man. Is he also a Jew?"
"No," Judith said. "He is not a Jew. He is a professional agitator, a professional survivor. What he failed to achieve in St. Petersburg, he hopes to achieve here. When we are beaten, when many of us have been killed, he will melt away and reappear somewhere else. He

is not a true revolutionary. If you can persuade your husband to hang *him,* you will be doing us a good turn. He calls himself Lenin. Remember that." She released Ilona and pointed down the darkened street. "That way lies safety, for you."

Chapter 6

ILONA RODITCHEVA BECAME AWARE THAT THE NOISE HAD STOPPED. The continuous explosions, the crashes and the bangs, the staccato ripple of rifle and machine-gun fire which had dominated Moscow for the past ten days, and which had grown to a climax over the preceding twelve hours, had ceased. Suddenly it was so quiet her ears hurt.

She sat up and rang the bell. "What is happening?" she asked when Catherine Ivanovna appeared.

The maid placed the breakfast tray on the table by the bed. "The rebels have surrendered, my lady princess." She regarded Ilona with some suspicion. She had expected the prince to be angry with his wife for visiting Kitai-Gorod at all, and certainly for becoming separated from her coachman and maid, for disappearing for several hours, and for returning late at night with her clothes torn and covered in mud. But Roditchev had forgotten anger in his alarm for her safety, had insisted she immediately go to bed and stay there, with hot-water bottles and tonics and a physician every day, and with Catherine Ivanovna to see to her every want—as if *she* had not also been knocked to the ground and trampled on and bruised and battered.

"Thank God for that," Ilona said. "All those people . . . what could they hope to achieve?"

"I do not know, my lady princess," Catherine said primly. She saw her chance for at least a small revenge. "But it is good that his excellency will now be able to return home."

Ilona drank her juice. Sergei had not been home for three nights. Three nights of blessed peace. But he had not touched her since the revolt began. So why was she happy it was over? Because she did not wish to think of that Jewish girl, Judith, or even the redheaded man, and certainly none of the other people she had worked beside for that unforgettable hour, lying dead on the cobbles? Now they had surrendered. But Sergei had promised to be merciful. "As merciful as I can be," he had said.

"That is good news," she said. "I think I will remain in bed for the rest of the morning, Catherine Ivanovna. You may attend me later."

She slept, and awoke to find her husband standing by her bedside. His uniform was soiled with smoke and sweat, and he looked tired but triumphant.

Ilona sat up. "I am to congratulate you."

He stooped to kiss her on the forehead. "And I am pleased it is over."

"Those pathetic people—I am so glad they finally learned some sense."

"I doubt they have learned any sense." Roditchev took off his tunic and rang the bell. "A hot bath. My God, how I long for a hot bath. Putting down revolts of civilians is no task for a soldier, you know, my dear. It is no challenge to kill people who are not mentally or physically equipped to fight. And they had courage. One cannot deny that. It was not until our cannon had reduced Kitai-Gorod to a shambles that they surrendered."

Ilona stared at him. "Cannon? You used cannon?"

"Well, what would you have me do?" He turned his head as Catherine Ivanovna presented herself. "Have Anatol Vasilievich draw me a bath," he said. "And be quick. I cannot stay long."

Catherine curtseyed, glanced at her mistress, and withdrew.

"You turned cannon on those people?" Ilona repeated.

"I invited them to surrender," he said. "And they wanted terms. Terms, after rebelling against the authority of their tsar! I told them to surrender, and they would not. They had held the city for nine days. They had killed several of my men. They were making Moscow —they were making me, my dear—the laughing stock of the empire. I could not permit such a state of affairs to continue. Questions were being asked. So yesterday afternoon I ordered the cannon brought down from the Kremlin and directed at barricades."

"You promised to be merciful," she said.

"As merciful as I could be. And using the cannon was the most merciful thing I could have done. They were going to die anyway. This way I *saved* lives. You should have seen them—those cobblestones *flew* apart." He smiled. "The rebels too."

"My God," she whispered. "Oh, my God." She had wanted only an end to the fighting because she had been there. She could not believe in anything the redheaded man had said. She could not wish for a revolution which would topple her family as well as the tsar. And yet all her sympathies had gone out to those men and women trampled to death by the Cossacks, and to the rest who had been prepared to fight rather than be murdered. Her sympathies, nothing more. She knew that even had she not been sent away, she would have fled the moment the soldiers arrived. But she had been able to salve her conscience by extracting from her husband his promise of mercy: that was the condition on which she had been allowed to leave.

And now they had been blown to pieces by cannon. Her brain filled with an image of the dark-haired Jewess lying sprawled and bloodied on the cobbles.

"They brought it on themselves," Roditchev said, not unsympathetically.

Ilona raised her head.

"The fact that they let you go," he said, "does not excuse them from being criminals. It did not mean that they would not have killed you, and certainly me, had they succeeded in gaining control of the city."

"Was there ever any hope of their doing that?" she asked.

"No. But they must have thought there was. Believe me, Ilona, it was necessary to make an example. Someone had to, sometime. If the authorities in St. Petersburg had made a proper example of these strikers two months ago, this revolt would never have happened. Leniency can be as grave a mistake as undue harshness. I know I was right. I have received telegrams of congratulations from all over the empire. There is one from the tsar himself. This event will make me famous."

Infamous, she thought. "What of the survivors?"

"The jail is overflowing—which is why I must hurry and get down there. I cannot hang them all, of course, that would take too long."

"Hang them?" she shouted.

"My dear girl, they are revolutionaries. Taken with weapons in their hands. And we did not catch them all. Some escaped. Some of their leaders escaped. I will have to interrogate the more intelligent prisoners and see what I can learn. You may think this thing is over, but for me it is just beginning."

"What will you do to them?" Her voice was low. "Tell me."

He regarded her curiously for a moment. "Our methods are not things that a lady would normally wish to hear."

What things, her brain screamed? The girl, Judith, was certainly intelligent. What would a man who took pleasure in beating his own wife do to a pretty girl whom he regarded as an enemy? She lay down and closed her eyes.

"I know it is terrible," Roditchev said, sitting on the bed and holding her hand. "But it is necessary. And you must always remember that they bring these things on themselves. No one asks them to make trouble. There is no reason for it. The empire is prosperous, everybody should be happy. They bring it on themselves." He squeezed her fingers, and she opened her eyes.

"I would like to leave Moscow for a while," she said. "I would like to visit my mother in Starogan. I have not seen her for three months." And I must get away, she thought.

But her husband was frowning at her. "Leave Moscow? That is quite impossible. There is far too much to be done here."

"I have nothing to do here."

"But I have. I am the military governor of this city, and if I were to send my wife away at this time it would be said that I had doubts about your safety. No, no, you ask too much. You will stay here until the city is completely back to normal."

Ilona lay down and closed her eyes. I ask too much, she thought.

But what could the Jewish schoolgirl ask for, as she was taken before the military governor of the city, and told that unless she accused all her friends and relations they would . . . imagination could take her no further.

But the Jewish schoolgirl was surely already dead, a bloody pulp surrounded by shattered cobblestones.

"Spring," Irina Borodina exclaimed, looking down from the balcony of the Borodin town house to the sparkling waters of the Neva as it made its way through the archipelago toward the Baltic. "I think spring is the best time of the year."

"I prefer summer," her sister-in-law said.

Irina gave a mock shudder. "In Starogan? My dear Ilona, Starogan is the most boring place on the whole earth. Don't you agree, Xenia Igorovna?"

As Xenia Borodina sipped tea, she seemed to peer over her cup at her cousin and cousin-in-law. With her big, buxom figure and her brilliant titian hair she always seemed to glow, but this afternoon she might have been about to burst, for all that she had said little since arriving. "Anywhere is boring, except St. Petersburg."

"Oh quite," Irina agreed. "How you manage to exist, my dear Ilona Dimitrievna, lost down in Moscow, is quite beyond my understanding." She rang the little golden bell, and a maid hurried in with a fresh pot of tea.

"And with only Roditchev for company," Xenia remarked, watching Ilona's expression.

"We manage to amuse ourselves," Ilona said. "And I am not entirely lost down in Moscow. Right now I am here in St. Petersburg with you. As you can see for yourselves." Lost down in Moscow. How right they were. Eighteen months, and this was the first time she had been allowed to leave. And even now, she had not been permitted to visit Starogan, but must come instead to St. Petersburg to stay with her sister-in-law, whom she detested.

But neither Irina nor Xenia must suspect even an iota of her misery.

"But when you are pregnant," Xenia said, "then you will be stuck there. I should go mad."

"At being pregnant?" Ilona asked, her tone indicating that from some of the rumors circulating round the capital it was amazing that such a fate had not already overtaken her cousin.

"That too," Xenia agreed without taking offense.

Irina made a moue. "It does not appear to be a fate that is in store for either of us. Would you believe that I have been married a year?"

"Fourteen months," Xenia said. She liked to be exact.

"And Ilona has been married eighteen months," Irina said. "What is the matter with us, my dear?"

"What is the matter with your husbands, you mean." Xenia gave a shriek of laughter.

"I would have supposed Roditchev . . ." Irina peered at Ilona. "He *does* whip you?"

Ilona's head jerked. "Certainly not. What an idea."

"Doesn't he? I was told on the best authority that he whipped poor Anastasia Roditcheva every night."

"And it didn't do her any good," Xenia pointed out.

"Oh, yes it did. She died in childbirth."

"Are you seriously suggesting. . . ." Ilona began.

The maid was back with more sandwiches and cakes. Irina waited until she had withdrawn.

"Well, you know, I think there may be something in it. After all, if your husband mounts up just after you have been whipped, well, your body must be more relaxed, more . . . well, receptive."

"I have never heard such obscene nonsense in my life," Ilona declared, hating her flush.

"I don't think you can dismiss any old wives' tales as nonsense," Irina said seriously. "They are all based on *some* evidence. And we are a good case in point."

Xenia giggled. "You mean Peter never whips *you?*"

"Peter wouldn't dream of it," Ilona said.

"I don't think Peter ever dreams of anything, about women," Irina said regretfully. "Do you know, he actually enjoys spending most of his time down in Starogan? He *likes* farming. I have seen him become more excited over a newborn foal than the sight of me in my bath."

"Are you very exciting in your bath?" Xenia inquired.

"Don't you think I could be?" Irina replied.

They were always having these utterly impossible conversations. In fact, Ilona thought, they were rather alike. If Irina was dark where Xenia was fair, they were both big and voluptuous, and they had similar reputations for dazzling men with their wit and their suggestions of promiscuity. Suggestions? She wondered.

"All baths are exciting," Xenia said dreamily.

Ilona and Irina exchanged glances. It had been obvious to each of them from the moment Xenia had arrived that she was simply bubbling with a secret. Something to do with baths?

"Tell us," Irina suggested.

Xenia appeared to be shocked. "Tell you what?"

"About this exciting bath."

"Oh . . . it was just a remark. Is Tattie coming to spend Easter with you?"

"Unfortunately," Irina said. "That is something else I wanted to speak with you about, Ilona."

Something else? Had she seriously been intending to discuss her failure to become pregnant? Or was it Peter's lack of fire as a lover?

"What has she done now?"

"Nothing. That is the trouble. She has spent two years at that silly convent, and she does not appear to have learned a single thing. I am afraid we shall have to do something about her. I have tried to speak to your Mama, but she merely says, oh, she is young yet, she will learn to apply herself as she grows older. Young? She is fourteen."

"What can we do with her?" Ilona asked.

"Well, that is a remarkable attitude to take about your own sister. I think we should find her a husband."

"Tattie?" Ilona cried.

"She is nearly a woman," Irina pointed out coldly. "Fourteen is a good age for a girl to be betrothed; she can be married the moment she is sixteen. That way she becomes a wife without having had a chance to be exposed to all the . . . well, the things that young women do get exposed to." She looked at Ilona.

"Like all of us, you mean," Xenia said brightly.

"No, I do not. Well, I am going to see if I can find Tatiana a husband. I am going to make that my task for 1907."

"I thought getting pregnant was your task," Ilona said.

"That is in the hands of God."

"It may not be," Xenia said. "Well, of course it is. But it might be possible to jog God's elbow, so to speak."

The two princesses stared at her in horror.

"I'm not being blasphemous," Xenia protested. "It's just that perhaps a priest—"

"Oh, don't start that nonsense," Irina said. "Don't you think I have lit candles? Enough to have illuminated this entire house on a midwinter evening."

"I am not talking about candles, or ordinary priests," Xenia said with dignity. "But you'll not deny there are some men with special powers."

"You mean a starets?" Ilona asked.

"That's right."

"Mumbo jumbo," Irina declared.

"Well . . . I know a starets who is really gifted."

"Here in St. Petersburg?" Ilona asked.

Xenia nodded.

"Where?" Irina demanded.

"Not far from here, as a matter of fact. Anna Vyrubova introduced me."

"Anna Vyrubova?"

"You couldn't have a better recommendation than that," Xenia pointed out.

"Anna Vyrubova may be a friend of the tsarina's," Irina said, "but she is a complete hysteric, in my opinion."

"I know she's very excitable," Xenia said. "But this time she knows what she's doing. Did you hear about the tsarevich's being ill?"

"A rumor," Irina said.

"It may have been a rumor, but it was true. Anna herself told me. He got some kind of a bruise and started to bleed. And nothing that the doctors did could stop it. The tsarina was beside herself with anxiety. And then Anna asked her to send for the starets, and he came, and touched the tsarevich, and prayed, and the bleeding stopped." She looked from one to the other. "It's a deadly secret of course. Just between us three."

And everyone else you have tea with, Ilona thought.

"And you think if he touches us and prays we will immediately get pregnant?" Irina asked.

"Well. . . ." Surprisingly, Xenia flushed. "He . . . he is a very strange man. But you can't doubt that he can intercede with God. He is quite marvelous. I could introduce you, if you liked."

"You? Not Anna Vyrubova?"

"I am accepted now," Xenia said with dignity. "I am a disciple."

"Good Lord," Irina remarked.

"Would you like to meet Father Gregory?"

"Father Gregory?" Ilona cried. "Not from Starogan?"

"Of course not, silly. This man is from Siberia. His name is Rasputin. Would you like to meet him?"

"Well . . ." Irina pretended to consider, "it sounds as if it might be amusing. What do you say, Ilona Dimitrievna?"

"Well. . . ." Supposing he *could* make her pregnant. She certainly wanted to become a mother. There was really nothing else to do with her life. And it would mean months and months of freedom from Roditchev. "It might be an idea."

"Then we'll go tomorrow," Xenia said. "Tomorrow afternoon, at teatime." She put down her cup and rose quickly. "I must rush. Don't forget. Tomorrow at three o'clock."

She kissed them both and hurried from the room, obviously in a state of high excitement. That, then, Ilona realized, was the secret she had been dying to confide all afternoon.

But what on earth could a starets from Siberia have to do with bathing?

"Now, you must remember that the starets is a law unto himself." Xenia was, if anything, more excited today than the day before. "You *must* obey him."

Irina gave a short laugh. "He isn't going to whip us, is he? I can't imagine what Peter would say to that."

"No matter *what* he does, you must *never* tell Peter about it," Xenia said, suddenly very agitated. "Just as you must never tell Prince Roditchev, Ilona. It would be better if you did not even tell him you had visited the starets."

"A secret society," Irina remarked, looking at Ilona, who flushed. But they were both in their best today, Irina in an oyster-colored chiffon-and-lace blouse, secured with an enormous blue velvet bow on her bodice, worn with a gray serge skirt, Ilona somewhat more formal in a green suit—a tunic over a skirt—worn with a fawn felt hat; Irina was bare-headed. She guessed that her sister-in-law, for all her bravado, was no less nervous, no less half-wishing that she hadn't agreed to come. And now, for Xenia to be suggesting this absurd secrecy. . . .

"Well, it is up to you," Xenia said. "Do you wish him to help you or not? He can only help you if you surrender yourselves to him, utterly."

"You are making me quite nervous, my dear," Irina said. "I suggest that we stay close together, Ilona. Then at least there is no risk of this Father Gregory getting us pregnant in person."

"Irina," Xenia snapped. "That was a beastly thing to say. And blasphemous, too. Father Gregory is a man of God."

"Then I apologize. How much farther?"

Xenia looked out the window. "It is right here."

And certainly Xenia's coachman seemed to have visited the house before. It was situated in the English Prospekt, set back from the street and reached through an enormous pair of wrought-iron gates which gave access to a metal driveway. But to Ilona's dismay she saw that there were several equipages there already, their postilions gathered for a smoke. They did not seem interested in the new arrival.

"Is it a party?" Irina asked. But her voice was brittle; she, too, had expected a private audience.

"Oh, there are always ladies trying to get in to see the starets," Xenia explained. "But you cannot without an introduction." She jumped down as her driver opened the door. "Come along."

Irina glanced at Ilona and shrugged. "Having come this far, my dear . . . we are going to share a secret. I have always wanted to have a real secret, and who better to share it with than my own sister-in-law?"

Ilona sighed, and followed the others through the open front door and up the stairs. The house was divided into several apartments. Rasputin's was on the third floor, and they arrived on the landing out of breath, to discover a closet filled with furs. It was a warm spring day, but certain types of women wore their furs even in summer, just to show the world that they owned them. The type of women who went to visit a holy man?

But she was visiting the holy man herself.

A footman opened a door for them, and Xenia led them into an antechamber. Ilona paused in consternation. There were at least twenty women in the room, all of them, judging by their clothes as well as by the coats they had left outside, very wealthy indeed. But they were just sitting, sipping tea which was being served by waiters, and staring at each other and the wall. Now their gazes turned to the new arrivals. Their stares were hostile.

"Xenia," Irina whispered. "Are you sure we are invited?"

"Of course we're invited. These people are always here," Xenia said loudly, and marched across the room to where some sort of major-domo was lecturing one of the ladies. "Anton."

The major-domo sprang to attention. "Mademoiselle Borodina." He seized Xenia's hand and kissed it. Then he looked past her. "And these are . . . ?"

"My friends, Princess Borodina and Princess Roditcheva."

Ilona looked around her in embarrassment. She hadn't really expected to be announced. Xenia was in many ways an idiot.

"Of course, princesses. Of course. The starets is waiting for you." He hurried across the room and opened the double doors. Immediately the crowd of women rose to their feet with a great murmur and moved forward. But Anton was too quick for them, blocking the doorway with his arms spread wide. "Patience, ladies," he said. "Patience. Will you enter, princesses?"

Irina hesitated, then gave a little shrug and stepped inside. Ilona followed, suddenly feeling like a very small child instead of a twenty-one-year-old woman who had been a wife for a year and a half.

She found herself gazing at a huge man, the biggest she had ever seen. He was dressed exactly like one of the peasants at Starogan, except that his white smock and black breeches were both made of silk, as far as she could tell, and his black boots were new and highly polished. The richness of his clothes apart, he did not seem to be in a proper state to receive ladies, for he had spilled red wine down his smock, and as he came closer she could smell the liquor on his breath, mingling with a remarkable scent of body odor, as if he had not bathed in some time. Yet she found that she could not look away. The starets might never in his life have cut either his hair, which hung from his head in great shaggy locks rather suggestive of a bear, or his beard, which was also long and shaggy. From the center of this forest the great face loomed at her, big nose and chin, somewhat pessimistic mouth, drifting down at the corners, blotchy red and white cheeks, and dominating the whole, eyes that were fiery pools of black.

"Princesses," Rasputin said, his low voice seeming to seep around them. "Welcome to my home."

He reached for Ilona's hand, and she allowed him to take it. To her consternation he pulled off her glove to kiss her hand, and she felt his tongue flick her knuckle.

"I . . . it is my pleasure, holy father."

"Good," he said, and released her to kiss Irina's hand in turn. "I have never before been so honored. Come in. Come in." Behind her the door closed softly, and the sound of the clamoring women disappeared. Ilona found herself inhaling, slowly and carefully, as she inspected her surroundings. It was a big room, high-ceilinged but sparsely furnished, with just a couple of settees against the wall, a Persian rug in the center of the parquet and a table on which there was a decanter of wine and several glasses. And despite the warmth of the afternoon, a porcelain stove glowed with heat against the far wall. Ilona felt herself immediately begin to perspire, and wondered if living in this constant heat might not be responsible for the man's smell.

She glanced at Xenia. The starets had not even troubled to greet her, but she seemed to be transformed by his presence; her eyes glowed and her lips trembled with expectation.

"You are very lovely," Rasputin remarked. He was still holding Irina's hand, but he was looking at Ilona. Now he released Irina, and sat on the settee. He patted the space beside him, and immediately Xenia took her place. Irina glanced at Ilona, and then sat down on the holy man's other side, leaving Ilona standing alone in the middle of the room. To her amazement, Rasputin put one arm around each of the shoulders pressed against his, and to her horror his left hand drooped down beyond Xenia's neck and began to unfasten the buttons of her blouse. "Will you not sit down, Princess Roditcheva?"

"I. . . ." Ilona looked from right to left, chose the other settee, and perched herself on the edge. She watched in fascination as the third button opened, and the great dirty fingers slipped inside; Xenia gave a little wriggle of enjoyment. Irina met her sister-in-law's gaze and pouted; she seemed to be saying, well, we are here, we may as well do what Xenia does. But the hand on her shoulder had not yet started to move. Ilona wondered what she would do when it did.

"I feel that you are hostile to me, Princess Roditcheva," Rasputin said.

"Hostile? Why ever should I be hostile?" The fingers were now definitely cupping Xenia's breasts. She really could not trust her eyes.

"Good," Rasputin said. "Mademoiselle Borodina tells me that you are concerned, both you ladies"—he gave Irina's shoulders a squeeze —"with your inability to give your husbands heirs. But you both appear to be healthy, and strong, and you are both very pretty. The fault must lie in your minds."

"My mind?" Ilona asked.

"The mind is the source of all good and all evil. It must be lifted beyond the reach of sinful thoughts. It must have reached the grace of God before I dare intercede with him on your behalf. Has your mind reached such a state?"

"I have no idea," Ilona said. She was determined he was not going to establish any sort of mental ascendancy over her. After all, he was just a muzhik from the steppes pretending to be a wizard.

Rasputin snapped his fingers next to Irina's ear. "Take off your hat."

"Holy father?"

"Do as the holy father says, my dear Ilona," Xenia said. "Free your hair."

Ilona hesitated, then slowly put up her hands, removed her hat and released the pins holding her hair, which promptly tumbled about her shoulders. She lay the hat on the cushion beside her.

"You are even more beautiful than I had supposed, my child," Rasputin said. "Show me more of you. Take off your clothes."

"Father?" Ilona's voice rose to a squeak.

"She is shy. Xenia, pour her a glass of wine. Pour us all a glass of wine."

As if mesmerized, Ilona watched the great hand extract itself from Xenia's flopping bodice. Xenia did not bother to fasten the buttons; with her breasts half exposed, she got up and went obediently to the table, where she filled four glasses and brought them back on a tray.

"Now drink," Rasputin commanded; he was fingering Irina's ear and she didn't seem to mind at all. Ilona obeyed, her head was spinning.

"You think it is wrong to take off your clothes before me, a holy man?" Rasputin asked.

Ilona knew she had to concentrate, to oppose him with arguments as subtle and as insidious as his own, to counter the mesmeric power of his eyes. But oh, when she got Xenia back to the house.

"Well, holy father. . . ."

"You think it is a sin?"

"Isn't it?" Ilona gazed at Irina, helplessly. Irina was smiling as the great hand moved from her ear to fondle her neck.

"Have you never sinned before, princess?"

Ilona gazed at him. "I suppose so, holy father. Everyone has sinned."

"Little sins," Rasputin said contemptuously. "Have you never committed a great sin?"

So that was his game. Or Xenia's game, certainly. Everyone suspected, wondered, but no one knew for sure. She did not even think Irina knew for sure; she could not imagine Peter's ever telling her. Well, they must take her for a nitwit. George was in the past. He could never be in the future. That secret belonged to her, and to those few who had had to know; not to two of the worst gossips in St. Petersburg.

"I have no idea what is a great sin, holy father," she said.

"When you have committed a great sin, my child, you will know it," he said. "And you can never hope to know God's greatness, God's forgiveness, until you have aroused his anger. God is not concerned with *little* sins. He wishes his children to commit *great* sins, and then pray to him for forgiveness, that he may know they are his children."

Ilona found her mouth was open, and closed it again. She had never considered that point of view.

"That is a priest's business," the guttural voice continued, "to intercept such terrible sins, and intercede with God our father for the forgiveness of the transgressor. No one can live without the blessing of God, not even you, Ilona Roditcheva. Drink your wine."

Ilona drank.

"Now take off your clothes. Because you are right, it is a great sin to take off your clothes for any man but your husband. You must sin, that I may pray to God to forgive you, and make you strong for the trials that lie ahead."

Ilona stared at him. Think, she told herself. She hadn't any intention of undressing before him. But how to escape without causing embarrassment? And suppose he was right about sin? Why had no one ever told her this argument before? Her own Father Gregory, who had listened to her confession down in Starogan, or the priest in Port Arthur who had attended her every Sunday, had never suggested it.

"She is shy," Rasputin said again. "Show her how to do it, Xenia."

Xenia undressed with amazing rapidity for one who was normally assisted by a maid. Tunic and petticoat and drawers cascaded to the floor. Then Rasputin was himself unlacing her corset, and she was sitting down to roll off stockings and garters in a single movement, to untie her boots and kick them off. She was a glowing goddess of pink and white beauty; Ilona could only stare at the big, thrusting breasts, the pouting belly, the thatch of surprisingly dark hair which coated her groin, the long powerful legs. Xenia was a goddess, as well as a member of one of Russia's oldest families. And she was. . . .

Rasputin snapped his fingers, and Xenia sat on his lap. "Feel me," he said, and she released his belt and thrust her hand down the front of his pants. Ilona thought she was going to faint. But she had never been able to faint, and anyway, she dared not faint now; she had no idea what they would do to her. So she looked at Irina instead. Irina's cheeks were pink and she was breathing heavily. But she would not move and she would not meet Ilona's gaze; the huge hand was now somewhere down the back of her blouse.

"Mademoiselle Xenia is committing a sin," Rasputin said, his voice lower than ever, while Xenia rested her head on his shoulder, her hand still inside his breeches, "for which she will receive the blessing of God. Now Ilona Roditcheva, you must resist me no longer. I command you, stand up and take off your clothes."

Ilona realized that she was on her feet, that her hands had moved without meaning to, and her fingers were releasing the buttons of her tunic. She gazed at them, Xenia's eyes shut as she committed her sin,

Irina's wide with anticipation, Rasputin's half closed as he enjoyed what one woman was doing to him and watched the other obeying him. Ilona discovered her tunic was loose.

"And then," he said dreamily, "you can come and assist Xenia. No, you must come now." He stood up without warning, and Xenia gave a little shriek and slid off his lap, hitting the floor with a bump, arms and legs scattered. Rasputin's breeches fell to his ankles, and Ilona gazed at the most terrifying sight she had ever seen; twice the size of any man who had ever been sent into the hospital in Port Arthur, or of either of the men she had known, huge and thrusting and, she knew even at a distance, unwashed.

"Quickly, Ilona," he said, kicking off his pants to move toward her. "Quickly. I cannot wait."

Ilona's mouth closed with a snap. She had barely rebuttoned her tunic when she reached the door and fled from the room.

How secure Moscow seemed. How securely dull. Ilona gazed from the windows of her first-class compartment as the train pulled into Moscow central, watched the spires she knew so well, identified the huge bulk of the Kremlin on its fortified hill over the river. And realized with a start of surprise that she was actually happy to return.

She had gone back to the Borodin town house that afternoon two days ago, told Catherine Ivanovna to pack, and caught the evening train. It had taken her three hours to remove herself from the house, and in all that time Irina had not come home. Irina had stayed with Xenia, to . . . she could not imagine what the pair of them might have spent their afternoon doing. What they would have been commanded to do by their master.

So Irina was now a disciple. She was a creature of that huge, obscene beast. It had happened, just like that. And it had nearly happened to her. Under the circumstances, she did not feel up to leaving Irina even a note. She could do that from the safety of her study, here in Moscow.

But what to do? Tell Peter? Tell Peter that the woman he had married was a good deal worse than the sister he had condemned? How could she? How could she even find the words? Or the proof. It would just cause another family row. And besides, if this Rasputin was the protégé of Anna Vyrubova, who was herself an intimate of the tsarina . . . Ilona pressed her fingers to her mouth in dismay. The tsarina? Sitting on that foul-smelling lap, her hands inside those silk breeches? That was utterly impossible.

And yet, what other conclusion could she draw? That he had women to attend to his lusts she had seen with her own eyes. That he was no respecter of rank she had just experienced herself. And that he had been to the imperial palace was apparently a fact. She did not know a great deal about law, but she supposed that in any court that would be regarded as an indisputable accumulation of circumstantial evidence.

The tsarina, the creature of a lust-crazed monster from the steppes. And therefore, through the tsarina, every woman in St. Petersburg. Eventually, every woman in the empire. And through them, their husbands. Why, even the tsar was rumored to pay attention to his wife's suggestions. Suppose she was told what to suggest by Rasputin?

Ilona leaned back in her seat, her mind suddenly aflame with an apocalyptic vision. As if Russia did not have serious troubles enough, without this new threat. But what had caused all those troubles? Was it not that very moral decay which had been eating away at Petersburg society for far too long? Peter thought so. And now his own wife. . . .

But Peter also considered *her* an example of that decay. As if her affair with George Hayman could ever be remotely compared with the obscenity taking place in the very heart of the capital. What, indeed, would George make of such a story, could he ever learn of it? He had always distrusted the Russian aristocracy, felt that so much power, so much wealth, had to equal so much corruption. And living with her family, experiencing the horrors of the siege with them, had changed his mind. George had gone back to America thinking he was wrong, that there was still courage and ability and decency and, above all, honor, controlling Russia. She had wanted him to believe that. Oh George, George.

But might that not be the answer to the problem? Write George, and tell him all she knew about Rasputin? Have him blaze it on the front page of the Boston *People,* whence it would reach every country in the world? Would that be an act of betrayal of Russia, or an act of patriotism, in that she might yet be saving it from the abyss? Was there really an abyss? Did what men and women presumed in the privacy of their own homes, even if one was a blasphemous priest and the other the wife of the premier prince in the land—or even the wife of the tsar—really lead a country to decay and disaster?

She had never felt more lonely, more in need of someone to talk to, to advise her, in her life.

And then, dared she write George? She had not replied to his birthday greeting two years before. It would have been too great a risk either to give a letter to Catherine Ivanovna to mail, as she normally did, or to attempt to mail it herself—she had never mailed a letter in her life. He had not written again. And she had been grateful for that, not only to avoid trouble with Sergei, but to free her own mind of temptation. Would he even read her letter, if she wrote to him now?

The train was stopping, and Catherine Ivanovna was standing in the doorway of the compartment. Catherine Ivanovna was not pleased with her mistress. She had enjoyed their visit to St. Petersburg, and did not like having it cut short. And she liked even less not knowing the reason for Ilona's sudden departure from her sister-in-law's house.

"I do not know if the carriage will be waiting, my lady princess," she said. "I did telephone, but the line was very bad."

Ilona adjusted her hat and pulled on her gloves. "Well then, you may telephone again, from the station," she said. "There is no great hurry."

This was another problem: Sergei was not expecting her back for two more weeks. And she had not even thought of a story to tell him. Why not the truth? But it was quite impossible to imagine Sergei Roditchev's reaction to learning about Rasputin.

A porter held the door for her. When he recognized her he gave a hasty salute, at the same time rolling his eyes in an effort to discover the location of the stationmaster. But that worthy was not to be seen at this moment. Ilona smiled at the thunderstruck young man, stepped past him, and walked slowly toward the first-class waiting room. She felt like a cup of coffee, and if the carriage were not waiting, it would take some time to get here.

"Princess Roditcheva." The stationmaster had at last been alerted and was at her side, anxious to open the door for the wife of the city's military governor. "A thousand apologies, my dear princess. We had not been told . . . *I* had not been told . . . I will find out whose fault it is, princess, and he shall be punished. Oh, you may be sure of that."

"It is no one's fault, my dear Viktor Michaelovich," Ilona said. "I decided to come home early, that is all." She gave him a roguish smile. "I have not even told my husband."

The stationmaster waggled his eyebrows. "And your carriage is not here? I shall see to it immediately. Perhaps you would like to wait in my office."

"I shall wait in here." Ilona had reached the waiting room. "Please do not let me detain you from your duties."

"Oh, my dear princess," he opened the door for her, "it will be my pleasure."

Ilona stepped inside, smiled at the woman behind the serving counter, glanced at the three other people in the room, and stared at the girl named Judith.

Their consternation was mutual. Judith had been drinking a cup of tea, which she put down with such violence that the liquid spilled. She seized her handbag and stood up. Ilona stood still to make sure it really was the same girl. An immense surge of relief and pleasure came over her. She was alive, and she looked quite unharmed. And in two years the rather lean girl had grown into a splendid woman, with handsome features and a blooming figure.

And she was in the first-class waiting room, wearing a poplin gown and a matching hat, and carrying a parasol.

"Judith," she said.

The girl opened her mouth, closed it again, while color flared in her cheeks. Then she gave a half curtsey. "Princess Roditcheva."

"Ah, you know Mademoiselle Stein," the stationmaster said. "That is nice. Someone for you to talk to." He bustled to the counter. "Coffee for the princess. Cream and sugar, princess?"

"One lump." Ilona sat down. Judith Stein. This was incredible. Jacob Stein, one of Moscow's leading lawyers, must be her father. "Do sit down, Judith."

Judith Stein hesitated, then cautiously lowered herself onto the chair beside Ilona's.

"Let me see," Ilona remarked wickedly, "it is some time since we met. Why, it must have been the Christmas before last."

"Yes, princess," Judith said, her voice low.

"And then it was only for five minutes." Her pleasure was sudden and complete and overwhelming. They shared a secret. A quite unbelievable secret. She glanced at the stationmaster as he placed her cup of coffee in front of her. "Thank you, Viktor Michaelovich. Please do not concern yourself with me any more. I am sure you are terribly busy."

"Oh, well, my lady princess, if you really do not mind." He looked through the door, saw Catherine Ivanovna approaching and gave a relieved smile. "Your carriage is here."

"Bother," Ilona said. "I so wanted to talk with you, Judith. I know! You will ride with me."

"Princess?" The girl's voice rose. "I couldn't possibly. I'm—"

"Are you going or coming?"

"I have just returned, princess. I am waiting for my father to come for me."

"Viktor Michaelovich," Ilona commanded. "Will you telephone Monsieur Stein and tell him that I have taken his daughter to my home for a chat?"

"Of course, my lady princess. Of course." He twisted his hands together.

"Come along, Judith," Ilona said, glaring at Catherine Ivanovna. Catherine Ivanovna was looking quite shocked, while the stationmaster was obviously impatient to hurry away and tell anyone who would listen that Princess Roditcheva had just ridden away with a Jew.

"It is not the best thing for young girls to be by themselves in railway stations," Ilona said severely as they walked together toward the exit, Judith having apparently given up any idea of protesting further. "How old are you?"

"I am eighteen, princess."

"Then you were sixteen when last we met? My God. You are obviously of a very independent mind. Do your parents not object?"

"My parents. . . ." She hesitated. "They do not know anything of my thoughts, princess. As for today, I traveled from St. Petersburg with a school friend, who has already left the station."

"I do not wish you to lie to me, Judith Stein. I would like us to be friends."

"Friends, princess?"

They had reached the street and the waiting carriage. Vasili Tigranovich was waiting to hand her up. "Would you mind riding on top, Catherine Ivanovna?" Ilona asked.

Catherine Ivanovna made a face, but climbed up onto the driving seat. Ilona sat down, patted the seat beside her, and Judith Stein joined her. "Thank you, Vasili Tigranovich." She waited for the carriage to start moving, for their conversation to be smothered in the rumbling of the wheels. "Would you not like to be my friend?"

"Well, princess, I. . . ."

"You do not see how it can be possible?"

"I do not see why you should wish to be my friend, princess. I am surprised you have not immediately denounced me to a policeman. Or are you taking me home to denounce me to your husband?"

The girl had regained her composure. But she was still very nervous; little beads of sweat were gathering on her upper lip.

"Why should I do that?" Ilona asked. "When last we met you saved my life. Not once, but twice, I think. And you'll remember I promised to help you, if I could."

"Help me?" Judith demanded. "Was it helping me to have your husband use the cannon?"

Ilona nodded and sighed. "I'm afraid that my husband does not often do what I would like him to. How did you escape?"

"Oh, I am like you, princess. I ran away early. My parents would have been anxious had my brother and I remained out on such a night."

"They did not know where you were?"

She shook her head. "I should not like them to know."

"I shall not tell them, Judith. But I think you were very foolish to become involved in something like that." She smiled. "As foolish as I."

"Foolish? Is it foolish to wish to do something for my people, my country?"

"They are my people too, Judith. And it is my country."

"Of course, princess. It is *your* country. They are *your* people. You do not consider yourself to belong *to* them or it. You think they belong to you."

For the second time in three days Ilona had been confronted with a point of view she had never previously considered. "Well," she said, "perhaps I do not look on it in exactly the same way as you do, but I certainly wish to see Russia great, and everyone in it prosperous."

"Great," Judith remarked bitterly. "What is greatness? Is it to have four million men under arms, to wage wars and make treaties? What is great about that?"

Ilona could not answer.

"And you speak of prosperity. Do you wish to see everyone living on your scale, princess? Or would you be willing to give up some of your wealth to live like a peasant?"

"Your father is a wealthy man, I believe." Such propositions could only be countered with facts.

"Yes." The girl's shoulders slumped. "I apologize, princess. You have been kind to me. I should not have spoken like that."

"I am glad you did. But I would like to know what made you wish to support a mob of peasants and criminals."

"They are not peasants and criminals," Judith said indignantly. "They are human beings like you and me, princess, who wish only to reach a decent standard of living, to have some control over their own destinies. To be treated as human beings."

"All of them? What of that redheaded man? That Lenin. Did he escape too?"

"Oh, yes. Lenin always escapes. He even escaped the country. He is in Switzerland again, writing his poisonous newspaper." She shrugged. "That is the trouble with popular, radical movements. They attract so many sorts of people. That is why it is so important for decent people to take part. To lead, if possible. Otherwise the Lenins of this world take control."

"And you are a leader?"

Judith flushed. "I am only a girl, princess."

"But you would like to lead." Ilona looked out the window as the carriage turned into the drive of her house. "Judith, I would like you to visit me."

"Princess?"

"Come to tea tomorrow afternoon. I would like to speak with you again." She smiled, and squeezed the girl's hand. "I shall not betray you. I give you my word. Now my carriage will take you home. But don't forget. Tomorrow afternoon, for tea."

"I'm told you gave a Jewish girl a ride from the station and sent her home in my carriage." Sergei Roditchev handed his wife a glass of sherry.

Ilona nodded. "Judith Stein. Her father is Jacob Stein, the lawyer. You must have met him."

"I know Stein. May I ask why?"

Ilona hesitated and sipped her sherry. She had her story fully prepared.

"I never told you before, but when I got caught up in that trouble, the Christmas before last, and I had to hide for an hour from the mob, Judith Stein was hiding with me. We both were trying to escape, but she helped me more than I helped her."

"Why did you not tell me at the time?"

"I didn't think it was important. Anyway, I was afraid she'd get into trouble. She was only sixteen then. She really shouldn't have been in the Kitai-Gorod at all."

"You're sure she wasn't involved?"

"Good heavens, no, Sergei. Why should she be involved? Just because she is Jewish? Her father is well off, isn't he? Anyway, she was only sixteen."

"I believe Stein has quite a good practice," Roditchev agreed. "In fact he must have made a great deal of money out of that rebellion. He endeavored to defend several of the people we arrested."

Ilona met his gaze. "That does not mean that either he or his children were involved."

"Of course not. I just find it disturbing that you should wish to befriend one of them. I find all your actions surprising. Rushing back from St. Petersburg with no reason, after begging me for more than a year to let you go. Riding in my carriage with a Jew—"

"She is coming here to tea, tomorrow," Ilona said. There was no possibility of keeping anything secret from her husband while he forced her to have Catherine as her maid. Her only defense was to be so open about everything that nothing appeared to have special meaning.

"Here? Really, my dear Ilona—"

"Listen to me for a moment, Sergei, I beg of you. You are the military governor of Moscow. My brother is prince of Starogan. Have either of you ever tried to understand the people you rule?"

Roditchev frowned. "I do not even understand you."

"Well, we are the rulers of this country. We believe we know what is best for Russia and its people. We treat them as children, don't we? Make laws for them to follow, tell them what jobs they can have and where they can live, and when they disobey us, we—you—punish them."

"That is my duty, yes."

"But no one ever troubles to find out what *they* would like to do, or where or how they would like to live."

"What a preposterous idea. Would you ask a child to decide his own upbringing? Anyway, I can tell you what they would say if you asked any of them where they would like to live and what they would like to do. They would tell you they'd like to live here and be me, or you."

"Would they, do you suppose?"

"No doubt of it. You ask your young friend if she wouldn't like to change places with you. And then ask yourself if you'd like to change places with her. Besides, this absurd Duma business is an attempt to find out what the people want. And it is not only absurd, it is dangerous. Once you get a peasant thinking, once you *teach* him to think, he can only think sedition. Peasants cannot have ambition; there is nowhere for them to go, and if they try to go anywhere, upwards or sideways or even downwards, they cause trouble."

Ilona sighed. Talking to Sergei was like talking to a brick wall. And he was entirely representative of his class. Why, she thought, he has never even troubled to try to understand me. She had never considered that before. But from their wedding night on, he had decided what was best. He had treated her like a child, and he still treated her like a child. She did not suppose Peter treated Irina like a child, but perhaps like a somewhat tiresome sister. So neither of you know, or care, what we do with our spare time, what holy men we visit and allow to debauch us, what strange redheaded scoundrels we may discover ourselves talking with. Oh, yes, you would *care*—but you would never wish to understand.

"Well," she said, "I would like to get to know these people better. And besides, it will be good for appearances. You may not accept it, Sergei, but Russia *is* changing. It has been changing for the last fifty years. I am sure your father was as angry about the liberation of the serfs as you are about the Duma. But it is people like Jacob Stein who are going to be sitting in the Duma. Don't you agree it would be a good idea to get to know how he thinks, what he hopes to see happen to Russia?"

Sergei Roditchev frowned at her for some seconds, then his brow cleared and he smiled, and leaned forward to chuck her under the chin. She was so surprised she nearly dropped her sherry glass. "Do you know, that is quite a brilliant suggestion? I always suspected you were an intelligent girl. My congratulations. Yes, of course. By all means entertain Mademoiselle Stein to tea. I shall look forward to hearing all about it."

How serious am I, Ilona wondered? Oh, very serious indeed. In the oddest fashion her life seemed to have reached a climax in the wine-drenched atmosphere of Gregory Rasputin's salon. She had supposed the climax of her life had been when she had laid on the settee in Port Arthur with George Hayman, while the world had crashed around her ears.

But now she realized that had been nothing more than an incident. Passion between two people could never be anything more than an incident. And even the love which inspired the passion, or which might grow out of the passion, could never be more than a base for life, like the keel which keeps a ship upright or the foundations which support a house. It was what one built upon that base that was important. So what *could* a woman build? Well, motherhood was a start. But she was not a mother, after having been a wife for a year and a half and a mistress for six months before that. So it seemed unlikely that she would ever become one. The power behind her husband's throne? The tsarina was that, and five times a mother as well. But the tsarina was an exceptional woman. If Ilona had ever supposed she could influence anything Roditchev intended to do, she had learned better during the Christmas insurrection.

What was left? Of course if one were a peasant the question did not arise. One labored from dawn until dusk at the side of one's husband, just to keep from starving. But what of ladies? Well, now she knew. They sat around and gossiped, they became bored, and they created diversions for themselves. Diversions like Rasputin. Diversions which, if allowed to take hold, would dominate the rest of their lives and leave them no more than creatures at the mercy of their physical urges. Now that she was prepared to think about it, she was realizing that almost all the women she knew were like that.

But not Ilona Roditcheva. Ilona Roditcheva would never succumb to such an insidious doctrine of waste. She would use her time well. To help her husband? No, she did not think she would ever really wish to help Roditchev. But perhaps, in the long run, to help Russia. There was an inflated view of her importance. But no human being who set out to understand another could ever be completely useless.

And this Stein girl fascinated her. Because she was neither a peasant nor a lady, but rather a member of that strange middle section of society which neither owned land nor belonged to it, but made a precarious livelihood by the use of their wits. She supposed, really, George had been one of those, or if not George, certainly his father, who had begun life selling newspapers on a street corner. But Judith Stein was so earnest, so anxious to discover something better. Ilona supposed such a point of view was absolutely necessary to counter the influence of the Rasputins of this world. And the girl was not even a Russian, really, however deeply her roots might be embedded in Russian soil; yet she apparently understood and could sympathize with the aspirations of the simplest muzhik.

All things to be understood.

"Jews," she remarked. "Do you know, I think you are the first Jew I have ever sat down to speak with? Isn't that odd?"

"Not odd at all," Judith Stein said. She had not settled yet, although she was on her third cup of tea. She was too fascinated by the house, the size of the rooms, the richness of the carpets, the splendor of the tea service, the value of the paintings on the walls, the subservience of the maids and footmen. She could not keep her eyes still, as they darted from one treasure to the next.

And perhaps, Ilona thought, she still cannot believe, as she is inside the house of the military governor of Moscow, that she will not at any moment look around and find a policeman at her elbow, stretching out his hand to arrest her.

"Why isn't it odd?"

"Because to people like you, princess, people like us do not really exist. Oh, you know we are there. But then, when you ride in your carriage, you are also aware that there are stray dogs hurrying out of your way."

"That is a very bitter point of view."

"We are a very bitter nation, princess." She flushed and drank some more tea. "You did ask me to speak frankly with you."

"I did, and I also promised never to take offense. I shall not take offense. Why are your people so bitter?"

"Would you not be bitter, princess, if your people had been chased from one end of Europe to the other for nearly two thousand years? Here in Russia our plight is worst of all. It is not merely that we are forced to live in the pale. Whenever anything happens, from a simple case of burglary to a peasant revolt, the authorities—the military governors—say, well, the Jews must have been responsible. They send out their Cossacks to arrest all the Jews they can find. Sometimes they just send them out to destroy Jewish communities. They don't necessarily kill us. They just beat us up and burn our homes."

"Why do you stay in Russia?"

Judith shrugged. "My father, as the Greeks would have said, has Medized. He has become a part of Russia's median society. Or he thinks he has."

"I meant you, personally."

"I do not suppose I will stay here all of my life," Judith said. "I have an uncle in America. I would like to go and live with him."

"America," Ilona said. "I think that would be a good idea."

"But then I think," Judith looked around the room, making sure they were for the moment alone, "that it would be running away. There is so much to be done here." She paused and looked at Ilona.

"And you suppose an eighteen-year-old girl can do anything here?"

"Probably not. But if everyone felt like that, nothing would ever be done, would it?"

"Perhaps not," Ilona mused. "I have been reading about your people, this morning. I got a book from the library. They are not only exclusive in their religious practices, but they are a very moral, very strict people. Yet you seem to have a great deal of freedom."

"Not really," Judith said, and smiled. "There was quite a fuss when I told them that I had been invited by Princess Roditcheva for tea. Mama wanted me to refuse. But as I said, Papa has Medized. So long as my gentile friends are above him in social station, he is content."

Ilona frowned. "Do you hate your father?"

"Of course I do not. I am sorry for him."

"Yet he has given you a good life. Do you regret that?"

Another shrug. "Sometimes."

"And he does seem to allow you quite unimaginable freedom, judging by what I have read."

"Not really," Judith said again, and flushed.

"It is inconceivable to me that an eighteen-year-old Jewish girl, especially the daugher of Jacob Stein, should be allowed to travel from St. Petersburg to Moscow by herself, or even with a school friend."

"Well. . . ." Judith's flush deepened.

"You never were on that train, were you?" Ilona insisted. "I do not think you have ever even been to St. Petersburg."

Judith set down her teacup. "It has been a lovely tea, princess, and I am deeply honored that you invited me." She stood up. "But if you'll excuse me—"

"Sit down," Ilona said. "Tell me what your father said when the stationmaster telephoned him. Because I do not think you were even supposed to be at the station by yourself."

Judith sat down. "He was angry, until I explained that I had been walking by and met you, that I had met you before, and that you invited me to have a cup of coffee with you. I told him you had misunderstood the situation."

"And he believed you?"

"Because it was you, princess. Princess—" She bit her lip. "I would be very obliged if you'd leave it like that."

"I shall. If you'll tell me who you were meeting."

Judith Stein's face seemed to close, and once again she gave a quick glance around the room.

"You can trust me," Ilona said.

"You, Princess Roditcheva?"

"I would like to be your friend," Ilona explained. "I would like to try to understand not only your people, but all the people in Russia. I would like to help you, Judith. Believe me. I know now that I cannot influence my husband. I cannot help you in that way. But I *can* help you. I know I can. If you would let me."

Judith frowned at her.

"This person you were going to meet," Ilona said. "Is it someone to do with socialism? A speaker, perhaps? If so, it must be a private meeting. You'd never dare hold a public one, at this moment. May I attend?"

"You must be . . . so you could report to your husband?"

Ilona sighed. "I will swear any oath you like that I will never tell my husband."

"And when he has you followed?"

"Even then."

"He will force you to."

"I don't think he will be able to do that." Ilona smiled. "He can do nothing to me he has not done already. Besides, I will not let anyone follow me. I promise you. I am trying to help."

Judith bit her lip, and then finally shook her head. "I could not possibly agree to that, princess. Not without. . . ."

"Very well. Ask who you like. Think about it. And come and have tea with me again tomorrow."

"I cannot come tomorrow."

"Because you are having a meeting?"

"No, nothing like that. I could come the day after."

"Then I shall look forward to seeing you, the day after." Ilona looked up as the butler appeared in the doorway. "Yes, Ivan Pavlovich?"

"My lady princess, the Prince of Starogan."

Ilona jumped to her feet in a mixture of surprise and dismay. She watched Peter crossing the room toward her. This was the first time she had seen him since his wedding, but even then she had observed, as her mother had also remarked, that he was showing the cares of his new position, with permanent frown lines gathering between his eyes. And now she could swear there was a streak of gray at his temples. But perhaps it was the light. He wore civilian clothes, and he had never looked as handsome dressed as a civilian.

"Ilona Dimitrievna, my dear. I am sorry to burst in on you like this." He checked, noticing Judith for the first time; his face took on an expression Ilona had never observed before. And then, amazingly, he flushed.

"Judith Stein, Prince Peter Borodin," Ilona said. "Judith just stopped by for a cup of tea." She laughed nervously. "And Prince Peter has just stopped by from . . . from where, Peter?"

"Oh, from Starogan. I am on my way to St. Petersburg. I thought I'd pay you a visit. Mademoiselle Stein, it is my great pleasure."

Judith started to curtsey, changed her mind, and held out her hand. She too was flushing.

Peter gazed at the hand for a few seconds and then took it and raised it to his lips.

"The day after tomorrow, princess," Judith said, gently extracted her hand, and hurried for the door.

"Well, really," Ilona said, when she had left. "You might have let me know you were coming."

"I only decided to leave Starogan two days ago," Peter explained. "And it occurred to me that I could travel just as fast as any letter. What an extraordinarily beautiful girl."

"Do you think so?" But when Ilona thought about it, she supposed that Judith was a very good-looking girl. "Why, I suppose she is."

"And her name is Judith?"

"She is Jewish, yes. Her father is a lawyer."

"And she is a friend of yours?"

"Shouldn't I have a Jew as a friend?"

"I just wondered what Sergei says."

"Sergei lets me find my own friends."

"And she is coming here to tea the day after tomorrow?"

"Yes, she is," Ilona said. "Well, it is very good to see you."

"Yes." Peter seemed to collect his thoughts. "It is good to be here." He held her arm to walk her to the settee, then sat beside her. "I would like to talk to you. Very seriously."

"To me?"

"Yes. It . . . I would like to talk to you about Irina."

"Oh yes?" But Ilona's thoughts were wandering in turn. She was just realizing that if Peter were here, then Michael Nej must be here too. She had not seen him since her own wedding.

Chapter 7

"IRINA WROTE TO TELL ME YOU WERE GOING TO STAY WITH HER IN St. Petersburg," Peter explained. "I wondered how . . . well, how the two of you got on."

"You came all the way from Starogan to Moscow to ask me that?" Ilona inquired.

"Well, not exactly." Peter got up to pace the room, hands clasped behind his back. "I told you, I was going to St. Petersburg anyway. And I wanted to see you again. I think it is very unfair of Sergei to keep you locked away like this."

"Then you should tell him so," Ilona said.

Peter stopped his perambulating and glanced at her with a slight frown. "You *are* happy?"

"For heaven's sake, Peter, what reply do you expect me to make to that? Let me say I am as happy, I imagine, as ninety percent of the women in Russia. The other ten percent are just lucky."

"You knew what you were born to, Ilona. But for that aberration —my God, what a stroke of ill fortune it was, the day that American came riding into Port Arthur."

"I'm sure it must seem so to you," Ilona said coldly. "Now, if you'll excuse me, I must see to your apartment."

"Don't go," he said. "I apologize. I wished to speak about Irina. You have recently been to see her. Would you say she is happy?"

"My dear Peter, she is one of the ninety percent."

"But why? What has she got to be unhappy about? I give her everything she asks for. It is not my fault that she finds Starogan boring. She knew Starogan was there before she married me."

"Wasn't she commanded to marry you?" Ilona knew she was being a perfect bitch, but he deserved it.

"I don't think so. That is not the impression I gained. But really, considering that we maintain virtually separate establishments. . . ."

"Irina suffers from a complaint which afflicts a great many women, Peter," Ilona pointed out. "She needs to be loved."

"I love her."

"Do you? I always supposed you were more honest than that. You needed to be married, and you chose the most attractive and eligible woman you could find. Had you ever thought of Irina Golovina before you suddenly required a wife?"

"Well, I . . . does Sergei not love you?"

"Whatever emotion Sergei feels for me it is certainly not love. But we have a passable relationship, because he at least loves my body."

"Ilona!" Peter was shocked.

"I had supposed we were having a heart-to-heart talk."

"Very well then. What of you?"

"If you are trying to ask me if I love his body, I would have to say, from time to time."

"My God. But you stay here with him, buried alive in Moscow."

"I stay here, my darling brother, because Sergei will not let me go."

"Not let you go?"

"Haven't you ever thought of commanding Irina to remain at Starogan with you?"

"Commanding her? She'd laugh."

"And what would you do then?"

"Well . . . what would Sergei do?"

"He'd lay me across the bed and whip me until I bled."

Peter peered at his sister. "I don't believe you."

"I can show you the marks."

"My God." He sat down again.

"I am not trying to cause a family row," Ilona said. "You asked me certain questions, and I am answering them truthfully. Besides, what a man does with his wife is their business, and theirs alone, as Sergei is always reminding me."

"If he is that cruel to you, I'm sure we could arrange a divorce."

"On what grounds?"

"Well. . . ."

"Am I supposed to bare my backside in court?"

"Really, Ilona, sometimes you shock me."

"Sometimes I shock myself. And even if I did undress for the judge, I doubt he'd do more than pat Sergei on the head. You're the one who's out of step, Peter Dimitrievich. I would recommend that you try a cane on Irina. It might do wonders."

"For heaven's sake, I cannot imagine what she would do. If that is all the advice you can give me—"

"The best advice I could give you, Peter Dimitrievich, is to try to find your wife sexually attractive. Get her pregnant. Make her go down to Starogan and *love* her. However you have to work yourself up to it, *do* it. And do it quickly."

Peter stared at her, his brows drawing together in that expression he had inherited from his father and which she knew so well. She got up.

"If you can't do that, then neither I nor anyone else can give you any advice." She left the room and came face to face with Michael Nej.

He had not changed at all. Even his expression had not changed, and he flushed slightly, as she had seen him do so often. I am the one who has changed, she thought. When last we met, despite George, I was still an innocent girl who believed that it was far easier to be happy than to be miserable. Now I know that happiness is the passing moment, instantly lost in memory. And if you have not yet found that out, Michael Nikolaievich, you are a very fortunate young man.

But his circumstances, at least, had changed. He wore a frock coat and a wing collar, displaying a gold watch chain across his vest, and carried his silk hat under his arm. He had leapt into the middle class.

"Michael Nikolaievich," she said. "How good to see you." Had he really said those words? Did he remember them now? Did he suppose she had actually heard them?

"Princess Roditcheva," he said. "I have dreamed of this moment."

She frowned at him, although it was a perfectly natural, if excessively polite, thing to say.

"You will come with me, Michael Nikolaievich," she said. "I will show you where Prince Peter is to sleep."

"Your housekeeper has already shown me, princess."

Oh, damn you, Anna Petrovna, she thought. "Nonetheless," she said, "I wish to look at it myself. I have not seen my brother for eighteen months. I would like him to be comfortable on his first visit here." She climbed the stairs in front of him, her skirt held in her left hand.

"Of course, princess," he said from behind her.

On the landing they encountered the housekeeper, who gazed from her mistress to the valet with raised eyebrows, but did nothing more than give a brief curtsey before descending the stairs. Ilona opened the door to the principal guest apartment, surveyed the fire, the flowers, then went to the inner door and threw it open to look at the bed.

"Will Prince Peter be comfortable?"

"I should imagine so, princess."

She turned to face him, standing just inside the open outer door. Now, why had she noticed whether the door was open? Because, as she had told Peter, a woman needs to be loved? And if Michael Nikolaievich was only a servant, at least he did love her. Loved her so much he had betrayed her?

"How are your father and mother? And Ivan and Nona?"

"They are all well, princess."

"And yourself?"

"I too, princess." Once again the quick flush. "I am to wed."

"You? To whom?"

"Zoe Geller, the schoolmaster's daughter. You remember Zoe Geller, princess?"

"Of course I remember Zoe Geller," Ilona snapped, suddenly quite out of sorts. "When is the great day?"

"We thought of the autumn, princess. Prince Peter has graciously given his permission and will attend. Zoe Geller will become the dowager princess's second maid."

"My mother's maid? Well, you must be very pleased and proud." Ilona stared at him. Is this truly love, she asked with her eyes? Or are you, too, putting up with what you must, knowing that your love is unattainable?

Michael met her gaze. "It is a man's duty, my lady princess, to marry and get sons."

Dear Michael. "Of course it is," she said, and crossed the room to stand beside him. "As we are such old friends, I shall try to persuade Prince Roditchev to come down to Starogan for your wedding as well. Or at least allow me to come. Would you like that?"

"I should like that very much, my lady princess."

"Then I shall come. Congratulations, Michael Nikolaievich." She held out her hand, and after a moment's indecision, he took it, raised his eyes to look into hers, then raised her hand and kissed the knuckles, still watching her. Ilona could feel the heat in her own cheeks, and he was not releasing the hand as quickly as he should. Gently she pulled it free. "Congratulations," she said again. "And while you are here, you must tell me how things are at Starogan. I shall arrange a time for us to talk."

Judith Stein waited in the small withdrawing room. She stood at the French windows leading to the terrace and looked out at the walls of the Kremlin. The table was laid for tea, and she had been shown in here by a slightly supercilious footman. Now she could be alone for a few moments, to enjoy her surroundings—because it was utterly false to pretend that she did not enjoy coming here. It was not just the obvious wealth reflected in the house, although she could not help but respond to that; her parents sought to emulate such a scale of living. It was the natural elegance with which these people lived. Where Momma and Poppa struggled to surpass their equals, Prince and Princess Roditchev took their positions, their furniture, the crystal goblets from which they drank their wine, no less than the money in their bank accounts, for granted. They had been born in such luxury, and they had no doubt they would die in it.

She should hate them. She felt guilty for admiring them at all. That a handful of people should possess such wealth, such all-embracing power, that they should be enabled to live their lives in careless disregard of anyone else, that this Roditchev should possess the authority to comamnd cannon to open fire on people who were Russian like himself and give them the choice between being blown to bits or hanged, ran counter to every human principle. She was utterly dedicated to opposing them, and eventually to bringing them down. She did not want to hurt them, however. She could understand their point of view, and in any event, her enthusiasm for socialism was always tempered with the reflection that its triumph would also mean the eclipse of her own mother and father, and all they had fought to achieve. Yet as it had to happen, as the whole weight of history dictated that inevitable event, it was far better that the movement be controlled by people like herself and her friends, who did not seek tumbrils in the street; who, if it became necessary to take over this house, for example, as a hospital or even as a residence for several families, would offer the Roditchevs alternative accommodation, and bring them down to a proper level slowly, by taxation rather than expropriation. Better than to have the future fall into the hands of people like that Lenin, who dreamed only of complete overturn, with the highest becoming the lowest, the lowest the highest, and the rope or the gun for any who would resist such change. Because people like the Roditchevs would resist any change. If pushed too far they would fight, and as they commanded the loyalty of the army, they could not lose. Lenin had talked about the army's being demoralized after its defeats in Manchuria, about its having lost faith in its officers and even in the tsar, and about how readily it would respond to the call to revolution. Well, he had been proved wrong. The day before he had disappeared from Moscow he had grumbled, "I doubt this nation will ever be ready for revolution."

She doubted it too. At least revolution as he interpreted the word—blood in the streets, rather than the gradual social change which was actually taking place. But there would always be other Lenins, men with a burning grudge against society, who would rather destroy than build. Parasites of death.

She turned guiltily as the door opened. After today her brief flirtation with the pleasures of the aristocracy would be over and done with. No doubt that was all to the good. She was realizing for the first time in the two years since she had become involved in the movement that her determination did not preclude a susceptibility to the good things of life.

"Judith Stein." Princess Roditcheva came across the room with arms outstretched, and after a brief hesitation, Judith allowed herself to be embraced and kissed on each cheek. "How lovely to see you," the princess said. "Do sit down." She sat herself and poured tea, keeping her voice rather low. "I shall not close the door, because that would encourage the servants to listen. It is a characteristic of servants that they will always overhear what they can. But from where I am sitting I can see into the hall, and therefore no one can approach close enough to overhear us. Now, when can I come to hear your lecturer?"

She thinks of it as a university class, Judith thought. What shall we learn today? Flower arranging? Cookery? Needlework? Or elementary revolution? That sounds interesting.

She sighed, but there was no help for it. As she had got herself into this mess, she had to get herself back out of it.

"First of all, princess, do you give me your solemn word that you will never repeat a word of what we discuss here? That you will not have me followed or investigated in any way?"

"Of course I do," Ilona said.

"Well, then, I am afraid I must tell you that I cannot take you to our meeting. It is absolutely forbidden."

Ilona leaned back in her chair. Pink spots had appeared in her cheeks. "Because my husband is military governor of Moscow? I have given you my word that he will never know anything of this."

Judith would not lower her gaze. "Because you are a princess, and were born to that rank. It is felt that you could not possibly sympathize with any of the aims likely to be expressed at our meetings."

Ilona drank tea. "You mean there will be talk of revolution. I am of the opinion that a controlled revolution might be a very good thing for Russia."

"I do not think what you would consider a revolution would be the same as what we would consider a revolution, princess." Judith got up. "I must go."

"You have not drunk your tea."

"Are you angry with me?"

Ilona considered her for a moment. "Yes," she said at last. "Yes, I am angry. Not with you, my dear Judith, but with your people, who refuse to trust me. I should have thought that, could I be captured for your cause, I would be a very valuable asset indeed. And if you fail to convince me that what you intend is good for Russia, well then, I should at least be a wiser person, and that can be no bad thing."

"I am sure, at this moment, princess. But people change. Their points of view change."

"I see." The pink spots were back. "So, after all, you do *not* trust me. You imagine I may have second thoughts and betray you to my husband."

Judith sighed. "It is a risk we cannot afford to take, princess. Now I must go. May I—" She bit her lip. "May I remind you of your promise?"

"A Borodin does not need to be reminded of a promise," Ilona said coldly. Then she smiled. "I would not like us to part on bad terms. I have said that I would like to be your friend, and I have not changed my mind. Will you come to tea again?"

Judith hesitated, then shook her head. "No, my lady princess. I do not think I should do that. Good afternoon." She debated about whether or not she should offer to shake hands, changed her mind, and left the room, closing the door behind her. Immediately a footman appeared with her coat and parasol; if they could not hear what was being said in the drawing room, the servants certainly kept a close watch on the hall. "Thank you," she said. "Good afternoon." She turned for the door and faced Peter Borodin. Now where on earth had he sprung from? Hastily she gave a brief curtsey. "My lord prince."

"Judith Stein." He held out his right hand while making a dismissing gesture with his left. The footman departed. Slowly she took his hand, and he raised hers to kiss it. "I had supposed you were staying for tea," he remarked.

"I must apologize, my lord prince, as I have just apologized to the princess. But I have urgent business elsewhere."

"Urgent business." He smiled at her. He was an extraordinarily handsome man. Quite the handsomest man she had ever met. A fitting brother to the beauty behind the door. And he was attracted to her. But he was a prince, with all that suggested of his relations with women he might consider as belonging to an inferior class.

"Even I can have urgent business, my lord prince," she said, and freed herself.

Peter himself opened the door for her. "I am sure you do," he said. "But I also have urgent business from time to time, Mademoiselle Stein. Legal business. Do you suppose your father might find the time to consult with me?"

"I am sure he would be delighted," she said. Delighted? He would be overjoyed. "His offices are not far from here."

"I would prefer to call at his home," Peter said. "My business is confidential."

Once again she was aware of the appraising stare. Judith's knees felt quite weak.

"I shall tell him," she said. "No doubt he will write to you for an appointment."

"That would be kind of him. I shall be remaining in Moscow for another week. Ask him to write me tomorrow, will you, Mademoiselle Stein?"

"Of course, my lord prince." She went down the front stairs, reached the drive, and looked back. He was standing in the doorway, looking after her.

Ilona remained seated by the tea table for some minutes after the door had closed. She had never felt quite so angry in her life, not even on the dreadful day George had been forced to leave Starogan, because then she had been riddled with guilt, whereas now she had only tried to help the silly girl. She had offered her friendship, to a Jew, of all people. It had been a genuine offer. And it had been refused. Because she was a princess, she was not considered trustworthy. Of all the absurd nonsense. Insulting nonsense, as well.

The poor fools could not even understand that she was their one hope, not of succeeding, but of surviving. She knew exactly what would happen at the meeting. Some rabble-rouser, like the redheaded man, would get up and by his oratory sway the majority into proposing yet another general strike or revolution, and they would take to the streets to be shot down in their hundreds by Sergei. Whereas if they would allow her to understand some of their points of view, some of their aspirations, and be guided by her into patience, everything was possible. As she grew older, her power and influence would increase. If Peter's marriage were already in a state of collapse, and if he were willing to sympathize with her point of view as regards Roditchev . . . well, Peter certainly was not as rigid in his thinking as Sergei. If for the moment he was being allowed to feel his way into his role as a landowner, there could be no question that very soon he would be required to take his place on the national stage, as the princes of Starogan had always done. Whether it would be a high command in the army, or a post in one of the ministries, like Uncle Igor's, or even a provincial governorship, he would then be in a position to influence events himself. It was in the hands of people like Peter and herself, not people like Sergei or people like Lenin, that the future of Russia lay.

And the fools had excluded her. Did they really suppose she would accept that? Her duty, to them no less than to herself, was to help them, whether they wished it or not. And fortunately, at this moment she had the means at hand. Michael Nej.

He loved her. He had said so. How did a servant love a princess? Was it a matter of dreams? Or merely an abstract sense of worship? No matter. He loved her, and with luck he would be the first of many. Because it was occurring to her that this was what she needed above all else, a band of faithful followers, bound to her by her greatest asset, her beauty. After all, what was the real cause of her misery? The fact that she was surrounded by Roditchev's creatures. And by constantly letting them know they were her husband's, she only increased her isolation. But even they, in time, could be seduced to her service rather than his. As for Michael Nej. . . .

But did she dare use him? He had betrayed her once before. Well, she would have to find out. If he betrayed her again, it would only be to Peter, and Peter would understand this particular escapade, she had no doubt of that. If he did not betray her, she would know she had one friend in the world. More than a friend. A man who loved her, and would do anything for her. A beginning.

She finished her tea and got up. Her anger had disappeared in the anticipation of action. She opened the doors to the hall and encountered her brother.

"You have not quarreled with that Jewish girl?" he asked.

"Why, no. What makes you think that?"

"I met her leaving. I had supposed she was staying to tea."

"She came to tell me that she could not. So much nicer than writing a note. I think she is a very charming and well brought-up young woman."

"Charming, certainly," Peter agreed, and walked beside her up the stairs. "I have decided to stay on in Moscow for a few days. You do not mind?"

"My dear Peter, I think that is a perfectly splendid idea. But what of Irina?"

"I am sure Irina is enjoying herself in St. Petersburg."

She certainly is, Ilona thought.

"And besides, when I get there, do you know what will happen? There will be tears and recriminations at the very mention of Starogan. I find it very tiresome."

They had reached the upper hall. "Well, there is always the cane," Ilona pointed out wickedly.

Peter turned away without a word and went into his apartment. That meant that Michael would be summoned at any moment. Ilona went to her sewing room at the end of the corridor, left the door open, and sat down with a piece of needlework on her lap. She could now oversee the head of the servants' stairs at the far end of the hall, and sure enough, five minutes later Michael hurried up. He passed the sewing room without looking in, disappearing in the direction of the guest apartments.

Ilona stitched industriously, was visited by Catherine Ivanovna, who wanted to know if the princess were finished with the tea things, reminding Ilona that she had forgotten to ring for the footman, and was sent away again because her mistress had a headache and wished only to do a little sewing in peace. Catherine departed, and a few moments later Michael also emerged, carrying Peter's boots to be polished.

"Michael Nikolaievich," Ilona said softly.

His head jerked, and he looked along the corridor.

"Come in here, Michael," Ilona said.

Michael hesitated, then came into the sewing room.

"I think you should close the door," Ilona said.

Another hesitation, then Michael carefully closed the door. He looked down at the boots.

"Put them on the floor," Ilona suggested. "And sit down."

Michael placed the boots on the floor and regarded the chair suspiciously.

"Do sit down," Ilona said gently.

Michael lowered himself into the seat, perching on the very edge.

"I can't imagine when you and I were last alone together, Michael," Ilona remarked. "It must have been in Port Arthur."

"I think so, my lady princess," Michael agreed.

"And a great deal has happened since then," Ilona said. "Then, we were children. Now we are both grown up."

"Yes, my lady princess."

"Have you forgiven me for wishing to run away and leave you all?"

"Forgiven you, Mademoiselle Ilona?" Unthinkingly, he had used the name he called her before her marriage. "Why, if I could think that you have forgiven me. . . ."

"I have," she said. "Oh, I was terribly angry with you at the time. But since then I have realized that you acted entirely for the best." What an accomplished liar she was becoming. "And I have also come to suspect that your reasons were personal." She would not take her gaze from his face, and watched him flush. Well, he deserved a certain amount of embarrassment. "Did you mean what you said at my wedding, Michael Nikolaievich?"

"I . . . I apologize, my lady princess."

"Now, why should you do that? I have not taken offense. I am delighted to feel that you are so concerned for my welfare. Can we not let bygones be bygones? Once we were the closest of friends. Once I knew that I could count on you for anything, Michael Nikolaievich. And even if it seems to be the will of fate that we are to be separated for much of the time, I would still like to feel that in you I have a friend on whom I can rely."

"You have, my lady princess." His face was shining. "I swear it, so help me God."

"I knew it." She smiled at him. "Then let us seal our renewed friendship, our renewed intimacy, with a new venture."

"My lady?"

"I would like you to do something for me, Michael Nikolaievich." She gave him a roguish smile. "Believe me, it is nothing that you would not care to assist me in. The only thing I must require of you is complete secrecy."

Michael looked uncomfortable again.

"Will you give me that promise, Michael?"

He seemed to shrug, as if to himself. "I will give you my word, my lady, that whatever you tell me will go no further."

"Or whatever I ask you to do?"

"If . . . if I can be assured it will not harm my family."

"It will not harm your family, Michael Nikolaievich."

"Then you have my word."

She leaned forward. "It is not a difficult task. As we do no entertaining, I assume you have a great deal of spare time at the moment?"

"The prince does not require much of me, no, my lady."

"Well, then, I would like you to find out something for me. It will involve keeping watch on a certain house, and following a young lady when she leaves it. Eventually it will involve gaining admittance to a meeting. This meeting, I will tell you frankly, Michael Nikolaievich, is a socialist gathering. Do you know anything about socialism, Michael?"

The quick jerk of his head told her that whatever he said, he did know something about it. "I have heard of it, my lady."

"Well, I wish you to attend this meeting, and learn what is said, and more important, learn where the next meeting is to be held. I think there is going to be one either tonight or tomorrow, and I should like to find out as soon as possible. You will have no difficulty in being accepted if you profess socialist views yourself. I give you my word that I will vouch for you if the police should raid the meeting."

Michael frowned at her. "May I ask why you require this, my lady?"

"I would prefer not to tell you at this moment. But I should very much like your help, Michael Nikolaievich. That way I can be sure that our past differences are forgotten, and that we can resume our old friendship. Will you help me, Michael Nikolaievich?" She leaned forward and took his hand. When she did that, she was the most beautiful girl in all the world.

The lawyer lived on the right bank of the Moscow River in Zamoskvorechye, a suburb of new villas built in stone as a contrast to the wooden houses of the older part of the city, and, to Peter Borodin's eyes, somewhat huddled together, with often no more than half an acre of garden to separate them from their neighbors. Here he knew he would find none of the old boyar families, who preferred, when their business or pleasure took them to the old capital, to live amid the spacious private parks of the Konushennaya. These new houses were the properties of the growing mercantile class, the men who had made their fortunes in trade out of the Kitai-Gorod, and those others who had made their fortunes out of the first group, the doctors who cured their ailments and the lawyers who handled their affairs.

Even a Jewish lawyer, it seemed, was allowed to escape the pale in which so many of his compatriots were confined. But that, Peter reflected as the carriage came to a halt, was another sign of the growing liberalism of his country. The liberalism supported, however discreetly, by his father and grandfather, and which had led their country to this sorry situation of being regarded as an ailing nation, second candidate only to the Turks for the title of sick man of Europe. But that would change, was already changing. The new prime minister, Peter Stolypin, while doing all he could to improve the dreadful financial situation of the peasantry, and allowing these very middle classes the right to make their views known by means of the Duma, yet retained the reins of power firmly in his own hands, and therefore the hands of the tsar, and punished those who would incite sedition against the Motherland with the utmost rigor of the law. It would be the duty of those who came after Stolypin to continue that double-pronged policy: increased prosperity for all, and woe to the dissident. His duty, in the course of time.

So think well what you are doing, Peter Borodin. The carriage was stopping, and he must either descend or order it to drive on. As he had demanded a private meeting, Stein had tentatively asked him to dine, and been delighted when he accepted. Now it was half past eight, time to go in. But do you know what you are doing, Peter Borodin? You are setting out quite deliberately to seduce a girl. Because your wife is patently bored with you, has been bored with you from the moment she found herself alone with you on her wedding night? Because you are afraid of her? As he was in a mood of honest introspection, that thought could be considered. Certainly he feared Irina's moods, her ready tears which left him helpless, her endless recriminations. Certainly he was happier when she was in St. Petersburg and he was in Starogan, happy except for the reflection that all the world knew of the distance between them, and speculated about the reasons for it.

But she was his wife, therefore what could he expect to obtain from Judith Stein except the sex he never enjoyed with Irina? Irina had a most attractive body, which was his to command, but she never allowed him that impression, but suggested by her every movement that she was granting him the very temporary use of it, however pained and bored she might be. He had hoped for so much, and had received so very little. Not even a son. So what made him suppose that this girl would be any different? Only that he was older than she. But why *she,* when he had seen her only twice, when he could buy whatever he wished, if it was nothing more than sex?

He wanted a great deal more than that. He wanted love. Ilona, with typical feminine casuistry, apparently did not suppose that men loved at all. They took when they felt the urge. Irina obviously felt the same way. Which, he supposed, was why men had mistresses. Because mistresses loved. Even if it was an act and dependent on what their lovers gave to them, it was still a most convincing act. A woman bought and paid for on a permanent basis, and knowing that, was the most precious possession a man could have. Peter was prepared to buy now, if it were necessary, even if he dreamed of a mutual attraction, a mutual love which would surmount any of the many obstacles which lay ahead of them.

Judith Stein was not just a woman. She was a Jew. A people of which Peter knew very little, except that the tragedy of their history had caused them to turn in on themselves, to live their own ancient way in the midst of foreign communities, to obey the laws handed down to them through countless centuries. Very moral laws. He knew that. Therefore, in the eyes of a rabbi, he would be asking this girl to commit a very great sin. And not only in the eyes of a rabbi. The Jews, by their very presence, were regarded as natural rebels against authority, as natural socialists. Was he not going against everything he now held dear in even considering it?

But consideration could only bring him back to the memory of that utterly appealing face, those bottomless pools which were her eyes, that strangely unfeminine look of defiance which crossed her face when she feared she might not be understood . . . and that obviously blooming young figure. He had never in his life met a girl to whom he had so immediately been attracted, with whom he had so instantly felt a rapport. She had to feel the same about him. And if she did not, how could she resist him, when he was a prince and she nothing but a lawyer's daughter? As a lawyer's daughter, how could she possibly be one of the run-of-the-mill Jews who sought only some kind of Jewish millennium? If further argument were needed, it lay in the plain fact that Jacob Stein had risen from the pale and achieved true respectability, here in Zamoskvorechye.

He wondered if the dinner would be kosher.

"You may wait, Vasili Tigranovich," Peter said, and got down. He walked up the front steps, and the door was immediately opened for him. Inside the house the electric lamps were already burning, and there was a glow of expectation, with the butler and a footman lined up to take his hat and cape, and Stein himself waiting in the inner doorway. A tall man, like his daughter, with similar features. A handsome man.

"Prince Borodin," he said. "Welcome, your excellency, welcome to my home. Come in, sir, come in."

The door was held wide, and Peter entered a neat little room studded with low tables on which were clusters of brass ornaments and photographs of past and present Steins in silver frames.

"My wife, your excellency. Ruth, Prince Borodin of Starogan."

Peter took her hand and bent over it, but did not kiss it. Ruth Stein was as tall as her husband but thin and angular, with permanent worry lines between her eyes. She was very simply dressed in a high-necked evening gown, and wore no jewelry at all.

"Welcome to our house, Prince Borodin."

"It is my pleasure, Madame Stein."

"My daughter, Rachel," Stein said.

Peter turned to the girl and frowned. Also tall, and destined to be as pretty as her sister, but clearly very, very young, hardly older than Tatiana, still all legs and arms.

"My pleasure, Mademoiselle Stein." He glanced at Stein. "I understood that you also have another daughter, Monsieur Stein."

"Indeed I do, your excellency. Indeed I do. And a son." He twisted his fingers together. "But they are out tonight, your excellency. It is to do with the synagogue. They are very conscientious about playing their part in the lives of the community. A thousand apologies, your excellency. A thousand apologies."

"I cannot imagine what Peter Dimitrievich is about," Roditchev commented. He waited for his butler to fill his brandy glass; he seldom spoke during the meal itself, as he suffered from indigestion. "If he wanted a lawyer here in Moscow there are several I could have recommended. There was no necessity to go to a Jew. And then, actually to accept an invitation to dine with the fellow—it's the height of absurdity."

Ilona raised her head. "Peter is dining with Monsieur Stein?"

"Indeed he is. Did he not tell you?"

"He did not. He merely informed me that he would not be at dinner. I did not wish to pry into his affairs."

"He is using my house as an hotel," Roditchev grumbled, "and doing my position no good at all. Dining with Jews!"

Ilona smiled at her husband. She certainly owed Peter nothing, and if Roditchev was going to start brooding on the Steins in any event, it was best to give him a reason.

"There is nothing sinister about it, Sergei. He is not even serious about employing Stein professionally. He has taken a fancy to the daughter."

"Eh? A Jew?"

"A very good-looking Jew. She is the girl I befriended at the station, remember?"

"My God." Roditchev finished his brandy. "My God. Your family really is quite irresponsible, Ilona. I shall have to talk to that young man."

"Oh, I don't think he will make any progress in that direction," Ilona said. "I doubt that she will be interested in Peter."

"He is a prince, my dear. And anyway, it is the principle of the thing that matters. If he wanted a mistress, why didn't he come to me?" He frowned at her. "Is there trouble between him and Irina?"

"I do not think so," Ilona lied. "He is just a man."

Roditchev gazed at her for some seconds, as if uncertain exactly what she meant, then he snapped his fingers. The butler hastily pulled back his chair and he got up.

"I shall bid you good night."

"Good night, Sergei. May I ask where you are going?"

"My club. Do not wait up for me."

Ilona held up her hand to be kissed. When Sergei had left she went on sipping her brandy and gazed down the length of the table. Peter really was an incredible fool, supposing that Judith Stein could ever even think of him as a lover. Even if she weren't Jewish, with all the moral strictures that implied. Ilona frowned. He could also be a dangerous fool. If he were to press too hard, and Judith were to lose her head and confess her socialist leanings . . . she must be warned. Well, she could do that herself, whenever Michael had some information for her. And come to think of it, he must have some by now; it was three days since she had set him to watching the Stein house in his spare time; if he did not make haste, Peter would depart for St. Petersburg and that would be that.

She nodded to the butler and he held her chair. "Send Nej to me, Ivan Pavlovich. I will be in the drawing room."

He bowed. As he had overheard the dinner conversation, he would have not the slightest suspicion that she wished to do anything more than check on her brother's movements. The footman held the door for her and she sat down on the settee. The footman hastily refilled her brandy glass and left the room as Michael appeared in the doorway.

"Come in, Michael Nikolaievich," she said. "I have a question to ask you."

Michael came across the floor and stood in front of her.

Ilona lowered her voice. "What have you found out?"

"I have been waiting to tell you, Mademoiselle Ilona. There is to be a meeting tonight."

Ilona raised her head. "Tonight? But . . . that is impossible."

"It is scheduled, Mademoiselle Ilona. There was one the night before last, which I attended. As you suggested, it was not difficult."

"There was no check on you?"

"Oh yes. They would only admit you if you gave the name of a socialist leader."

"Do you know any socialists?"

"No, my lady. But I know the name of one. A man called Lenin, who lives in Switzerland, but has published a book."

Ilona stared at him. "Lenin? What book? Have you read it?"

Michael looked suitably shocked, copying the tactics Geller had used in Starogan. "Oh no, my lady. But I have heard of it. So I used his name and was admitted without further questions."

"Was Mademoiselle Stein there?"

"Yes, my lady. With her brother. There were several people there.

And another meeting was arranged for tonight, because the speaker is returning to St. Petersburg tomorrow morning."

Ilona bit her lip. She hadn't expected such short notice. But on the other hand, if Judith were not going to be there tonight—and she could not possibly be there if she were entertaining Peter at dinner—she would never have a better opportunity of going unrecognized. If she had the courage. She realized that she had never before in her life actively called upon her courage. It had failed her when George left Starogan, and on the night of the uprising everything had happened too quickly for her to reflect on just how dangerous her situation was.

"What time is the meeting?"

"Eleven o'clock, my lady."

Ilona looked at the clock over the mantelpiece. It was eight thirty. Sergei seldom returned from his club before one in the morning.

"Is it far?"

"No, my lady. But—"

"Yes?"

"You cannot go in a carriage."

"I know that, Michael. Don't take me for a fool." Anxiety was making her testy. She smiled at him. "I will be ready at ten thirty. Wait for me by the back door." Once before she had asked him to do that. "Don't fail me this time, Michael Nikolaievich."

"I shall not fail you, my lady."

She nodded. "Then leave me." She waited for him to go, rang the bell, got up and left the room. Catherine Ivanovna only caught up with her halfway up the stairs.

"My lady?" she panted.

"I am very tired, Catherine Ivanovna. I shall retire early tonight."

"Of course, my lady princess." Catherine scurried at her heels into the bedroom, helped her undress, held the toothpaste and flannel for her, tucked her into bed and opened the windows sufficiently to allow the warm evening air to flood the room, placed the jug of water and the glass by the bedside. "Will there be anything else?"

"No, thank you, Catherine Ivanovna. Good night."

"Good night, my lady princess."

The door closed. Ilona waited for five minutes, then leapt out of bed and dressed herself. Her heart was pounding. Suppose Roditchev came home early? Or Peter . . . she hadn't thought of that. She chewed her lip, fingers still buttoning away. But Roditchev had not visited her bedroom since her early return from St. Petersburg. He claimed to spend almost every evening at his club; clearly he had found himself a mistress, and nothing could be more fortunate, in her opinion. As for Peter, he would hardly come in to see her if he were told she had retired. There really was no risk at all. And besides, it was an adventure. If she did not have adventures now and then, she would go mad with boredom.

She left off her corset, wore her most nondescript gown, but could not find an equally nondescript hat. Suddenly she was struck with an idea. Peasant women wore kerchiefs tied over their heads. She found a large kerchief, tucked her hair out of sight, and secured the knot under her chin. The kerchief was silk, but it would soon be dark and no one would be able to discern the material easily. She had no suitable coat, even her church-going cloak being too obviously expensive, so she draped a summer shawl around her shoulders and surveyed herself in the mirror. She thought she looked quite remarkably common. It was a pity her boots were so highly polished, but they could be scuffed on the street. Oh, and no jewelry. She took off her rings and placed them in her bedside drawer.

The upper landings were empty; if the servants dared not retire until the two princes returned, they would be below stairs drinking vodka and gossiping—except for the footman, who was always on duty in the front hall. Ilona used the staff staircase, tiptoeing down the carpeted steps, listening at every landing, and hearing Ivan Pavlovich holding forth in his pantry, to the accompaniment of much laughter and clinking of glasses. No one was going to hear her. She drew a long breath, ran down the final flight and past the kitchen door, reached the basement and the door into the service yard. This was ajar, and she stepped through to find herself standing next to Michael, who wore a flat cap instead of his usual topper, and a cloth coat.

"Are you sure, my lady?" he whispered.

"For heaven's sake," she said. "Come on." She felt desperately excited, and even happy. They had not gone on an escapade together since they had climbed that tree, ten years before. That had turned out badly—as had her attempted escape from Starogan. The third time would be lucky.

They crossed the yard. A small gate in the wall led to the street. Michael held it for her, and they were on the pavement. The dusk gathered around them, and other people walked by, either for a promenade or on their way home from work. Not one of them gave a second glance to the couple by the gate, obviously Roditchev servants allowed out for the evening. Ilona felt a great surge of relief traveling through her entire body. She wanted to laugh with the sudden feeling of freedom. For a whole three hours—no, it would be safer if they were gone only two hours—she would not be Princess Roditcheva. She was as free as any other woman in the world, as free as if she had been Mrs. George Hayman.

And she had an entirely personable young man as her escort. A young man who loved her. She tucked her arm through his, and smiled at him when he gave a start of dismay.

"That is how young people walk together, Michael Nikolaievich," she said. "I have seen them. And we are two young people out for a walk together, are we not?"

What was she really up to, Michael Nej wondered. And did it really matter when she walked beside him, her arm tucked into his? He could even let his fingers brush against her glove.

He had not anticipated such a reaction from himself. After eighteen months, during which he had known she hated him, she had become a memory. More often than not he used the memory for hateful fantasies. He remembered that night in Port Arthur, and he replaced the American with himself, and then he imagined her, all white flesh and disordered underclothes, fighting him, as she undoubtedly would have fought. But he was too strong for her, and in the end she had to submit, and he . . . but memory, or imagination, could take him no further; he had no experience of female flesh closing on his.

But to see her had been to love her all over again. And then, to be summoned to her sewing room and told to close the door, to inhale her marvelous perfume, to be able to look at her and look at her and look at her, and then to be given the chance to atone for his earlier crime in sacrificing her to a man like Roditchev. Not that he regretted that for an instant, now. Had he let her go with Hayman he would never have seen her again. This, the feel of her flesh against his, could never have happened.

So what was she after? In the beginning he had not cared. But soon he had understood. She was as cold-blooded and as treacherous as she was wanton. There could be no doubt about that. She had found out that Prince Peter had taken a fancy to the Jewish lawyer's daughter—that would not have been difficult to discover, as it was the talk of the servants' table—and she was determined to ruin the girl by proving her socialist affiliations. Ruin. Michael did not like to think what Judith Stein's fate was going to be. Exile at the very least, hanging more likely. After spending days, perhaps weeks, at the mercy of a monster like Roditchev. And he was helping that tragedy to happen.

But did it matter, beside the fact that he was promenading with Ilona, walking with her hand now definitely resting in his? He didn't care about the Jews. He had no inclination toward socialism. The socialists would overturn the world, and he had no desire to have this world overturned. With socialism in control, supposing that were ever possible, there would be no Prince Borodin of Starogan needing a valet, so there would be no silk hats and woollen tailor-made suits and first-class compartments for Michael Nej. There would be no great occasions and there would be no hundred-rouble tips from grateful officials who, through his offices, had been brought close to the prince.

And there would be no Ilona.

No, no, he thought. This Stein deserved her fate on both counts, Jewry and socialism. She might not have been able to help the first, but she had chosen the second, and she must abide by the consequences.

They walked across the bridge, and Ilona wanted to pause and look down at the rushing water. She released him to lean against the balustrade, and he wondered if he dared put his arm around her waist.

"I never knew what a pleasure it was, walking in the city on a summer's night," she remarked.

"You must make a habit of it, my lady princess," he said.

"And you must not call me my lady this evening, Michael Nikolaievich. Use my name. Besides, walking is only a pleasure when the company is congenial. Whom would you have me walk with, Catherine Ivanovna?"

Use her name. He wondered if he dared. He had lost his nerve at the bridge, but now that they were walking again he took her hand and passed it under his arm, then held it. She glanced down at their locked fingers, but made no remark.

"It is not far now, Ilona Dimitrievna," he said, and felt his heart turning somersaults. If only it were possible to stay in Moscow all summer.

"We don't want to be too late," she agreed, and actually gave his hand a squeeze. Or had it been a simple reflex action caused by her excitement? No matter. But they had now left the residential part of the city and plunged into the dock area which clung to the river bank below the Kremlin, giving berth to the traffic which used the Moscow River as a road. And there was the side street down which their stroll would end.

"You had better let me do the talking," he suggested.

"Of course."

He released her hand reluctantly, stepped in front of her to knock on the door. The peephole opened.

"Chernov," he said, and drew a long breath. "Remember me, comrade? Tonight I introduce my wife."

He dared not look over his shoulder. The face at the square hole was glancing from him to Ilona, then the bolts were drawn. "Welcome, comrade."

Michael waited for Ilona, held her hand again, and escorted her into the small, poorly lit room. There were about thirty people already seated in the well of the hall, while on the dais at the far end there were another dozen, arranging chairs and tables and glasses of water. Among them he recognized the girl, Judith Stein, and her brother. Ilona recognized them too. She gasped and tried to pull free.

"You knew they would be here," he whispered.

"I did not. I did not think she could be. I must leave," Ilona said.

"You cannot. They would be suspicious. Sit here by me at the back. They will not be able to see your face."

"My hair—"

"They cannot see that either, unless you take off your scarf. There is no danger, Ilona Dimitrievna. None at all."

She sat down in the straight chair beside him. The chairs were so close together their shoulders touched, and he could feel her trembling. He put his arm round her and held her close.

"There is no need to be afraid, Ilona Dimitrievna. You did not mind my pretending you are my wife? It is safer."

"No," she said. "I did not mind." But now her interest was caught by developments on the dais. The organizers, Judith included, were taking their seats, and the speaker, a short, plump man with horn-rimmed glasses and a pointed beard, was advancing to the edge of the platform.

"Comrades," he said.

"Comrade," the room said in unison.

"It is good to see so many of you," the speaker said. "Good. It is a sign that even the setbacks we have been experiencing cannot affect our cause. As I have said to those of you who came the night before last, we shall rise again. But for the moment, comrades, we must counsel patience. Stolypin is our enemy. He is a man of energy, of strong will, of determination. It is always wise to recognize your enemy's strengths. He was put into power after the events of 1905, just to ensure that such a thing could never happen again. And comrades, we were premature then. There is no point in hiding the truth from ourselves. The future of Russia, of socialist Russia, cannot be secured by blood. It must be secured by reason, by work, and eventually, by the power of the ballot box. We have made progress. We have our Duma. The suffrage is not what we would have wished, and Stolypin would reduce it further. But it is there, and it will not go away. But comrades, I tell you this: Stolypin will go away. Eventually, he must. It may take a year, five years, even ten. But one day there will be no Stolypin, and whenever that happens, there will still be us. Perhaps not me, perhaps not you. But it is our business to ensure that when the next opportunity arises to further our cause, by peaceful means, by democracy, by socialism, there are sufficient of us ready and willing to act."

He paused, and took off his spectacles to clean them. Michael discovered he had been so interested in what the fellow was saying that he had forgotten to hold Ilona as tightly as he might.

"And now, comrades," the speaker resumed, and was checked by the blast of a whistle.

The entire room rose together, kicking over chairs, looking toward the door, which suddenly shattered beneath an enormous impact.

"Police," someone screamed.

"Run," another urged the people in front of him.

"This way," shouted Judith Stein, opening an inner door and, amazingly, waiting for the others to go out first.

Ilona seemed to be paralyzed. Michael had to grab her arm and push her forward, kicking tumbled chairs out of their way, while behind them there came the crash of more panels splintering.

"Hurry," said the girl, her voice amazingly calm. Then she looked into Ilona's face and her jaw dropped. Ilona fell over the edge of the dais and landed on her hands and knees. Michael pulled her up, and she faced the girl.

"Bitch," the girl said. "I hope you rot in hell, princess."

Ilona tried to speak, but Michael was already pushing her through the crowded rear door. From behind them there came a shout and a gunshot. Michael and Ilona had now reached the safety of the corridor, but he turned around just in time to see Judith Stein's face as, still standing on the other side of the door, she closed and locked it; her face had grown icy cold and impassive, and yet dreadful in its hate and its apprehension of what would soon be happening to her.

The corridor was dark, and filled with people, stumbling and cursing. And now there came a fresh banging from behind them.

"That girl," Ilona gasped. "She thinks—"

"Be quiet, Ilona Dimitrievna," Michael snapped. He did not wish her to identify herself to anyone else here. He could see a patch of light in the darkness. It was a yard into which the running men and women were escaping, making for the wall on the far side. Michael dragged Ilona across, held her thighs and heaved her up. She straddled the wall, her skirt tearing, and he jumped up beside her and pulled her down on the other side. They fell together on their hands and knees on a steeply sloping grassy bank. They scrabbled at the grass with their fingers but failed to gain hold. Ilona gave a wailing scream and slid feet first into the river, making hardly any splash at all as her skirt ballooned about her. Michael jumped in beside her, pushing her away from the bank. He looked up. The police were lining the wall, and he saw the flashes of their revolvers, although his ears were singing so loudly he could not hear the explosions. But they were firing at the governor's wife. He wondered what they would say if they knew that.

Ilona had swallowed water and was gasping for breath. She kept trying to make for the bank, and Michael kept steering her into the middle of the stream. "For God's sake," she gasped. "I'm drowning. My boots are full of water."

"You'll not drown," he said. "I'll not let you drown. But we are safer here. Go with the current."

"Where?" she gasped, doing a breast stroke as best she could, weighed down as she was by her clothing.

"Away from the lights," he said. "There's a park downstream. They won't look for us there."

He tried to listen to what was happening behind them. The shooting had stopped, and it was difficult to identify any noises above the general hum of the city. It was better to concentrate on swimming, keeping Ilona afloat, and looking for the park; he dared not consider the consequences of this night.

"There," he said, and guided her to the bank.

The night was now utterly dark as the last of the street lamps had disappeared, and above them there loomed only the darkness of the trees. Ilona gave another gasp, and her head disappeared beneath the surface. He clutched her shoulders to pull her up, and touched the bottom; she had apparently done the same and lost her buoyancy for a moment. He pulled her to the bank and knelt in the soft mud, holding her against him. Her head rested on his shoulder. Ilona Roditcheva was in his arms.

"She thought I'd betrayed her," she whispered. "My God. She thought I'd betrayed her. But I didn't. I didn't." Suddenly she thrust him away. "You," she said. "You little swine! You—" She swung her hand, but he caught it, and caught her other hand too as she tried to strike him with it.

"I didn't, Ilona Dimtrievna," he said. "I swear I didn't. Betray her? How could I have taken you to a meeting which was going to be raided by the police?"

The effort of her swinging fists had absorbed the last of her strength, and once again she sagged against him. Her scarf had disappeared in the escape and her hair touched his lips, wet and lank and smelling less of perfume than river water.

"How could I, Ilona Dimtrievna?" he whispered. "I love you."

She seemed to subside against him, her head hidden once more in his shoulder. For a moment he could not grasp what was happening. But this was that night in Port Arthur over again. Her nerves had been stretched past breaking point by tonight's events, and when that happened, as he knew so well, she wanted, needed, love. Physical love. But love.

Even from Michael Nej?

Very cautiously he released her wrists, allowed his arms to go around her body, hugged her against him, while they knelt in the mud and the water flowed past their thighs.

"I love you," he said again, and kissed the hair away from her ear. He felt her hands on his back tightening him against her. He wanted to scream for joy, and yet was afraid to go any further. But they could not stay in the river for the rest of their lives. Time was fleeting.

Carefully they rose, then stood, their bodies still pressed against each other. But her head was moving, her cheek leaving his. It had to be now or it would be never. He moved his own head, caught her mouth with his. Her lips were already parted, and she made no attempt to close them. Her tongue was anxious, eager, demanding. And now surely she could feel him against her and know what was going to happen, what had to happen.

Her lips slid away. "Oh, my dearest, dearest girl," he whispered.

"I'll help you up." He moved his head back, gazed at her in the darkness. He could hardly see her face, still could not grasp that all that beauty was yielding itself to him. And he could not see her eyes at all. But she was not turning her head away or attempting to resist him. However unbelievable it might be, it was happening. Ilona Roditcheva was giving herself to him, in her desperate search for love. "Turn around," he said.

She obeyed without question. He grasped her thighs and lifted, and she got her knees up, started to slip, and reached down with one hand to pull her skirts up to her waist and allow her knees to grip. He looked at the white stockinged legs, the mud-stained boots, and could wait no longer. He gave a gigantic heave, and she gasped and landed on her stomach, clear of the water. Michael scrambled up the bank behind her, and she turned over on her back, wet hair resting on the earth, eyes still lost but face waiting for his to approach, and skirts still up around her thighs. A mud-stained, soaked Ilona Dimitrievna, as far removed from the magnificent creature of the drawing room as it was possible to be, and yet the same girl, the same thighs and long legs, the same heaving breasts. She was not naked, and he could not properly undress her. And even if he could have done so, he could not have seen. How he wanted to see, to remember, to cherish. But that was for the future. Tonight he could feel. He had never felt a woman before.

Chapter 8

HOW COLD IT WAS. THE NIGHT SEEMED TO HAVE BEEN GOING ON FOR-
ever. But for Judith Stein the night had only just begun. It stretched
in front of her for the rest of her life, she supposed, black and
moonless and cold.

At the moment it was no more than dusk. She sat on a bench in a
corner of the room, watched by the group of policemen gossiping on
the far side. They were the men who had brought her in. They were
the men who had searched her at the meeting hall. They had enjoyed
themselves. Here was a pretty young woman, and a Jew in the bargain, caught in their hands as a moth might get caught in a mesh
screen. Who could tell what terrible weapons, what treasonous manifestos, she might have concealed about her person? So they had
spread-eagled her on the table and searched her. She had supposed
she was about to be raped, and had braced herself for an ordeal
which would leave her only half a woman, but the better able to hate
them. She had not been raped. To have raped a young woman on arrest would have been criminal, and these men were policemen of the
tsar. Searching her had been the correct procedure, sanctioned by the
law.

And at the end of it all she had nevertheless been only half a
woman, but for now she lacked the capacity to hate. As she had been
released and told to get up and dress herself, as she had pulled up

her torn drawers and fastened her buttons, with the men watching her and commenting, she had felt only shame. And now, far worse, she felt only fear. Since the search, no one had touched her. She had been left here, waiting, for Prince Roditchev. He had been at his club, but he knew of the raid, and he would soon be here. To pull the wings from his captured moth.

She was not without weapons of her own, she kept telling herself. Except that she was sure she could not tell him anything he did not already know about his wife; she could only suppose that everything the princess had done, from the moment they had encountered each other at the station, had been on her husband's orders. She could only threaten to stand up in court and accuse her prosecutor of using his own wife as a spy. That was hardly a weapon.

The policemen stirred and came to attention. Judith's stomach seemed to contract as if a gigantic hand had fastened itself upon her, and she felt sick.

"Up," said the sergeant.

She stood up, wondering why, since they were going to torture her anyway, she did not merely defy them and remain sitting, let them drag her to her feet. But she did not want any of those men ever to touch her again.

Several officers came in, but she recognized Roditchev immediately. He walked at their head, wearing evening dress, and smoking a cigar. "Well?" he demanded.

The sergeant beside her stood to attention. "This girl, your excellency."

Roditchev peered at Judith, then at the sergeant. "This girl? You raided a socialist meeting and have come back with one girl?"

"One of the leaders, your excellency. She held the door while the others escaped."

Judith gazed into the clear blue eyes. They were like the sky in the dead of winter.

"What is your name, child?"

She had her answer ready. "Lenina."

"Your first name?"

"Anna."

"Anna Lenina?" His hand reached out to grip her chin; he turned her head up and then from side to side. "I do not believe you." Still the terrifying smile, the more terrifying because she knew that he was intending to reassure her—for the moment. "But your name is not important, child. I will record you as Anna Lenina if you wish. What I want you to do is write down the true names of everyone who was at your meeting tonight. How many people were there?"

"I do not know," Judith said.

"Well, I will be satisfied with twenty names. Sit down and write those out for me, and I will let you go home to your bed. Do you not wish to leave this place, and go home to your bed?"

Judith gazed at him, and just for a moment felt her resolution begin to slip. How she wished she could have the power of transporting herself. How she wished she had never gone out tonight. How she wished she could be snug in her own bed, knowing that this nightmare was only a nightmare, that it would end when she woke up. But it was not going to end when she woke up. Nor could she put any faith in the governor's suggested promise of immunity for herself if she betrayed her associates. Instead she knew she must force the issue; only then was there the slightest hope of safety.

"I have a defective memory, your excellency," she said. "But you do not need me for information. Why do you not ask your wife?"

The smile faded and the brows drew together; they were the heaviest brows Judith had ever seen. "My wife? Do you know her?"

"I know that she was at the meeting, your excellency."

His face betrayed nothing. But she thought she had made some progress; she could not be sure in which direction. Roditchev glanced from side to side. "Has she been searched?"

"Yes, your excellency," said the sergeant.

"Then clear the room." He glanced at the officers, who were beginning to whisper to each other. "You too, gentlemen. I would speak with this young lady alone."

The men shuffled to the door and closed it behind them. General Prince Roditchev seated himself at the sergeant's desk, his hands clasped in front of him. "Sit down. Repeat what you just said."

"Princess Roditcheva was at our meeting." Judith's heart began to race, and she slowly lowered herself onto the bench. "Did you not send her, your excellency?" Was it possible that the princess had *not* betrayed them? Then what have I done, she wondered?

"If I did send my wife," Roditchev said, "obviously I do not wish it to be shouted to the world. That displeases me, Anna Lenina, or whatever your real name is. That name I now would like you to tell me, together with the names, the real names, of twenty other people who were at that meeting. And I do not wish you to mention my wife's name again. Do you understand me?"

Judith met his gaze. "She was there, your excellency. Her name will head my list. Her name will be the only one on my list."

Roditchev got up. Judith followed his progress with her eyes, and made herself remain sitting. He stood above her. "Do you really suppose you can defy me?"

"I *must* defy you," Judith explained.

Roditchev stared at her for several seconds, then walked to the door and opened it. "Come in here, sergeant," he said.

The sergeant entered and stood at attention.

Roditchev pointed. "Strip that woman," he said. "And tie her to that bench, face down. Show me her ass, sergeant."

Judith's heart pounded. The sergeant was moving toward her. But he could not be allowed to touch her. Not yet. That would be to add humiliation to horror. "I can undress myself, your excellency, if you require it."

Another victory? She was beginning to doubt the quality of her victories now. But she had again surprised him.

"Then do so, child," he said.

Judith stood up. She had never in her life undressed in front of anyone, not even her sister. And after she had undressed they were going to savage her in a way that would make the other policemen's search seem like a slap on the hand. But there was nothing she could do but endure, and endure, and endure, and pray that she would not betray her friends, or worse, her family, for that the governor would now include her family in her crime could not be doubted. Somehow she had to shut these men from her mind, pretend they were not here, that the coming pain would be nothing more than severe toothache.

She drew a long breath, willed herself to move her hands—and heard the door open. It crashed back upon its hinges, and the sudden noise, added to the thought that there would now be someone else in the room, made her gasp and then as quickly release her breath.

"What are *you* doing here?" Roditchev snapped.

"I was told to come," Peter Borodin said. "By Mademoiselle Stein's brother."

No, Judith thought. Oh my God, no. She closed her eyes.

"Mademoiselle Stein?" Roditchev was clearly puzzled.

"That is her name, Sergei." Peter's voice was closer; Judith refused to open her eyes. "What have you done to her?"

"Very little, yet. But she is a socialist agitator. I will have some names from her. If I have to whip her backside raw, I'll have them."

"You disgust me, Roditchev," Peter said. "What crime has she committed? She attended a meeting. A meeting of socialists. My God, what a terrible sin."

"You condone socialism? You condone riots and rebellions?"

"No," Peter said. "Anyone who rebels should be hanged. But socialism—there are many people in this country who wish to discuss change and yet have no intention of employing violence. What *you* are doing is an incitement to hatred. I shall take her home."

"You—you have no authority here," Roditchev said.

"I am on my way to St. Petersburg at this moment," Peter said. "To have an audience with the tsar. I am to be offered a post. Which post I cannot say. But I am to see the tsar."

"I have had telegrams from the tsar," Roditchev said. "Telegrams of congratulations."

"For suppressing rebellion, Prince Roditchev. Not for humiliating young girls."

For a moment there was silence. Judith refused to open her eyes. She did not wish ever to open her eyes again.

"And will you also tell the tsar that your sister was at the meeting?" Roditchev said at last.

"Do you expect me to believe that?"

"It is true enough. This girl has said so."

"And what will *you* do to the princess? Flog her? She tells me that is a favorite pastime of yours."

"What happens between my wife and myself is no concern of yours," Roditchev said.

"When your wife is my sister it is a concern of mine," Peter said. "I will not have it. Now, Sergei, release this young woman to me. You have no evidence against her, beyond the fact that she has attended a meeting. A meeting also attended by your wife and my sister. If you still believe that such a meeting could have discussed sedition or rebellion then you are a blackguard, and I shall report it to the tsar."

Another brief silence, and Judith found that her eyes were open, and that Peter was looking at her. Gradually she was becoming aware that her system was relaxing, her muscles slowly unknotting themselves, the dreadful fear seeping from her mind. Prince Peter was here, like the most shining of avenging knights.

What additional problems would his appearance bring her?

"Of course," Roditchev remarked. "The girl is your mistress. Be sure that I shall also make a report to the tsar."

"You may report to whomever you wish, Sergei. But you'll not again proceed against either Mademoiselle Stein or any member of her family. Understand that, or I shall personally call you to account. Are you ready, Judith?"

"You are using rank to undermine the course of justice," Roditchev protested. "I would be within my rights to have *you* arrested."

"I suggest we discuss the matter later." Peter glanced at the sergeant. "In more privacy. You'll excuse me, Sergei."

He held the door for her. A prince, holding the door for Judith Stein. She stepped through and looked at the officers gathered there. They might have been staring at a ghost. Prince Peter was at her elbow, guiding her down the corridor and then down the steps, while every moment she expected to hear Roditchev's bellow commanding them to be stopped. But she had never known the power of being a prince of Starogan. Instead of being stopped, doors were opened for them, and the coachman was waiting to help her up into the carriage. Only when she was seated on the soft leather cushions, Peter beside her, did she feel she could truly breathe.

"Will you not be in trouble?" she asked. She felt it was necessary to say something before he did.

"Good heavens, no," he said, and gave instructions to the driver.

"I . . . I do not know how to say thank you to someone who has just saved me from death. Or worse."

"Is there a worse thing than losing your life?"

"Oh, yes," she said. "Losing your life is nothing. It is what happens before then."

He nodded. "It is difficult to draw a line with men like Roditchev. When there is a revolt, we expect him to put it down with an iron hand; this is necessary. When there is not a revolt, we must watch him all the time to make sure he is not acting as though there were. It is difficult."

"He is your brother-in-law."

"Yes," Peter said, his voice hard.

She glanced at him and found him looking at her. He smiled,

relieving the anger in his expression. "I have ordered us to be driven to your home. Is that where you wish to go?"

As if life for Judith Stein could ever be that simple again. Yet he had to be answered. "Should I not wish to go to my home?"

"I thought, perhaps, you might wish to wait awhile."

"With you?"

"I would wait with you, if you wished. Your parents were somewhat upset when I left them."

"And will they not continue to be upset until they know I am safe?"

"I think they were less upset to think of your being arrested than to think of your being a socialist. Are you a socialist?"

"Yes," Judith said. "Will you drive me back to police headquarters?"

"Why should I? I am just curious to know why a girl like you, who has a very good life—and could have a better one—would wish to be a socialist."

"If you had known what I was, would you have rescued me?" She had to keep provoking him. It was her only defense.

But he would not be provoked. Another smile. "Yes. I would have rescued you, Judith Stein, if you had been arrested with a bomb in your hand. I have fallen in love with you."

No preamble. No compliments. No hints. Just a bald statement. She had to wait for a few moments to allow her heart to settle down.

"As I think you have guessed," he said gently.

"This is only the third time you have spoken with me," she said.

"What does time have to do with it? One *knows* when one sees the person for whom one has been waiting an entire life." He picked up her hand. "I knew."

"You knew that you wanted to possess my body, Prince Peter."

She could be as frank as he, with equally devastating results. He leaned back against the cushions, away from her.

"Because that is how men love those who cannot be their wives, your excellency," she said. "And I agree with you. Knowing that you wish to possess a woman is something which you should feel instantly, and no doubt continue to feel, until the possession is achieved."

"You are a feminist."

"Should I not be, Prince Peter? I am a female."

He sighed. "A damned aggressive one, if you'll pardon me." He smiled. "But the more interesting for that. And how does a woman love? How do you love?"

"I do not know."

"You have never loved. So then, are you not prepared to give it a try?"

"I must give it more than that, your excellency."

"I would like you to."

"Therefore it must have the sanction of my religion, my family, my conscience. Can you not understand that, your excellency? You would like me to be your mistress. To do that I must entirely cease to be Judith Stein and become instead Prince Borodin's woman. My lord prince, what are you planning to give up for me?"

He gazed at her for several seconds, a slight frown gathering between his eyes. And she waited for his anger.

But it never came. "You are right," he admitted. "I would give up nothing for you. I cannot. Can you not understand, Judith? I am prince of Starogan. I am about to commence a lifetime of service to my tsar and my country. I believe I am entirely qualified, by talent as well as by birth, to perform that service better than anyone else. It is an immense responsibility, and you should know how much there is to be done. I am married to a woman I do not love and can never love. But I must be married to her, remain married to her, because that, too, is part of my responsibilities as prince of Starogan. Yet I need love. I need to love with all of myself, as I love you. And I need to be loved, by the woman I love. I know what I am asking you to give up. I can only say that you will never want for anything, that you will be protected for the rest of your life, and your family as well, and that I will cherish you and love you for the rest of my life as if you were my wife. I can give up nothing for you. But I can invite you to step with me out of the mud and the muck that is common humanity, onto a mountain top of beauty and companionship."

She did not doubt a word of what he said. He would love her for the rest of her life. He was that sort of man. And he would give her a lifetime of fur coats and jewels and silks and satins and carriages waiting for her wherever she went. More important, as his mistress she might even be able to help people, in a way she never could as Judith Stein.

But would she want to? Having taken that one step of raising herself from among them, of putting herself beyond that pale, would she ever wish to think of them again? Or even look into the mirror again?

Peter had been watching her expression. "But like Christ, you deny," he said. "You refuse to be tempted."

Her head turned sharply. "That was unfair."

"And beastly. And blasphemous. I apologize."

"I . . . I have no right to seek a personal happiness when there are so many miserable people in Russia."

"That is childish, if you'll pardon me, Judith. You cannot live for all of them. They certainly would not live for you. If you refuse me now, you are going to throw yourself even more vehemently into the socialist movement. You are going to become a radical. You must, because it will be the only way you can justify to yourself the enormous sacrifice you have made. And then you are going to be arrested again, inevitably. And then, perhaps, I may not be there to rescue you."

"Perhaps?"

"I will always rescue you, Judith, if I can."

"Even when you have your mistress to love?"

He shrugged. "It appears I am not intended to have a woman to love. So you see your decision will have an effect on me, too. I will throw myself even more wholeheartedly into my duties and responsibilities."

"Words," Judith said. "No one knows what is going to happen, to themselves or to anyone else."

"You have an opportunity, now, to know what is going to happen to you. But you will not take it."

"I can't. I can't, I can't, I *can't*." Tears rolled down her cheeks.

Peter felt in his breast pocket and handed her a silk handkerchief. "Here is your house," he said. "Judith, I must go to St. Petersburg tomorrow morning. I shall be there for some time. But I would like your permission to call upon you when I pass through Moscow on my way back to Starogan. May I?"

She dried her cheeks, and gave him back the handkerchief. "I cannot change my mind, your excellency."

"May I call?"

She hesitated. "If you wish."

"Then you may expect me. And Judith, for God's sake, do nothing foolish while I am away."

* * *

"I love you, Ilona Roditcheva. I love you." A servant's plea of love. A *servant*. But even as he had whispered the words he had been taking possession of her, as no man had ever done before.

No man? Ilona, lying on her stomach, sank deeper into the softness of her bed. It was just over two years since George had last held her in his arms. Could she admit to having forgotten him already? That was nonsense. She would never forget George, however often she told herself it was the sensible thing to do. The obvious thing to do. She would never see him again, and to cherish his memory above all others would be to enter a life of self-torture.

But to give herself to another man! She had never given herself to Roditchev; she had been taken. And a servant. And to have enjoyed it. But was it not the most marvelous thing in the world, to have the right to compare two such men? Was there any woman in the world so fortunate?

No other woman Princess Roditcheva should know. And she considered Xenia and Irina to be loose! My God, Ilona Dimitrievna, what have you done?

She pushed herself up in bed and knelt, the covers slowly slipping from her shoulders. Her fingers drove deep into her golden hair, still damp however hard she toweled it.

Michael had been so very gentle, though no more gentle than George. But George had been strangely hesitant, had seemed to hold himself back, knowing that he was doing wrong in the light of his religion, of her upbringing and position, taking refuge in the fact that their marriage would make it all right . . . but perhaps knowing, in his heart, that their marriage was easier dreamed of than accomplished.

She had led him on. She had wanted. She had loved. Oh yes, she had loved, with all the passion of her passionate nature. She craved physical love—the touch of a man who worshipped her—as a drowning man might crave air. There was no use denying it. She wanted to be loved, not savaged. And since George's departure she had known only savagery. It would almost have been easier for her if she could be like her cousin or her sister-in-law, or any of the other fly-by-nights of St. Petersburg society, who craved only sensation, would permit a grope from anyone so long as his was a new face, a new touch. If that had been her craving, she could have found satisfaction long ago.

And yet, not even Xenia or Irina would ever have had sexual intercourse with a servant.

She flopped back down in her bed and buried her face in the pillow. The more fool they. But had she led Michael on? Not intentionally, she was sure. But it had happened, because he had wanted it so very badly, and because she . . . had she also wanted it so very badly? She knew the answer to that question was probably the most important she would ever have to decide. But once it had begun there had been no holding back. Michael had not been hesitant. He had whispered in her ear that she was his eternal dream come true, now lying in his arms. Perhaps the darkness had helped, and her own tumultuous emotions. His hands had wandered everywhere, from her shoulders and her breasts to her knees and even her ankles, as if he were blind—he had been blind in the darkness—and had been imprinting her image on his memory forever.

But then, she reminded herself, Michael Nikolaievich was her oldest friend. Why, had they had the slightest idea of how to go about it, they might well have made love when they were children. And now that she was tied, for the rest of her life, to a monster . . . well, Michael would simply be there, for ever and ever and ever, whenever she wanted him. Whenever she needed him. No, that was not true. He was Peter's valet. She might not see him again for years; Peter and Sergei were not exactly getting along.

She raised her head in dismay and propped her chin on her hands. Peter and Sergei. Like heavy black rain clouds hovering, waiting to drop their burden of misery on her head. But was there anything to fear? After their return to the house, she had undressed in the servants' hall, and Michael had taken her clothes away to be destroyed. But before he had done that he had held her in his arms again. Ilona Roditcheva, naked, in the arms of her servant. She had wanted to stay there forever.

He had taken her clothes and she had crept up to her room and washed off all the mud she could find and rinsed her hair and got into bed, waiting all the while for the sound of Sergei coming home. The sound of disaster. But of course Sergei would be at police headquarters, interrogating people. Sergei would be enjoying himself in his own way. Therefore she could enjoy herself in hers. My God, what an old married woman she had become.

Well then, who else could point a finger at her? The girl, Judith Stein. Oh my God, she thought. Judith had certainly been arrested.

Judith would be screaming her name the length and breadth of the police station, as they . . . Ilona had no idea what they would do to her, or even if they would have to do anything to her. In any event, she had too many problems of her own, to spare much thought for Judith Stein.

Once again she knelt, fingers clawing at her scalp. Should she deny it? Dismiss the whole idea as nonsense, claim the girl was only trying to save her own skin? Yes, she thought, and slowly lay down again. Yes, deny it.

Then what of Judith Stein? Gallant Judith Stein. The girl she had been going to befriend and understand—and help. But Judith Stein was clearly beyond any help now. Judith Stein was bound for Siberian exile, at the very least, after enduring the worst from Roditchev. They would be closer than ever in experience, even as they were separated by thousands of miles. They must fend for themselves.

And she did not have only herself to think of. She had Michael Nikolaievich as well. Were the truth ever to be known, his fate did not bear contemplation. Michael Nikolaievich. She lay down, nestling in her bedclothes. Oh, you are the most rampant whore that ever lived, Ilona Dimitrievna. But he loves you. And he has made you happier than at any moment in more than two years. Michael Nikolaievich. She frowned; Sergei had still not come home, and it was dawn . . . could she not summon him?

What madness. What criminal madness. She had not felt such a lightheaded desire to toss away all convention and caution since the night she had given herself to George. A similar night. Oh, George, George. But at least she now had Michael.

A tap on her door. She turned, heart pounding, rolling over with such violence that she almost fell out of the bed. Desperately she grabbed the covers and pulled them over herself. "Yes?"

"May I come in?" It was Peter.

"Peter?" She sat up. He was fully dressed in his evening clothes and looked tired. "Where have you been? Not at the Steins all night?" My God, the Steins.

"In a manner of speaking," Peter said. "Ilona, I would like you to get up and get dressed, and have your maid pack your clothes. Just enough for a journey. We will send for the heavy things later."

Ilona blinked at him. He was not making sense.

"Please hurry," Peter said. "I would like to catch the early train."

"And I am to accompany you?"

"Yes."

"I do not understand. Sergei will never permit me to leave again so soon."

"What Sergei will or will not permit is irrelevant."

"But he's my husband."

"Not any longer. You are my sister. Now do as I ask."

Ilona pushed the hair from her eyes. "What has happened?" Her heart and her mind were starting to perform all sorts of leaps.

"Let us say that I have learned that everything you said about your husband is true. I can only apologize for inflicting this marriage upon you. Now I intend to make amends. I wish you to accompany me to St. Petersburg, and there I will set the situation before the tsar, and request that your marriage be annulled. There are no children of the union, so there should be no problem. Certainly I am determined that you shall spend not another night beneath this roof."

Ilona discovered that her jaw had slipped open. She closed it. There did not seem to be anything to say. She could only have screamed for joy.

"I realize this is very sudden," Peter said. "I apologize for that also. I only wish you had brought the situation to my attention some time ago. I shudder to think what you must have experienced these last couple of years. It shall not happen again though. Now get dressed."

Ilona found her voice. "But . . . my maid, Catherine, is Sergei's creature. Will I take her with me?"

"You had better. I think you will find that she will be your creature once she does not have Roditchev behind her. In any event, it does not matter. Michael Nikolaievich will be with us, of course, and he is a good fellow. Quite capable of looking after you as well as me, I do assure you. Now hurry."

The door closed, and Ilona felt her back sliding down the cushioned bedstead. Michael Nikolaievich. She was going to St. Petersburg with Michael Nikolaievich. And once she had thought herself the most unfortunate of women.

Ilona Roditcheva laughed.

Tsar Nicholas II got up from his desk, walked to the great windows at the rear of his study, and looked out at the garden, hands clasped behind his back. Prince Peter Borodin glanced at the imperial secretary waiting beside the desk, and received a brief shake of the head. So he remained standing to attention. He wore his full dress uniform as a captain of the Preobraschenski Guards, a glitter of gilt breastplate and freshly pressed white serge. He listened to the sound of laughter and shrill shouts coming from the garden, where the imperial children were at play. It was an intensely happy sound. But the tsar did not look happy. He had not looked happy all morning.

"How delightful they are," Nicholas mused. "How delightful." He turned. "What does one do with a little boy, Prince Borodin, who wishes only to play and enjoy himself, but who must yet be coddled as if he were still a babe? Have you heard anything of our problem?"

"Well, your majesty—"

"Rumors," the tsar said. "And they must remain rumors, prince. It would be no good thing for Russia, for the world, to suspect that my heir may never be completely healthy."

"Surely, your majesty—"

Nicholas sat down. "I am being pessimistic, of course. My doctors assure me that his ailment is but a childish weakness which will pass as he grows to manhood. But, you see, Prince Borodin, I am a pessimist by nature. I think it is probably a better thing for a monarch to be a pessimist striving to be optimistic than the other way around. Do you agree?"

"I think that is a wise observation, your majesty."

Nicholas raised his head. "Do not be a sycophant, Prince Peter. Never a sycophant. Your father and your grandfather spoke their minds, as you came in here this morning, I believe, determined to speak your mind. I have read your statement."

"Then, your majesty. . . ."

Nicholas leaned back. "Do you know where I should be now, Prince Peter? I should be at The Hague. These peace conferences were my idea. How absurd, is it not, that the first European nation to find itself at war after I had convened the Conference should be my own? But I should be there. Upon conferences such as this depends the future of the entire world. Have you read Bloch?"

"I'm afraid not, your majesty."

"Read him, Prince Peter. He has written an apocalyptic vision of what will happen when next there is a war between European nations. It is terrifying. There must never be another war between major nations. The concept is too horrible. I should be there. But I must be here. I am dissolving the Duma."

"Your majesty?"

"It has not been a success. I took the decision this morning."

"But your majesty, your word—"

"Do not misunderstand me, Prince Peter. I promised my people a Duma, and a Duma they shall continue to have, but clearly we made a mistake about suffrage. You cannot give landless peasants the vote. That is absurdity. They have no stake in the country, or the future of the country. I have considered this matter for a very long time. I have consulted. The next Duma will be elected on a restricted suffrage. Landowners and men in responsible positions. Of course the people will not like it. There will be strikes and riots. The socialists will have a field day. So they must be suppressed. Not violently—just suppressed, until the country at large understands that it is their own best interests I have in mind. But it is an awesome task I have set myself—would you not agree, Prince Peter—to give my country prosperity and even liberalism, and yet not permit license."

"Indeed it is, your majesty."

"But I would not have gone to The Hague in any event," the tsar said. "How can I leave my son? Even with Father Gregory here, how can I leave my son?"

"Father Gregory, your majesty?"

Nicholas waved his hands. "A starets. But one of exceptional healing powers. A remarkable man." He leaned forward and shuffled the papers on his desk. "You did not come here to talk about my domestic problems. It is very unusual for a woman to seek a divorce from her husband. And on what grounds? That her husband is too zealous an advocate of the cause of justice?"

"I appended that, your majesty, as an example of what my sister has had to suffer."

"Should a man not beat his wife?" The tsar gave a wry smile. Everyone in the empire knew he was securely under the thumb of the tsarina. "It is an old established custom, especially in Russia. You tread upon dangerous ground here, Prince Peter, in disturbing the sanctity of the marriage bed."

"Your majesty, I—"

"And even more dangerous ground in interfering with the processes of justice. I have here a report from Prince Roditchev as well. You will know what it contains."

"Your majesty, all the people of Russia, even Jews and socialists, are entitled to be treated as human beings, as subjects of yourself."

The tsar gazed at him for some seconds. "Admirably said," he remarked at last. "But weakened when the Jew and socialist you would defend is of so great an interest to you."

"The girl is not my mistress, your majesty. Nor has she ever been."

"Nor will she ever be?"

"That I cannot say, your majesty. I will not lie to you. I know her. She is a friend of my sister's, and she is attractive and educated and cultured. But that is of less importance than the fact that she had broken no law in attending a meeting. Prince Roditchev had no proof that anything was discussed beyond, perhaps, a desire to broaden the functions of the Duma. Surely, your majesty, groups of your subjects may get together from time to time and discuss changes they would like to see. The ultimate decision as to those changes remains in your hands. And surely nothing can transcend the rule of law."

"There are times, Prince Borodin, when you sound like a socialist yourself. And this business of Princess Roditcheva also having been at the meeting—I do not understand that at all. But no matter. I have considered the situation." The tsar paused, and Peter understood that he had discussed the matter with his wife. "And we feel that perhaps your sister has been exposed to more than her rank allows. There is no possibility that Princess Roditcheva is pregnant?"

"None, your majesty."

"Yes, well, the lack of children eases the matter, as I'm sure you understand. However, we feel that it would be premature to end a marriage that is so full of promise, so obviously good for the empire. Thus we are prepared to permit a separation for a period, shall we say, of six months. This would avoid the unpleasantness of a divorce, and especially one in which there is the messy business of the wife— your sister, Prince Peter—having to testify as to physical cruelty. No, no, that would not do at all. Let us give both parties time to consider the matter. However, during this period, Prince Peter, your sister will conduct herself with the utmost propriety. Is that understood?"

"Of course, your majesty."

"And you, Prince Peter, will refrain from championing causes which are by their very nature inimicable to good government. Am I understood?"

"Yes, your majesty."

"Good," said Tsar Nicholas. "Good. No doubt you will also be able to restrain the princess's interest in social change. Well then, let us sit down now and discuss the real purpose of your visit to St. Petersburg—an appointment worthy of your rank and abilities. Sit down, Prince Peter. Sit down."

"My dear," remarked Princess Irina Borodina. "What a scandal. All St. Petersburg will be ringing with it by tomorrow. But tell me, my dear Ilona, did Sergei Pavlovich not make a fuss?"

"There was the most terrible scene," Ilona confessed.

"Wouldn't he have been within his rights to prevent your leaving by force?"

Ilona shrugged. "I suppose so. But he couldn't really, not with Peter there."

"What a forceful fellow this husband of mine seems to be," Irina said reflectively. "I wish he would show it more often." She leaned closer to her sister-in-law, lowering her voice. "You never mentioned anything to Sergei about Father Gregory?"

"Of course I didn't."

"Or to Peter?"

"No. Irina, you're not still seeing that man?" As if she didn't already know the answer.

"Well," Irina fanned herself, "there can be no doubt that he possesses the most remarkable powers."

"Are you pregnant?"

"I can hardly be, my dear, seeing that today is the first time I have seen Peter since Easter. But I have no doubt that I soon shall be. And you?"

Ilona flushed. "Sergei and I have not been terribly close the last few months. And now . . . but what does he do? Or make you do?"

"There you have it," Irina said. "Father Gregory seldom does anything, although he does like to touch us. But he likes us to bathe him."

"To . . . ?" Ilona's jaw dropped.

"That is his dearest pleasure," Irina said dreamily. "He likes to be bathed by about four ladies. It is quite indescribable, the feelings it arouses."

"I can believe that," Ilona said. "My God. You mean, you. . . ."

"Oh, he has to be touched. And more than touched. Because

when we do that, you see, we are committing a great sin, and afterwards he can pray for our souls, and for our desires as well."

"And you *believe* that?"

Irina smiled at her. "Without Father Gregory, I do believe I should go mad with boredom, my dear. Will you not come to tea with us this afternoon? After all, now you are a woman on your own, and it will do you good. I know that Father Gregory will be delighted to see you again. He was very upset when you walked out that day."

"Did you undress for him then?"

"Of course I did. And sat on his lap. I told you, I can't describe what it was like. I would have to be a poet. It's . . . well . . . have you ever swum naked?"

"Yes."

"Well then, only more so. You know, the utter relaxation of it. The *abandon*. Because you know you are being very, very wicked, and yet you know that it is all right, that he is taking the sin on his shoulders, that you can just enjoy it. Oh, how you can enjoy it."

Ilona stared at her in amazement; Irina's eyes were half shut, and her voice had dropped to little more than a whisper. And yet, she reflected, who am I to criticize? Would I not stand, and probably look, exactly like that, if I dared to describe my feelings when I am with Michael Nikolaievich? And if I also know that I am committing a sin, I do not even have the satisfaction of feeling that I am being absolved for it. And I do not care.

Irina seemed to wake up. "I hear Peter," she said brightly. "You are about to learn your fate."

Ilona stood up and turned to face the door. It had not really occurred to her before that the tsar might insist she return to Roditchev. He could not possibly ask her to do that. She would rather commit suicide.

Once she had thought she would rather go to a convent. But now, having held Michael in her arms, having discovered that George Hayman was not the only man in the world who could give her moments of happiness, how could she go back to Roditchev?

The footman opened the double doors and Peter entered the drawing room. His face was as serious as ever, but he was clearly elated. "Irina, my darling." He held out his hands, and Irina hastily got up and ran to him, to be kissed on each cheek. "I am appointed aide-de-camp to the Grand Duke Michael."

"Grand Duke Michael?" Irina cried, leaning away from him. "But he is governor general of Poland."

"That is correct, my sweet. We shall make our home in Warsaw."

"Warsaw?" Her voice rose higher.

"Yes. Well, not immediately. His majesty understands that I will have a great deal to do, both at Starogan and in, well, my domestic affairs." He glanced at Ilona. "We take up our position in the new year. That will give me six months to arrange things down at Starogan, and install a steward to look after the estate while I am away. You had better come down with me, Irina. Yes, that will be an excellent idea, because Ilona is returning to Starogan also. You will be company for each other."

"Starogan?" It was Ilona's turn to cry out.

"Yes. You will have to live there for the time being. His majesty refused to countenance the idea of a divorce. But he feels that a short separation will have the desired effect. He has promised to speak with Roditchev. It is all that we could have hoped for. When you return to him he will be a perfect gentleman."

Oh God, Ilona thought. I am to go back. It does not matter when, only that it is going to happen. But at least I am being given a few months in Starogan, and with Michael, before we are separated forever. With Irina cluttering up the place?

"I have never heard anything so ridiculous in my life," Irina declared. "I have no desire to live in Warsaw. I certainly have no desire to spend the rest of the summer down in Starogan. I have no intention of leaving St. Petersburg. Anyway, think how lonely Tattie would be without me to take her out to tea whenever she has an exeat?"

Ilona, brooding on her own misfortunes, half turned her head as a monstrous suspicion suddenly flickered across her mind. But it was too disgusting to contemplate. Not even Irina would dare risk anything like that.

Peter was glaring at his wife, who was glaring at him.

"You *must* come to Warsaw," Peter said. "As aide-de-camp to the governor general I will have to do a great deal of entertaining, and I will need you."

"All right," Irina said. "So I have to go to Warsaw. My God, the end of the world. But at least let me spend the rest of the summer here. Please, Peter. I'll join you for Christmas, I promise."

Peter hesitated. He glanced at Ilona, then shrugged. "Oh, very well. I'm afraid you are going to find life a trifle boring, Ilona. But you do understand that I could not possibly leave *you* in St. Petersburg, under the circumstances. And I will see about bringing Tattie along."

"I do understand, Peter," Ilona agreed. "And I shall be happy to return to Starogan. I could never be bored."

She had really taken the news awfully well, Peter reflected, as he gazed out the window of the first-class smoking carriage, the fields beginning to give way to houses at the outskirts of Moscow.

But then, she had not really had a great deal to hope for. She had never supposed it would be possible to obtain a divorce from her husband on the grounds of his ill-treatment, and had been prepared to accept the fate forced upon her to the best of her ability. Perhaps, Peter thought ruefully, I acted hastily in taking her away at all. It was the sight of Judith Stein starting to undress herself so that she could be whipped, the thought that his own sister might be forced to suffer such humiliation and such pain, which had made him see red. He had very nearly challenged Roditchev, and that would have been the disaster to end all disasters, with both of them disgraced if not charged with attempted murder.

The fact was, he supposed, Ilona had been born under an unlucky star. Having been granted so much beauty by a benign providence, it was really too much to hope that she would also be granted happiness. He did not regret the quarrel over Hayman. Had she not been besotted with the fellow, and confused by the tragedy of Port Arthur and the even greater tragedy of her father's death, she would herself have understood that for a Borodin to marry an American was quite impossible. Perhaps Roditchev had been a hasty choice, but the truth of the matter was that there were probably faults on both sides. Ilona could be the most uncooperative woman. He certainly would not like to be married to her. So undoubtedly she had annoyed Roditchev and discovered to her grief that she was antagonizing the wrong man. Probably, Peter thought, everything will happen for the best, as it always does. The tsar would have a word with the prince, and he and Ilona would be able to resume their marriage under much better circumstances.

And for the time being, she would have a six months' vacation in Starogan. She was clearly delighted about that. So delighted that she had even, apparently, forgiven Michael Nikolaievich for the part he had played in preventing her silly elopement two years ago. It really was most gratifying to see how friendly they were once again, just as they had been as children. All for the best.

And in his affairs, too, he thought, with some satisfaction. An appointment as aide-de-camp to the tsar's brother was a far better start to a career than being sent as provincial governor to some outpost of the empire. Warsaw was the very hub of the continent; the French and the Germans were constantly bickering, Austria was glaring at the Balkans like a hungry alligator, and Russian interests needed to be reestablished as the major consideration in Europe. He knew that even Irina would like it, once she got to know it. Irina, for all her sophistication, was really very naive in considering St. Petersburg the only city on earth.

Irina. It really was amazing how things resolved themselves. Only a week ago he would have been prepared to write off his own marriage as another too hasty mistake. But during the three days he had spent in St. Petersburg, except for her pointblank refusal to return to Starogan, no woman could have been more loving. Perhaps she had missed him after all. Certainly she seemed to find much more pleasure in his caress, actually seemed to want him to touch her body. And Irina had a most splendidly voluptuous body, made to be touched.

So even that was going to turn out well. With a wife like Irina, did a man really need a mistress? Not for a while, at least. And besides, although the tsar had not mentioned the matter again, he had dropped the heaviest of hints. Russian princes did not have liaisons with Jewish agitators. It had been the maddest thing he had ever considered, a wild impulse born out of his marital misery. And she had refused him. That was the most amazing thing of all. He had nothing to reproach himself with. If he had embarrassed her, he had equally embarrassed himself by intervening on her behalf, saving her from an unimaginable fate. She could ask no more of him. It was time to start thinking of himself, of his future.

It wasn't as if she had been prepared to say yes. He had supposed she might, when he left Moscow. He had thought that he would be able to break her down, make her see what a magnificent life he was offering her. But was she—and the embarrassment of the tsar's disapproval—really worth it?

The train was slowing, and Michael Nikolaievich was standing in the doorway. Being the prince's valet had done wonders for Michael.

In his frock coat and silk hat he looked almost a gentleman, and he had gained confidence as well. In fact, he was gaining confidence all the time; Peter had noticed quite a change in him just over the past week.

"We are coming into Moscow, your excellency," Michael said. "Shall I summon the porters?"

"Why?" Peter asked.

"Your excellency gave me to understand that we would be stopping off for a day or so on the way back," Michael said patiently.

"Did I?" Peter asked. "Well, I have changed my mind. I am sure Princess Roditcheva has no desire to stop off. No, no, Michael Nikolaievich, we shall remain on the train."

Michael bowed and withdrew. Peter lit another cigar and looked out of the window at the houses. A mad impulse. That was all it had been.

Six months in Starogan. Six whole, glorious months in the most beautiful place on earth. Ilona was not prepared to worry about the new year. Six months was a long time. Anything could happen by Christmas. And if she did indeed have to return to Roditchev, well then, she would at least have these six months to look back upon.

She had been afraid, in the beginning, that even after two years she might find the memories too painful. She had been here last as a virtual prisoner, and immediately before that had been George. And in this respect her apprehensions were correct. Whenever a door opened behind her, she turned, expecting to see that red hunting jacket, that smiling face. At the table she kept looking at Tattie sitting opposite her, and remembered George sitting there, looking at her. And at night . . . but at night there was Michael. As he slept in the house, their meetings were easily managed; no one roamed the corridors at Starogan after midnight. They could spend almost every night together, almost as she had done with George.

Would he ever forgive her, if he knew? Could he? Could he ever understand what she needed, that without Michael she would go mad —or worse, she supposed, actually become a socialist or an anarchist or something like that. And Michael was a magnificent lover. He sought only to please her, apparently found all his own pleasure in her sighs and her climaxes, wished only to be allowed to stroke that velvet flesh, touch the flowing yellow silk of her hair, be with her. Which was all she wanted from him. They had nothing to talk about, because there was nothing they dared talk about. They had no past, and they had no future. They had six months. She would make those six months the happiest she had ever known, by living only for the day.

But summer in Starogan would have brought joys even without Michael. She had forgotten that there could be such peace. She had forgotten that there were still places in Russia where one could walk down the village street and see nothing but smiling faces; no trace of the revolution had ever reached Starogan. She had forgotten the pleasures of strolling through the apple orchards or riding her favorite horse through the farm and across the rolling pastures beyond. Even the growing modernity of the place had not really changed its character. Peter was a determined modernist; he had installed electric lights powered by a generator in the cellar; instead of horses drawing the plows he had steam-driven tractors, and now he drove to and from the village in a fifty-horsepower Rolls-Royce, especially imported from England. Mama and Grandmama preferred the carriage, but Ilona delighted to wrap herself in a long chiffon scarf, hide her eyes behind goggles, tuck her hair into a leather cap, and sit beside him as he careered along at speeds of up to thirty miles an hour, leaving a plume of yellow dust to mark his progress. Sometimes they even drove down to Sevastopol and spent the night in an hotel. Here was freedom, at last. True freedom.

Once again she returned to her dream, that perhaps Roditchev might die and leave her that freedom.

Even the annual summer inundation by the Igor Borodins could not temper her happiness. Aunt Anna might roll her eyes and make loud asides about these *modern* women who preferred to live apart from their husbands, but she knew none of the reasons which had caused Ilona to leave Moscow, and fish as she might, no one was going to tell her. And if Xenia might look the most bored young woman on earth, Ilona enjoyed the pleasure of being the only one there who knew why, and Xenia was certainly not going to antagonize her cousin, who could bring disaster down about her ears with only a word to her mother. Uncle Igor even seemed to have become reconciled to the fact that Peter was prince of Starogan, and Tigran was good-humored if slightly pessimistic. He made the mistake of broaching the subject of George to her, remarking that he had liked the fellow and that it had been a damned shame the way things had gone. But she indicated that she preferred not to discuss the matter, and Tigran was far too much of a gentleman to say anything he thought might offend.

The only discordant elements were Viktor, Catherine Ivanovna and Tattie. Poor Viktor was just being his usual self, as Ilona well knew. Whether he actually discussed socialism with his friends at the university, or whether he was only repeating what he had read in the newspapers, he obviously wished to talk about it only in the hope, invariably fulfilled, of annoying his father. But Ilona did not want even to hear the word. After all her resolutions that she would never slip into the moral trough that Xenia shared with Irina, that she would find her salvation in understanding and helping the people her husband had to rule, she found her happiness with Michael Nikolaievich. To someone like Judith Stein, that was probably blasphemy. How could one person's happiness stand against the well-being of an entire people?

But surely, Ilona argued to herself, if everyone in the world concentrated on being happy, then the world would have to be a happy place, and there would be no need for revolutions and secret meetings. To which Judith would undoubtedly reply, because only people like you, my dear princess, can possibly find happiness at the snap of the fingers; the rest can find only misery. To which Ilona would reply, in her private conversations, oh, shut up, I do not really wish to discuss it; there is nothing *I* can do about it anyway. But I didn't betray you. Any trouble you got into was through some fault of your own.

So she said to Viktor, whenever he began, "Oh, shut up, do. I don't wish to hear about it. You sit there and talk about revolution—I was *in* the revolution, in Moscow, and it was a dreadful affair. You should experience revolution before you start talking about it."

When she spoke like that, even Uncle Igor nodded at her in approval.

Catherine Ivanovna was a constant reminder that her future was in Moscow and would eventually have to be faced. Ilona, indeed, debated with herself whether she dared send the girl back. But since it appeared Ilona really would have to return to Roditchev, Catherine could not possibly be made into an enemy. Of course she remained a spy; there could be no doubt about that. But Ilona had no fears; Michael visited her after midnight, and she removed her nightgown before greeting him, donning it again after he left, and after she had washed herself most carefully. There were no telltale crushings of material, no telltale scents to give her away. And during the day she was the model of propriety, while Michael, to their mutual agreement, spent whatever spare time he had in the company of Zoe Geller, discussing the preparations for their wedding, which would take place just before Christmas, a date Ilona had personally selected, as it was immediately before she had to return to Moscow. So Catherine could report nothing more serious than that her mistress was happy in Starogan, and Ilona did not mind the whole world knowing that.

Tattie, however, was a serious problem. She presented the same world-weary appearance as Xenia, and indeed seemed to come to life only in Xenia's company. They were constantly exchanging secret smiles and knowing glances, yet Xenia, ten years the elder, always professed to be utterly bored by Tattie's company. And when she was in St. Petersburg, Tattie undoubtedly was extracted from her convent by Irina for tea on every possible occasion. But what action should Ilona take? To reveal what she knew about Rasputin and his coterie would cause an explosion which might well blow the family right apart. So Tattie might take off all her clothes for the starets and then bathe him—but was that more horrible than herself being at the mercy of Roditchev? Rasputin apparently never had intercourse with any of his disciples, so there was no risk of the loss of her virginity. For all Ilona knew, Tattie was being well-prepared for whatever other monster she herself would eventually have to marry.

Ilona was discovering that she was becoming adept at adjusting her conscience in favor of what she wished to do. She was living her own life. And in her private search for happiness, she was certainly in no position to cast stones.

But it was distressing to see Tattie, always so bubblingly vivacious, decline into a disinterested young woman. She never played any of her own compositions any more, seldom even practiced the piano. She mooned, clearly waiting for September. It was quite a relief when Tattie and Igor's family finally had to depart for the station and the train back to St. Petersburg. Now she would really be alone, Ilona thought, with only Mama and Grandmama and Peter—and Michael Nikolaievich. And there were still three months of her separation to go. The best three months.

They kissed good-bye on the front porch, and squeezed into the carriages for the drive to the station, while Viktor and Tigran went with Peter in the Rolls. The dust clouded into the still air, and

Grandmama snuffled into her handkerchief. But Mama looked oddly distracted. Had she also observed the change in Tattie?

"Ilona," Olga Borodina said, "I wonder if I could have a word with you? Will you come upstairs?"

She *has* noticed, Ilona thought. Good lord. What am I to say when she starts asking questions? She had never been any good at lying to her mother.

"Close the door, Ilona Dimitrievna," Olga said. "And sit down." But she, remarkably, remained standing.

Ilona sat down.

"I had meant to speak with you before," Olga said, "but not with the rest of the family here. How are you feeling?"

"Me? I feel fine," Ilona said. Whatever was she thinking about?

"Hmm. Have you noticed nothing odd these past couple of months?"

"Odd?"

"Catherine Ivanovna tells me you have not menstruated for two months, my dear Ilona. You must have noticed that."

Ilona stared at her. She had supposed it was because she had been so happy.

"Don't you understand, you silly girl?" Olga said, a trifle sharply. "You are pregnant."

Ilona sat very still. She was looking at her mother, but she no longer saw her. She could only think, oh my God.

"There is no need to look quite so distressed," Olga Borodina pointed out. "I think it is probably a very good thing. Just what you and dear Sergei Pavlovich need. But under the circumstances I think it is absurd for you to live apart any longer. With your permission I will ask Peter to telephone Sergei and ask him to come down here, at which time we must hope this entire scandal will be resolved."

Ilona made herself focus. You don't understand, she thought. My God, you don't understand. It isn't Sergei's child. It can't be. Or it could *just* be, if it had happened the very last time I slept with him. But after two years, that was absurd. The child was Michael's. It had to be. Michael's child. Ilona Dimitrievna was to be a mother at last— by her brother's valet.

"Do you not agree that would be the best thing?" Olga inquired gently.

Ilona raised her head. No, she wanted to shout. No. Sergei is not the father. Let me stay here and be a mother, with my lover there to see me and know me and love me.

But that would be a disaster for them both. A Borodin might divorce her husband on the grounds of cruelty and manage to survive socially. But if she divorced her husband—or was divorced by her husband—after bearing an illegitimate child, she had no course but to disappear forever into the limbo of unwanted whispers. And once the child was known to be illegitimate, intolerable pressure would be brought to bear on her to name the father; what that would mean for Michael did not bear consideration.

Yet she wanted the child. How she wanted the child. If all summer she had been knowingly deluding herself that it was possible for her to return to Roditchev and live with him and even be happy simply by looking over her shoulder, now at last she possessed something tangible to live for. How she wished George had made her pregnant. No, that was foolish. They would simply have taken the baby away and locked her up in a convent. But now . . . should Michael be told? Of course he must be told. He must know that between them they possessed a secret which could never be divulged, but which was *theirs* for the rest of their lives.

Ilona felt a sudden overwhelming sense of responsibility, almost of ecstasy. She had counted her life ruined from the day Peter returned from the Japanese prison camp. She had done nothing more than exist for nearly two years, until Michael had so strangely come back to her. And then that night of the raided meeting she had committed the greatest sin of her life, far greater in the eyes of her society than giving herself to George. In Moscow she had betrayed her family and her class and the very structure of the nation—and she had loved it, had wanted to shout it from the rooftops, her defiance as much as her happiness. Yet she had never doubted for a moment that eventually she would have to pay for it. Instead, she was being rewarded. God had after all forgiven her. She was to have the child she had always desired, and it was not even to be Sergei's. Her life would at last take on some meaning, double meaning, triple meaning, because of her secret. And the child would be hers, all hers, to raise against Sergei and all that he stood for.

She felt her eyes fill with tears as she smiled at her mother. "Yes, Mama," she said. "I think that would be best."

It was necessary to endure the congratulations of Grandmama and Peter. Marie Borodina's eyes gleamed as she kissed her granddaughter on both cheeks. "My dear child," she said. "My dear, dear child. I am so happy for you. So very happy. I have always said that everything always turns out for the best. Dear Sergei is going to be absolutely delighted."

"So will her majesty," Olga said proudly. "She always said this match would turn out well."

"Yes," Peter said. "I am sure that Sergei will be delighted." He smiled at her as he kissed her on the cheek. "It makes me look something of a fool, but I am glad for it."

"Never a fool, Peter," she said. "I am grateful for your intervention, and for the tsar's help. I will tell him so next time we meet."

"Which may well be soon, now that you are to be reconciled with Sergei. Believe me, Ilona Dimitrievna, you have made me the happiest brother in the world. If only Irina would now follow your example, I should be the happiest man in the world."

Irina. Rasputin. Could her visit to Rasputin really have had this effect? She had done nothing he had commanded. She had not submitted to him. But perhaps . . . no, that was absurd. Besides, Irina had not become pregnant.

Midnight, and Michael. They sat together on the edge of her bed, and he said not a word until she had finished speaking. Then he very gently kissed her on the lips. But then, all his kisses were gentle.

"You are mine now," he said. "Mine in a way you can never be another's. Are you pleased about that, Ilona Dimitrievna?"

"It is what I always hoped for," she said.

"Then you cannot want to return to that monster Roditchev."

How his attitudes had changed. She could not imagine the Michael of their childhood referring to any member of the aristocracy by just a name.

"I do not want to return to Prince Roditchev, Michael," she said. "But as I must, I am at least happy that I can return in favorable circumstances."

"Do you suppose he will mistake the child for his?"

"Of course he will. It would never occur to a man like Sergei that there could be any other explanation." She ruffled his hair. "Your coloring is not so different, and if the features are neither Borodin nor Roditchev, well then, they will have to belong to some throwback. Believe me, he will never doubt it for an instant. And besides," she smiled, "I will tell him that it is his."

"And love him tenderly to make sure he believes you."

Ilona frowned at him. It was the first time he had ever spoken to her with any sharpness.

"I have to go to bed with my husband, Michael, from time to time," she said.

"Or he will beat you. But perhaps you enjoy being beaten."

"Now you are being silly," she said. "This should be a joyous occasion for both of us. I am carrying your child. Our love has been blessed by God. Our sins have been forgiven."

"God?" he demanded. "Sins? In what way have we sinned? Do we have to be blessed by God because I am the son of a serf and you are the daughter of a prince?"

"We have committed adultery. That is a serious crime."

"I do not believe adultery is a crime," he said. "And neither do you, in your heart. You cannot."

She flushed. She should have remembered he would know all about her affair with George, even though they had never discussed it. The servants must all know.

"I do not know what I believe," she said. "I only know that we have loved illegally, and that our love has been blessed. I am sorry to be returning to Moscow three months early, but we could no longer lie together with me pregnant, in any event."

"Why not?"

"Because . . . well, we might hurt the baby. Besides, I'm not sure I would wish to."

"So our love must come to a stop, here and now."

"Of course not. We will meet again."

"When, do you suppose?"

"Well. . . ."

He held her shoulders. "If you loved me, if you believed in our love, you would defy these princes and counts that surround us. You would tell your brother the truth, tell him to make Roditchev divorce you."

"So that I could marry you?"

It was his turn to flush, but he would not lower his eyes. "Is that so unthinkable?"

"It is utterly absurd. On every count. What do you suppose would happen to you were either Peter or Sergei to know the truth? You are the son of a serf, as you have just reminded me. George Hayman is the son of a millionaire, but they talked of imprisoning him, of having him beaten up by the guards. What do you think they would do to you?"

"And of course," Michael said, "as I am the son of a serf you could not bear to live with me. Sleep with me, yes, live with me, no. I might not be able to look after you as a princess should be looked after."

Ilona lay down in the bed, tucking her feet beneath the covers. "You are determined to quarrel, Michael Nikolaievich. But I do not wish to quarrel with anyone tonight, least of all with you. Come to see me tomorrow, when you are in a better humor."

Michael stood up. "I am dismissed," he said bitterly. "By my mistress."

"Yes," Ilona said. "If that is how you wish to put it. You are dismissed. Come and see me tomorrow night. If you wish to."

The trouble with you, Michael Nej, Michael reminded himself, is that you are a dreamer. Last summer your dream suddenly came true, and you began to believe in dreams. But all dreams have awakenings.

He had always known Ilona Dimitrievna for what she was, certainly since that night in Port Arthur. His mistake had been in assuming, hoping, that throughout her life she had been looking for something, and that suddenly, mysteriously, unbelievably, she had found what she wanted in him. Unbelievably was the word. Because she had not been looking for any one person. She craved the romantic excitement of physical love, and when that love also had to be illicit, the romantic excitement was only heightened. Why, he presumed, the one man in all the world she could never love, even supposing he were a Greek god, would be her husband. Therefore he was well out of it, should be grateful that his dream had been brought to an early awakening.

But she carried his child. And more than that. She carried his love. When he thought of those long white legs, that pouting belly, those heavy breasts, and above all, that silky hair, whether yellow on her head or brown on her groin, he wanted to weep, to lie on the floor and tear his own hair, at the thought that it could never again be his. That was certain, now, because his foolish pride had kept him from visiting her room again, and this morning when she had said goodbye to the servants she had merely swept by him with a haughty look. Princess Roditcheva was angry.

Ivan was polishing boots on the floor at the foot of his chair. Ivan had not progressed at all from his boyhood occupations in Port Arthur. He never would, Michael supposed. He had been tried as a footman, but he was clumsy and his fingernails were always dirty. Alexei Alexandrovich had not approved. So it was back to the job he knew best and apparently liked best.

"Well," he remarked, spitting on the boot and regarding it for a moment before rubbing with sudden energy. "I am glad they are gone. Not because of Ilona. No, no. She grows more lovely with every day. But for that Catherine. My God, what a shrew. I don't suppose you have heard what she has been saying?"

"I am not interested in Catherine Ivanovna," Michael remarked. Indeed, he had spent a good deal of the summer avoiding her; she made him uneasy.

"Well," Ivan said. "Catherine is saying that she very much doubts the child can be Prince Roditchev's."

"What?" Michael frowned at him. "Whatever are you talking about?"

"What she is talking about," Ivan said, patiently and logically.

"I doubt she knows anything about her mistress, really."

"Oh, come now," Ivan said. "She is her maid. Just as you are Prince Peter's valet. You know all about Prince Peter. About his love affairs."

"He doesn't have any."

"But if he did, you'd know about them. Anyway, this Catherine claims to know all about Ilona. And she says she wouldn't be at all surprised if this baby Ilona is going to have isn't Prince Roditchev's. What do you think about that?"

Michael frowned at him. He was beginning to feel sick. "You mean Ilona has ano . . . had a lover?"

"Now there's the strange thing," Ivan said. "Catherine Ivanovna wouldn't say. That's odd, eh? She talks about everything else. But it would be a bold man to cuckold Prince Roditchev, eh? Have you heard how he carries on in Moscow? You remember the rebellion two years ago? He blew them apart with cannon. And those he captured, did you hear what he did to them?"

"Yes," Michael said, and got up to stand at the scullery window and look out at the apple orchard.

"He held them down and put broken glass up their backsides," Ivan said.

"Oh, shut up," Michael snapped. "Those are just rumors. No one who wasn't there could know what he did to them." But Ilona had told him what he did to her. The very thought made his blood boil. Even Prince Peter had been heard to refer to him as a monster.

And now . . . no wonder Ilona had been terrified to name the father of her child. And he had been angry. How he wished he had gone back to her room, at least once. Baby or no baby, he knew she would have let him love her. She didn't know how to say no.

But where did that leave him, if Catherine Ivanovna knew? Or even suspected?

"It must be wonderful," Ivan said dreamily, "to have such power. To look at someone, and be able to say, I am going to do whatever I feel like to you, and there is nothing you can do about it, because you are in my power. Wouldn't it be marvelous to be able to say that to Ilona?"

"You are a dirty-minded little rat," Michael said, and boxed his ears, sending Ivan's glasses spinning into the corner. But hitting Ivan was no answer. He went outside, hands deep in his pockets, and brooded as he walked among the apple trees. A good deal of what Ivan said made sense. It would be marvelous to have that much power, not to torture people, but to be able to force Roditchev to divorce Ilona, and marry her himself, and bring up his own child as he wished. More dreams. Some people were born to power, and others, the majority, to obey. At least in Russia. He looked up into an apple tree, heavy with fruit which would soon come tumbling down. Society had been like that in other countries—in France, for example—and it had changed. The people had made it change. But that man who had spoken at the Moscow meeting had been against revolution. He looked forward to a gradual development of liberty. The silly fool. Only a few days after his speech the tsar dissolved the Duma, and decreed that the next one would be elected by property owners only. That was a step backwards, and the tsar could make as many steps backwards as he chose.

Or as his wife chose, as the joke went.

My God, he thought, you are thinking like a socialist. No, not even a socialist, but a radical. My God. But where in Moscow he had hated the very idea of revolution because it would upset his privileged position, he now realized how wrong he had been. A man of brains and courage would always find a privileged position. The important thing was that a revolution could, would, give him Ilona.

More dreams. How could the valet of the prince of Starogan spark a revolution? There was no one in Starogan who wanted to revolt against anything, except himself.

He turned to look back at the house when he heard the sound of the car engine. Prince Peter was returning from the station; Ilona was on the train, on her way to Moscow, to convince her husband that the child was his. And Ilona could convince anyone of anything, merely by wrapping those long white legs around her victim. And Roditchev would, as ever, have the best of all worlds, pretty girls like Judith Stein to torture when he chose, and the most beautiful woman in Russia to love. In Moscow.

Michael realized he was weeping, tears of sheer anger and frustration. In Moscow, the people had revolted once, and surely hated enough to revolt again. He thought he would settle for another revolt, even if it were no more successful than the last, if it could only bring him the opportunity to kill Roditchev and regain possession of Ilona, for just a single night.

In Moscow. If he dared.

He dried his tears and went into the house. Peter was downstairs talking with his mother and grandmother, but as Michael had anticipated, soon enough the bell rang from his master's bedchamber.

"I shall be riding this afternoon, Michael Nikolaievich," Peter said, frowning at his embryonic mustache; he would never need to shave his chin more than every other day.

"Yes, your excellency." Michael drew a deep breath. "Your excellency, I would like to leave Starogan."

"We shall be leaving Starogan in January," Peter said, still stroking the mustache gently. "To go to Warsaw."

"What I meant, your excellency, was that I would like to give up service." Michael was amazed by the evenness of his voice.

At last Peter turned from the mirror. "What?"

"I . . ." he fumbled, but would not let his resolution slip. "I would like to go, your excellency. To . . . to see something of Russia."

"Are you mad?"

Michael waited.

"You cannot just give up your position like that."

"It is not illegal, your excellency."

"Of course it isn't illegal, Michael. It just isn't done. The Nejs have always lived at Starogan, and worked for the Borodins. It is quite unheard of."

"There will still be Nejs at Starogan, your excellency, working for the Borodins."

"Do you suppose your father will approve? And what of your betrothed? Are you meaning to take her with you? You're not even married yet."

"I am not going to marry Zoe Geller," Michael said, and clutched at the straw of reason that presented. "I have realized, your excellency, that I do not love her. Therefore, I cannot stay here."

"What nonsense. You don't have to love a girl to marry her, Michael. You are far too idealistic. You must marry to have sons, to carry on your father's name." Peter paused, and a shadow flitted across his face as he was reminded of his own situation. "Anyway, your father will never agree."

"My father cannot keep me here, your excellency. I would like to leave. If I may suggest, your excellency, my brother, Ivan, would make an excellent valet."

Peter blinked at him. "You are making me very angry, Michael Nikolaievich. And you are being absurd. See the country? There can be very few men who have seen as much of Russia as you."

"Nonetheless, your excellency—"

"And how could you possibly earn a living? Where will you go?"

Michael was not going to be caught in that trap. "I thought of going to Sevastopol, your excellency. I am sure I can obtain work in the city. I am young and strong and intelligent. I—"

"You are a fool. If you go, Michael Nikolaievich, you go. Do not suppose I will ever have you back on Starogan. Do not suppose I will ever lift a finger to help you in any way. You can starve in the gutter as far as I am concerned."

"Yes, your excellency." Michael hesitated. "I will say good-bye, your excellency."

"Oh, get out," Peter said. "Just get out. You are a fool, Michael Nikolaievich. An utter fool. You will end up badly, mark my words. You will end up on the gallows."

Chapter 9

"IF YOU COME ON DECK, MR. HAYMAN," THE PURSER SAID, "YOU'LL see the roofs of St. Petersburg."

George Hayman closed the book he had been reading, a turgid tome called *Materialism and Empirical Criticism,* by someone calling himself Nikolai Lenin; during the voyage he had set out to read everything written about Russia during the past five years, even the thoughts of a self-confessed revolutionist exile like Lenin. He put on his cap, for the April breeze off the Baltic was brisk. The purser held the door for him, and together they strolled up the promenade deck to look over the bows at the land which was appearing on every side.

"Over there," the purser said, pointing north, "is Finland. And here on the starboard bow is the island of Kronstadt. That's the main Russian Baltic naval base."

George leveled his binoculars.

"Ahead of us are the mouths of the Neva River. There are three, actually, but we take the southern one, because that is where the main seaport is. There are bridges across the others."

"And all this freezes?" George asked.

"It certainly does. Why, it was frozen solid only a few weeks ago. We will be one of the first ships to get through in 1911. There, now you can see the houses."

And indeed they did seem to be rising immediately out of the sea.

"The land is very low lying," the purser explained. "It was nothing more than a vast swamp when Peter the Great decided to build a city here. I wouldn't like to estimate how many lives it cost. And even nowadays it floods from time to time. Can you see that enormous building way over on the left? That is the Fortress of St. Peter and St. Paul. It was built to defend the city from the sea, but now that they have Kronstadt and all the other works out here, it is a prison. A place you do not ever want to find yourself inside, Mr. Hayman, if you can possibly avoid it."

"I'll bear that in mind," George said. "And that rather overdone place to its right?"

"That's the Winter Palace. For God's sake, don't criticize it once you leave the ship. It's on the mainland, you know, and the fortress is on an island opposite."

"Do you know, Hennesey," George remarked. "You are making Russia sound very much like a police state."

"Well, isn't it?" The purser frowned. "Weren't you here before?"

"Six years ago. But I was down in the south."

"Six years ago," Hennesey mused. "That would have been just about the time of the revolution, as they call it. A pretty abortive revolution it was. But it gave the tsar the opportunity he wanted. It's a police state all right. This man Stolypin, the prime minister, is a tough one. A brilliant man, make no mistake about that. He's performing wonders in agriculture, and given time, he'll probably raise the standard of living throughout the country. But say a word against the regime and it's half a dozen policemen knocking on your door, and knocking on more than that once they get hold of you."

"How do you know all this?" George said.

The purser winked. "The poor devils are always trying to get out. But they don't find it too easy to raise either the cash or the papers. So they try other ways. We've had at least six stowaways in the last three years."

"What sort of people?"

"Jews, mainly. They seem to be the national scapegoats for everything that goes wrong."

"What do you do with them?"

"We take them with us. The old man is a humanitarian, I guess you'd say. So maybe they are revolutionists. It wouldn't do our consciences any good to hand them back to the Okhrana to be torn apart. Oh, it's an unhappy country. And if you'll take my advice, Mr. Hayman, you'll leave that book you've been reading on board, even if you are an accredited newspaper correspondent."

"But this Lenin left Russia years ago."

"Not that long. He was here during the rebellion a few years ago, they say, and I can believe it. He has quite a reputation as a troublemaker, and his name is one the secret police don't even like to think about. Take my advice, Mr. Hayman."

He saluted and went about his duties, leaving George to look at the slowly rising land. An accredited newspaper correspondent. Russian correspondent of the Boston *People*. Incredible. Incredible that he should have bullied his father into giving him the position immediately on his return to America six years ago, and then have been refused a visa by the Russians; and that now, after all this time, they should suddenly have relented. On instructions from whom?

Even more incredible was the fact that he still wanted to come. Six years ago he had been desperate to return any way he could, to be near Ilona. The refusal of his visa had thrown him into the nearest thing to despair he had ever known. But he had pulled himself together, a recovery dictated by his common sense no less than his natural resilience. It had been an episode. Perhaps the most glorious episode of his life. But it was over. He had been her girlish fling, the object of Ilona's overheated emotions at a crucial time of her life. He supposed he had been an utter cad to have taken advantage of her. As if any man with red blood in his veins could possibly resist Ilona Dimitrievna when she *wanted*.

Besides, he had not intended to be a cad. But she had made her feelings clear, first of all in writing him that stilted letter in Sevastopol, regretting any inconvenience she might have caused him, and then in not bothering to reply to his letter of congratulations on her marriage. If she had chosen to settle for the life to which she had been born, he could do no less.

Since then his career had involved him in some of the most fascinating events of his time. There had been the Algeciras Conference in 1907, which had settled the question of Morocco, a bone of contention between France and Germany which had seemed likely to start the conflict of 1870 all over again, with the nightmare of a general European war—a catastrophe unknown since the death of Napoleon nearly a century earlier—lurking in the background. Then there had been the visit to the Belgian Congo, to write at first hand the ghastly exploitation of rubber workers revealed to the world by Roger Casement. And last year had been the trip to England for the funeral of Edward VII, his first visit to that small country which was the home of his ancestors, and which seemed to hold so much of the world in its palm.

And there had been Elizabeth. Mother's choice, certainly. Elizabeth's family name was Lee, and she came from Virginia, after which nothing more needed to be said about her background. With her slender, dark beauty she had been the greatest possible contrast to Ilona, even if in her surroundings—the plantation house and the horses, the dogs and the acres of cotton—she had sometimes seemed similar. Presumably they had been in love, briefly. There had been so much in their favor. "The handsomest couple in the world," the *People*'s gossip columnist had gushed, predictably. Two wealthy families, each as enthusiastic as the other. A life of perfect domestic bliss ahead, following what would undoubtedly have been the society wedding of the century.

Yet they had parted almost without regret, within hours of his father's casual suggestion that the Russian post was now available, if he still wanted it. Perhaps Elizabeth had known all along that his heart was elsewhere. Certainly she had chosen that moment to make her stand, to indicate that she wished him to give up being a correspondent and concentrate on the management of the paper. As Ilona had once suggested.

But Elizabeth wasn't Ilona, and besides, he had already been feeling the adrenalin pumping through his veins at the prospect of once again standing on Russian soil. He had tried to explain; he was in love with the country itself, with everything about it, from the great brooding wastes of the steppes to the rippling wheatfields of the south. Now he would see St. Petersburg, this fantastic dream of a determined tsar, created out of a swamp and a river to dominate the Baltic.

America had a similar immensity, but it lacked the quality of imminent tragedy. Presumably the conquest of Siberia, which was still going on, had not cost any more blood and misery than the conquest of the Great Plains and the Southwest. The difference was that the Americans had undertaken that conquest of themselves, in their hungry desire for new lands and new wealth. It had been brutal, but it had been a spontaneous upsurge of energy by a whole people. The Russians had embarked upon the conquest of this great country at the will of their tsars, had shed their blood and their tears with no prospect of enriching themselves, but only their masters.

And so they rebelled, from time to time. And were shot down in their hundreds, or hanged in their hundreds, or exiled to Siberia in their thousands. His original judgment had been correct. One understands more of a country on a very brief acquaintance than by learning to know it too well. The Borodins were the most charming people he had ever met, but they had revealed their claws in their treatment of him when he overstepped what they considered the bounds of polite behavior. He really did not care to imagine what they would do to a rebelling serf. And their friend, the obnoxious Roditchev, Ilona's husband, was the military governor of Moscow, who had put down the revolution of 1905 with an iron hand. Ilona! Had she been in the city during the revolt? What had she thought of it all? She had revealed, if not exactly liberal tendencies, a remarkable capacity for thinking about things; he had had no doubt that he would convert her to at least a Republican point of view within a year of their marriage. What had Roditchev converted her to?

Ilona. At the end of it all there was no point in deceiving himself. He was back in Russia entirely in the hopes that he might be able to see her once more. She could never be an episode. She was the most wonderful creature he had ever met or would ever meet.

He wondered if he would have gotten his visa if the Russians had been able to read his mind.

"His excellency will see you now, Mr. Hayman." The secretary stood to attention, frowning above his little mustache.

"Thank you." George stood up and straightened his tie. Was he nervous? He did not think so. The mere fact that he was being admitted was reassuring.

Tigran Borodin stood up to welcome him to the large, airy room; one of the windows was open to admit some of the still chill spring air, but there was a blazing fire in the hearth.

"George Hayman," he said. "My dear fellow." He came around the huge desk to shake hands. In six years he had put on weight, and taken to waxing the ends of his mustache. His whole being exuded well-fed prosperity and total confidence. "How very good to see you again, after all these years. I knew you were returning to Russia of course. In fact, I knew you were back. I wondered if you were going to call. Do you know, if you hadn't, I was going to invite you to one of my bachelor evenings."

"Good of you," George murmured.

"But sit down, my dear fellow. Sit down." He gestured at a leather-upholstered armchair, perched himself on the edge of his desk, and held out a box of cigars. His secretary hovered with clippers and matches, waited until George was puffing, and then left the room, closing the door behind him.

"May I inquire after your family?" George asked.

"My family? They are well enough. Did you come here to inquire after my family?"

George flushed. "Well—"

"You know of course that Peter is in Warsaw."

George nodded. "Aide-de-camp to the governor general."

"That is correct. And Ilona is married."

"I knew that also. To General Prince Roditchev."

"Again correct." Tigran eased himself off the desk, and went around to take his seat behind it. "And presumably, happily married. There was some friction at first. There were even rumors of a possible separation at one time. But then she became pregnant and recently they seem to have gotten on much better."

"Oh," George said. "Did she—?"

"Indeed she did. A little boy. Mother and child well, as the saying goes. Tell me, is it true you proposed to her?"

George frowned, uncertain as to the depth of the water he was about to enter.

Tigran smiled at him. "That is the family rumor. And the given reason for your somewhat precipitate departure from Starogan."

"I suppose it's near enough to the truth," George said.

"Hmm," Tigran said, communing with himself. "Well, she lives in Moscow now. And as I say, is apparently a contented wife."

"I am here as Russian correspondent of the Boston *People*," George pointed out. "Not as a jilted lover."

"Of course, my dear fellow. Of course. If I can be of any assistance at all—"

"I'd appreciate some information from time to time. These military conversations with the British—something of a volte-face in Russian foreign policy, wouldn't you say?"

Tigran stroked his mustache. "What makes you think that?"

"Well, for heaven's sake, you and the British have spent most of the last hundred years at each other's throats. And they are allied to the Japanese."

"The Japanese business is over and done with," Tigran pointed out. "It can never happen again, simply because now we would be prepared for it. Foreign policy, my dear Hayman, is not a static matter. It moves with the times. It has to. It is quite true that we are having, as you put, conversations with the British. This is no bad thing.

Our aim is the preservation of peace in Europe. To ensure this, we must prepare ourselves for any eventuality."

"Even the remote possibility that you and the French might find yourselves fighting with the British against Germany and Austria? Now there would history have come full circle."

"History has a habit of doing that," Tigran remarked. "The important thing is for everyone to be aware that it can happen, and will happen, should events ever get out of hand; there you have the surest guarantee that things will be kept very much *in* hand. I will be frank with you, Hayman. Here in Russia things did not go well for the first ten years of the present reign. Do you remember that conversation we had down in Starogan? I do. I asked you for a weather forecast. You never gave it to me. But if you had, it should have been a brief unsettled period ahead, with showers and even some heavy rain, followed by fine and bright weather spreading to all parts. I'll admit, I was very worried then. But now things are better. No doubt we needed the shock of losing to the Japanese to shake ourselves out of our inertia. Shake his majesty out of his uncertainty, as well. And he has certainly recovered. He has got it right at last, found the best man for the tasks he wants accomplished—Peter Stolypin. There you have one of the greatest men Russia has ever produced. A man who knows how to keep the people happy and the country prosperous at the same time. I would estimate that Russia has never, in all her history, been so contented, so prosperous, and so powerful as at this moment. And I will tell you this, Hayman: we mean to keep her that way."

George leaned forward to deposit ash in the tray. It was reasonable to suppose that the purser, looking in from the outside, and Tigran Borodin, one of the pillars that held the inside up, would have different points of view. His task was to discover which point of view was the more accurate. And to do that he had to probe, at whatever risk.

"I am sure you're right," he agreed. "How sad it is that prosperity always seems to go hand in hand with corruption."

"Corruption?" Tigran's head came up, like a dog scenting its quarry.

"Here in St. Petersburg. You have no idea the rumors which circulate in New York."

Tigran leaned back in his seat. "Rasputin," he said.

"Do you know him?"

"Everyone knows the holy father, Hayman. And everyone knows what is said of him."

"But none of it is true?"

"A great deal of it is true. The man is what he is, a Siberian peasant with a gift of sacred magic, if you like. Every so often he gets drunk in public and behaves like a boor. Because he is a boor. But he is still a great man."

"I was thinking of some other rumors."

Tigran leaned forward again. "All great creatures attract jackals, which tear futilely at their flanks, simply because jackals cannot abide greatness. Let me tell you the truth about Gregory Rasputin. It is true that he affects women more than men. His success depends upon faith, utter and abiding faith—entirely what our Lord demanded, incidentally—and it is a fact of life that women are less skeptical than men; they are more willing to believe. Thus his salon is besieged by women, day and night, and no longer are they only interested in faith. Now that he is one of the most powerful men in the land, they are seeking advancement for their husbands, their sons, their brothers, themselves."

"The temptations must be enormous," George observed.

"That I cannot say. In public, at least, he does not seem especially interested in his conquests. But I can assure you that he is the soul of propriety. Why, my dear fellow, he is on terms of the closest friendship with her majesty. Now do you honestly suppose the tsarina would have anything to do with a lecher? The tsarina?

"And just to confirm what I saw, I can tell you that my own sister is one of his most ardent disciples. Xenia spends two or three afternoons a week with him."

"May I ask what she does there?"

"She assists him with his enormous correspondence." Tigran smiled. "Would you believe it, the fellow can hardly read? There is a true prophet, eh? But as for Xenia, can you imagine she would waste her time with the man if he did not have a compelling power?"

"No," George said thoughtfully.

"So there you have it. It would be doing Russia an immense service, you know, were you to quash all these obscene rumors once and for all. I personally would be most grateful."

"I certainly came here to report only the truth," George said. "Perhaps I could meet with your sister."

"Of course. Well," Tigran frowned, "in time. There was some comment when they learned you were returning to Russia." He stared into George's face. "They all immediately assumed that you were in some fashion bent on pursuing Ilona." He flushed. "You know what women are."

"I do indeed," George said. "Then I shall have to be patient, and prove myself a good boy."

"Hmm. Wait a moment though. There's Tattie."

"Tattie?"

"You haven't forgotten Tattie? She is at school here in St. Petersburg, and she spends her spare time with us. She certainly hasn't forgotten you. And she spoke up for you. 'I like George,' she said. 'I always liked George. I wish he had been allowed to marry Ilona.' She'd love to meet you again."

"Well," George said. "It would be a pleasure, I'm sure."

Tigran smiled at him. "Don't sound so unenthusiastic. She's eighteen now, you know. Growing up. And more important, she is also a disciple of the holy father."

From the park outside the city proper, the view over the Neva was breathtaking. The houses gleaming in the morning sunlight, the river mouths winding their way beneath the bridges as they fed into the gulf beyond, the ships discharging cargoes in the port area, and beyond, the fortress islands with their bristling guns, reinforcing the defensive majesty of the battle fleet lying at anchor beneath the shadow of Kronstadt. Presumably it was an even more breathtaking sight in the dead of winter, George thought. A comparison he would be able to make, since he would be here for a while.

To see Ilona? He did not suppose he had fooled Tigran for a moment. But Tigran was prepared to be his friend—as was Tattie. He had almost forgotten Tattie. And now she was eighteen. He remembered the untidy bundle of arms and legs who had bubbled with excited joy, at least when he had first known her. And now . . . he heard the clip-clopping of horses' hooves and turned, nervously tapping the ground with his stick. Two figures were approaching.

She wore a green habit and a black top hat. Black boots glinted in the sunshine; a red scarf drifted away from her throat. Her hair was almost invisible, caught in a snood on her neck. George gulped, and all but dropped his stick. Ilona. Ilona reincarnated as she had been on the day he had first seen her, standing on the patio of the doomed house in a doomed city.

But it was not Ilona.

"George," Tatiana Borodina screamed, disengaging both her stirrups at the same time and jumping down in a flurry of flying skirts. And she was not Ilona in other ways. The same height, the same figure, the same hair, the same basic coloring, but Tattie took after her father more than her mother; her chin was square instead of pointed, her nose slightly upturned instead of straight, her eyes pale blue instead of turquoise. And her smile was all her own; it made her already wide mouth seem to split her face in two. "George," she said again, and held out her hands.

George looked at Tigran to see how he was reacting, but Tigran merely smiled as he reached from his saddle to hold his cousin's bridle. George squeezed the gloved fingers and had himself drawn closer for a kiss on each cheek.

"George," she said a third time. "I always knew you'd come back. You haven't changed a bit."

"You have."

"Well . . . I've grown up, wouldn't you say?"

"I would say. Most enchantingly."

She blew him a kiss. "I like compliments."

Tigran cleared his throat abruptly.

"Oh, you can leave us, Tigran," Tattie said. "Can't you?"

"Well, I have got some work to do."

"We shall walk together," Tattie said. "Tigran is terribly afraid that I'll get into mischief. Everyone thinks I'm going to get into mischief. You know I won't, George."

"I won't let her," George said.

Tigran considered, then touched the brim of his hat with his crop. "I will invite you to one of my soirees," he said. "I would like to hear your impressions of Russia." He touched his horse's flank with his spur and walked it down the bridle path.

"Have you come back to see Ilona?" Tattie tucked her arm under his as they walked, the horse obedient at their heels.

"I have come back as a newspaper correspondent," George said carefully. She pouted.

"But you'd like to see her, wouldn't you? I know she'd like to see you."

"Would she? I am told she is happily married."

"To Roditchev? My God. She is absolutely miserable, I would say."

"She's a mother."

"Yes, but. . . ." She squeezed his arm. "These things happen when you are married. She tried to run away to join you, you know."

George stopped walking and looked down at her.

"Fact," Tattie said. "I was going to come with her."

"You?"

"I've always wanted to visit America, so I could play what I want to play, and not some stuffy old composer. But she made the mistake of asking Michael Nej to help her, and he told Peter. There was the most terrible fuss. And Peter told her if she didn't write to you and put you off forever, he'd have you arrested and beaten up." She gazed at him eagerly. "I've never told anyone about that. They used to ask me all the time. But I never told anyone. The only person I've ever told is Father Gregory."

"Father Gregory," George muttered. But he was not thinking about Father Gregory. Ilona had tried to run away to join him. Oh, my God, she had tried. Six years ago.

"Tigran says you are very interested in Father Gregory," Tattie said.

Think. Concentrate. Control the wild beating of your heart. She had loved him after all. She had tried to elope with him. But surely the important word was *had*. Six years ago. Since then she had been married. She was a mother. But he would see her again. And together they would remember, even if they could never speak of it.

But no one, not even Tattie, dear, delightful Tattie, should suspect.

"He's a phenomenon," he said. "Reporters are always interested in phenomenons."

"He is the greatest man I have ever known," she said, her face aglow. "Would you like to meet him?"

"Is it possible?"

"I'll arrange it for you," she said, and gave his arm another squeeze. "Father Gregory always does what I ask him. I'm his favorite."

What did he expect? George had no idea; he preferred to keep an open mind on the matter and not prejudge the issue. Nevertheless, he had certainly expected more dignity. The crowd of cigarette-smoking grooms and chauffeurs gossiping in the drive, the elegant house—he understood that the starets had prospered sufficiently to have moved from his early, humbler apartment on the English Prospekt—the antechamber full of anxious women who stared at the male intruder with unmistakable hostility, disturbed him as much as the effusive greeting he received from the major-domo.

"Monsieur Hayman. How good to see you. We are expecting you. Come this way, monsieur, come this way." He snapped his fingers, and a footman hurried forward to take George's hat and stick.

Instantly, he was surrounded by the women, and gained a brief insight into Pentheus's feelings just before the maenads tore him apart.

"How can *he* gain admittance?"

"I have been waiting for two hours."

"I have been waiting for two days."

"Oh, please Monsieur Anton, can't you just squeeze me in?"

"Monsieur Anton!"

"Monsieur Anton!"

Roubles were thrust at the major-domo; fingers clawed at George's sleeve in an attempt to thrust him to one side. But Anton was apparently used to such demonstrations.

"Back, ladies," he shouted as he might have addressed a pack of dogs. "Back to your seats, or the holy father will be displeased with you. He will send you all away."

The hubbub subsided and they retreated, glaring at George. He wiped his brow. "Does this happen often?"

"They are hysterical," Anton said contemptuously, opening the inner door. "It is best to ignore them."

"But will they ever gain admittance?"

Anton shrugged. "The holy father inspects them from time to time, and if he likes their looks, he will admit one or two. But he is far too busy to answer every petition."

The door closed behind George, and he found himself in the inner room. He inhaled the scent of humanity and Madeira wine, and watched as a man who had to be Rasputin left an inner doorway and came toward him, both arms outstretched.

"Monsieur Hayman."

George hesitated, unprepared for the size of the man, his smell, his general uncouthness; for although his smock and breeches were clearly silk and looked new, they were rumpled, as if he had just left his bed fully clothed, and stained with wine. His hair and beard had evidently not been combed in some time.

Rasputin's huge face split into a smile. "But you are welcome, Monsieur Hayman. Welcome." Before George could come to a decision, he was folded in the bearlike hug and kissed on each cheek. "You are a friend of my little Tattie's, and more important, you are the lover of Princess Roditcheva." He held George's shoulders, thrust him to the full length of his arms, frowned at him even as he smiled. "That was very sinful of you. But you are a lucky man. One of the luckiest men I can imagine. You'll take a glass of wine?"

"That would be very kind of you," George said.

Rasputin released him, and went to the table to pour two goblets of Madeira. He handed George a goblet and raised his own. "Wine, Monsieur Hayman. It is one of the few pleasures of this world. A jug of wine, a beautiful woman, and a soft bed, eh?"

George sipped, reminding himself that if he had never heard a priest talk like this before, Rasputin *was* an unusual priest. And so far it was only talk.

"I had expected Mademoiselle Borodina to be here," George said.

"Aha." Once again the surprising combination of frown and smile. "You would possess the other sister as well? Is there no end to your lust?"

George realized he was flushing. "I would not dream of laying a finger on Tatiana," he said. "It is just that she invited me to visit you, so naturally I supposed—"

"And she is here," Rasputin said. "Of course she is here. Where else would she be? Come." He opened the inner door and ushered George past him. George stepped inside and stopped in surprise and dismay. This room was clearly Rasputin's bedchamber; it smelt strongly of the man himself, and contained a vast divan bed, in a state of complete disarray, pillows and coverlets scattered. There was no furniture in the room except, incongruously, an upright grand piano against the far wall, and beside it, Tatiana Borodina. But a Tattie whom George had never seen before, for while her hair was as loose and untidy as it had been when he first met her, this was a full-grown woman, who was wearing, so far as he could ascertain in a single glance, but a single garment; a swathe—it could hardly be called a negligee—of diaphanous white silk which shrouded her from her neck to her ankles but left almost nothing to the imagination. And Tattie, he realized, was considerably more voluptuous than Ilona had been at that age.

"George," she said, and left the piano to come toward him, arms outstretched.

George closed his eyes as he was hugged and kissed; he had to prevent himself from touching her by an exercise of will.

"Be careful of him," Rasputin growled. "He wishes to bed you."

"Do you, George?" Tattie cried in delight.

George opened his eyes. "Your friend is being amusing," he said.

"Oh." Tattie pouted.

"Ha, ha," Rasputin roared. "But *she* would like to bed *you*, my friend. Tattie would like to bed anyone. She simply wishes to bed." He wagged his finger at the pair of them. "But I have forbidden it, until she is wed. I will have no sinfulness among my disciples." His hand swung down to slap her bottom crisply. She jumped, but she did not seem to resent it. "Now go and play for us."

She gave George a quick smile, ran to the piano, sat down, and immediately started playing. She used no music, but instead allowed her eyes to close and her body to sway as her fingers rippled over the keys. The music was not recognizable; it was a wild outburst of sound in which discords were hurled against each other with only the faintest suggestion of a melody, and yet the rhythm, combined with the girl's arching, waving back, the movement of her buttocks across the stool, the tossing of the mane of yellow hair, left him quite entranced.

"Is she not magnificent?" Rasputin asked. "I see a great future for her, Monsieur Hayman. Her own people would not let her play as she wishes. But I do. I seek to release all that is primeval in her, Monsieur Hayman. Because that is her true genius, and her true delight. Do you play?"

"A little. Nothing like that."

"I will give you music. You play, Monsieur Hayman, and Tattie will dance for us. Here is a many-sided genius."

George Hayman sat at the desk in his hotel apartment and lit his eighth cigarette that hour. The writing pad in front of him remained untouched.

He was endeavoring to remind himself that he was a journalist, that his business was to report what he saw and heard, and that indeed a report on Rasputin had been one of the items his editor had most urgently requested. Well, that could be done easily enough. He did not suppose he could add a great deal to what was already known of the man. That he possessed a towering personality as well as a towering frame was obvious, and that his whole life was built on lust could hardly be doubted. But those were things everyone in America who had heard of him already took for granted. They wanted details, succulent morsels of titillating delight for them to whisper at each other across their back fences. He could supply that also, could relate how the holy father kept an almost naked girl to amuse him, and not just a girl, but a member of one of Russia's oldest and noblest families, who obeyed his every whim like a slave.

What they did, what he made her do privately, did not bear consideration. George's mind was sufficiently filled with the image of her dancing, gracefully to be sure, but obscenely, her flying garment often held above her waist as she waggled either bottom or belly, her hair flailing to either side of her face and even sweeping the floor as she went through her gyrations, her heavy breasts scraping against the thin silk, her features an unforgettable mixture of concentration and pleasure. Until she collapsed, panting, across the monster's bed, and Rasputin sat beside her. That had been the most unforgettable moment of all.

Such an account would certainly increase the *People*'s circulation. But at this moment he was not interested in the paper. He lit his ninth cigarette.

Tattie had been corrupted, and was in the process of being further corrupted. The only saving aspect of the entire situation was that she was apparently not the man's mistress. Whatever he did to her, whatever he made her do for him, Rasputin was apparently well aware of the limits beyond which he dared not go. As if it mattered. Tattie was sexually dominated by this man, a man who, in his own secret, disgusting fashion, was dominating all of St. Petersburg. And St. Petersburg in turn dominated Russia.

Undoubtedly he had to be stopped. Tigran might boast that his country had never been more prosperous or more stable, but Tigran had allowed himself to believe what the tsarina's circle said of the holy man, had never tried to find out the truth of the matter. Could any country count itself prosperous and stable when its very core was rotten?

And just as, undoubtedly, Tattie had to be rescued before it was too late. She was still a very young woman. There was time. If it could be done.

He lit his tenth cigarette. Rescuing Tattie was far more important than amusing the American public. But how? He himself had been allowed to return to Russia on sufferance; he did not suppose attempts by him to discredit Rasputin would accomplish anything better than his rapid expulsion. Approach Ilona? That was in itself dangerous, even if it was something he hoped to do, in time. Besides, he did not see how that could accomplish anything toward ousting Rasputin, even if she were to believe what he had to say.

But Peter. Peter guarded his sisters, or at least the honor of the family, with utter determination. Peter would certainly act, quickly and promptly, could he be brought to suspect that Tattie was being debauched. How to do it? Only by the most dishonest of methods, the anonymous letter. Peter would certainly not accept any communication from George Hayman.

George leaned back in his chair. Why bother? Why involve himself in something so devious, and so disgusting? His own part in it could only discredit him. Did he really care that much for Russia? Or for the Borodins? Ilona was not involved, and Tattie, well, certainly Tattie thought herself happy at the moment, being allowed to do what she really wished. But then came the recollection of Tattie sprawled across the divan bed, arms and legs flung wide, while Rasputin sat beside her and rested his hand on her thigh. It was at that moment that George had left, to the obvious surprise of both of them. And since that moment he had been in a turmoil of uncertainty and anger.

The chair legs hit the floor as he flung himself forward. He stubbed out the cigarette and picked up his pen.

Princess Irina Borodina peered through the window of the first-class compartment as the train pulled into the station. "Petersburg," she said. "Do you know, my blood tingles every time I even see it. Oh, Peter, you are a *darling,* bringing me back for a second visit this year." She sat down again and glanced at her husband. "I do wish you'd tell me why, Peter Dimitrievich."

"I have a duty to perform," he said. "I have told you. Ah, Feodor Alexandrovich, you will see to the bags. Is there a car waiting?"

"Certainly, your excellency. Everything is arranged." His new valet was tall and thin and lugubrious, a man as far removed from Michael Nej as it had been possible to find. Michael Nej of all the stupid fools, Peter thought, as he always did when he was in the mood to be angry. Disappeared without a trace, undoubtedly starved to death in some gutter, a source of permanent disgrace to his family; in a matter of months old Nikolai had seemed to double in age.

Peter got up. "Shall we go?"

"Am I allowed to ask where?"

Irina's initial delight at finding herself in St. Petersburg was starting to dissipate into the worried suspicions she had been experiencing throughout the three-day journey from Warsaw. She had never seriously attempted to understand her husband. He was one of the most boring young men she had ever met. Even in bed he was boring, for he was apparently unaware that women had any desires of their own, and his own nature was so gentle and polite that he never revealed extreme passion. She often wondered what it would be like to be married to someone like Roditchev; how unfair it was that Ilona should always have the best of everything. Peter's only redeeming features were his rank and his wealth; she did not suppose she could truly complain, as those were the reasons she had married him in the first place, and she had always known that she could not continue to live her own life in the capital forever. Indeed, during the past couple of years she had managed to become quite reconciled to Warsaw society, was enjoying a gentle little flirtation with Count Georgi Panin, and, confident now that Peter would never notice, was looking forward to carrying the friendship a stage further than exchanging letters and furtive caresses. At least, she *had* been entertaining such a plan until Peter's sudden announcement that he had obtained leave from the governor general and was returning to St. Petersburg immediately. Was it possible he had noticed after all?

She had thought he might beat her. Or at least shout at her. Instead, he had spent the whole journey sitting in a corner of the compartment, brooding on some catastrophe. But it really wasn't fair for a husband to keep a catastrophe private from his wife.

"I have somewhere to go," Peter said. "But I shall drop you at the house first. I shall probably be bringing Tattie home with me when I come, and I wish you to look after her."

"Tattie?" Irina's heart gave a disturbing lurch; she was in constant correspondence with Xenia. "Isn't she at school?"

"I think it is time Tattie left school," Peter said. "She is eighteen years old. Four years ago you were talking about finding her a husband."

"That was before you carried me off to Poland," she pointed out.

"Well, it was a bit premature then. But I think it is time now."

"And we have come here for that purpose?"

Peter allowed himself to be draped in his cape by Feodor Alexandrovich. He held the door for his wife. "Yes," he said.

Irina bit her lip and lowered her veil over her face. Something had happened. Something terrible. If only she had some inkling of what it was. Something to do with Father Gregory? But Xenia had given no hint that he had got himself into trouble, or at least, no more trouble than was usual. He was continually getting drunk in public and upsetting the tsar, but the tsarina always managed to have it smoothed over. He had even been dismissed once, the previous year, but almost immediately the tsarevich had been taken ill and Father Gregory had hastily been recalled to his bedside.

In fact, Irina realized as she hurried behind her husband, as long as the tsarevich's health depended upon the starets's presence, there was really *no* crime he could commit which would involve his dismissal.

Therefore it had to be something else, something Tattie had done.

They left the station, passed a line of bowing stationmasters and porters and reached the motor car. The chauffeur was saluting as he held the door for her. "You will drive first of all to my house," Peter said. "And then you will take me to—" he felt in his breast pocket and pulled out a piece of paper, "—the Gorokhovaya."

"The . . . ?" Irina turned as she sat down, nearly slipped off the seat. "The Gorokhovaya? But that is. . . ." Once again she bit her lip.

Peter sat down beside her. "Yes?"

"I . . . I have heard that that is where the holy father, Gregory Rasputin, lives."

"That is correct," Peter said.

"Well . . . but . . . you're not going there?"

The car was moving through the crowded station yard and on to the street.

"I *am* going there," Peter said. "You may as well know the truth. I have received information that Tattie has been visiting him, that she spends all her spare time there, in fact, and that she is allowing herself, well, I do not know what to think or believe. I intend to have a few words with Uncle Igor, I can promise you that. After I have fetched Tattie. And after I have taught this fellow a lesson."

"Oh God," Irina said. "Oh, my God. You cannot."

"What?"

"Think, Peter!" She threw her veil over her hat. "Isn't he a favorite of the tsar?"

"I intend to have some words with his majesty as well," Peter said. "It is a disgrace that he should allow himself to be surrounded by charlatans and scoundrels. He is far too trusting."

"Oh, my God," Irina said again. "It will mean—" She clutched his arm. "Peter. Let me come with you."

"To Rasputin's house? Good lord, no. I don't wish you to be involved, my dear. You must be at home to look after Tattie when I bring her there. I've no doubt she'll be upset."

"Upset," Irina muttered. "Peter, if there's going to be a scene—any trouble—I want to be there with you. Please. *Please.*"

They had turned onto the Nevski Prospekt, and the car was slowing.

"I will not hear of it," Peter said. "Your business is to look after Tattie. You may leave this Rasputin to me."

"His majesty is waiting for you," said Count Gutchkov. For years, the count had been one of the pillars of the court; he had served as far back as Alexander II, Nicholas's grandfather. Today he looked at once grave and concerned, but not entirely unsympathetic.

Peter tucked his cap under his arm and marched forward. Of course his majesty was angry. But his anger would very soon be redirected. And the capital would be rid of an utter scourge.

The doors were opened; the desk was in front of him. To his right a red curtain shut off a third of the study. Was *she* there? Peter had heard that the tsarina had taken to attending all her husband's audiences, in order to give him the benefit of her advice. But he hoped she was not there today. This meeting with the tsar might well involve some delicate matters.

Nicholas looked tired. But then, he always looked tired. He also looked severe, with no hint of the usual twinkle in his eye.

"Well, Prince Peter," he said. "It appears, whenever I meet you, that there is some domestic disturbance in the air. But this time I think you have gone too far. I really cannot have my princes of the empire arrested for brawling."

"The arrest was a mistake, your majesty. As soon as my rank was discovered—"

"The arrest was not a mistake, Prince Borodin. Perhaps your release was."

"Your majesty, if I may be permitted to explain the circumstances—"

"The circumstances are, Prince Borodin, that you entered a private house and assaulted its owner. Do you deny this?"

"I do not, your majesty, but—"

"And this house did not merely belong to a private person, Prince Borodin. It belonged to a starets, a holy man—a holy man, Prince Borodin, who has received our personal recognition as someone of exceptional ability, exceptional goodness. Do you deny *that,* Prince Borodin?"

"No, your majesty, but if I may be allowed to explain certain facts—"

"What facts?"

"The fact, your majesty, that this man, this so-called starets, far from being the holy man you suppose him, is a black-hearted villain and a lecher, a seducer of young women and girls, a drunkard and a—"

"I think you should stop there, Prince Borodin. Or you may say something you will regret, if you have not already done so. Such calumny upon a starets is even more heinous an offense than attempting to assault him."

"Calumny, your majesty? No doubt your majesty is unaware that I discovered my own sister in this monster's private apartments."

"I am aware of that," Nicholas said. "I understand that Father Gregory has been teaching Mademoiselle Borodina music."

"Music?" Peter cried. "Your majesty, if that is music, I am . . . but it matters nothing what he was teaching her about music. Your majesty, my sister, a girl of eighteen, was wearing . . . well, hardly anything. And she was alone. Alone, your majesty, in a bedroom with this . . . this charlatan."

"Tell me, Prince Borodin, does your sister go to confession?"

"Why yes, your majesty, she does, but—"

"And is she not alone with her priest on these occasions?"

"Of course she is, your majesty, but there is a grill between her and the confessor."

"Are you seriously suggesting that Father Gregory would conduct himself improperly with your sister? Or with any woman?"

"Well, your majesty—"

"Because if I were you I should think very carefully first. Father Gregory's methods are unorthodox, I will agree. But he is a starets, a law unto himself, and I have the utmost confidence in him. So has my wife, I may add. I do not become hysterical when he is alone with one of my daughters, as he often is."

"Hysterical, your majesty?" Peter felt his face burning with a mixture of anger and embarrassment.

The tsar hesitated. His head started to turn in the direction of the red curtain. Then he checked himself. "Yes, Prince Borodin," he said. "I cannot help but regard your behavior as hysterical. Have you had your sister examined?"

"I have, your majesty."

"And?"

Once again Peter felt the heat in his cheeks. "She has not been seduced, in that sense, your majesty. But—"

"Therefore you stand condemned out of your own mouth, prince, of a vicious and premeditated assault upon a starets. You are only fortunate that his servants managed to restrain you before you injured him, or before he injured you. I will hear no more upon this subject, but I am bound to say that your behavior raises serious doubts in my mind concerning your earlier complaints regarding Prince Roditchev. I wonder at my innocence in believing you."

Peter stood to attention. "Are you accusing me of lying, your majesty?"

The tsar made a deprecatory gesture with his hand. "I would not accuse any Russian nobleman of deliberately lying, Prince Borodin. What I am saying is that your judgment regarding these matters is seriously at fault. Which raises questions as to your judgment on wider, more important issues. I am not competent to pronounce upon your relations with your sister. You are the head of your family and it is a matter for you alone. But I must accept the evidence that you are not temperamentally suited to positions of high responsibility in the state. I am sorry, because I had the highest respect for both your father and your grandfather, and the name of Borodin has for three centuries ranked high in the affairs of our empire. But my first concern must be the welfare of that empire and the people who are my subjects.

"I have therefore decided that it would be best for all of us if you were to return to your estates at Starogan, where I am sure there is a great deal to be done. I feel that you should concern yourself with domestic matters for a period of not less than three years, at the end of which time you may have gained some sense of perspective, and we may be able once again to welcome you to St. Petersburg—and even to find some employment suitable to your rank and ability."

Chapter 10

A LAST BLARE ON THE HORN SENT A GROUP OF CYCLISTS SCATTERING away from the pavement, and the Daimler pulled over to the side of the street.

"Will this do, my lady princess?" inquired Alexei Pavlovich. He was a young man, one of the new breed able to cope with the intricacies of a motor car, which had proved far beyond the understanding of old Vasili Tigranovich.

"This will do very well, thank you, Alexei Pavlovich." Ilona waited for him to open the door for her, and smiled at him as she stepped down, her basket draped over her arm, her head shaded from the sun by a huge straw hat. Vasili Tigranovich was also one of those who did not approve of Princess Roditcheva's habits, whereas Alexei Pavlovich could accept that times were changing. If he found her a surprising woman, he was content enough to be in her company. "I will be here again at six."

The chauffeur saluted and returned to the wheel. The passers-by, including the disturbed cyclists, had gathered in a respectful ring to watch the wife of their military governor emerge. Now they shifted their feet uncertainly as she turned her smile on them. Even after two years, Princess Roditcheva's regular visits to the Kitai-Gorod, without even the company of a maid, much less a detective, remained the talk of the city. Opinion varied, from old men who wondered what her husband was thinking of to allow it, through old women who concluded she must be mad, to the young who thought her apparent interest in them, her visits to the bazaars and the emporiums, to the churches and even to the synagogues, her long chats with passers-by selected at random, the most hopeful sign they had ever seen. In the beginning there had been a great deal of speculation over whether or not capital could be made from her so strange behavior. There had been no lack of those who spoke of kidnapping and ransom, even of murder. But the vast majority would have none of it. It was argued that Prince Roditchev would never let his wife wander the streets of the city unless he had made some arrangements to protect her, and thus it would be senseless to fall into his trap. Besides, it was apparent even to the hotheads that if there was scarcely a soul in all Moscow did not hate the Prince, there were very few who actually hated the princess, or wished her any harm. She was a ray of sunshine who entered their lives, three times a week, with her smile and her basket, from which she would dispense charity to anyone who appeared in need of it.

Ilona was well aware of the comment she inspired; apart from what she herself overheard, there was the gossip relayed to her by her servants and even by Roditchev. Sometimes it troubled her conscience. But clearly she was not cut out to be a revolutionary. The thought of ever again experiencing a night like that of the meeting sent shivers down her spine. Besides, the socialists did not need her help. She had written a note to Judith Stein offering her sympathy and assistance, and she had received no reply.

Well, she no longer wished to help them. And whenever her conscience grew truly troublesome, she could always remind herself that the course she had chosen was not an easy one; it required all her cunning and concentration, for it was quite dangerous. And utterly selfish. But so satisfactory. Once she had thought Michael no more than an episode. A necessary episode, to be sure, for the preservation of her sanity. Once she had thought that in bearing his child she had fulfilled herself as a woman, not only as a mother who loved that child, but as a wife who wanted to avenge herself, however secretly, upon a husband she hated.

Now she knew better. Michael, in his effect upon her senses, was like alcohol or a drug on the weakminded; once tasted it could never again be forsworn. But there was more than that. To meet him again, once again to experience the joy of those gentle hands, the insistent plea of utter devotion, would have been sufficient. To have him also abandon his position—the only decent position he could ever hope to achieve—change his name, and follow her back to Moscow to live off her charity, just so he could be with her and could see his son from time to time—that was true love. Michael Nikolaievich loved as no man could have loved before, as no woman could truly expect to be loved.

Did he hope for love in return? Perhaps this troubled her conscience more than anything else. Does the drunkard love the bottle from which he drinks, or merely the life-saving liquid it contains? Would it not have been better to have told him, from the very moment of his reappearance in Moscow, that he was a fool?

But since he had reappeared in Moscow, since he had abandoned everything worth having in his life, in pursuit of the one thing he could never truly possess, what else could she have done? She fed him, she protected his secret, and she risked much to be with him. If she knew that this was not love, could never be love, it was at least a sufficient substitute for Michael Nej. And there remained herself. Through Michael she was avenging herself upon not only Roditchev, but upon Peter and her family, and even upon George, for not having abducted her by force. That was unfair, of course, but it was part of her self-justification. They had made her what she was, what she had to be. Well, she had made more of her fate than anyone would have dreamed possible.

She paused at Schiffer's Emporium to make a few purchases, and pass the time of day with Monsieur Schiffer. Then it was on to Ascharin's for another chat. This was part of her routine, to disappear into various shops for up to half an hour at a time. Thus when she reached the bookshop, no one expected her to return to the street for some time.

Did she ever fear discovery? Did she not know that she must be discovered some day? Did she not continue on her way in defiance of that inevitable confrontation with Roditchev? Not that she feared betrayal by Petrovski. Petrovski was one of those old men who worshipped youth and beauty—and superior rank. That Princess Roditcheva should have chosen him for her confidant would have made him the happiest man in the world, even without his monthly remuneration. He watched over the lovers like a mother hen, and Ilona had no doubt he would die rather than let her husband know of their secret.

"Monsieur Petrovski," she said, and gave him her hand to kiss. "Have you some new books in today?"

There were several other customers in the shop.

"Indeed, your highness, indeed. A parcel arrived but this morning. Will your highness inspect them?"

"I should like to."

"Of course, of course, your highness. My clerk will show you. Michael Nikolaievich Chernov! Princess Roditcheva would look at some books."

This was all part of the game, the subterfuge she practiced all the time—that Michael should be busy whenever she entered the store, should have to be summoned to attend to her, should reluctantly leave the customers he was serving, to escort her to the rear of the shop, should open the door to the office for her, allow her inside, close the door behind him, and take her in his arms. It was a practiced drill, which continued behind the door. For there was another door, into a further inner room, where there was a bed. Within a minute of Petrovski's first call she was naked in his arms; and as they both wanted, and needed—because they saw each other only twice a week, because of their clandestine meetings, because of the dangers involved—within another two or three minutes they were spent and exhausted, lying against each other, gasping for breath and sweating in the mid-afternoon heat.

"Five minutes," Michael said bitterly, gazing at the low ceiling above their heads. "Five minutes." He stroked a bead of sweat from her cheek, allowed his hand to wander higher, and was checked by her quick glance. He could not touch her hair, lest it become disarranged.

Ilona sighed. He was becoming increasingly frustrated by the limited nature of their love. An entirely masculine discontent, she supposed. She herself accepted that the brief moments they shared were all they could ever dream of enjoying.

"Do you know why I came to Moscow?" Michael asked. "I came to take you by force. I came to have you always, and completely. I would have started a revolution. Is that not an indictment?"

This was becoming too constant a theme.

She kissed him on the nose. "It is a blessing. You would have been hanged."

"Not if I had succeeded."

"I cannot understand this talk of revolution," she said, sitting up and hanging her legs over the side of the bed. "I cannot understand why there need be talk of revolution. I am happy. You are happy. Everyone is surely happy, so long as they have sufficient to eat and someone to love. But I do not understand how you can even imagine it could succeed. You saw those people at the meeting. Do you still go to such meetings?"

"Sometimes."

"Michael! You don't."

"What else have I to do?"

"My God. One day you will be arrested."

"And you will defend me."

"I? How?"

"You will think of a way, my darling princess."

Ilona got up and started to dress.

"Are you in that much of a hurry?" he asked.

"When you talk like this, I am in that much of a hurry. Sometimes I think you are demented." She stood above him, her petticoat in her hands. "Do you love me, Michael Nikolaievich? Really and truly?"

"Do you not suppose so, Ilona Dimitrievna? Have I not given up all for you?"

"Then let us have no more talk of revolutions." She stepped into her petticoat and adjusted the straps on her shoulders. Michael caught her hand.

"And do you love me, sweet princess of the five minutes?"

"Three years," Irina Borodina said for the hundredth time. "Three years." She stared out the train windows at the rooftops of Moscow. "Don't you realize that you and I have been banished? How can you talk of a temporary retirement to the country? You have been banished! *I* have been banished."

Tattie remained sitting in her chair, her face closed. She did not yet seem to appreciate the magnitude of the blow which had fallen.

"Banished," Irina continued. "All the empire, all the world, will know of it. It will be front-page news in every newspaper. Prince Peter Borodin, banished to the steppes. You will never be able to hold up your head in public again."

"You are being absurd," Peter said patiently. He could not blame her for being angry. He knew how much St. Petersburg society meant to her. "People have been banished before, and returned to favor in the end. I did my duty. I have no regrets about that. I can only hope and pray that his majesty never lives to regret that he did not listen to me."

"Returned to favor," Irina sneered. "Three years. Three years— 1914. I shall be thirty-six. God almighty, I shall be an old woman."

"Oh, really, Irina, you are behaving quite hysterically. How can three years make you into an old woman if you consider yourself a young woman now?"

"Consider myself?" she shouted, turning to face him. "Consider myself?" She glared at the door as it opened to admit Feodor Alexandrovich. "What do you want?"

"I wish to inform his excellency that it is time to leave the train, my lady."

"Leave the train? Here? Whatever for?" She pointed at her husband. "You are trying to humiliate me. Why should I leave the train? Why should I put up with your sister and her abominable husband? Have them sneering at me, asking questions? I won't."

"You will," Peter said. "I have business in Moscow, and I may not be able to return here for some time, as you yourself point out." He got up. "So I would be obliged if you'd stop acting like a child and try to become what you are—Princess Borodina. Come along, Tattie. We are going to see Ilona."

Tatiana got up without a word.

"Three years," Irina moaned as she put on her hat. "Three years."

"A sad business." Sergei Roditchev smiled at himself in the mirror as he poured sherry. "Sad, but then, one must always be careful when one seeks to oppose the might of the church." Silly young fool, he thought, as he held out the glass. But Peter Dimitrievich had always been a silly young fool. Something like this had been bound to happen. Roditchev could only hope that *he* would not be involved in the general disgrace. He wondered it if might be a good idea to visit St. Petersburg.

"It has nothing to do with the church," Peter said. "I am told that the archbishop would cheerfully disown the scoundrel. It has to do with some hold this Rasputin has over her majesty. And I can tell you, Sergei, that what I saw with my own eyes makes me shudder at the possibilities."

Sergei held up his forefinger. "You are coming dangerously near to treason, Peter Dimitrievich, and you must remember that I am still the military governor of Moscow." He smiled. "I sometimes think that I am going to be the military governor of Moscow for the rest of my days."

"Because you made such a success of it," Peter said bitterly. "Is there still unrest?"

Roditchev shrugged. "No unrest—they know I will not tolerate it. They have their little meetings, and they talk a lot. I usually manage to have a spy there to tell me about it. I arrest half a dozen of them a year, and hang perhaps two."

"Can you really treat it that lightly?"

Another shrug. "It is a game. A game they insist upon playing, so I must play too. And if I must play, then I might as well enjoy it, don't you agree? Now tell me about this fellow Hayman. You know he is back in Russia?"

Peter nodded. "When did you find out?"

"Oh, Igor Petrovich, your uncle, informed me immediately. Have you seen him?"

"I have not. And I have no intention of doing so. Ilona is well?"

"Ilona is blooming. Did you not think so when you met her?"

"She looks very well. How did she take the news?"

"I haven't told her."

"Well, she will know now," Peter said, "since we have left her alone with Tattie and Irina."

"I doubt it will make any difference to her now," Roditchev said. "If I thought so I would go to St. Petersburg tomorrow and make that Yankee feel very uncomfortable, too uncomfortable to remain in Russia. But I am quite sure Ilona has outgrown him. She is happy as she is. I will admit to you, my dear Peter, that I made some mistakes in the early days of our marriage. I made the mistake of thinking Ilona was just another woman. But of course she is far more than that. I should have known better. I am only grateful that I found out in time. I am grateful to you, my dear boy, for showing me my mistakes, by taking her away from me for a while. Ilona needs the freedom to express herself, to act. She is a superb mother. My only regret is that she has not yet had another child. But dear Ivan Sergeievich is the apple of both of our eyes, as you can imagine. The plans I have for that boy, Peter, when he gets a little older . . . I will tell you of them."

"You were telling me of Ilona," Peter said.

"Oh, yes. Well, as I was saying, apart from managing my household and bringing up my child, she busies herself with what she calls good works. It is amazing. She wanders through the city, by herself, mind you, without even her maid."

"Good lord," Peter said. "Can you permit it? Isn't it dangerous?"

"One would think so. I certainly thought so, in the beginning. I used to have her followed by one of my agents. But do you know, the people seem fond of her. She can go to places I would not dare visit."

"But what does she do?"

"She visits the elderly and the sick. She talks with the young in the marketplace. She administers charity. And she does her own shopping. It is quite expensive, I can tell you. But it is worth it, because she repeats to me everything she has seen or heard. Would you believe it? I maintain a force of some fifty spies, whose sole duty is to position themselves in shops and marketplaces and repeat to me what the people of Moscow are saying. They cost the government a fortune. And here is my own wife, doing it better than any of them, for nothing."

Peter scratched his head. "I cannot pretend to approve, Sergei. I still think it is dangerous. And somehow . . . underhanded."

"Police work is always underhanded. And Ilona genuinely enjoys it. I have said, she is a woman who needs to do something with her life. Since she has found that something, I am sure a man like Hayman will no longer interest her. If you don't believe me, ask her yourself. We'll go and ask her now."

"This evening," Peter said. "I must do some business first."

Roditchev frowned at him. "You have business here in Moscow?" Then why do I not know of it, his expression indictated.

"I placed some affairs in the hands of an attorney. Jacob Stein, you remember?"

"Stein?" Roditchev's brows cleared. "He handled some property for you. As I said at the time, it was stupid to employ a Jew. I have no doubt at all he robbed you." He smiled. "But of course, I suspect you placed even more affairs in the hands of his daughter."

"Don't be obscene." Peter got up and straightened his tie. "I hope she has not been indulging in any more conspiracies?"

"We shall have to wait and see. A leopard seldom changes its spots. A leopardess even more seldom."

"I was talking about the past three years."

"Ah well, for most of that time she has been out of my jurisdiction. After her arrest, her parents sent her away to stay with an uncle in St. Petersburg."

Peter frowned at him. "Judith Stein is in St. Petersburg?"

"I am informed that she is in Moscow now. She returned about six weeks ago. I have tried to make up a file on her activities in St. Petersburg, but frankly, Peter Dimitrievich, those fellows don't know their asses from their elbows. They kept no surveillance on her, although the moment she left here I sent them a copy of her file. So as I say, we shall have to wait and see. Since her return she does not appear to have attended any meetings. She spends a great deal of her time in the public library, reading and making notes. But I am watching her, you may be sure."

"I did not doubt it," Peter said. "But you should remember that I also am watching her, Sergei Pavlovich. Even from banishment in Starogan, I am watching her." He smiled at his brother-in-law. "And I shall not be banished forever."

"Itchykitchykoo," Irina said, dangling her finger in front of the little boy. "Itchykitchykoo. Ow! Damnation! He's bitten me."

"Ivan Sergeievich," Ilona said. "How could you?"

Ivan started to wail.

"Teeth marks," Irina said, holding up her hand. "He's broken the skin."

"He has very good teeth," Ilona said proudly.

"I didn't mean to," Ivan wailed. He glared at his aunt. "I hate you."

"Well," Irina remarked, "I think he should be whipped. Really I do. I shall speak to his father." She flounced from the room.

Ilona gathered her son into her arms. "There, there. But you really shouldn't bite auntie. She's not all bad." She raised her head to gaze at Tatiana, standing by the window and apparently oblivious of the fuss in the room as she looked out at the Kremlin. Tattie had certainly changed. The vivacious girl seemed entirely lost in the solemn, distracted woman. It was possible to believe everything Peter said of her. But hadn't she known as much for years, without even bothering about it before? Everyone had his own life to live. It was a creed she had put into practice on that unforgettable night when she had attended the socialist meeting, and it was not something she could change now.

But now! George was back in Russia. Irina had watched her closely as she told her, seeking some telltale flush, and had seen none. She was sure of that. Because the news, the suggestion of what it meant, was only just sinking in. George had come back. For his newspaper. Only that. But, she reminded herself, there was no other way he *could* have come back.

George. But where did that leave Michael? And where did that leave her? After four years of utter hedonism, utter selfishness, she was in no mental state to resist temptation.

But Michael.

"I took George to see Father Gregory," Tatiana remarked casually, still looking out the window.

Ilona's head jerked, and Ivan, crying gently to himself, gave another wail.

"You've seen him?"

"Of course," Tattie turned away from the window. "Tigran arranged it."

"Oh." Ilona rang the bell abruptly. "Take baby, will you, Natasha Petrovna," she told the nursemaid. "He is upset. Take him into the garden."

"Of course, my lady princess." The girl gave a brief curtsey, and left with the little boy.

Ilona waited for the door to close. "Tell me—is he the same?"

"Exactly the same," Tattie said. "Well, older. And . . . well, older. More certain of himself. But he still loves you. He only came back because he loves you."

"Loves me?" Oh my God, she thought. My instincts were right. He has come back because he still loves me.

"Do you still love him?" Tattie asked.

Ilona glanced at her sister. What could a child like that know of love? But Tattie was eighteen, the same age she had been when she had fallen in love for the first time.

And the last time? She got up and joined her sister at the window. What difference did it make? Even if he loved and she loved, what difference could it make? Quite apart from Sergei, there was Michael. In her despair at losing George and being bound to Roditchev, she had committed herself to a quite irrevocable course of action. Could George ever understand, ever forgive her for that? Easy to cuckold Roditchev, again and again and again. Every week for three years. Easy to do. Amusing to do. Delightful to do. But cuckold Michael? She was far more married to Michael than ever to her husband.

"You *do* still love him, don't you?" Tattie said.

Ilona chewed her lip. Suddenly, she could remember George as if it were yesterday. The quick smile, the moments of seriousness, the gentleness of his touch . . . but also the uncertainty, the hesitation. But George would have changed. He had grown more sure of himself, Tattie said. As if Tattie could possibly know about such things.

But he was back. That was all that mattered. Then what of Michael? Could she possibly contemplate such an act of disloyalty?

Why had George been sent away in the first place? Only because of Peter's pig-headed morality. Which had now got him banished from court. There was a moral for you.

And how could she really talk about disloyalty to Michael? Once she had committed the act of disloyalty to her husband, could there be such a thing as loyalty again?

Now there was true morality, she thought bitterly, Michael had been her salvation. To dream of abandoning him now was not just disloyalty—it would make her into a whore. He was the father of her child.

"Listen," Tattie said. "I can help you."

Ilona turned to look at her.

"I will help you," Tattie promised. "If you'll help me."

"I have no idea what you're talking about."

"Peter is taking me back to Starogan," Tattie explained. "I am to be punished because I went to see Father Gregory. He is going to marry me off, he says, and right away. It'll be someone horrible, I know it will be. Besides, I don't want to marry at all. I don't see why I should. Xenia has never married, and she's nearly thirty. She's quite happy working for Father Gregory. I want to do the same."

Ilona collected her thoughts. "You are a very wicked girl," she said severely. "Working for Father Gregory! Allowing him to . . . to fondle you, you mean. You, a princess of the empire, letting a filthy Siberian peasant put his hand down the front of your dress."

For a moment Tattie's face closed, then her expression relaxed. "I won't be angry with you, Illie," she said. "You just don't understand. You will, one day. One day everyone will understand about Father Gregory. And even if you won't help me, I'll help you. Peter can't keep me in Starogan forever. I'll get away, you'll see."

"He'll have you locked up," Ilona said.

"I'll get away," Tattie said confidently. "Father Gregory will see to that. You'll see. Would you like me to help you?"

"How can you help me? To do what?"

"I could write George for you. I have his address in St. Petersburg."

"It would be simpler to give it to me," Ilona said. "Not that I really want to get in touch with him."

"You do," Tattie said. "I know you do. You want him to come back and love you again. And you talk to me about being wicked. Can there be a worse crime than adultery?"

"Oh, you are a wretched child! You don't know anything about what you are saying. Adultery—what a word! Go to your room and leave me alone."

Tattie shrugged. "I don't really think it's a crime, you know. I don't see why people have to get married at all, why they can't first live with whomever they choose, for as long as they choose. That's how I intend to live, even if Peter does marry me off. I think if you don't see George while he's here, if you don't take this opportunity to run off with him, you're a fool. You'll never have another opportunity. Not while you're young." She went to the door and hesitated. "I'll help you, Illie. If you want me to. And if you'll let me stay here with you for a while."

"Are you in there, Judith?"

Rachel Stein knocked on the door of her sister's bedroom, then opened it and looked in. At seventeen Rachel had attained the family height, but without a commensurate filling out of her body; she remained as she had been as a girl, all arms and legs, her gaucheness increased by her somewhat awkward movements, accentuated at this moment. Like the rest of her family, she was afraid of her sister. No one knew what had happened the night Judith had been arrested. She had never spoken of it, even to her mother. And no one knew what had passed between Prince Peter Borodin and her either. Or what had sent him to her rescue, apart from Joseph's hysterical appeal as he had stumbled into the house, soaking wet from the river.

But they could suspect. They had all heard enough tales of the military police methods, and of Prince Roditchev's own peculiarities. And the logically minded, like Momma for example, could think of only one reason for Prince Peter to interest himself in the affairs of a radical Jewish girl. Thus she had been sent away, from the disgrace she had brought on her family, the disgrace she had brought on herself.

And then she had come back. As a stranger. But the truth was, Rachel thought, she had been a stranger even before she had gone away. Perhaps she had been a stranger for years and years, though not to all of them; she and Joe had always been close, as she was only a year his elder. And of course after that dreadful night the family had known that together they had been indulging in socialism, consorting with anarchists and revolutionaries, for several years. The next day Poppa had whipped Joseph. But he had not touched Judith, because from that night Judith had been a stranger even to her brother. The thought of what must have happened to her that night made Rachel's blood run cold.

But however much she kept her family at arm's length, existing in the invisible cocoon she had wrapped around herself, she seemed to have achieved some equilibrium of spirit. She was entirely bound up in her books; she sat at her desk surrounded by volumes she had borrowed from the library and others she had bought out of her allowance. They had become her life. And when Poppa had suggested, mildly, that it might be a good idea for her to find something to do with herself, had hinted that he might be able to give her a position in his office as a clerk, she had merely smiled at him, almost pityingly, and said, "But I *am* working, Poppa. Very hard."

"At what?" he demanded.

"You'll see when I am finished," she promised, and even Poppa had not felt sufficiently authoritative to press the matter. Rachel had overheard him talking to Momma, and saying "What *can* I do with her, when I do not know what she has known, what she has suffered? We might as well have a stranger in the house."

"But she is your daughter," Momma said.

"Of course she is. And she is welcome to stay with us for as long as she chooses. But do not ask me to treat her as anything different than what she is, a stranger."

Poppa was afraid of her too. Afraid of breaking through that cocoon, of learning things he did not wish to know, of opening a Pandora's box of shame and horror. Just as Rachel was afraid of opening this door, intruding upon so private an existence.

But Judith did not even raise her head. She continued to write, slowly and carefully, copying some sentences from the book at her elbow. "You may come in," she said. "What is it?"

"That man is here to see you."

Judith raised her head. "Mordka Bogrov?"

"Is he your boyfriend?" Rachel asked.

"No," Judith said. "You had better show him up."

"He comes here so often." Rachel looked from right to left. "And right into your bedroom."

"I am sure Momma would not wish Mordka Bogrov in her drawing room," Judith pointed out. "Go and fetch him."

Rachel raised her eyebrows, then shut the door behind her. Judith closed her pen. There was no point in being angry. The poor fools like Bogrov did not understand that she was working for them in her own way, that she would have a far greater impact upon the future than they could ever have, with their meetings and their threats and their conspiracies. She had not even been able to make Joe understand. She supposed she had not tried very hard. But it was an impossible task. They thought she was afraid. They did not blame her for it; some of them had been interrogated too, and they knew just how unpleasant it could be. They were sorry for her.

They could not understand that fear did not enter into it at all. She could admit to herself that she had been remarkably lucky. She did not know what Roditchev would have done to her had Prince Borodin not come in at that moment. She knew what his men did to her when they had searched her, but this she did not wish to forget. That memory was part of her resolution, her determination, which would have to carry her for the rest of her life. But men like Mordka Bogrov would not understand that either.

Nor would they have understood her refusal of Prince Peter. She supposed they would have understood had she accepted the prince's proposal and turned her back on them entirely. If she had not been prepared to do that, then they would certainly have condemned her for not accepting such a position, with all the wealth and influence it would entail, and then using that wealth and influence to further the cause. So instead they must suppose she had given Prince Peter whatever he wanted and then been cast aside, and out of fear and the hope that he might come back to her in the future, had turned her back on them and all they were fighting for.

And yet they hoped to reconvert her.

She watched the door open. Bogrov was as nervous as Rachel had been. He was a little man, with a heavy mustache and a furtive air. A born conspirator, he had become the natural leader of the Moscow cell.

"Come in," she said.

He sidled into the room and closed the door behind him.

Judith pointed with her pen. "I think you are a fool coming here, and a blackguard. You are a radical well known to the police. And you have the nerve to come to my parents' house in broad daylight? What are you trying to do?"

He licked his lips and looked around the room for a chair. The only chair was the one in which Judith was sitting. Only the bed remained, and he had never dared sit on the bed. He twisted his cap in his hands. "You did not come to our meeting."

"And that gives you the right to come here?"

"It is very important. I asked Joseph to speak with you . . . did he not speak with you?"

"He tried."

"And you would not listen. You must listen."

Judith placed her elbows on the desk and leaned forward. "Why should I listen to you, Bogrov? I think you are a fool. I think Joseph is a fool. I think you are all fools. Do you not know that the police are aware of all your meetings? That they send spies to most of them? That you are marked men, already with ropes around your necks, which can be pulled tight whenever Roditchev wishes? So I was once a fool as well. That does not mean I have to be a fool all my life."

Bogrov sidled closer to the bed, but still did not risk sitting down. "I do not believe you. I have never been arrested. Neither has your brother. Those who are arrested are careless. They make mistakes, and the police pick them up. I do not believe in making mistakes. And I do not believe that you have turned your back on us. I cannot believe that, Judith. I believe, despite all, that you are on our side. And we need you."

"Bah."

"Listen to me." He sat on the bed, perhaps without meaning to, his cap reduced to a rag between his hands. "We cannot go on the way we have been. Because we do make mistakes, we are infiltrated by police agents, if not here, then in other places. We are being crushed out of existence, slowly and surely. Why? Because we do not organize ourselves, do not combine into one great movement. Because, as Nikolai Lenin says, we are not fit to be revolutionaries."

"Nikolai Lenin? You read that rubbish?"

"I have one of his newspapers here."

"You take out that thing and I will scream for help," Judith warned. "Nikolai Lenin. Not fit to be revolutionaries. He sits in safety in Switzerland and writes nonsense like that. He can afford to. Is *he* fit to be a revolutionary? If he were, would he not be here, with us?"

"Words are important," Bogrov said. "A revolution cannot be fought with bombs and guns alone."

"That is about the first sensible thing you have ever said, Mordka Bogrov." Judith hesitated. But she knew she was going to tell him what she was doing. For three months she had been dying to tell someone. "Can you keep a secret?"

"It is my business," Bogrov said.

"Well. . . ." A last hesitation. "In my opinion bombs and guns are quite useless. They lead to anarchy and then to repression. Your little band of gunmen cannot possibly take on the army, and the army will always fight for the tsar. What we must do is persuade public opinion that our cause is just. Do that, and we have won, because even the tsar must give in to public opinion in the end, if it represents the majority of people in the country."

"That is a dream," Bogrov said.

"It need not be. That is why we need a literature of revolution, not a newspaper filled with inflammatory statements. I am writing such a book. It will be a book no one can decry, because it will be based upon facts, not fantasies. I am proving what is wrong with Russia, and not just what is wrong with the government. I am going to prove that free trade, undertaken by a free people, will benefit the entire country, the tsar as well as the muzhik. I am going to prove that the reason Great Britain is so wealthy is because she permits free institutions, free elections, free speech, even free newspapers. I have spent the past three years reading everything I can find on government, economics and revolution. I would estimate that I have forgotten more about revolution than you have ever learned, Bogrov. I know all the mistakes, and the mistakes are made over and over again, by each revolutionary group. Shall I tell you why? Because you approach revolution as an emotional matter, an outpouring of bitterness and hate. Revolution is a science, Bogrov, if it is going to be successful. And it must represent all the people, not just a few Jews and a few radicals and a few exiles."

She paused for breath, half afraid of what she had said, because she had never in her life said it to anyone before. Bogrov stared at her for some seconds. Then he said, "When will you finish this book?"

"I don't know. It will take some time. I am prepared to make it my life's work."

"Your life's work? My God. Do you suppose the revolution can wait that long? When you finish it, who will publish it?"

"I will find a publisher. I promise you. Even if I have to have it published outside Russia."

"Just like Nikolai Lenin, eh? And who do you suppose will read it? The police, in order to suppress it, and people like me, who do not need to be converted. Do you suppose the tsar will read it? Do you suppose Stolypin will read it? You *are* a dreamer, Judith Stein."

Judith bit her lip. It was, as she had always supposed, impossible to make them understand.

"It will be published, and it will be read, outside Russia," she said, "and it will influence people outside Russia, and those people will talk, and the talk will get back to Russia. Revolutions do not happen overnight. Not successful revolutions. They take time. The French Revolution did not just happen in 1789. It had been prepared years before, by Voltaire and Rousseau. Their books were banned in France, but without them there could never have been a French Revolution. That is what we need here in Russia: a literature of revolution."

"You are even more of a dreamer than I had supposed," Bogrov said. "You would happily let us all go on suffering for thirty, forty years, while you write your book. I have never heard such nonsense in my life."

"Well," Judith said, "if you do not approve of my way of doing things, I suggest you leave. And do not trouble me again."

"Now, you listen to me. . . ." Bogrov stopped at the knock on the door. Instantly his shoulders hunched, and his face took on an even more furtive expression. "Who is it?" he whispered.

"Who is it?" Judith called.

Rachel entered and gave a nervous giggle. "Your busy day. You won't believe it, Judith. Prince Borodin is downstairs. Asking for you."

Bogrov stood up with a strangled inhalation, cap dropping to the floor. Slowly he bent to pick it up, watching Judith. She sat absolutely still for some moments. She could not believe it. When he had promised to return within a few weeks, following her arrest, she had refused to make a decision, because it had been such a great decision. She had been prepared to wait. And he had not come, which had made it that much easier to acquiesce in Poppa's decision that she should go away and stay with Uncle Poldi for a while. Uncle Poldi had asked no questions, and neither had Aunt Golda. They had assumed that she had gotten herself into trouble. Well, they had not been very far wrong.

So *that* decision had been made for her, and out of that had come all the other decisions. Peter Borodin had foretold a future for her. A future of intrigue and misery, and eventually disgrace and possibly death. She would prove him wrong. She would leave her mark upon history itself, and upon Russian history most of all.

And she would never see Peter Borodin again.

So why were her knees suddenly too weak to support her?

"Then it is true," Bogrov said, "what they say of you. You *are* the prince's mistress. And you speak to me of writing books, on revolution."

Judith glanced at him. "Oh, shut up," she said. "You are talking nonsense. I have not seen Prince Peter in four years."

"Prince Peter," he said contemptuously.

"Prince Borodin." She pushed back her chair and got up. "Where is he?"

"I have shown him into the sitting room," Rachel said, glancing from one to the other.

"It would not do for the prince to find me here, would it?" Bogrov sneered.

"No," Judith agreed. "It would not be good. For either of us. Rachel will take you out the back way."

She would not permit herself to show any femininity before Bogrov, but on the landing she paused to peer at herself in the mirror. Her hair was untidy, and she smoothed it with her hands. There was ink on her fingers, but she could do nothing about that at the moment. And she wished she were wearing something better than a housegown, but that could not be helped either. Besides, she did not wish to attract him. She wished to repel him. Utterly. She ran down the stairs, hesitated again in the doorway to the sitting room. The prince stood by the window, gazing at the lawn and the garden. He wore civilian clothes, and looked older than she remembered.

She drew a very long breath, smoothed her skirt with her hands, and entered the room.

"Your excellency?"

He turned, his face lighting up. "Judith." He crossed the room in three quick strides, stood before her and took her hands. "Judith Stein."

She gave a half curtsey, and he raised her fingers to his lips. "Four years," he said. "I must have been mad."

"I am surprised you ever wished to see me again, your excellency," she said, and freed her hands. "Will you not sit down?"

"Will you not call me Peter?"

Resolution. How she needed resolution. "I do not think that would be proper." She walked around the settee and sat down in a straight chair, leaving him with no alternative but to sit opposite her. "May I offer you a glass of wine?"

He shook his head. "I am on my way back to Starogan. I shall be there for some time." He gave a little shrug. "You will know soon enough that I have been banished from court, and from all official appointments, for three years."

"Banished?" she cried. "You?"

"I attempted to check the evil that is spreading throughout St. Petersburg like a disease. You have lived there for the past three years. You must have heard of the starets, Gregory Rasputin."

"I have heard of him," Judith said cautiously. "But—"

"Everything you have heard is quite true," Peter said. "I have seen it with my own eyes." Another shrug. "His majesty will not believe it."

"And so you are banished? That is monstrous. Medieval."

"In many ways, my dear Judith, Russia is still a medieval society." He got up and began to pace the room. "I apologize for not coming to see you four years ago. I think then I was confused. Uncertain." He paused. "Besides, your refusal was fairly definite."

Judith felt herself flushing.

"But I have thought of you often." He stood above her. "I have been thinking of hardly anyone else. I thought . . . well, that by now you would be married, and have forgotten all about me. But I am told you are not married. Have you forgotten all about me?"

"You saved my life," she said. "I could hardly forget that."

"And you are not married? Not even betrothed?"

She shook her head.

"And no longer indulging in seditious activities. That is very wise of you."

Judith bit her lip. "That does not mean I have altered my opinions."

"I should hope not. But you will agree that there could be no excuse for my changing mine, either."

She waited. Resolution. Oh, for resolution.

"As I have said, I am returning to Starogan. And I am not supposed to leave there for three years. I cannot, for example, return to Moscow. To see you again I would need you closer at hand."

"Is not your wife returning to Starogan with you?"

His mouth hardened. "My wife and I do not see eye to eye. Our marriage was a mistake. She does not love me."

"Do you love her?"

"Of course not."

"Perhaps you should try."

He frowned at her. "I did not come here for a lecture, Judith. I came here to ask you, once again, to be . . . to join me in making both of us happy. With you to turn to, I should not care if I had to spend the rest of my life in Starogan. Indeed, I should rather enjoy it."

Oh, why had he come back, to weaken her resolve, to interfere with her work? Why, why, why? But suppose Bogrov was right, and she could accomplish nothing? Then she would be devoting her life to a complete waste. And as Peter Borodin's mistress? He was, for all his self-centeredness—which she supposed was a concomitant of being a prince—for all his stuffiness and stiltedness, a truly noble man, a truly noble Russian, who like her could see the disaster for which the country was headed. As his mistress she could do nothing but good. And for herself as well. As his mistress she could even continue with her great work; Peter would never object.

And since he was already out of favor, she could not possibly harm him, even by association.

Peter Borodin's mistress. Only a fool would ignore such a glittering prospect. It required but a simple act of will. "I, Judith Stein, reject, turn my back on, and in every way forget my family and friends, my upbringing and my religion, my beliefs and my ideals, and from this moment forth devote myself to the welfare of a single man, because he loves me and is a man I could easily love in return, and because he is wealthy and powerful, and will protect me and mine, even if they do not wish his protection. And because, someday, some good may come out of our union."

Reject, turn my back, and in every way forget my family and friends.

"I think champagne may be in order," Peter said, having watched her face closely. "We shall celebrate. This will be a night you will never forget."

"I cannot," Judith said. "I cannot, I cannot, Prince Borodin. Not now and not ever."

Tatiana's fingers raced over the keys, while she sang in a high, clear voice. " 'Come on and hear, come on and hear, Alexander's Ragtime Band. Come on and hear, come on and hear, it's the best band in the land.' "

"My God," Ilona remarked. "What is that?"

"It's a song," Tattie pointed out, pityingly. "It's called ragtime. That's its name, 'Alexander's Ragtime Band.' "

"You wrote that?"

"Of course not. It was written by an American named Irving Berlin. Actually, I think he was a Russian originally, but he left here as a child."

"However did you obtain the music?"

"Father Gregory got it for me. Father Gregory can do anything. That's why you're all so wrong about him, Illie. He isn't a bad man. All he wants to do is good."

"I am not going to discuss Father Gregory," Ilona said severely. "And I have never heard such rubbish in my life."

"Well, that's what I'm going to write," Tattie declared. "I've already started. And I'm going to dance to it. Father Gregory says there is a famous dancer named Isadora Duncan, who interprets music in her own way. Well, I'm going to be famous too. I'm going to be even more famous, because I'm going to write the music first, and then dance to it, while this Duncan woman only dances to other people's music."

"Tattie," Ilona begged, taking her hands, "you can't. You simply can't. You're Tatiana Borodina. You're the sister of the prince of Starogan. You can't go about the place dancing with hardly anything on."

"Oh, stuff and nonsense," Tattie said. "The prince of Starogan? He's been banished from St. Petersburg. The Princess Roditcheva married after having an affair with an American. There's something wrong with us, Illie. Can't you see that? We're not like other people. We're different. And I'm so *glad* we're different. I think we should be as different as we wish to be. I mean to be different. The moment I'm twenty-one I'm going to do just what I choose. Father Gregory will help me. You'll see."

Ilona gazed at her. So young, so utterly lovely, and so utterly determined to live. Well, she thought, was not I utterly determined to live, at her age? I have no right to condemn my sister for being my shadow. I have no wish to condemn her in any event. Don't I still wish to live? Only I have settled for a false existence, a life of lies and subterfuges, all the way from the nursery to my lover's bed, and what can possibly come of it? What happens when Roditchev finds out about Michael, as he must eventually? What happens when Ivan Sergeievich starts to grow up? Will I ever dare tell him his name is really Ivan Michaelovich? And what do I do with Michael, who daily becomes more demanding, less content to play the role I chose for him? No, no, he chose it for himself. But now he regrets it.

"Excuse me, my lady princess." Catherine Ivanovna hovered in the doorway with a silver salver filled with letters.

"Is there anything for me?" Tattie cried, jumping up from the piano stool and hurrying across the room.

"I think so, mademoiselle. From St. Petersburg."

Ilona had already taken the letters from the tray and was sifting through them. There were the usual crop of invitations, and some notes from the guests of the small supper party she had given for Peter and Irina before their departure for Starogan. Roditchev's letters all went to his office, and the remaining envelope was addressed to Mademoiselle Tatiana Borodina, in a handwriting that even after six years she recognized instantly.

"Thank you, Catherine Ivanovna," she said, wondering if the maid could hear the pounding of her heart. But Catherine merely bowed and withdrew.

"Give it to me," Tattie said.

"Sssh." Ilona walked to the far end of the room and sat on the window seat; it would have been far too obvious to close the door.

"Is it from him?" Tattie scrambled beside her in a flurry of skirts.

"For heaven's sake, keep your voice down," Ilona begged. "Here. You may open it."

"I should think so, since it's addressed to me." Tattie's fingers tore at the envelope, and extracted a sheet of notepaper folded once.

"Is that all?" Ilona asked in dismay.

She opened the paper and another note slipped out from between the sheets.

"There!" Ilona seized it from the floor and opened it. Her heart was pounding so hard she could scarcely read, and her eyes seemed covered in a misty vapor.

> My darling, darling girl. What a fool I have been, ever to believe that you turned away from me. Oh Ilona, my dearest love, when I think of what must have happened to you these six years, I feel my heart constricting until I think I will die. And when I think that but for Tattie I would never have known—my dear, I can only say that whatever you wish to do, I will do. Would to God I had done it six years ago, but looking over our shoulders will accomplish nothing now. You are married, and you have a son. It may be that Tattie is wrong, that you are already regretting having encouraged me to write this letter. If you would prefer me to remain a dream and a memory, I swear

I shall abide by your decision. All I would ask is that I may see you once more. I know your problems and your dangers. I ask you to risk nothing, if you do not choose. But a week from today I shall be in Moscow. I shall be sitting at a table in Kitai-Gorod, with a bottle of vodka in front of me, at three o'clock in the afternoon. I ask only that you walk by, my lady princess. Were you to smile at me, I would know I was in Heaven. Were you to exchange a word—but I dare not dream so high. A week today, Ilona, my dearest, dearest love.

A week from today—the letter was postmarked three days previously. Four days from now. Ilona discovered that her eyes were full of tears.

"Quite a lecture," Tattie grumbled. "I do not think I should have taken him to meet Father Gregory. George really is a very stuffy fellow. I shall have to take him to task when I see him. He is coming to Moscow?"

"Yes," Ilona said.

"And we are going to see him?"

"Oh yes," Ilona said. "We are going to see him. Or at least, I am."

Was she nervous? My God, she thought, no one could know how nervous. But she could hide her face behind her summer veil, and only she knew how her fingers seemed to be sliding about inside her gloves.

Would he be there? Of course he would be there. And would he do as she wished? She did not doubt that.

If only she knew what she wished, what she truly wished. But for the moment it was only to see and talk. After six years they would both have changed greatly. Neither of them could anticipate more than a meeting.

And even Michael could have no objections to that. He *would* object, because he was in the mood to object to everything. But he would be losing nothing, as it was not one of her regular afternoons at the bookstore. Her decision to go out looked, to the Roditchev household, like a spur-of-the-moment one, caused by the heat of the summer afternoon, perhaps the upset over her brother's banishment. And Michael would never, *must* never, suspect that he was in danger of losing everything.

Was he in danger? To cuckold a husband she loathed was one thing; to throw over her lover, and the father of her child, for another man—even if that other man was the only human being she had ever loved as a woman, rather than as a daughter, or a sister, or a mistress. But perhaps after six years the love had died. Oh, it must have died. There was no chance of its having survived. But she could not know that until she had seen him again, talked with him again. Michael would understand that. Michael *must* understand that. And anyway, she reminded herself, Michael had always been George's friend. If he had refused to help her elope, it had been because of his love for her, not because he had wanted to hurt George. And surely that selfish act gave her license to act with equal selfishness herself. Not that she had any intention of doing that, of course. She wanted only to see and talk.

"Six o'clock, my lady?" asked Alexei Pavlovich.

Ilona nodded. She stood on the pavement waiting for her heart beat to slow down, and smiled at the usual accumulation of spectators. She began to walk slowly. Ahead of her were the restaurants which, at three o'clock on a summer's afternoon, overflowed onto the street. Ahead of her was George.

She stopped to talk with some holidaying schoolchildren. Her gloves were swimming, and she could feel sweat gathering at her neck. She walked on, reached the first set of tables, swept them with her glance, and paused to discuss business with a delighted headwaiter.

On to the next set, another conversation, this time with an army officer out walking with his fiancee, then to the next—and George. He sat, as he had promised, by himself at one of the outside tables, a bottle of vodka in front of him. His glass was full, but only one glass had been poured; she did not think he had drunk more than a sip. He was staring at her as she approached.

Ilona checked herself, only feet away. This was necessary, if only because her knees would not carry her any further. He did not seem to have changed at all. Possibly there was more tension in his face, but that was natural on such an occasion. His hair was shorter than she recalled. And somehow she had expected him to be wearing his red hunting jacket, which was how she remembered him best, rather than a gray suit and a soft hat.

"Will you take a drink of tea, your highness?" The headwaiter hovered at her elbow.

"I think not, thank you," she replied. "Perhaps when I have finished my stroll." She moved closer, her fingers sliding into the top of her reticule to secure the note tightly into her palm as she drew up to him. "You, sir, are surely not a Russian."

He was on his feet in an instant, having, it seemed, to take a very long breath before he could speak. "Guilty, ma'am. I'm an American."

"An American," she said. "How splendid, to meet an American on a sidewalk in Moscow." She reached out, picked up the vodka jug, at the same time allowing the note to slide from her palm and onto the table. She held the jug to her face and raised her veil to sniff, watching him as she did so. "And drinking vodka. Beware, my American friend. It only looks like water."

The note had disappeared. "I have discovered that, ma'am."

Ilona smiled at him. Her nerves had stopped jangling, and she was aware of a bubbling exhilaration growing, spreading throughout her system. "Then enjoy it, Mr. American. I will bid you good day."

She continued down the street. Had anyone seen the exchange? The waiter? She did not think so. And George would not be so careless as to open it immediately. Now there remained only Michael. But in the long run, Michael would always do what he was told.

"Your highness?" Petrovski peered at her over the tops of his spectacles, and then looked at the calendar on the wall.

"Have you no books for me today, Monsieur Petrovski?"

"I . . . ah. . . ." Petrovski glanced around the shop, and lowered his voice. "I have sent Michael Nikolaievich out on an errand, your highness. But he will soon be back."

She could not possibly have been more fortunate. "Then I would like you to send him out on another errand immediately," she said. "And I *will* look at your new books, monsieur."

Petrovski took off his spectacles, polished them, and replaced them on his nose. "Whatever your highness wishes."

"I am expecting a visitor, monsieur," Ilona said softly. "An American gentleman. When he comes, will you send him into the storeroom?"

Petrovski seemed to have trouble swallowing. But he nodded. "Of course, your highness. Of course."

"Thank you, Monsieur Petrovski. And really, there is no need to tell Michael that I have been here at all. After all, it is not one of my regular visits. I shall be back the day after tomorrow."

"Of course, your highness." Petrovski hurried in front of her to open the door. Ilona stepped inside and the door closed behind her. Now she had only to wait. Her heart had stopped pounding and she felt quite cool and entirely weightless, as if she were floating on a cloud. In five minutes, George would be in her arms.

Ilona Roditcheva reached up to take off her hat and release her hair.

Michael Nej whistled as he walked along the street, his satchel under his arm. The satchel was full of roubles collected from Monsieur Petrovski's various debtors; it had been a good afternoon's work, and it was a good afternoon in any event. It was impossible not to feel happy on a bright summer's afternoon. Even Michael Nej could not be unhappy.

And what did he have to be unhappy about? Did he not possess the most beautiful woman in Russia? And a princess in the bargain. He loved her. And she . . . well, maybe there was some cause for unhappiness. He could not be sure of her love. She gave herself to him, endlessly and passionately—but always for brief moments. It was a ritual, a habit, something she could not resist. As he had first thought, she had the morals of a Tartar whore. But she was irresistible when she wanted. And she wanted him.

So what was he grumbling about? A wasted life? Would it have been any the less wasted as Peter Borodin's valet? Once it might have been possible to suppose so. Once it might have been possible to think that as Peter Borodin's valet he could be a power behind the chair of one of the most powerful men in Russia. But Peter Borodin had revealed the fatal flaw in his own character, the rigidity which had now caused him to be banished. Valet to a prince banished to his estates for the foreseeable future was no way to influence events.

Then what of his dreams of revolution? That had been sheer absurdity. He, Michael Nikolaievich Nej, was going to overturn Russia, start a fire which would race across the country, just so that he could kill his beloved's husband and make her his mistress? Well, had he not accomplished the desired end? Roditchev lived, but Ilona was his mistress.

What had he got to be unhappy about? Only a nameless concern that he was not fulfilling his destiny by merely working as a clerk in a bookshop and waiting for his mistress to come to him. It made no sense. Mordka Bogrov might talk about murder and mayhem, about spontaneous uprisings which would sweep the tsarists from the streets of Moscow in a welter of blood, but Mordka Bogrov was just as crazy as all those other radicals and anarchists. What could he hope to achieve except bloodshed—their blood, his blood? Had it not all been tried before? And here in Moscow. And had not Prince Roditchev blown them apart in their hundreds with his cannon, and then hanged the remainder? What could they hope to achieve?

Michael rounded the last corner and approached the Petrovski bookshop. He frowned as he watched a man, dressed quite differently from any Russian, enter the shop. A familiar man. A man he had seen before, too often, and too intimately. George Hayman.

How dark it was inside the inner room. And how hot. Ilona had already taken off her driving jacket. Now she fiddled with the buttons on her blouse. But that was absurd, and indecent. And far too forward. It was years since they had last seen each other. She had no idea what changes in his attitude might have taken place in that time. Why didn't he come? She seemed to have been waiting for hours. But perhaps he was not coming. Perhaps, having seen her again, he had realized that he did not love her, after all. Perhaps. . . .

The outer door opened and closed, and she almost gasped. Then there was a very light knock on the inner door.

"Come in," she said. Her voice was steady. She stood straight and watched the door open, watched him come in, watched him close the door behind him. "George," she said, and prayed he would simply hold out his arms.

He held out his arms, and a moment later she was against him, her face turned up for his kiss.

"Oh, my darling, darling girl," he said. "If only I'd known."

"Six years," she said. "Just a moment in time, my dearest."

He kissed her mouth, then her nose, each eye, her chin, gently, lightly, but possessively. "Six years," he said. "They were forever. If only I'd known they would end."

His hands were on her shoulder blades and slipping lower, to the depths of her back. Then suddenly they came up again, to scoop the loose golden hair. "I think I must be dreaming."

"Then dream, George," she said. "Oh, dream."

He held her away from him. "Are you sure, my darling?"

"Sure," she said. "Very, very sure." And did not add: because I have to know.

But almost immediately her apprehension disappeared. She had always considered undressing the most awkward aspect of lovemaking. To undress in front of another person, especially a man, was to reveal too much of one's personality, just as he in turn revealed his.

Perhaps that, above all else, had worried her, when she had thought about meeting George again. They would meet as strangers, in this same little room she had shared with Michael, and they would have to undress in front of each other. Before, at Starogan, she had always come to him in the dark.

It had never occurred to her that he might undress her. That his hands would gently unfasten her blouse, gently ease it from her shoulders as his head came down gently to kiss the tops of her breasts. That his hands would release her skirt, would gather her petticoat, sliding his hands up the silk of her legs, and lift it over her head. Michael never did these things. Michael preferred to watch.

Then it was time to pause while he held her in his arms, his own jacket mysteriously discarded, her nipples little darts of desire against his shirt. He'll never manage the corset, she thought. But the corset was removed as effortlessly as everything else, and she was naked in his arms, except for her stockings. These were removed as she sat on his lap, and while he kissed her; she only knew they were gone when his hands were free to return and cup her breasts, not squeezing or caressing, but just holding them, while she felt the surge of desire grow until she was about to burst.

He could not work miracles. He had to lay her on the bed while he stood up to finish his own undressing, and she could admire, and remember, the hard-muscled torso of the dedicated athlete.

She closed her eyes. She always closed her eyes with Michael. She wanted to feel, oh, how she wanted to feel, but she did not want to *see,* to know what was being done to her, what she was accepting, from her brother's valet. She did not want to see his face as he entered her. She wanted always to re-create the dark intimacy of that night on the riverbank.

She opened her eyes again. This was not Michael. This was George, his face radiant with pleasure as it came closer to hers, and already she could feel him on the verge of entry. She threw her arms around his neck to bring his face down to hers, to kiss him again and again, while she spread her legs as wide as the narrow bed would permit. Yet he would not be hurried, but moved gently, stroking her into desperation before seeking his entry.

It was the quickest climax she had ever known, and the most tumultuous. She thought she cried out in sheer pleasure. Then she brought her legs back together to imprison him—not that he sought to escape, for he continued to hold her as she had never been held before.

Six years. A moment in time. But what a moment. Six years ago she had fallen in love with a man who was different from any man she had ever known. But they had both been children, she knew that now. Today they were children no longer. Today, everything she had ever wanted was here in her arms. If she dared to hold it. If she could make herself dare.

Ilona Roditcheva stood by her son's cot and looked down on the sleeping little boy. How peaceful he looked. And how like Michael. Only she would see that, though, because only she would think of looking for the resemblance. It was there nonetheless.

Once she had thought Ivan was all she wanted. She had returned to her home and her husband in the full confidence of the growing life in her womb. Roditchev had been afraid to touch her then. In view of their previous troubles, and of the memory of Anastasia's dying in the act of giving birth, for his second wife to lose her child would damn him forever. The tsar, and even more important, the tsarina, knew the secrets of his bed, and Ilona had been safe.

She had been safe even after the child was born, because of that knowledge. Her husband seldom slept with her, preferring the company of the mistresses he maintained in various houses around the city, girls he could no doubt beat and mistreat to his heart's content, without the risk of an imperial frown. It was that precious freedom she would forfeit, should she attempt to escape, and fail.

She leaned over the bars and pulled the sheet to his throat. Zoe Alexeievna, the head nurse, curtsied, and seated herself in the rocking chair under the night light. Ilona left the room and walked slowly along the hallway toward her own room, where Catherine Ivanovna was waiting. No doubt Catherine Ivanovna was still Roditchev's spy, but she, like all the other servants, was aware of the change in the relationship between her master and mistress these past three years, and she had adjusted her attitude accordingly. She had realized that she might spend the rest of her life serving Princess Roditcheva, and having produced a son, the princess could only grow in power as the years rolled by. It was at last possible to relax enough to think, even in Catherine Ivanovna's company.

Think about giving up that power, Ilona Dimitrievna. But that is the least of what you are giving up, should you fail. What had she thought, only yesterday? To cuckold a husband is one thing, to do that *and* desert a faithful lover, the father of your child, is another.

"My lady is pensive tonight," Catherine Ivanovna observed as she released her mistress's hair, removing the soft pads around which the pompadour was built. That pompadour had been rebuilt with George's help, and none too successfully. Would Catherine notice?

"I am very tired," Ilona said. "It is the heat." She put up her arms to have the lace nightgown dropped over her head.

"Will my lady take a cup of iced tea?"

Ilona shook her head. She did in fact feel like some tea, but she wanted to get rid of Catherine, wanted the privacy of her own bed, and the darkness. Yet the moment the electric lights had been turned off and the door closed, she was out of bed and standing at the open window, allowing the cool night breeze to ripple through her nightgown and caress her body. Despite her tiredness, she felt so *alive*. Even her mind, while wishing a quiet solitude in which to remember and savor and think, was joyously alive. She had realized this afternoon, for the first time, that however gratifying it might be to be loved, the pleasure could not compare with that of loving, and when that love was returned, the pleasure was almost painful.

Then how painful must be the agony of loving and being unsure of love's return? For the first time she could understand something of Michael's discontent. She gave him her body. She had borne his child. But had she ever loved him? If she could not know, how could he?

She gazed at the twinkling lights of the city, listened to the blare of car horns and the roar of their engines from beneath her and inhaled the faint tang of exhaust fumes. George was out there somewhere, perhaps also standing in the window of his hotel room, thinking of her, remembering this afternoon. He would be doing that because he loved, and he would know that his love was reciprocated. Did he doubt her now? Could he? He had loved her, and believed in her, once before. But had she loved and believed equally? She had thought so. A combination of youth and weakness had forced her to accept her fate so meekly. Surely that could never happen again. The dangers of deserting Sergei, of escaping Moscow and reaching either the Austrian border or a ship bound for America, even with Ivan in tow, did not seem so immense. George had not even mentioned that possibility. He had wanted only to look at her, to hold her in his arms. Yet she knew it could happen. She was no longer a child, and he no longer had anything to lose; he had come back only for her sake. If she decided to do it, George would take care of everything. And this time they would succeed.

If she decided to do it. If she decided to cut herself entirely adrift from family, friends, position, birth and upbringing. What nonsense: her family was as good as ruined, she had no friends and her position was at the mercy of Roditchev. What did birth and upbringing matter after she had given herself to Michael? But there was the past. George knew nothing of Michael. He would have to be told.

Then where was the obstacle? Michael himself. Her fingers curled into fists and came together, the hands slowly rising to press against her breasts. She owed him nothing. He had betrayed her in the first place, created all the circumstances which had led to the misery of her life, to her decision to seek a physical solace for her ills. That he had been the one to benefit by her design had been an accident of time and place. Had Peter chosen Ivan Nej for his valet, it could even have happened with him. With Ivan Nej? That was an almost impossible thought. Almost. Wasn't it time she was at last perfectly honest with herself, and admitted that whoever had helped her escape from the meeting hall that night would have received his reward?

And become the father of her child?

She turned away, reached her bed, and fell forward across it, her face pressed to the coverlet.

Why wasn't life like a game of chess, where, when one was in a losing position, one could say, "I resign," and set the pieces up for a different encounter? How she wanted to be able to set the pieces up again.

How she wanted to be able to make up her mind.

"We must be prepared to strike." Mordka Bogrov leaned from his platform and peered into the smoke-filled interior of the small room. "We must be prepared to show Russia, to show the world, that we can act instead of talking."

He paused to take a drink of water and wipe his brow. He certainly needed to show that he could act as well as talk, Michael thought. But act with what? There were only seventeen men and two women in the hall, the remnants of the old radical party. And these were all poor muzhiks, the dross of the city. There was no middle class leavening left, as in the days when that Jewish girl and her brother had helped organize these meetings. They had been stung, and they would not risk it again.

So sixteen muzhiks and two of their wives, one madman, and one bookshop clerk were going to overturn Russia. And perhaps not even a bookshop clerk any more. Hayman. How he hated the very thought of the man's name. To see him in the flesh, entering *his* shop, to be told by Petrovski that he must leave again immediately on some quite unnecessary errand, to wait in the throng of passers-by until she had come out, as he had known she must. . . .

In his rage and his misery, had he possessed a revolver he would have shot her dead. Certainly he would have killed Hayman. But instead he had done nothing but weep. He was not the stuff of which heroes are made.

"And it can be done, comrades," Bogrov was saying, his voice lower now. "One blow, one act of determination, one spark, thrown into the air at this moment, will detonate an explosion which will rock Russia from Smolensk to Vladivostok. It can be done."

But had he really expected anything different, Michael wondered? Had he not known, from the very beginning, just what she was? A gentlewoman with the mind and the lust of a Tartar whore. And the beauty to make men dance at the snap of her fingers. And the total selfishness to enjoy them without a care for what happened next.

But she was the mother of his child. Did that count for nothing?

"So I ask you this, comrades," Bogrov said, his voice sinking lower yet, "who is the linchpin of the entire imperial system, which keeps our people in a state of servitude? It is one man, my friends. One man, and one alone."

"The tsar," someone said. And crossed himself.

"The tsar certainly heads the system. But he can only be served by men stronger than himself, more ruthless than himself. More hateful. And for five years now he has possessed such a man. Stolypin, comrades. It is Stolypin who rules Russia. It is Stolypin who tramples us into the dust, who hangs us and sends us to Siberia. Without Stolypin, the tsar would be like a lion which has lost its teeth."

"It has been tried before," someone else said. "They only succeeded in blowing up his daughter."

"Blowing up," Bogrov said contemptuously. "Bombs. Bombs are for cowards, comrades. And as you have just said, they are inaccurate, uncertain. Only the bullet will do for Stolypin. A bullet fired by a resolute and capable hand."

No, it didn't matter, Michael realized. The child was hers, not his. He had served his purpose. Now that the American was back, he had to retire into the outer darkness where the sons of serfs belonged. Princess Ilona Roditcheva had bigger fish to fry.

Then what was his remedy? A letter to Roditchev? He hated the prince, if possible, more than he hated Hayman. And if he told the whole truth, his own son would be thrown out like garbage. He knew enough about Roditchev to be certain of that.

"But there is more," Bogrov said. "There comes a time, only occasionally, when one knows the moment is ripe for action. When one knows that great schemes can be launched and brought to fruition. How may Stolypin be executed? It presents no great difficulty. He rides in his carriage in public often enough. He is surrounded by his guards, to be sure, but yet a good man with a revolver can accomplish the deed. So much for Stolypin. But is his death sufficient? Might not the tsar be able to find another like him? As someone has just said, above Stolypin there is the tsar. There will be the secret of our success, comrades. Always in the past we have struck at one evil, and one alone. That has been the limit of our ability. And the other evil, either the minister or the monarch, has remained to trample upon us. But think, comrades, think. Think of a Russia suddenly without either tsar or Stolypin, ruled by a sickly little boy, by a regency council in which every man will be intent upon furthering his own ambitions, feathering his own nest. Think of the opportunities we shall then possess."

So he would do nothing, Michael thought bitterly. He would crawl away into the darkness, and dream of what might have been, dream of some holocaust which might have enabled him to take Ilona and Ivan with him, just the three of them, as in his brother Ivan's childish fantasies or the romantic tales he had read in old Count Dimitri's library. A man, a woman and a child, against the world. But the world of nature, not of men. A world in which they could survive, leaning on each other, because there was no other path to survival. Holocausts of that nature only occurred in dreams or romances.

"Do you suppose you will discover the tsar and Stolypin riding together in the street?" one of the women asked contemptuously. "You are a dreamer, Bogrov."

Mordka Bogrov stopped leaning on his lectern and stood straight. His twisted face broke into a smile, a terrible smile. "I am a dreamer, comrade, who has the patience to wait for his dreams to come true. The tsar and Stolypin never appear in public together. Well, hardly ever. But I will tell you when they are going to appear together: on the evening of September third, at the opening of the new Kiev Opera House. September third, my friends. Just two weeks away. Think of that. They will be there together, with the tsarina and the tsarevnas. Why, the entire criminal crew will be in one box. Two resolute men, comrades, each armed with a six-gun, could change history on that day. They could destroy everything that is wrong with Russia, leave only the little boy, without even the solace of his mother. Two men, comrades, could raise a holocaust which would sweep away everything that we hate and fear, everything that we are determined to resist and destroy."

He paused for another drink of water, and Michael discovered that despite his misery, he was listening to the fellow. Old mad Bogrov. Dreaming of revolution and mayhem and murder. But wasn't that what he also wanted, if he supposed it could be done?

"Two men," Bogrov said, "and two revolvers. I have the revolvers." Theatrically he paused, then reached into his satchel and produced the two weapons, gleaming in the flickering candlelight. And he achieved the reaction he wanted, as a whisper of inhaled breaths filled the air. "And I have one of the men. Me, comrades. I am not afraid to lead our crusade. But I need a companion. I need someone to stand at my side and deliver the fatal blow which will topple this edifice we carry on our shoulders, and bring it down into the dust beside us. Who will stand beside me and strike a blow for freedom?"

Michael Nej found himself on his feet.

Chapter 11

"STAND UP AND LET ME LOOK AT YOU," MORDKA BOGROV COMmanded.

Michael stood reluctantly. He was sure Bogrov would be able to see his knees tremble.

"Hmm." Bogrov straightened his white tie and walked slowly around him. Michael still could not estimate how much renting the tail coats and silk hats, the beautifully laundered stiff white shirts, the ties, the lacquer for their hair and the patent-leather shoes had cost, just as he could not estimate how much this hotel room and the train fares from Moscow had come to. Suddenly Bogrov, the most down and out of men, had found a source of wealth.

"But I have always possessed it," he explained. "I have been saving it for years. For just this occasion. I have starved, Michael Nikolaievich, rather than spend that money."

But now it had been spent. They possessed nothing in the world but their return fares to Moscow. Under the circumstances it seemed almost sacrilege to be wearing this finery, straining at every seam, over their ordinary clothes.

"That looks all right," Bogrov said at last. "Almost perfect. And in the dark, who's to know?"

Michael stared at himself in the mirror. Almost perfect. He had never looked quite so perfect, he thought. If only Ilona could see him now. But Ilona would never see him again. Nor, he supposed, would she ever wish to, whether or not they were successful. But at least he was going to show her that he was worth something, even if he did not suppose she would appreciate it much.

"Nervous?" Bogrov asked.

"Why should I be nervous?"

"You are sweating," Bogrov pointed out. "Here." He poured two glasses of vodka.

"This will make me sweat more," Michael protested.

"It's a cool evening. You'll feel better outside. And the liquor will give you some courage. There is nothing to be afraid of."

"I am not afraid," Michael insisted.

"Well, put this in your waistband."

Michael took the revolver carefully. He had handled it before; Bogrov had made him practice. But he was still nervous of it. He had never actually fired it.

"Check the chambers," Bogrov said. "Your life may depend on it."

Michael broke the gun and rolled the six chambers. From the inner end of each, the brass cartridge case gleamed at him. "Do we take any spares?"

Mordka nodded. He opened the box and gave Michael another twelve cartridges, taking a similar number for himself.

"Now you understand," Bogrov said, "when they stand for the anthem, I will shoot Stolypin, and you will shoot the tsar. I will then shoot the tsarina, and you will shoot the Grand Duchess Olga. I will shoot the Grand Duchess Tatiana, and you will shoot the Grand Duchess Marie. Three shots each. Then we run for the exit. Our remaining bullets will clear the way for us, and when we are in the corridor we will have time to reload. Then we will throw off these clothes and make our escape, shooting if we have to. But it should not be necessary, as they will be looking for men in evening clothes."

The Grand Duchess Tatiana. He had never seen any of the grand duchesses, but the very name was too close to home.

"Do we have to kill the girls?"

"Yes," Bogrov said. "They are old enough to take control, and they are creatures of their mother. Then, when we leave the theater, we go to the station and catch the night train for Moscow. Understood?"

"Yes, but. . . ." Michael chewed his lip. "Do you not suppose it is known that we have left Moscow? I had to tell Petrovski I was leaving. The police will find out that we were in Kiev on the night of the murder."

"Do you take me for a fool?" Bogrov asked. "I have thought this through very carefully. We shall return to Moscow and we shall disappear. We shall go to the house of Jacob Stein, the lawyer."

Michael frowned at him. "Stein? But he is not one of us."

"His son and daughter are ours."

"His daughter?" The girl, Judith Stein. "She has renounced us."

"She is still one of us. And she will help us if we go to her. She will have to. She dare not turn us away, for if we betray her to Roditchev, she is as dead as we are."

"How can she help us? They will search every Jewish house in Russia." And I am not even a Jew, Michael thought bitterly.

Bogrov tapped the side of his nose. "She can help us more than anyone. Because she is Prince Peter Borodin's mistress."

"I do not believe it."

"Well, it is true. I have been at her house when the prince came to call."

"Prince Borodin? But has he not been disgraced and sent to Starogan?"

"Bah. What is disgrace to a prince of the empire? He dared to criticize the tsarina's lover. Nothing more than that. But with the tsarina dead, and the tsar as well, Prince Peter will be called upon to assist in governing the country. And we will be with his mistress. There will be no better place from which to start a revolution."

"But if she is his mistress, then she can afford to throw us out. He will certainly protect her from Roditchev."

Bogrov smiled at him. "Judith has secrets, Michael Nikolaievich; enough seditious literature, written by herself, to hang her. She will not throw us out. And she will not dare compromise her lover. She will help us. Just trust me. I have thought this thing through. Now, are you ready?"

No, Michael thought. I will never be ready. I have never fired a revolver before. I have never even considered taking a life before. No, that was a lie. He had considered killing Roditchev. Was Stolypin, or his employer, the tsar, any different?

And who knew what might lie at the end of it all?

He drained the vodka. "Yes," he said. "I am ready."

It was not yet fully dark, and the evening looked as though it were going to be a bright one. The street outside the theater was crowded, not only with people waiting to see the glittering royalty arriving for the opening night, but with policemen, mounted and on foot, patrolling the space in front of the foyer, where the cars and carriages drew up in turn to disgorge their splendidly dressed passengers. The atmosphere was close and the noise immense. My God, Michael thought, we shall never get through this mob when we try to leave.

"Fortune favors the brave," Bogrov muttered. "We shall simply disappear into the crowd when it is time. Are you ready?"

Michael nodded. He did not trust himself to speak. Wearing two suits of clothes on such an evening would have made him unbearably hot under the best of circumstances; he could feel sweat trickling down his shoulders. But he knew it was mainly caused by fear. They had not arrived by carriage. What would happen when a policeman stepped forward and tapped them on the shoulder? He feared Bogrov, that was the trouble. Bogrov would shoot first and think afterwards. How in the name of God, Michael wondered, had he managed to get involved in something like this with a man like him?

They pushed their way through the crowd, Bogrov apologizing courteously. The people parted good-naturedly enough. They were two young men going to the theater. So they didn't have a carriage; that was no reason why they should not be going to the theater. They were wearing the right clothes.

They reached the edge of crowd; there remained the street to be crossed. Above them the glowing lights naming the opera and the lead singers beamed at them; the entire theater was an explosion of light. The street was as bright as if it had been noon.

"Walk as if you own the earth," Bogrov said. "Confidence is the thing."

Confidence. Michael made himself square his shoulders, and as an afterthought pushed back the brim of his silk hat with his stick to give himself a more jaunty air. He could hear the comments of the onlookers, wondering as to their identity, and from a distance he could hear the fanfare of trumpets.

"Just in time, gentlemen," said the police captain on duty in the foyer, and saluted. Bogrov gave a brief nod and stepped past him. Michael gave him a smile.

"Damned horse threw a shoe," he said. "Tonight, of all nights."

The captain smiled sympathetically, and then they were lost again in the throng of guests, trying to present their tickets to the majordomos on each doorway, gossiping and chattering, looking over their shoulders.

The bugles were coming closer.

"We won't get inside in time," Michael whispered frantically.

Bogrov said nothing, but continued to push at the people in front of him.

There was a clatter of hooves and a car drew up. Entry into the theater was forgotten as heads turned to watch Stolypin and his wife step down. Peter Stolypin. Michael realized with horror that he had never even seen the man he had helped plan to kill. But then, he had never seen the tsar before either, or the royal women.

Peter Stolypin was a large man, at once tall and broad. His hair was receding, and was worn short in the German fashion; one of the main causes of discontent among people like Bogrov was the increasing influence at court of the Germans, all brought about by the tsarina, a German by birth. Stolypin's mustache was waxed and pointed, his clothes fitted him as if he had been poured into them, and he possessed the manner of someone who knew his position, his strength and his power, as he graciously acknowledged the greetings of the theater manager and the leading performers, of the police chief and the various princes who had gathered here tonight. In contrast, his wife, small and slight, glanced from left to right in nervous anxiety. Not even her gown or her jewels could hide her obvious discomfort.

"He has a broad chest," Bogrov whispered.

People jostled them as the throng grew thicker. They were never going to get inside in time for the anthem. But perhaps the anthem would be delayed until everyone had taken his or her place.

The fanfares were now upon them, and the imperial Daimler was drawing to a halt. Equerries and aides hurried to open the doors, and the tsar stepped out. How small he was, Michael thought, at once short and a trifle insignificant. But for the blaze of orders and ribbons on the breast of his coat there would be no telling he was anyone important. Not so the tsarina; her face was as tightly drawn as Madame Stolypin's, but settled into lines of determined arrogance; the diamond tiara sparkled in her hair just as her fingers and her gown glistened with other stones.

And then the girls. He swallowed as he watched them, hurrying behind their parents, chattering to each other, laughing as they gave their hands to be kissed. Three of the loveliest and most unaffected young women Michael had ever seen. They wore white—which would shortly be stained red. He closed his eyes.

Bogrov gripped his elbow. "Now," he muttered. "We'll never get so close again."

Michael opened his eyes in terror. The tsar had stopped to speak with his minister. The two men were together, half turned away from the crowd, heads close—and no more than twelve feet from where he and Bogrov were standing.

"No," he said. "For God's sake. . . ."

But Bogrov had drawn the revolver from his waistband, and with his left hand had given the woman standing in front of him a violent push. She staggered forward with a gasp of dismay, and both the tsar and Stolypin turned even as a policeman ran forward, stopping as he saw the revolver.

Bogrov fired.

For a moment Michael thought that Bogrov had missed, for Stolypin seemed to slap himself on the chest. Then he took a stumbling step forward, and blood welled from under his fingers, suddenly covered his white shirt front.

"Shoot," Bogrov screamed. "Shoot them down."

But as Stolypin stepped forward, Michael had stepped back into the crowd. He knew he was not going to shoot, not the tsar and certainly not any of the girls. He had always known, deep in his heart, he was not a murderer.

The night dissolved into pandemonium as people recovered from their shock. There was another shot, and Michael supposed Bogrov had fired again. But Bogrov was gone, lost beneath a crowd of men and women who had thrown themselves upon him. Stolypin was also down, and the tsar knelt beside him while policemen formed a ring around them. Another policeman was holding the arm of Madame Stolypin, whose eyes were closed. The three tsarevnas huddled together, clutching each other's hands, surrounded by police. And the tsarina stood as straight as ever, staring into the crowd. Staring at him, Michael realized, for he also had remained standing.

But I have not drawn my weapon, he said with his eyes. You do not know it was I Bogrov was calling upon. You do not know.

Yet the force of her gaze drove him backwards, and when he saw her speak to one of the policemen surrounding her, he turned and ran.

The crowd around the theater surged forward. They screamed and yelled and wailed, but saw no reason not to welcome Michael into their ranks. For a moment he was carried back toward the theater, and he had to work his elbows to get through the crush and find himself some air. When he looked back at the lights, he saw policemen already pushing their way into the crowd, looking, thrusting people this way and that.

They were after *him*. Michael turned, elbowed more people out of the way, reached the open space beyond, and looked over his shoulder once again. He saw Bogrov being dragged to his feet by two policemen. Bogrov's face was bleeding and his coat was ripped. The policemen had only just saved him from being torn to pieces by the crowd. In order to tear him to pieces themselves?

Michael reached the safety of a side street. He discovered he was trotting and made himself slow to a walk. A man in evening dress, running, was bound to be suspicious. But it would soon be dark, and he would find an alleyway where he could strip off his outer garments, and become what he was, a simple muzhik, who could not possibly be associated with the well-dressed assassins of the prime minister.

But they had only got Stolypin. They had failed. *He* had failed. He had failed Bogrov no less than he had failed Russia. But he now knew that they never had a chance of succeeding. He might have shot the tsar, but there would never have been a chance of a second shot, and the tsarina would have been left. The tsarina was a far more fearsome figure than her husband. Russia had been ruled by women before; in more than one case, by women who had disposed of their husbands in order to seize power. Those had been famous times for Russia, but bad times for anyone who dared object. Pugachev, who had led a revolt against Catherine the Great, had been exposed in an iron cage for all the world to mock, until he had died.

An alleyway. Michael sighed with relief. Behind him, the noise was dwindling. He must be half a mile away. He was safe. Poor Bogrov. But Bogrov would never betray him. Bogrov was a man of steel.

"Halt there! You!"

Michael turned and gazed at a policeman. His entire system seemed to slow as he suddenly felt very cold.

The policeman came closer, his oil lamp casting a glow in front of him. "What are you up to back there in. . . ." He hesitated as he saw the evening dress. "Good night to you, monsieur," he said.

Michael drew a long breath. "Good evening."

"I apologize, monsieur," he said. "But we have been told to question every man found on the streets of Kiev this evening."

"Indeed?" Michael asked, pleased with the even tenor of his voice. "Has something happened?"

"I believe so, monsieur," he said. "There has been a great tragedy at the theater. They are saying that Monsieur Stolypin has been shot."

"My God," Michael said. "Have they caught the assassin?"

"One of them, monsieur. But it is said there are two. So if you would accompany me to the station."

"The station?" Michael's heartbeat, which had returned to normal, suddenly started to race again.

"It is not far, monsieur."

"But . . . you have spoken with me here. You know that I am no assassin. My dear fellow, I am in a hurry. I must get home. My wife has been taken ill. Surely you will not insist upon taking me to the station."

"I must, monsieur," the policeman said. "I have been ordered to do so." He came closer. "Come along, monsieur."

Michael thrust his hand into his waistband and pulled out the revolver. Once again his heart was slowing, but amazingly, he felt quite in command of himself. "I cannot," he said.

The policeman looked at the gun in surprise, then made a sudden attempt to draw his own weapon. Michael squeezed the trigger. The explosion sounded like a cannon shot in the confined space of the alleyway, and the policeman gave a curious gasp as he arched forward, his gun only half out of his holster. He hit the cobbles.

My God, Michael thought: I have joined the rank of the assassins after all.

Judith Stein sat at her desk and wrote, slowly and carefully. Quite apart from the passage she was copying, from a book by Robert Owen, she genuinely liked writing, liked forming letters and then words, all neatly put together in rippling curves and brisk straight lines.

She worked on a daily schedule, going straight from her bed to her desk without doing more than cleaning her teeth and putting on a dressing gown. She worked through until lunch, composing and setting down her own ideas during the first half of each morning, when her brain was fresh and at its most active; later on, as she got tired, she would do the copying. But copying was almost the pleasantest part of her work, because she could allow her thoughts to wander, while the mere fact of writing down her subject enabled her to absorb it and remember it and use it to develop her next chapter.

She could allow herself to be self-critical at times like this. To wonder what she was doing, and whether the enormous expenditure of time would ever be justified. Whether she was a fool, or merely a coward.

She was twenty-two years old, and both the evidence of her own eyes, as well as the reaction of men with whom she came into contact, told her that she was attractive. Her father was wealthy. And she refused to marry or even to become engaged. No one could understand, neither her parents nor the young men they invited to their house for dinner.

And Peter Borodin? Had he been able to understand? He had been angry. A prince of the empire, returning for a second time to plead his love for a Jewish girl. And for a second time refused. There would never be a third time. There could never be a third time, because she did not suppose she would have the strength of mind to refuse him again. But as a third time was not possible, her refusals, her self-sacrifices, had to be worthwhile. And that could certainly not be achieved by agreeing to marry some nice boy who would want her to have several nice children and manage his nice home. Then her life would be truly wasted.

But if Bogrov were right, and her great work would never see the light of day . . . she discovered she was chewing the end of her pen. Bogrov could not be right. Bogrov had never been right in his life, because he never considered any matter deeply enough to understand it fully. Bogrov swam on the surface of events, but dangerous nonetheless, dangerous because his jaws were always snapping away, at friend and foe alike.

So she must find her happiness here in this study, with these books, her true friends, her only friends. And she *was* happy. Or at least content. So why wonder what it might be like to have a man, a prince, take her in his arms and kiss her on the lips, and then . . . but she knew nothing of what more he might do. And she was afraid to think about it too deeply. Thoughts like that occasionally brought back memories of the hands and fingers of the men who had searched her, of the look in Prince Roditchev's eyes as he had commanded her to undress. Mankind, lusting, was evil. She had the evidence of her own experience.

Noise from downstairs. A sudden, loud, violent sound, as if the cook had dropped a platter. And then Momma's voice, high and anxious, and a scream from Rachel. Judith leaned back in her chair, frowning. Undoubtedly some domestic tragedy. Should she go down? Would they wish her to go down?

She listened to feet on the stairs, boots. Slowly the pen slipped from her fingers as she stared at the door. Her mind teemed even as her body broke out in a violent sweat. She could only think, my God, Bogrov. Bogrov has betrayed me.

She gathered the papers together, held them in both hands, hesitating. There was nowhere she could hide them where they would not be found. She pushed back the chair, stood up, and continued to gaze at the door as it hurtled inwards. It had not been locked, but they had not troubled to turn the handle, and now one of the hinges had come off. The door sagged. And three men in uniform stood there.

"You cannot go in there," Momma was crying from behind her. "You cannot break into a girl's bedroom."

Momma gasped, and Judith commenced to hate. Hate was the only emotion which could possibly sustain her now. She watched one of the policemen coming toward her, realized she still held the papers in her hands. She threw them at him. Sheets of white paper, covered in her neat handwriting, cascaded about him. He merely shook his head, and the papers settled on the floor behind him. Then he was before her, hitting her on the face.

Her head swung sideways with the force of the blow, and her eyes misted. Tears. But she would not cry. Then her stomach seemed to explode in pain, and she realized he had hit her in the belly. Her knees gave way and she fell against him. His hands caught the front of her dressing gown, fingers seizing the material and the breast beneath, then threw her to the floor. She opened her eyes in time to watch the carpet racing upwards at her, got her hands between it and her face just in time, yet still received a jolt which, added to the breathless pain in her abdomen, left her helpless, unable to move, gasping and wondering if she were dying.

If only she were dying. She looked at boots, and supposed she was seeing double. But of course there was more than one man. She knew they were speaking, and she knew Momma was screaming, but she could hear nothing but a confused, high-pitched humming in her ears. She watched the men stoop and seize her arms to pull her to her feet. Their fingers were biting into her flesh, and she had to feel pain, but she felt nothing except the agony in her stomach.

She was on her feet being dragged toward the door by two of the policemen. The third was gathering her books and papers into a satchel. Her feet came out of their slippers and she jarred a toe. Desperately she tried to stand and had an ankle kicked from under her by one of the boots, sending fresh pain welling up through her leg; they preferred to drag her.

Hair had flopped across her face; she blew it away with her gasps and gazed at her mother. Momma's face was also twisted with pain, and flushed with fear and humiliation; great tears rolled down her cheeks. But she was not being held by any policemen, and neither was Rachel, behind her. Thank God for that, Judith thought.

Ruth Stein was speaking, telling her something, but she still could not hear her. And then she was past her, and flopping down the stairs, bare toes bumping from one step to the next. She gave a quick glance at the pantry doorway, where the servants were gathered in horror-stricken concern. She looked away, and gazed instead at the front door, also half torn from its hinges, at the bright September sunshine beyond, at the crowd which had gathered to watch the police at work.

For the first time she was conscious that she was wearing only her night dress, and that her dressing gown was open. The sun, shining on her, would silhouette her body through the linen. She closed her eyes, as if by doing so she could shut out the eyes looking at her; she felt the heat on her head and face, felt her feet bumping on the stone of the steps. The fingers seemed to drive deeper and deeper into her flesh with every second. She knew she was going to scream. But she could not scream. She could never scream. To scream would be to surrender.

At the foot of the steps there waited a horse-driven van and two more policemen. The back doors were open, and Judith was picked up and thrown inside. Her knees struck and she fell on her face, legs still dangling outside. A man's hand closed on her thigh, fingers on the inside, high up so that he could hold her buttocks as well, while one of the fingers went between. The grip was immensely powerful, the shock of pain and revulsion unbearable, as he picked her up and thrust her forward into the van.

Judith screamed.

The police orderly opened the door and stood to attention. George Hayman straightened his tie, hoping he did not look as nervous as he felt. The very last thing he had ever supposed he would be doing was calling on his mistress's husband in a professional capacity, but there was nothing else he could do. Events had an unfortunate habit of interfering with the most carefully laid plans.

General Prince Roditchev stood behind his desk. He looked prosperous, well-fed, contented. It was occurring to George that those were descriptions which could apply to almost any Russian aristocrat. Even after their leader had been struck down?

"Mr. Hayman," Roditchev said. "What brings you to Moscow?"

"Why, the news, of course."

Roditchev smiled. "You arrived here three weeks ago, Mr. Hayman. Are you suggesting you are prescient?"

George flushed. "I have been in Moscow for three weeks, yes, general. My job is to get about the country, see people, learn what I can."

"Sit down," Roditchev said, and sat down himself. "It was remiss of you to visit my city and not call. After all, we are old acquaintances. And of course you are an old acquaintance of my wife."

George's jaw tightened. He had never supposed this meeting was going to be a comfortable one. And matters were not helped by his more recent guilt. Did Ilona have any idea of what would happen if they were discovered?

But Ilona . . . to hold her once again in his arms. To know that she loved him. She had hardly changed at all, unless to become even more beautiful, and she had become much more certain in her lovemaking. Because of lessons learned from her husband? He had always loathed the man. Now he thought he might hate him. And yet this was the man Ilona was actually betraying.

Would she wish to continue betraying him? It was impossible to decide what went on behind those deep blue eyes. In that way she *had* changed. She had become a woman of secrets. But no doubt that change had also been forced upon her by her husband.

And even if she was contemplating it, was it something he dared ask her to do? To encourage her to risk this man's rage was criminal. George had already, unwittingly, brought disaster to her family.

"No doubt," Roditchev observed, "you supposed you would not be welcome. My dear Hayman, the past is the past. I think you should come to see us. I am sure my wife would like to renew your acquaintance. I think you should come to dine. Tonight."

George got his thoughts under control. "Tonight? But with all that's happening—"

"And what is happening, Mr. Hayman?"

"The prime minister?"

"Is gravely wounded. But the state will continue to function. And we have the assassin. He has been most cooperative. He has given us many names of others in his group. They originated here, in Moscow. Would you believe that? I am not pleased, you may be sure." He continued to smile. "But we have arrested most of them. Out of evil there sometimes comes good. I have been accused in the past of being too severe, Mr. Hayman. Thus the tsar himself has requested me not to arrest people on suspicion, or to use . . . shall I say, stringent methods in obtaining information. So these people have lived in my city, and prospered, for too long. Now the orders have been given to destroy them."

"And you are doing that?"

"Of course. Would you like to see?"

"To . . . ?" Once again, George felt his jaw clench.

Roditchev stood up. "You are a newspaper reporter, Mr. Hayman. You should see life in all its aspects. Have you ever met an assassin?"

"I don't think so."

Roditchev laughed. "You have, you know, Mr. Hayman." He went to the door and opened it. The orderlies outside came to attention. "But that is the most dangerous thing about revolutionaries. You never know what they are when you meet them."

"I really wouldn't know," George said. But he was interested despite himself. Roditchev was being amazingly cooperative.

"Well, I am going to show you." The general was leading him down the stairs, with an orderly immediately falling into place at his heels. "They come from all walks of life, these people. Some are the very dregs of our population. Others are from respectable middle-class households. One wonders what drives them on, what turns them into criminals." They passed the ground-floor level and continued their descent. The air became filled with the smell of disinfectant, and even on a warm morning it was chilly. "And others, even more amazingly, are from the very bosom of our best families."

They reached the bottom level and were now some twenty feet beneath the street level, George estimated, where a green-clad jailer was waiting for them. Now all the warmth was gone from the morning, and not even the disinfectant could hide the stench of unwashed bodies and unemptied slop pails, the stench of fear, which seeped up the corridor in front of them. But the sounds were the most horrible of all, the moans and wails, the occasional screams, of human beings in agony and terror. George inhaled, prepared himself for some very nasty moments. But surely Roditchev knew he would report everything he saw and heard. Obviously Roditchev did not care. Roditchev was working according to a plan.

Did it involve frightening George Hayman?

They walked past three of the cell doors, their heels dull on the stone. Before the fourth door they paused, and Roditchev snapped his fingers. The jailer immediately opened the peephole and looked inside, then nodded and inserted his key into the lock. The metal rasped, and the door swung inwards.

"Don't go inside this one," Roditchev said. "He is, after all, a desperate man, and in his more lucid moments he has shown a tendency to suicide."

George stared at the huddled figure in the far corner. There was no furniture in the cell, not even straw, and no slop bucket either; the place looked and smelled like a stable. But George did not suppose the man cared very much. He was naked, his body a white wisp layered with black hair. There was a great deal of hair, from his head to his beard to the heavy down which covered his shoulders and his arms and legs. But not even the hair, or the gloom of the cell, could disguise the bruises and welts which covered every inch of exposed flesh, made his face into a large, reddened mess, left bloodstains on his beard and buttocks.

"Mordka Bogrov," Roditchev said. "The assassin himself."

George had to lick his lips. "Why is he here?"

"He has been returned here since he is a Muscovite. He is, as I have said, busily implicating his accomplices. Reluctantly, of course. But then, every man has his breaking point."

"Are you allowed to torture him? Won't he have to stand trial?"

"They will hardly strip him naked at his trial. As long as he can stand. . . . His face is a nuisance, of course. But then, he was assaulted by a mob, with his smoking weapon in his hand. One or two bruises will be expected. And most of them will have faded somewhat by the time he reaches the dock."

"Won't he tell his lawyer what's happened?"

Roditchev snapped his fingers again, and the door swung shut. "I have no idea what he will tell his lawyer, Mr. Hayman. But I very much doubt if his lawyer will take any notice of his complaints. All prisoners complain. And besides, he shot Monsieur Stolypin. There can be no sympathy for one such as he. Now, this one will amuse you, I think."

They had paused before another door, and George prepared himself for another grim sight. And found his jaw slipping down in a horror greater than he had felt even at the sight of the murderer. He was looking at a young woman, hardly more than a girl, he guessed. Like Bogrov, she was naked, her shoulders shrouded in long dark hair, but her body was pitifully white, except for the red stripes across the flesh of her buttocks. She sat against the wall, half turned away from them, but she was not quite so crushed as Bogrov, for as the door opened her head started to turn, only to face the wall again quickly.

"Now here is a case in point," Roditchev said, stepping into the cell. "This girl, believe it or not, is the daughter of Moscow's leading lawyer. I assure you, Mr. Hayman, that Jacob Stein cannot believe it. Or so he says. Say good morning to Mr. Hayman, Judith."

The girl seemed to press her face even closer to the wall of the cell, but a tremor shook her body from her neck to her ankles.

Roditchev stood above her. "People like Judith are bonuses to my profession, Mr. Hayman. Not only because she is extremely good-looking. That is always pleasant. But because she is intelligent. It is possible to have a conversation with her, even while questioning." He reached down, thrust his fingers into the girl's hair, pulled her head around and up to show the bruise on her cheek. "Now that is unforgivable. My men are sometimes far too enthusiastic. But that will certainly fade before she comes to trial." He released the hair, and Judith's head flopped downwards. "I shall be coming to see you again this afternoon, my dear," he said.

The head quivered.

"What more can you do to her?" George asked, his voice thick.

"Why, my dear fellow, I have done very little to her as yet. Just a warm-up with my cane. Unfortunately, she is being stubborn. She insists she had nothing to do with Bogrov. But he gave us your name, my dear. Can't you see that once he did that you were condemned?" He looked down at her for a moment, and shook his head. "Do to her? Why, Mr. Hayman, if you cannot think of a hundred and one things to do to a pretty girl, then you are hardly a man. I had her in my grasp once before, you know. And she slipped away. Ever since then I have looked forward to having her back. I knew it had to happen. Oh, she and I are going to have an amusing time together. Would you not like to come back this afternoon and watch?"

"Thank you, no."

"Ha, ha! Well, come along. We cannot spend all day enjoying the charms of Mademoiselle Stein. I have someone even more interesting for you to meet."

The door swung to. George blinked, and still saw the girl, crouching against the wall. Beauty and the beast. But this was no fairy tale with a happy ending—except that I may be able to help a little, George thought, by printing everything I have seen. But would anyone believe me? And would my denunciation have any effect upon the tsarist government? Certainly nothing he might write could be published in time to help Judith Stein.

Another door was opening. "Here is the true surprise of the conspiracy," Roditchev said. "A man with a long family tradition of service, a man with a good position and not, one would have supposed, a care or a grumble in the world. But of course you know him, Mr. Hayman. As I said, revolutionaries are not always easy to spot. This man was my brother-in-law's servant, Mr. Hayman. You must have met him during your stay in Starogan. His name is Michael Nej."

The butler threw open the double doors to the drawing room. "Mr. George Hayman."

George wished he had had more time to prepare himself—as if there could be any real preparation for this evening. He had spent the afternoon in his hotel room, thinking. About the girl in Roditchev's cell. About Roditchev looking at her. And about Michael Nej. Again a pitiful, naked figure, though at first sight he had seemed less injured than either the assassin or the girl. But then Roditchev had probed the man with the end of his cane, causing him to sprawl on his back so that his swollen testicles and the blood on the inside of his thighs could be seen.

Had Michael recognized him? George could not be sure; the eyes had been dull. But there was one point on which he could agree with Roditchev. How on earth could a man like Michael Nej, whose entire life had been devoted to the service of the Borodins, become involved in a murder conspiracy directed against the highest in the land? Roditchev had not been very forthcoming on the subject. Perhaps he would be more expansive over dinner. Supposing, George thought, I can even bear to look at the fellow.

But since he had come here, it was an act which had to be carried through. Was he afraid of him? He did not suppose so; to be able to face him on equal terms would be a pleasure. But he no longer doubted that Roditchev's motives earlier in the day had been to inspire fear, to demonstrate his power and his ruthlessness, even his pleasure in inflicting pain, in maltreating his victims.

How much did Ilona know of the real man? How could she *not* know of him, as she had lived with him for six years? How much of his sadistic pleasure had *she* endured? She had said nothing of it during the few times they had been able to meet, in the back room of the bookseller's, during the past three weeks. She had wanted to speak of nothing but him, to know what he had been doing during the time they had been apart. She had not wished to speak of herself. "I have been a wife and mother," she said, and he left it at that. Because until this morning he had not fully realized what being a wife to this man might involve.

But was that not another aspect of Roditchev's undoubtedly deep-laid plans? He would show Ilona's erstwhile lover what she had lived with for six years, and what, by a logical projection, she must therefore condone, perhaps even enjoy. Could that be possible?

"Mr. Hayman." Roditchev was on his feet and advancing toward the door. "Ilona, my love, you remember George Hayman, the American from Port Arthur?"

Had she been warned? George decided that she had, because her features were quite composed, even if her face was a trifle pale, as she came forward. She wore an evening gown of crushed strawberry satin, decorated with bands of silver and mauve embroidery and a pink satin rosette bow on her left shoulder. Her necklace of pearls matched the pearl and ruby bracelets on each wrist, and her hair was gathered in that soft golden pompadour he adored.

"Mr. Hayman," she said, coming forward. "Welcome back to Russia."

She extended her hand, and he gave it a gentle squeeze, meeting her gaze as he did so. And wondering, why do we pretend? Your husband knows you have lain in my arms, as I know you have spent years lying in his. You know us both better than you have ever known anyone. The only true secret is ours, that we have renewed our love. Were we even remotely as civilized as we pretend, it would be a matter for discussion, not secrecy.

But was Roditchev, on the evidence of what George had seen this morning, even remotely civilized?

"I am only sorry my return has been so long delayed, princess," he said.

"Ha, ha." Roditchev shook his hand. "But you are here now." He snapped his fingers, and the butler held out a tray with glasses of champagne. "You'll remember that Mr. Hayman is a newspaper correspondent, my love. Thus he has a nose for news. So here he is in Moscow at a moment of great crisis."

"At least the murderers did not harm the tsar," Ilona remarked, leading them toward the chairs. "As they meant to do."

"Is that so?" George asked.

"Oh, indeed," Roditchev said. "Bogrov has confessed it. Together with the names of his accomplices. I have not had a chance to tell you, my love, but we have managed to arrest them all. You'll never believe whom we have managed to turn up."

Ilona gave George a quick glance, as if wondering whether he was included among them, then looked back at her husband. "I am sure you are going to tell me, Sergei."

"Of course. Well, one of them is the girl Judith Stein." He paused, and smiled at his wife. "The Stein woman is an old friend of my wife, Hayman."

George watched the color fade from Ilona's cheeks, and then return in a rush. "Judith Stein? How could she have possibly been implicated? Did you not say it was two men?"

"Two men who planned and carried out the crime, to be sure. But there were many others in the plot. This girl Judith Stein was to give them shelter afterwards. Do you know why? Because she is Peter's mistress and was sure that he would help them. As he helped her once before, you may remember."

Ilona stared at him. "Judith is Peter's mistress?"

"Of course. Did you not know that?"

"But . . . she confessed that to you?"

"Well, of course she didn't. I must say, my love, she is a most stubborn girl. She has refused to confess anything, no matter what I . . . no matter how strongly I urged her to be sensible. But that is what Bogrov says. And how can there be any doubt? Do you really suppose that Peter would have risked his majesty's wrath to rescue a girl from the police if he did not have a possessive interest in her?"

"But . . ." Ilona's brain was obviously whirling. "It just doesn't make sense. Judith Stein lives in Moscow. And Peter has been here once in the past four years. That is a love affair?"

"Ah, my dear, but Judith Stein has spent a large part of the past four years in St. Petersburg, where Peter visited quite often. I can see that you are worried, and of course I shall do my very best not to implicate him. It would not be very helpful, would it, under the present circumstances? But do you know, Peter may have had a fortunate escape. That girl is the worst of the lot, in my opinion. Her bedroom was absolutely filled with seditious literature, a good deal of it written by herself. She is an absolutely dyed-in-the-wool revolutionary. I am seriously wondering whether I should not arrest her entire family. They must have known what she was up to. But that can wait. I have something even more interesting to tell you. No, no, Mr. Hayman, why don't *you* tell her?"

"Me?" George asked.

"About the second assassin."

"Have you caught him?" Ilona's tone was eager.

"Of course. He killed a policeman and then boarded the night train for Moscow. We had no trouble in picking him up. His name was given as Chernov. You'll never guess who he really was—Michael Nej. Peter's former valet. I must say, your brother is going to have to do some explaining."

Had she betrayed herself? If she had, neither man gave any sign of it. But Ilona did not know how she could not have betrayed herself. Her first reaction had been a violent pain in her chest, which had been followed by a desire to vomit. She had hastily drunk some champagne, which had made her feel worse, but had gone some distance in hiding her horror and confusion.

Then she had been forced to sit through the meal. It had been the longest, most dismal meal of her life. She had anticipated a difficult evening from the moment Sergei had told her who was coming to dinner. She had thought it absurd of George to have called on his greatest enemy, and forgiven him because he was a newspaperman who loved his work. But nothing she had anticipated could have measured up to the evening itself.

It was all her fault. She did not doubt that for a moment. With that careless selfishness she had developed over the years, she had been relieved when Petrovski told her that his clerk Chernov had suddenly asked for a vacation and gone away. Undoubtedly Michael had seen George entering the store, and had decided to disappear for a time. Either to let them get on with it, or to decide what he wanted to do about it. She had no fears on that score. Michael was not a violent man. There was no risk of his attacking George. And Michael had slipped away into the darkness before. He had done that at Starogan, and reappeared six months later in Moscow. Michael liked to go away and lick his wounds, but at the end he would always come back to the woman he loved. And his absence had been a blessing. It had left her able to consider the matter dispassionately, to make her decision without outside influence, with the knowledge that if she decided against George, Michael would always return to her. She had known she was being utterly unreasonable in her determination to do only what was best for her and for her son. But she had lived her entire life, certainly since George had left Starogan, on that basis, and it had not turned out so very badly. For anyone.

But that he should have run away and joined an anarchist group! Of course, he had always belonged to some such group, had attended meetings regularly enough. But Michael Nej, a man of peace, a man who had never been able to hurt a fly, shooting a policeman? After setting out to kill the tsar himself? It was incredible. And horrifying.

The men talked to each other and to her, and she smiled and replied, and heard nothing of what they were saying. She prayed only for the privacy of her bedroom. But it was George sitting between Roditchev and herself, George, the man she loved. She must remember that. Especially now, when she was prepared to throw away husband and position and wealth and even safety for him. She had not yet told him; she was going to do that at their next meeting. But surely he knew.

And Roditchev? Roditchev wished only to talk about Judith Stein and Michael Nej. Roditchev was being as pleasantly unpleasant as he could be. To her alone? Or to George? She decided it was to both of them, but not because he knew anything of their present relationshp, or even about her and Michael. He was tormenting his wife, as he liked to do, with the suggestions that he had already tormented her friend and her family's servant, that he might even gain enough evidence to proceed against Peter himself—"Although, my love, I would of course quash that possibility before anyone else thought of it"— and in tormenting her he was also tormenting her lover, forced to sit there and watch her squirm.

It was all a game, but played to a deadly purpose. Roditchev could have no doubt but that George had returned only to see her. So he would probe, and probe, and probe, searching for a single careless word, arising from a single outburst of anger or despair. So she must match him, smile for smile and quip for quip, and so must George, neither of them once betraying their true feelings.

But George's feelings were only concerned with her. What would he say, and what would Roditchev *do,* could they suspect the hell that was raging in her heart?

At last the meal was over, and George was saying good night. Sensible George, resisting all Roditchev's suggestions that he stay on for another glass of brandy.

"I have a great deal to do tomorrow, prince," he said firmly. "And so have you, no doubt, questioning those suspects."

George could afford to treat those suspects—even Michael—as just people, who had no meaning in this world, their world. But he was gone, having kissed her hand, secure in the knowledge that the day after tomorrow she would be at the bookstore.

Would she be at the bookstore the day after tomorrow?

"I am sure Mr. Hayman is right, and you are exhausted," she said, leading her husband toward the stairs.

"Exhausted, no. I am pleasantly tired. It has been a good day. A successful one, and an interesting one." He followed at her elbow. "Questioning that Jewish girl was most interesting. She is an extraordinarily pretty woman. It has made me quite, well. . . ."

Oh God, Ilona thought. Oh God, no. He cannot mean it. Not tonight. I could not stand that.

"And then, seeing you with Hayman—it is easy to see that he still adores you. Do you still adore him?"

They had reached the landing. A footman stood at attention to their left, and Catherine Ivanovna was hovering in the doorway of her bedroom.

"Please, Sergei," she murmured, "not in front of the servants."

His hand gripped her elbow, tightly. "Do you?"

She turned her head. "Of course I do not. That was a long time ago. I was only a girl."

"Because if I thought you did. . . ." He released her and walked into her bedroom.

He does mean to, she thought. What am I to do?

"My dearest wish is to be able to arrest Hayman on some charge or other," Roditchev said, sitting on her bed. "Even if I could not make it stick, I would like to have him in my cells for one night. One hour would do. It is a dream I have." He smiled at her, and snapped his fingers. "Go to bed, girl. I will undress your mistress tonight."

Catherine Ivanovna simpered and hurried for the door.

Roditchev crooked his finger. "Come over here, my love."

What am I to do? Ilona thought. Submit, of course. And what can I do about Michael but pray?

George had never seen such a crowded courtroom. No doubt the authorities had been acting wisely in moving the trial from Moscow to St. Petersburg. Despite Roditchev's boasts that he had the city under complete control, they had been afraid of massive demonstrations in support of the accused while the eyes of all the world were upon their country. They had certainly managed to exclude the muzhiks.

But it seemed all of St. Petersburg's nobility were present, as well as a goodly crowd from other parts of the country. From his vantage point in the press box, George could make out Igor Borodin, with his wife beside him, and Xenia sitting next to her brother Tigran. But there were many other familiar faces; it seemed to him that the only people of note not present were the imperial family themselves and Rasputin.

And Ilona was here, her face hidden behind a veil, sitting next to Tigran. Roditchev was not to be seen. He had been a prosecution witness and had probably already left the building. But Ilona had been far more affected by the tragedy than he would have expected. He doubted it was due to fear that her brother might be implicated, even though his name *had* been mentioned several times in evidence. But George remembered the intimacy she had shared with Michael Nej. That was the true source of her grief. But she must also be afraid not for Peter or Michael, but for herself. It had turned out, to George's amazement, that Michael had spent the previous three years working under an alias for Petrovski the bookseller. Poor Petrovski had also been arrested and released after questioning, since he clearly knew nothing of the murder plot. Nor had he mentioned Princess Roditcheva. Although it was clear to George that she must have been well aware of Michael's employment in the bookshop.

Did that mean she was also bound up in some way with the revolutionary movement? But what way? Could she possibly have known about the assassination scheme?

In any event, the trial was over. It had, he supposed, been a mockery. Certainly he intended to report it as such. Granted that the man Bogrov had been taken with revolver in hand having just fired the shot; but the evidence against the other ten accused was purely circumstantial. Even the evidence against Michael was incomplete. He had been arrested with a revolver on his person, and one bullet had been fired. But the ballistics test had been very inexpertly carried out, as far as George could ascertain. The bullet which had killed the Kiev policeman had passed right through his body and smashed into the wall beyond, providing very little to go on. But that it had been fired from Michael's gun, had been conceded by the defense lawyers, as they had conceded all the other points raised by the prosecution; apparently they were more concerned to prove themselves good citizens than to save their clients from conviction. And they had certainly succeeded in their self-appointed task. George could not see what might save the prisoners now.

He supposed the end was going to be almost a blessing, though. From where he sat he could see their profiles as they stood and faced the sentencing judge. There were no traces of bruises now, except for the scar on Bogrov's cheek, but as Roditchev had promised, that had been explained away to the satisfaction of all present. But what of those parts of their bodies the judges could not see? What of their minds? He was less interested in Michael than in the girl. Her face was composed. Her lips were tightly pressed together, and her hair was neatly brushed. Her dress was pressed and clean, provided especially for the trial. And only he, of all the people in the court at this moment, knew even a little of what she had suffered, of the agony that must exist in her mind, of the hatred that must simmer there as well. And of the anxiety with which she waited for her fate.

The judge's attention was passing slowly down the line; the first eight were sentenced to terms varying from five to ten years in Siberia. The principals were left until last.

"Mordka Bogrov, have you anything to say before sentence is passed upon you?"

The judge waited, but Bogrov said nothing.

"Then it is the sentence of this court that you be taken from here and hanged by the neck until you are dead."

The first death sentence. The court rustled, and the judge tapped his gavel. But Bogrov could hardly have expected anything different; Peter Stolypin had died of his wounds.

"Judith Stein, have you anything to say before sentence is passed upon you?"

The girl stirred and seemed to awaken from a deep sleep. "I am innocent of any desire to kill Monsieur Stolypin," she said, her voice low but perfectly clear. "Or of any disloyalty to the tsar. This I swear."

The judge waited for a moment to see if she would continue, then cleared his throat. "It is the sentence of this court that you be taken from here and hanged by the neck until you are dead."

The girl's head jerked as she stared at him. Her manacled hands moved upward as if to clutch her throat, then fell down again. There was a wailing cry from the back of the court, and Judith's head turned before straightening again. George watched a tear trickle down her cheek. To have suffered all that, and then to die at the end of it.

"Michael Nej, have you anything to say before sentence is passed upon you?"

"Death to you all," Michael shouted with surprising anger. "Death to all tsarist monsters." He gave a little gasp, and George realized the warder standing behind him must have hit him in the kidneys. His hands closed on the bar of the dock and Judith Stein held his arm to steady him.

The judge was waiting, patient as ever. "Then it is the sentence of this court that you be taken from here and hanged by the neck until you are dead."

The silence that followed the last sentence was broken by a curious thump from the spectator's gallery. Heads turned, George's among them, and then he stood up. Ilona Roditcheva had fainted.

Chapter 12

ILONA RODITCHEVA OPENED HER EYES CAUTIOUSLY AND GAZED AT her husband.

"How do you feel?" he asked.

"I . . . it was the heat, Sergei. And then, to think of Michael Nikolaievich being hanged . . . I have known him all my life."

"It is always a mistake to become too attached to servants," Roditchev pointed out. "But I do understand, my sweet. I remember when my charger Sviatopolk died. I was quite upset. Well, I have a great deal to do. I suggest you remain in bed today. We have the journey back tomorrow."

She clutched his hand. "Tomorrow?"

"Of course. The trial is over. I should be in Moscow."

"But. . . ." She chewed her lip, and he waited.

"Yes?"

"Nothing," she said. "It's just that I feel so weak. And my head hurts."

"You struck it on the seat when you fell. It caused quite a to-do, believe me." He chuckled. "Do you know, the guards thought the distraction was some kind of a plot to free the prisoners? They became quite agitated."

"Sergei," she said, "do you think I could remain in St. Petersburg for a few days more?"

To her surprise he continued to smile. "With Ivan?"

"It would be nice. I'd like to rest."

He appeared to consider, then nodded. "Very well, my love. Your health is my chief concern. You lie quietly, and you'll soon feel better. I'll send Catherine Ivanovna to you."

She rolled on her side, looked at the window and listened to the door close. Now she could think, but she did not really wish to. Thought involved memory. Selfish memory. Except for Judith and Michael, she had never seen any of the prisoners before, even Mordka Bogrov. The others did not interest her. Did Judith interest her? The expression on her face? The lost look in her eyes? What had happened to her in Roditchev's cell? And yet she had retained sufficient control over herself, enough determination to survive if she could, to restate her innocence at the end. Peter's mistress? It was incredible. Incredible that Peter should have taken a mistress at all, incredible that a girl like Judith would surrender herself to a man like Peter. It just went to show how little she knew of any human nature but her own.

But was not her own sufficiently incredible? It had all seemed a game, a magnificent contest of will and excitement, with, at the end of it, the fullest possible gratification of her physical needs. Oh, one day the bubble would burst, but it was not something she had been prepared to worry about—until George's return. George had made her realize just how wanton she had been the previous four years, had left her bitterly regretting every moment of it. And now that George was back. . . .

The door opened. "I have brought you a cool drink, my lady," Catherine said. "Would you like some ice for your head?"

"Has the prince left the house, Catherine?"

"Yes, my lady."

"Then I would just like to be left alone."

"Of course, my lady." Catherine placed the tray on the table by the bed. "And no visitors."

"Visitors?" Ilona rolled over again and sat up. "What visitors?"

"A gentleman called. The American gentleman who came to dinner in Moscow, my lady."

"And you sent him away?"

"The prince said you were not to be disturbed, my lady." Catherine Ivanovna smiled at her. "Besides, do you not remember, my lady? This man is a reporter. He is merely seeking copy for his paper."

Ilona chewed her lip. "I . . . I would like to see him," she said. "I would not like to have him printing anything about my fainting."

"Well, my lady. . . ."

"Did he say he would come back?"

"He did, my lady, but—"

"Thank you, Catherine. When Mr. Hayman returns, you may call me. I am sure I shall be feeling better by then. Now leave me."

"Yes, my lady," Catherine said coldly.

Ilona lay down again and heard the door close. George had been here. Did Roditchev know that? Of course he did. Hence his so ready agreement to her remaining in St. Petersburg. He had watched George and her at dinner, and was now laying a trap for them, into which she was obligingly falling. The fool. He would discover the bait could run away with the catch.

Her mind was made up. She could no longer stay in Russia. The entire country had become hateful to her. Now was a time for serious thought, serious planning. But thought was irrelevant. What would they say of her, the Russian princess who deserted her husband and her family and her position to elope with an American journalist? It would be the scandal of the century. People would write articles about her. Why, they might even write books. Ilona Dimitrievna Roditcheva, the most famous woman of her time.

Not in Russia. The most infamous woman of her time, in Russia.

And would she give a kopeck for a word they spoke, or read, or thought? She knew Russia for what it was, a seething mass of misery relieved only by hysterical outbursts of violence or degeneracy. A brother who was intent upon making a fool of himself, a sister who was mad as a hatter . . . and a mother. But Mama had chosen the life she had been forced to live for the past six years. There was the pattern of history: obey one's parents, whatever hell their decisions condemned you to. But this was the twentieth century. In England, so she had read, women were risking prison to further the cause of their freedom. There could be no eternal justification for misery. One's duty was to live one's life to the fullest extent.

So, no thoughts. Plans. Plans to share with George when he came back. Plans for that American ship George had spoken of. It traded regularly with Russia, and he was friendly with both the captain and the purser. Their escape would be the simplest thing in the world. They would not stop until they got to America. Ivan Sergeievich would adore America.

Ivan Sergeievich? My God, Ivan Michaelovich. But the child did not know, and he could never know, now. How his father had been a servant who was hanged for murdering a policeman? Was that an ancestry to be proud of or to hate? That would depend on what she told him as he grew up, the point of view she adopted. Would she ever tell him the truth? How she sailed away from Russia and left his father to die?

It was an albatross to hang around her neck for the rest of her days. But what could she do? She had not been involved in Michael's revolutionary plans. She had known nothing of what he intended. And now he was to die. What could she do, except, perhaps, visit him in his cell, and since he was a condemned man, that would require authority from the governor. Roditchev could obtain it for her if she dared ask him. But she did not want to see Michael again, if he was to die. She was Ilona Borodina, first and last. All her life she had followed her own way, her own instincts, her own fortune. Michael had attached himself to her star and had prospered for a while. Then he had flown away on his own and come crashing to the earth. There was nothing she could do about that.

Except that she knew he had not flown away of his own accord; he had been *cast* away.

What could she do?

"Mr. George Hayman," announced Catherine Ivanovna, in tones of the strongest disapproval. She thought it was just bad luck that this upstart American should have returned while Prince Roditchev was still out. And to have to show him upstairs to the princess's private sitting room was the last straw.

"George." Ilona was dressed and looked as elegant as ever. She gave him both her hands, and he raised them to his lips.

"I had to discover how you were."

"I have a bruise on my head. Can you see it?"

But she had arranged her hair too cunningly; the entire pompadour swept forward to droop over her left eye.

"No."

She smiled. "Then there is nothing the matter with me. That will be all, Catherine Ivanovna. You may leave the doors open."

Catherine curtsied and left the room.

"Open?" George asked, softly.

"We must up here. If we sit by the window no one will be able to hear us."

She led him across the room and sat down. He remained standing for a moment. The Roditchev town house lacked both the grandeur and the situation of the Borodin residence; it stood in a quiet side avenue, well away from the harbor; Ilona's window looked out on a croquet lawn. He wondered if she and Roditchev played. It was almost impossible for him to imagine them in such a serene domestic pastime. Yet certainly they must have their moments of contentment. And this afternoon she was quite remarkably cool and composed, almost like the girl he had first known in Port Arthur. Perhaps it had, after all, been only the heat had made her faint.

But now he must upset her all over again.

"Have you heard the news?"

She raised her head. "What news?"

"It is only a rumor at the moment. I have not been able to find any confirmation, although I called at the Borodin house. But Peter is supposed to be in St. Petersburg."

Ilona frowned. "Peter? That is impossible. He was banished."

"So I understood."

"But if he comes to St. Petersburg without the tsar's permission . . . my God."

"What would happen to him?"

"I have no idea. I don't think any such thing has ever happened before. It must be because of that girl Judith Stein, the one who was condemned to death. She was supposed to be his mistress, but I never believed it. Now I think it must be true." She got up and walked to the window, looked down at the garden.

"I'm terribly sorry," George said. "If there is anything I can do—"

She turned violently. "There is nothing you can do. Or I. Or anyone. I sometimes think Peter must be a *complete* fool. But he must sort out his own affairs." Her tone softened. "After what he did to us, I am surprised you even think of helping him."

"He's your brother."

"Yes. My brother." She sat down again and poured tea, which neither of them wanted. "When is she to be executed? The girl, I mean."

"Ten days time."

"Ten days?"

"Well, I believe they are still being interrogated."

Still being interrogated. For ten days. With only the rope at the end of it. Ilona got up again. She moved over to the window and stood there, biting her lip. He had never seen her so agitated before.

"What are you going to do now?" he asked.

"I?" She turned, her face filling with color.

"I mean, are you going to stay in St. Petersburg a while?"

She gazed at him for some seconds, as if she had not understood what he had said. Then she sat down again. "Sergei wishes to return to Moscow tomorrow morning."

"Oh. Under the circumstances, I'm not sure I should go down there for a while."

"Are you afraid of Roditchev's suspicions?" she snapped.

"Only insofar as they affect us, my darling," he said gently. "He can make life very difficult for you. And I imagine he can have me deported all over again."

Once again the long gaze. She drank her tea, still watching him over the rim of her cup. Then she put down the cup with great care, and at last lowered her eyes. "Then perhaps we should anticipate both those eventualities."

For a moment he could not believe what he had heard. He put down his own cup with a clatter.

"Or are you not prepared to risk that?" she asked, her voice low.

"Risk that? My darling girl . . . but you are Princess Roditcheva. If you were to run away. . . ."

"I have thought the matter through," she said. "I no longer have any desire to be Princess Roditcheva. I never did have. If you can find a way, George, I will come with you wherever you wish to go. I ask only to be allowed to bring Ivan with me."

"Ivan? But. . . ." His thoughts tumbled over and over. To steal a man's wife was one thing; to steal his only son. . . . "He'll never let his son go."

"He will not know until it is too late."

"It'll be a legal matter, my darling. Your running away will be a legal matter too, but it can be fought in the American courts, if we can manage it. And I do not see any American judge ordering you to return to a husband you loathe. On the other hand, I don't see any judge granting you custody of your husband's child, after you have done the running away. Believe me, I'm trying to spare you unnecessary pain."

Once again the long, appraising stare. He had a most peculiar feeling that her thoughts were entirely remote from his, that she just happened to be in the same room. But that had to be nonsense. She had just agreed to elope with him. Ilona Roditcheva, the most beautiful woman in the world, had just agreed to throw over family, position and honor to live with George Hayman. Presumably at some time soon he would be able to understand just what that meant. For the moment he could only repeat it to himself, over and over again.

A great tear emerged from Ilona's left eye and rolled down her cheek.

"Ilona?"

"Close the door."

"The door? But you said. . . ."

She got up, walked across the room and closed the door herself.

"For God's sake, Ilona, what is the matter?"

She stood by his chair for a moment, and more tears came tumbling down. Then without warning her knees gave way, and she knelt, her head on his lap, while she cried. And through her tears, she spoke.

Count Gutchkov pulled each end of his mustache in turn, and then blew his nose. "I really am most terribly upset about this, Prince Peter," he said. "I knew your father, and I knew your grandfather."

Peter waited. He had to endure this sort of thing whenever he encountered anyone even ten years older than himself. But eventually the count needed to blow his nose again.

"His majesty will not receive me?"

Gutchkov sighed. "You are persona non grata, Prince Peter. Indeed, his majesty is extremely angry. You have disobeyed a direct order. This cannot be tolerated. His majesty has instructed me to tell you that unless you are on a train back to Starogan by this evening, he will have you placed under arrest."

Peter gazed at him for some seconds, and the count blew his nose again.

"As for the future, well, who can say. His majesty is very angry. But it is possible that in time he may relent."

"Time?" Peter said angrily. "You sit there and talk to me of time, with a woman's life at stake?" He tucked his helmet under his arm and walked past the desk toward the huge double doors.

"You cannot go in there!" the count cried.

"Stop me."

The guards came to attention. They were of the Preobraschenski, and here was a captain in their regiment.

"Guards," Count Gutchkov said.

The men hesitated and Peter stepped between them, threw the doors open, and looked down the sweep of red carpet toward the imperial desk. The tsar was inspecting some papers, with three men standing immediately behind him and looking over his shoulder. One was his secretary; the second was Monsieur Sturmer, a German who had become a naturalized Russian and was in the confidence of the tsarina. He was currently minister of the interior, but rumor had it he would succeed Stolypin. The third man Peter did not know.

All raised their heads to gaze at the intruder.

"Your majesty," Peter saluted.

Nicholas blinked at him. "Are you mad?" he asked. "Do you wish to be imprisoned?"

Peter marched further into the room and stood at attention. He could still feel a slight draft on his back and knew that Gutchkov would be waiting in the doorway behind him.

"You may do what you wish with me, your majesty," he said. "I seek only to prevent your allowing a horrible miscarriage of justice."

The tsar placed his elbows on the desk, his fingertips extended. "You are an unhappy, deluded young man," he said. "It is a great tragedy for your family."

"Hear me for five minutes, your majesty," Peter begged. "Then do with me as you wish. This girl Judith Stein is innocent of any crime. I have read the evidence given against her. Your majesty, it is a lie from start to finish. She has never been my mistress. I swear this as the prince of Starogan, your majesty. I . . . I have asked her to be so on two occasions, and have been refused each time. This man Bogrov must be aware that I visited her house, but she could not possibly have provided the assistance he sought."

"Innocent?" Sturmer sneered. "Are you aware that this woman was engaged in compiling one of the most seditious documents I have ever read? I suggest you peruse that manuscript, Prince Borodin."

"And then assure us that you are innocent of sharing in those ideas, Prince Peter," said the other man.

Peter gazed at them in turn, then looked back at the tsar. "If my loyalty is in question, your majesty, then place me on trial. As for Mademoiselle Stein's writing, have they been published?"

"She was taken in time to prevent that," Sturmer said.

Peter continued to look at the tsar.

"You have no proof that she ever intended to have them published except Bogrov's evidence, your majesty. But even if she had, I have never heard of anyone being hanged for publishing seditious literature. If she is guilty of that, your majesty, then punish her accordingly. But do not stain the history of your reign with such an abominable crime."

"Abominable crime?" the tsar inquired, his cheeks pink. "And what of the murder of my prime minister, Prince Borodin? Perhaps you do not consider that an abominable crime."

"The murder of Count Stolypin is as abhorrent to me as it is to you, your majesty. I do not ask clemency for the man Bogrov. I do not ask clemency for the man Nej, although he was once my servant, and his family have been my family's servants for as long as anyone can remember. They are guilty men, your majesty, and must abide by the consequences of their act. Judith Stein is guilty of nothing more than setting down her thoughts and her hopes on paper."

"Do you love the girl, Prince Peter?"

Heads turned, and the tsar hastily got to his feet. Peter also turned. The tsarina had stepped through the red curtain and stood a few paces to his right.

"Your majesty," he said.

"Because if you do not, there is something very odd about your behavior," Alexandra said. "I would have supposed that of all the men in Russia, you have the most to live for, to prosper for, to look forward to. More even than—" she hesitated, "the highest in the land. And you would throw it all away for a girl who is neither of your class nor your religion, whom you are willing to concede is a revolutionary, and who you claim has never favored you with her surrender. If that is not love, it is madness."

Peter inhaled and slowly allowed his breath to escape. "I love the girl, your majesty. It is not an emotion which can be dictated by class, religion or political points of view."

"Indeed it is not," the tsarina agreed, and Peter remembered that she had changed her own religion, and no doubt her own political beliefs, to marry the tsar of Russia. "If the love is true. Does your wife know of this love?"

"No, your majesty."

"But she will know of it now, after this madcap dash across Russia."

"Yes, your majesty."

"And presumably you are willing to desert her, and your sisters, and your mother and grandmother, for the sake of this Jewish girl?"

"No, your majesty."

Alexandra raised her eyebrows.

"I am aware of my responsibilities as prince of Starogan, your majesty. Had I been prepared to abandon them, I should have done so long ago. Had I been prepared to abandon them, Judith Stein would be either my wife or my mistress by now. Had I been prepared to abandon them, your majesty, this tragedy could not have happened."

"Sanity, at last," the tsarina said. "And do you suppose, or hope, that were we to reprieve this girl and send her to Siberia for ten years, that when she came back she would be disposed to change her mind in your favor?"

"I expect nothing from the future, your majesty. But I ask for her life because she is innocent of any desire to harm yourself or his majesty, of any desire to harm Russia. I am sure of this."

"Well, Prince Peter, you have earned our respect," the tsarina said, "as a man who is capable of what seems to be an absolutely pure and true love, and that is a rare emotion, certainly when it has to be exposed to so fierce a light as has yours. Perhaps you should once again address yourself to his majesty, who of all men is able to understand so great a love, and is, above all others, a man of mercy."

Peter stared at her for a moment, his heart starting to pound. Then he turned back toward the desk. "Your majesty—"

"We have listened to your plea with interest and sympathy, Prince Peter," Nicholas said. "And I would not wish knowingly to have the blood of any innocent person on my hands. God knows it is inescapable often enough. She will be reprieved. But she will spend the rest of her life in Siberia. The rest of her life, Prince Peter."

"Your majesty has been as gracious as I knew you would be, once the facts were placed before you. May I be so bold as to beg one last, minor favor?"

"Yes?"

"May I see Mademoiselle Stein?"

The tsar glanced at his wife.

"You are the stuff of which romances are written, Prince Peter," the tsarina said. "Yes, I think that may be allowed. But when you have spoken with her, you will return to Starogan and resume your exile. You will endeavor to love your wife and restrain that sister of yours. You will be prince of Starogan, Prince Peter. It is a duty, as you yourself have said, which should occupy the rest of your life."

George Hayman leaned back in his chair, his arms tight around the woman. She sat on his lap, her face lost in his neck. She had stopped speaking, and he thought she might also have stopped weeping. As he had always known, but as it was always easy to forget, her cool exterior did nothing more than hide the molten emotions beneath. And into what strange paths those emotions had led her over the past six years. What tragic paths.

And yet, he thought, what paths of glorious independence. But the question which now had to be answered was: where they would lead her in the future? Where did he want them to lead? Beside him, to be sure. For all that he had now learned of her, he still knew she was the only woman for him, just as he was sure he was the only man for her. Ilona Roditcheva, selfish and sensual, beautiful and helpless, had been adrift for too long. He would bring her to safety and put his trust in the future. But there was only one way that this could be accomplished without a lifetime of recrimination. He must try to save at least one of the people trapped in Roditchev's web.

Even if his name was Michael Nej, and he had been Ilona's lover, and had killed a man.

She stirred and sat up now. There were tear stains on her cheeks, and her hair had started to come down. But her face was once again composed.

"Would you like to leave?"

He had anticipated some such suggestion. "Just now you invited me to stay forever."

How huge her eyes were. "And now?"

"You have but to tell me what you want me to do."

Another long stare. Then she freed herself altogether and got up. "What can I do? What can we do?"

"A man, or a woman, can generally do anything, if they wish to badly enough. Do you wish to help Michael?"

"He is the father of my child."

"That is not an answer."

Her shoulders rose and fell. "I love him. In your absence, I loved him. Perhaps I love him still. Not as I love you, George, but . . . oh God, what can you think of me?"

"I do not think of you, my darling. I love you."

"And you would risk your life to help me get Michael out of prison?"

He smiled at her. "It has been recommended that I take a look at the inside of the Peter and Paul. I have a professional interest."

She turned away. "But how? How can it be done? You would need an army to storm the Peter and Paul."

"Armies are clumsy things. One man may often go where an army never could."

She faced him, frowning. "One man?"

"It is very simple, really. One man goes to see a prisoner, and half an hour later one man, wearing the same clothes, leaves. That ship I spoke of, the *Henry J. Wilkins,* is in St. Petersburg now. She leaves the day after tomorrow."

Her mouth opened slightly. "But the man who remained behind. . . ."

"Will be a very unpopular fellow with the Russian government. But somehow I doubt they would hang an American journalist."

"They'd send you to Siberia."

"I doubt even that, my darling. The tsar seems fairly anxious to stay on good terms with our people, and Father has known President Taft for years. I think they'd probably rough me up a little, and put me on the next boat for America."

"Rough you up? Have you any idea?"

He nodded.

Ilona shook her head. "You're being absurd. You're being absurdly masculine. You want to prove yourself as good a man as Michael. For God's sake, do you have to prove that? Will getting yourself reduced to a physical wreck prove anything?"

He flushed. She was uncomfortably near to the truth. "I don't think anyone is going to reduce me to a physical wreck, Ilona. There will be people anxious to take a look at me."

She chewed her lip. "It is absurd. Absurdly dangerous. Why should you? After what I've told you, you must loathe him."

George shrugged. "Maybe we won't ever be friends. But we have a lot in common, wouldn't you say?"

"Oh." She walked up and down the room. "Anyway, it would never work. You're twice his size."

"I'm a little taller, that's all. I'll be wearing a coat, and a couple of extra turn-ups on the pants should do the trick."

"You would never even be allowed to see him. He is a condemned man. As for being left alone with him long enough to change clothes—"

"Ah, that's where you come in. Can you obtain the necessary permission? After all, he was your brother's servant, and I am a newspaperman. Surely you can pull a few strings."

"A few strings?" Ilona stopped and stared into the fireplace. "I am not that popular in St. Petersburg."

"There must be someone. Roditchev?"

"That would be madness."

"Well then, who?"

"You could count on the fingers of one hand the number of people who could give you the right to a private interview with a condemned man." She ticked them off. "The tsar, the tsarina, the military governor of St. Petersburg, the governor of the prison." She paused, frowning.

"Would none of those do?"

"No." She gave him a sudden glance. "Are you sure, George? You would do this thing, take this risk, for Michael Nikolaievich?"

He shook his head. "I would do it for you."

She turned her head and looked again into the fireplace. "Then you must arrange for me to go as well. My son and I, on this ship."

"With Michael Nej?"

"I love you, George. If you do not believe that, then our conversation is pointless."

"My darling."

"But I cannot remain here, especially if you are in prison. Let me be in America to wait for you, to work for your release."

"If that's what you want, you'll be on that ship with Nej. All you have to do is get me permission to visit him."

Ilona nodded. "There is one person I can think of who could get us the permission we want."

"Who?"

"It does not matter. Go home now, George. The permission will be delivered to your hotel tomorrow morning."

It was his turn to frown as he got up. "I wish you'd tell me what you propose to do."

"It does not matter what I propose to do," she said fiercely. "The permission will be there, tomorrow morning. I promise you that."

Ilona summoned Catherine Ivanovna. "I shall be going out for a while, Catherine. Assist me to dress. My new blue gown."

"Going out, my lady? The new gown? But . . . the prince said you were to stay in bed and not be disturbed." She gazed disapprovingly at the uncleared tea cups.

"He said that because I was not feeling well this morning. Now I am feeling perfectly well. Kindly do as I ask."

Catherine made a face, but she could never be sure, nowadays, whose side the prince would take. She assisted her mistress into her latest gown, a royal blue silk tunic dress with a peg-top skirt and a loose kimono bodice worn over a pink lace blouse. Her hat was also pink, with a royal blue pompon, and she also wore her newest velvet boots, laced on the instep.

"May I ask where we are going, my lady?" Catherine inquired, for Ilona was a quite breathtaking sight.

"You may not. And *we* are not going anywhere. You will remain here."

"My lady? You cannot possibly—"

"Catherine Ivanovna, you are shortly going to make me very angry. Will you kindly do as I ask? Now go and tell Alexei Pavlovich that I need the car."

Catherine opened her mouth, changed her mind, and hurried from the room. What a tale she would have to tell Roditchev this night. But Ilona was no longer afraid of Roditchev. She had no doubt that she could satisfy him as to her reasons for going out, and besides, it was amazing how irrelevant he had become, now that the decision to leave him had actually been taken.

She was filled with a glowing ecstasy. She and George were working together at last, not only to help Michael, but to make their own lives for themselves. Whatever she was about to do was a part of that plan, and as such would be understood and forgiven by George.

She discovered she was tapping her gloved fingers on the armrest in the back seat of the Daimler; it was still light, and people wished to look inside the expensive car at the beautiful princess. If she was not terribly worried about Roditchev, there was no denying she was very worried about the next hour, and what she might have to endure. But could she endure anything, even from a grotesque monster, that she had not already endured from her husband?

And was her nervousness not just a little tinged with anticipation? Was there anyone in all the world who did not, deep in his or her heart, yearn to be absolutely wicked, just once in their lives? Especially when the act of wickedness was necessary to accomplish nothing but good?

She found her handkerchief and patted sweat from her neck and her upper lip. It was far too warm for late September. When the weather broke it would do so with a vengeance.

The car turned into the drive and came to a stop. The chauffeur opened the door for her and stood at attention.

"I do not think I shall be very long, Alexei Pavlovich," Ilona said. "I would like you to wait."

"Of course, my lady." He hesitated, uncertain, as she was unaccompanied, whether he should see her to the door. But she merely smiled at him, and at the other lounging chauffeurs, then walked across the drive and up the short flight of outside stairs. The door was, as she had expected, unlatched, and she stepped into an elegantly furnished hall, but with the usual accumulation of furs, and the usual hubbub of conversation from the drawing room on her left. Here was where she would need far more courage than in facing Rasputin.

She drew a long breath and stepped inside. Her beauty, not less than the quality of her clothes, brought conversation to a halt as heads turned. Most of the women recognized her, and when they resumed talking, it was in whispers.

"Madame?" the major-domo looked down his nose at her.

Ilona smiled at him, hoping that no trace of the rampaging butterflies in her stomach was showing on her face. "Do you not remember me, Anton? I am Princess Roditcheva."

"Princess. . . ." he looked thunderstruck. "The holy father is expecting you?"

"I'm afraid not. But I would like to see him, most urgently."

"Ah," Anton said. "He is. . . ." He glanced at the inner door. "Ah," he repeated, "I will see what can be done. Will you not take a seat?"

"Thank you."

"And a glass of wine? We have finished serving tea."

"I will have nothing, thank you." She had no doubt she would be forced to drink quite a lot later on. She sat herself in a straight chair as far removed from the other women as possible and looked directly in front of her, aware that she was being watched by everyone in the room, while their whispers seeped toward her.

"Princess Roditcheva."

"Her husband is military governor of Moscow."

"The man who caught the murderers."

"They say she fainted at the trial."

"Borodin's sister, you know."

"Is that so? I never realized that."

"And now he is in St. Petersburg too."

"About to be sent to prison, I've heard."

"A prince? That is impossible."

"Oh, but the tsar is furious."

"Well, that's why she's here. To beg the holy father for help."

Ilona almost smiled. They were completing her tale for her. However much he might disapprove, Roditchev would have to believe her. But now was not the time to think of Roditchev. The noise in the room was halted again by a bellow from the next room; the holy father apparently did not like to be interrupted.

The women watched the door, and after a moment Anton reappeared. There had been only one bellow, and Anton was smiling.

"My lady princess," he bowed to Ilona.

For a moment she could not move; her knees would not give her sufficient strength. Then she made a supreme effort and reached her feet. The gazes seemed to be scorching her flesh. She walked slowly across the room, and the inner door opened again. A woman emerged, hardly more than a girl, Ilona thought, and vaguely familiar; she must come from a family of her acquaintance. The young woman's hair was disordered and her clothes had obviously been dragged on.

"Bitch," she whispered as Ilona passed her, to where Anton was holding the door. Then it had closed behind her, and she was inhaling that never-to-be-forgotten scent, gazing into that never-to-be-forgotten face. But today he was even more repulsive than she remembered. He had already drunk a great deal of wine, she estimated; his eyes were bloodshot and as usual he had spilled some down his smock. He swayed and belched as she entered the room, and his clothes were as disordered as those of the girl who had just left.

"Ilona Roditcheva," he said.

"Father Gregory." She was delighted with the evenness of her voice.

"Ilona Roditcheva," he said again, and held out his hands. She advanced slowly, had her fingers seized, and was drawn forward more quickly. This time he did not attempt to kiss her hands, but instead she was pulled against him, to be kissed on each cheek, and then suddenly he released her, and his arms went around her shoulders to embrace her while his lips found hers. She felt her hat slipping, but her arms were pinned in the bear hug which was driving all the breath from her body, while his foul breath seemed to be blocking her nostrils.

And then she was released without warning. She could hardly maintain her balance as she watched him walking to the table to fill two glasses with wine. Was she angry? She knew what had to happen. But she was angry at his complete arrogance.

"The holy father is very confident," she remarked.

Rasputin returned toward her and held out a glass. "You came back, Ilona Roditcheva. And I know why."

"Indeed, father?"

He gave a guffaw and sat down on the settee, patting the place beside him. Once again her knees threatened to betray her, but she made herself cross the room and sit. "Your brother is a very wicked fellow."

"Do you really think so, father?"

He chuckled deep in his throat and moved so that his thigh rested against hers, while his arm went around her shoulder, the fingers immediately dropping down the front of her dress.

"Let me say that he is a very unwise young man. I do not know that I will be able to do anything for him. After all, my lovely princess, he did attempt to assault me."

The fingers were sliding down her shoulder and across the tops of her breasts to the buttons of her blouse. Sit still, she told herself. Sit still and enjoy it. But remember to bargain.

"I think the prince should have horsewhipped you," she said. The fingers gave a little squeeze, and she jumped. "But I also think my brother is old enough to look after himself. I have not come here to assist him."

Her top button was undone, and the fingers were stroking her throat. "You have a reason, lovely princess. All women who come here have a reason."

The second button was open.

"I wish to ask a favor of you, holy father," she agreed. "A very small favor."

"One I am sure I shall be able to grant." The third button was open. He was touching the tops of her breasts. Her stomach seemed to be rolling over and over.

"I wish you to obtain permission for a visit to the Fortress of St. Peter and St. Paul."

"Indeed?"

The fourth button was gone, and her bodice was too loose to restrain him. As I intended, she reminded herself, as I intended. The hand was sliding down.

"It is to visit a man called Michael Nej—one of the people condemned for the murder of Monsieur Stolypin."

His fingers, engaged in cupping her right breast, suddenly seized her nipple and pinched it. She gave a shriek of pain and dropped her drink. The wine stained her gown.

"You. . . ." She tried to get up, but the hand was still holding her by the breast, while the weight of his arm on her shoulder pinned her into the seat.

"Your brother's servant?" Rasputin asked.

Ilona got her breathing under control. "And an old friend."

"How old?"

"He. . . ." But this was also all a part of the plan. "He is the father of my son."

The hand went limp. Ilona Roditcheva had succeeded in shocking the holy man from the steppes. She seized the opportunity to wriggle away from him and get up, brushing the last of the wine from her skirt, although the dress was stained.

"Are you a liar as well as a whore?" he asked.

"It is the truth."

The huge eyes gloomed at her. "And you wish to sleep with him one last time, before they stretch his neck?"

"No. I do not wish to see him again. But I must send him a message. I wish the permission to see him to be in the name of George Hayman. And it must be a private interview."

Rasputin thrust his hand into his beard and appeared to scratch. "George Hayman? Your lover before the servant?"

Ilona's head jerked. "How did you know that?"

"It is my business to know. You would send one lover to bid farewell to another? Are you a woman or a demon from hell?"

Victory? She could only continue on her course. "I am a woman for whom men are happy to perform little duties."

"Little duties," Rasputin remarked. "Undress."

Ilona's chin came up. "Will you obtain the permission?"

"Undress. Then we will talk about it."

Ilona chewed her lip. But there was a limit to how long she could hold back. To antagonize him would be disastrous. She drew a deep breath, slipped her bodice from her shoulders, and took off her blouse. It can be no different, she told herself, from undressing before Michael or George. Or Roditchev. I am a full-grown woman who has known enough men not to be nervous of this man.

But she was hurrying. She could not prevent herself. And then she had to sit down on the settee opposite to unlace her boots, well aware that he was watching her every movement. But an even greater ordeal was to have to stand up and face him; she suddenly felt cold.

"You are magnificent," Rasputin said. "Quite the loveliest woman I have ever seen, with the exception only of your sister."

Ilona waited. She could not afford to be offended by him now.

Rasputin crooked his forefinger. "Come and sit on my lap."

"Will you give me the permission?"

He smiled at her. "I think that may be possible, my lovely princess. After you have sat on my lap."

The Fortress of St. Peter and St. Paul was reached by a bridge over the Neva. It was the most forbidding citadel George had ever seen, and as he stepped down from his cab he thought that over the main gateway there should be a sign saying, "Abandon hope, all you who enter here."

He was about to enter here. Not for the first time he wondered if he knew what he was doing. After what he had seen in Roditchev's cells in Moscow, consciously to put himself in the power of the military police . . . but Roditchev was on his way back to Moscow by now, and George had taken every precaution, by making sure his fellow American journalists knew just where he was and what he was doing. Besides, he could not withdraw now. He did not know what Ilona had had to do to obtain the letter of permission which was folded in his pocket, but she had done it, and she was on board the *Henry J. Wilkins*. The ship sailed at five o'clock, on the tide, and it was three o'clock now. All he had to do was enter the prison. All Michael Nej had to do was leave.

It had been surprisingly simple so far. The authority was signed by the military governor of St. Petersburg himself, and would no doubt have opened the door to hell. George had braced himself for an ordeal similar to that he had undergone in Roditchev's jail in Moscow, but here the corridors were wider and the cells larger, and if the warders looked no friendlier and there was the inevitable smell of disinfectant everywhere, the place lacked the atmosphere of total fear that he had been so conscious of on the previous occasion.

His relief had come too soon. Now he was walking past the condemned cells: these prisoners had all been interrogated, with all the horror that suggested, and several of them were to die. But the very gloom of this section—the darkened corridors and the low ceiling which made him stoop, was to his advantage; he had in any event put on his simplest suit, his least distinctive coat and hat.

"Are the three anarchists here?" he asked.

"The man Bogrov is here," the warder said. "And here is the man Nej."

"And the woman, Stein?"

"I do not know what has happened to the woman. She was removed yesterday."

To be interrogated again? George wondered.

The key was turning in the lock, and the door was swinging in. "It is to be a private interview," the warder said, as if trying to convince himself. "You are not afraid he may attack you?"

"Why should he attack me?" George asked. "I am only a newspaper correspondent."

The warder shrugged. "I will return in fifteen minutes."

George stepped inside and the door clanged shut.

Michael Nej sat on the cot in the far corner, his head drooping. He wore prison clothes, hardly more than pajamas, and his face was a stubble of beard. But George had anticipated this.

Slowly the tired head raised. "I have nothing more to tell you," he muttered, the words escaping before his eyes could even focus.

"Do you remember me?" George asked.

Michael reached his feet. "I would like to kill you," he said.

"Well, I'm here to give you that chance," George said. "But not right now." He felt in his pocket and produced a razor. "Get that stubble off. Hurry."

Michael stared at him.

"You heard the man," George said. "Fifteen minutes. Get shaved, and we'll change clothes."

"But . . . you?"

"Do it."

Michael took the razor and scraped at his chin. "Why should you help me?"

"Ilona asked me to."

Michael lowered the razor and gazed at him.

"She's going with you," George said. "She and the child. They are on an American ship called the *Henry J. Wilkins,* which is sailing from St. Petersburg in an hour and a half. In my pocket are your tickets and some money. For God's sake, shave."

Michael resumed. "I do not understand."

"Well, you'd better. Ilona is booked all the way through to New York. Do you wish to go to America?"

"What would I do in America?"

"Well, the ship stops at Hamburg and Le Havre before crossing, so you can leave whenever you like." George took off his coat and jacket. "I think I should tell you that Ilona and I intend to get married as soon as she can arrange a divorce."

Michael had finished shaving. "And my son?"

"That is up to you. I suppose it depends on what you intend to do. What do you intend to do?"

"I am a convicted revolutionary." Michael undressed in turn. "I have no profession but that."

"You were a valet."

"Do they have such things in America?"

George began to fit himself into Michael's clothes. "Indeed they do."

Michael also started to dress. "Well, I have no intention of ever working for anyone again."

"Oh no?"

"They have made me a criminal. You and Ilona, as well as everyone else," Michael said vehemently. "Well, if the world wishes me to be a revolutionary, I shall be one."

"Against the world?"

Michael glanced at him, flushed. "I have no fight with the world. My fight is with Russian despotism."

"But you'll agree you can't stay here. Let me adjust that tie."

Michael gazed into George's face. "There are men who fight against tsarism without being in Russia."

"I've read some." George stepped back, frowned. "I suppose that's as good as it'll ever be."

"Switzerland," Michael said. "Nikolai Lenin is in Switzerland. And many others. I shall go to Switzerland."

"And continue being a revolutionary?" George helped him into the overcoat. "Do you really suppose that is going to be a good life for a little boy who has been brought up in the lap of luxury?"

Michael tried on the hat. "What other life can there be for him?"

"He has a mother."

"Who is going to live with you. You would give my son a home?"

"I would give Ilona's son a home."

Michael was fully dressed. "Will I pass?"

George nodded.

"And you will just sit here and wait for the warder to come? They will beat you up."

"I've played football."

"But why?" Michael asked. He hesitated. "Do you not know that it was I betrayed you to Prince Peter?"

George said nothing.

Michael sighed. "I saw you and Ilona on the settee in Port Arthur.

I hated you then. And when you continued being her lover in Starogan, I wrote Prince Peter and told him."

"My God. Why are you telling me this now?"

Michael shrugged. "You are prepared to risk your life for me. Even a muzhik can have honor, Mr. Hayman."

"Has it ever occurred to you, Michael Nikolaievich, that by writing that letter you started this whole crazy mess?"

Michael chewed his lip. "And you will send her away with me, to safety. With me? You are a fool, my friend."

"I love her," George said. "Don't you?"

The cell door crashed open, and George sat up, a sudden alarming thought clanging through his brain: there was worse to come. He had anticipated some rough treatment. He had not even been surprised when they refused to allow him to walk from the condemned cell down to this one, but instead dragged him by his feet, so that his head bumped on every step and he could be kicked by those walking behind. When they had explained to the consul that he had fallen down a flight of stairs, they had not been altogether lying.

But he had not supposed it would take so long to be freed. He had estimated a few days, and instead nearly three weeks had passed. The worst of all was not knowing what was happening outside, how his family and friends were faring in their quest for his release, and what had happened to Ilona. For all his confidence in her, in his low moments he could not help remembering that he had sent her off with the father of her child.

He saw boots. Two pairs; the usual two men in the room. He tilted back his head and gazed at General Prince Roditchev.

"Close the door," the prince said.

The warder obeyed, and George forced himself to his feet. He had not supposed Roditchev would risk it. But now he understood he was going to need all his courage and his will power.

Roditchev felt in his pocket and pulled out a piece of paper. "I have here an order for your release."

George's jaw sagged, and he had to bring it up again.

"Oh yes, my friend," Roditchev said, replacing the paper in his pocket. "It seems you have powerful allies. A president who will appeal to his majesty for clemency on behalf of a young man in love, and journalists who will threaten to publish your own descriptions of life in my cells if you are placed on trial. I wish I could know which of those two actually influenced the tsar. But no doubt you knew that one or the other would obtain in your favor before you ever risked your neck."

George got his breath back. "I had hopes."

"Of course you did." Roditchev unfastened his belt. "So let us consider your achievements, Mr. Hayman. You have robbed me of my wife, and even of my heir, who it appears was never my heir, even as you enjoyed Ilona's charms before I ever possessed them. You have brought about the escape of one of the most depraved men in the country. You have made me the laughing stock of all Russia. The Roditchev name has suffered a catastrophe from which it can never recover. I sometimes think that you have been my evil genius, Mr. Hayman. And when I remember that you and I sat, stirrup to stirrup as the Japanese army crossed the Yalu, before you even knew that Ilona existed, when bullets were flying all around us, and you could so easily have stopped one, even from behind . . . what would a man not give to know what the future might hold."

He was to be released. Here and now. George's brain was only just comprehending what had been said.

"But there it is," Roditchev remarked. "You would appear to be one of those men for whom life holds nothing but success, whereas I. . . ." He sighed. "You will leave this cell, and you will go out of the main door of the prison, and you will find your friends waiting for you, and they will escort you to a ship—I am sorry to say that you are being deported from Russia, never to return—and you will sail across the ocean, and in New York or wherever it is you maintain your lair you will find my wife waiting for you. Oh yes, my friend, she will be there. The *Henry J. Wilkins* sailed from London yesterday on the last leg of her journey. There is nothing I can do to stop her now. The most beautiful woman in all Russia. All yours, for the rest of your life. Are you going to be happy?"

George could only stare at him.

"I have pondered long," Roditchev said, "as to my best course of action. The honorable way would be to challenge you. But duels are illegal, and the killing of an American would be considered murder in the international press."

"What about the killing of a Russian?" George asked.

Roditchev smiled. "You consider yourself a marksman? I have heard that you are. But after three weeks in this prison, would your hand be steady, Mr. Hayman? Do not be afraid. I have been forbidden to shoot you. And who am I to go against the law? But I have been granted the solace of an interview with you before you depart. I am told the Americans are a sporting race. Thanks to the reports of you and your brother journalists they may regard me as an ogre. But you have robbed me of my wife. So I suspect I will not forfeit the sympathies of the American public if I suggest we settle our differences here and now, man to man." He removed his coat and belt and laid them on the cot.

George glanced at the warder standing against the door.

"Oh, do not fear him, Mr. Hayman. His function is merely to ensure that we are not interrupted."

"Because you assume that after three weeks in here, I won't be in very good shape."

"My dear Mr. Hayman," Roditchev said. "That is unworthy of you." He lowered his head and ran forward. George got his hands together, and brought them down on Roditchev's neck; but the force of the charge carried him back against the cot, and he sat down heavily. The cot collapsed and George found himself on the floor, Roditchev on his knees in front of him, head pressed into his side, arms locked round his waist as he exerted all the strength he possessed. And already stars were beginning to shine in front of George's eyes, and his head was spinning. With an immense effort he turned to one side, carrying Roditchev with him. Desperately he clasped his hands together and struck again and again at the base of the bull neck. Roditchev grunted but still held on, still squeezed, and George realized he himself had only a few seconds of consciousness left. But Roditchev must guess that.

He gave a great sigh and with the last of his breath allowed his eyes to flop shut, and his entire body to subside. For a moment longer Roditchev continued to squeeze, and he thought he had lost. Then the bear hug relaxed and he could breathe again, great surges of air which distended his nostrils and his lungs at the same time.

He felt Roditchev push himself away.

"He is unconscious," said the guard. "He has fainted."

"But you are not going to say that," Roditchev pointed out. "You are going to say that he fought like a madman, eh? That it was necessary for me to beat him into insensibility."

"Of course, my lord prince."

George opened his eyes in time to see the boot coming toward him. He caught it, using all his strength to prevent it from crashing into his face, and twisted it and Roditchev away from him. The prince turned around once and cannoned into the wall. George struggled to his feet, caught Roditchev's shoulder, and turned him. His fist crunched into Roditchev's jaw, and the prince hit the wall and started to slide. George moved forward, and the guard left the door and came toward him.

George ducked under the first haymaker, jabbed his left into the man's stomach, and hit him on the chin as his head came forward. The guard struck the door and slid down it, while George looked at his fist, the burst knuckles and the dripping blood.

"You are more resilient than I thought, Mr. Hayman," Roditchev said, getting up. Another charge, but this time George was prepared. He clasped his battered hands together, swung them left to right, caught Roditchev on the side of the head and sent him blundering into the wall. The prince turned, face inflamed with pain and anger. George stepped in to meet the charge, hands still clasped, but low, in front of his groin, to come upwards with all the strength at his command.

The combined fists caught the prince under the chin, and he arched backwards, his head striking the wall as he slowly collapsed into a sitting position. It was time to stand still and draw a long breath before he stooped to pick up the prince's jacket and remove the precious document from the pocket.

And then it was time to open the door, and step into the corridor, and inhale the scent of freedom, and know that Ilona was waiting for him.

"I am to allow you five minutes, my lord prince," the guard said, and opened the door.

Peter ducked his head and stepped into the waiting room. It had been cleared of people; the rest of the political exiles were already on the platform, where the train was hissing as it prepared for the long journey which would take it into the depths of Irkutsk. The exiles would arrive there just as summer ended. After two weeks of rain, they would be plunged into the coldest winter any of them could ever have known, when the temperature would drop a hundred and more degrees below freezing. They would be forced to work outdoors, cutting down the virgin forest, building houses, roads, bridges, creating a civilization in the wilderness, while frostbite nibbled at their noses and ears and fingers, and their guards punished them for the slightest transgressions. And as they attempted, among themselves, to make some sort of civilization of their own.

Perhaps this last thought was the hardest of all to bear.

Judith Stein sat on a bench in the corner. Already she had changed from a well-groomed, pretty young woman into a permanent prisoner; the good clothes replaced by a shapeless gown, the elegant shoes by ill-fitting boots. Her hair was gathered beneath a kerchief. She had lost weight, and looked almost as thin as her sister.

Peter went to close the door but was checked by the hovering guard. "The door must remain open, my lord prince."

Because of George Hayman's success in freeing Michael Nej? There was a cruel twist of fate. Would it not have been similarly possible to free Judith?

He crossed the floor and stood in front of her. She watched him approach but made no move.

"It was all I could achieve," he said.

"And I am grateful." Her voice was low.

"Grateful, to be sent to a living death?"

"I know what it cost you, my lord prince. I am at least going with people who share my opinions. You must remain here, pilloried by all the world you call important. What will you do?"

Peter shrugged. "I have enough to do at Starogan."

"And your wife and family?"

"My wife?" He gave a brief laugh. "She has applied for a legal separation. She does not wish a divorce, you understand, as she still would like to spend my money. As for my family, well, you have heard about Ilona?"

Judith nodded. "Why do you not follow her example?"

He frowned at her. "A prince of Starogan, emigrate? I have a duty here, to Russia, to my people, to my mother and grandmother. Even to Tattie. Whatever she has become, she is the only sister I have left."

Judith sighed. What hope did she, or the next generation of Mordka Bogrovs, or even Michael Nej, escaped to Switzerland and no doubt plotting his next act in company with people like Lenin, have against so much duty, so much sense of responsibility?

"But what will you do?"

"Me, my lord prince? I will survive. As you have said, it is a living death I go to."

"But you are not like those people outside."

"I must become like them."

"You are Jewish."

"There are many Jews among us. Even more in Irkutsk."

"But . . . your entire life. . . ."

Judith Stein got up. "I will make myself a good life, my lord prince. I will work, I will dream a little, and in time I imagine I will marry, and bear strong sons. And who knows what the future may hold? I may well come back some day."

"Marry," he said. "Judith. . . ." He hesitated.

"Yes, my lord prince," she said. "I was a prisoner of General Prince Roditchev for several weeks."

"My God. Roditchev?"

She shook her head. "No man, my lord prince. He used his cane."

"His cane?"

"He used his cane for a good many things, my lord prince. To deflower me was merely one of them."

"And you do not hate?"

Judith appeared to consider. "Oh, I hate, my lord prince," she said at last. "I do not suppose even Prince Roditchev thinks he cures his victims of revolutionary tendencies by what he does to them. Or by sending them to Siberia. I hate."

"Judith." He reached for her hand, and after a moment she allowed him to take it.

"I do not hate you, Prince Peter. Had I taken your advice, accepted your offer, I would not be here now. I do not hate you."

"Judith, I shall try to obtain permission to visit you."

"In Irkutsk?"

"Yes, in Irkutsk."

Judith smiled at him. "I would not do that, Prince Peter. It is a very long way. Wait for me to come back, and see if you are still interested."

He chewed his lip, his grip tightening. She knew what he wanted, and allowed herself to be drawn closer. His kiss was chaste, a mere brushing of the lips. Judith freed her hand and stepped away. "I must go."

"Will you come back, Judith? Will you?"

She hesitated. "I don't know, my lord. I don't know if I will ever have the chance. But don't grieve for me. My spirit isn't going anywhere. It is staying here in St. Petersburg, and Moscow, and even Starogan. That is more important than my body. Even for you, Prince Peter, that is more important."

Land, rising out of the western mist. And suddenly, land all around the ship. Ahead, seeming quite enormous because of the surprise of her appearance, the statue of a woman, her right hand held high.

"Your first visit, princess?" asked the purser. As if he did not know.

"Yes," Ilona said.

"Here's a telegram," he said. "And welcome to America."

He walked back along the deck and Ilona remained, staring at the Statue of Liberty and the island of Manhattan looming out of the murky fog. The envelope remained unopened in her hand.

Throughout the journey she had refused to look over her shoulder, refused to consider what she had left behind. Mama and Grandma. Peter and Tattie. Her horses and her dogs. The Nejs.

Her heart lurched. And Starogan.

And Judith Stein, sentenced to hang by the neck until she was dead. And Sergei Roditchev, sentenced to hate, and hate, and hate, until he was dead.

And Michael. Even though he had fled with her. Even though, for two weeks they had been within touching distance every day.

Scurrying feet brought Ivan tumbling up the deck to her. "Mama," he cried in Russian, so incongruous on this American ship. "Mama, that is America."

"That's where we're going," she said.

"Will Papa be there, Mama?"

Ilona opened the envelope and took out the telegram.

"LEAVING LONDON TODAY STOP," it read. "BE WITH YOU IN A WEEK."

She looked over her shoulder, half-expecting to see Michael Nej standing there. But he wasn't. He would never be standing there again.

"Yes," she said. "Your father will be here soon."